Of Bonds and Bondage

by

Rita Baker

Bloomington, IN Milton Keynes, UK

authorHOUSE

AuthorHouse™
1663 Liberty Drive, Suite 200
Bloomington, IN 47403
www.authorhouse.com
Phone: 1-800-839-8640

AuthorHouse™ UK Ltd.
500 Avebury Boulevard
Central Milton Keynes, MK9 2BE
www.authorhouse.co.uk
Phone: 08001974150

This book is a work of fiction. People, places, events, and situations are the product of the author's imagination. Any resemblance to actual persons, living or dead, or historical events, is purely coincidental.

First published by AuthorHouse 2/9/2006

ISBN: 1-4208-8565-0 (sc)

Printed in the United States of America
Bloomington, Indiana

This book is printed on acid-free paper.

With this poem, I dedicate the book to my husband, a lawyer, without whose guidance this novel could never have been written.

TO HARRY

In loving you I've learned, full well,
The measure of my constant heart,
That I have never loved before,
Not in whole, or, indeed, in part.

I've learned the strength of your embrace.
I know the comfort of your hand.
I know the meaning of our love
Goes far beyond the wedding band.

I have no dream where you have no part.
I have no thought where you have no place.
No hope that does not enfold you.
I have no life but by your grace.

Love is not love that does not last,
Or alters with the tricks of life.
So come what may, until my death,
I am, my love, your constant wife.

CONTENTS

FOREWORD

Of Bonds and Bondage, which takes place between the years 1952-1982, is not only a tale of mystery, love, hate, and revenge, but also of relationships and the fine thread that separates good from evil.

While all the characters and events are fictional, the story is based upon my observations of human nature and the circumstances that can drive a person one way or the other.

CHAPTER ONE

The stale smell of one of his grandfather's hand-rolled cigars still lingered in the air of the enclosed elevator cab. Frankie Leeman smiled to himself as he stepped inside, remembering the entire family begging his grandfather to stop smoking. "Now you listen to me," he said, jabbing the lit end of a cigar in their face, "I don't drink, I don't gamble. As for women, they take too much effort to please for someone my age; but a man needs at least one vice to keep him from going crazy."

The private elevator came to rest at the top floor of the office building owned by the Bocacci family. He slipped through the still-opening doors and went down the corridor to the boardroom.

A shaft of early morning sunlight streamed through a window at the far end of the room, leaving the rest in shadow. Frankie shuddered; it was not his favorite time of day; the office staff wouldn't arrive for another two hours yet and the place had the feel of a morgue about it.

He turned on the light, dropped into a seat at the boardroom table, stretched out his legs, and, clasping his hands behind his head, gave thought to what he would say to his uncles when they arrived.

He knew he wouldn't have long to wait; the Bocacci men were always on time, arriving, as if contrived, in order of seniority. Joseph Bocacci, patriarch and founder of an extensive road haulage business, demanded punctuality, and his sons would never think of being anything but just that.

Aldo, the youngest, was the first to arrive, and being of a sullen nature, he rarely spoke unless spoken to first. He nodded to Frankie and took a seat opposite him, wearing a scowl that went deeper than usual. He resented those early morning calls; they interrupted his daily routine, not to mention the more than ample breakfast that his wife prepared for him with dedicated regularity. The couple were childless and food was their main interest in life, a fact borne out by their obvious overweight.

Vinnie came next. He was as slim and lithe as Aldo was fat and cumbersome, with a natural exuberance that breathed life into every corner of the room. He was a bachelor and, in his own words, "still playing the field." It must have been a big field; he was pushing fifty. "Hey Frankie!" he cried as he came waltzing through the door. "How goes it?"

Reacting to the pure vivacity of this favorite uncle, Frankie straightened up and smiled broadly. "Okay Vinnie," he replied. "How goes it with you?"

"What can I tell ya? Good! Good! Good!" he said breezily; then with a wide grin, he slapped Aldo on the back before taking the seat next to him. Aldo responded with a sour look at his aggressor, and Vinnie, amused, gave Frankie a knowing wink.

Johnny arrived, his face grave, his shoulders hunched as though he carried the worries of the world on his back; indeed, he felt that he did. He was a widower of some fifteen years with one son, Guido, whom he spoiled to make up for the lack of a mother. Guido was a source of constant concern to him and was the reason for the meeting that morning. He glanced at the clock on the wall. "Thought I was late," he said with a sigh of relief, then took a seat next to Frankie and adjusted his wristwatch.

"Does anyone know what this is about?" asked Vinnie; but before Frankie could reply, Joe came through the door.

Most days you wouldn't suspect that this short, energetic little man was anything like his seventy-eight years, but that day, his dark, deep-set eyes, which dominated a still-handsome face, had lost their usual calm and perspective, replaced by a troubled expression that added to his years.

Frankie, the apple of his eye, was the only one who made an effort to rise, to which Joe gestured for him to remain seated.

When at the age of four Frankie lost his parents in a car accident near their home in Italy, it was Joe who came to bury them and take Frankie back with him to America, where his childless daughter, Lucretia, and her husband, Albert Leeman, adopted him. Since then, a strong bond remained between him and Joe, and it was he who put Frankie through law school, from which he graduated five years ago and was now a fully active partner in the family business. Frankie was bright, as bright as Joe had been as a young man newly arrived from Sicily, and with the death of his wife, he relied, more and more, upon this grandson for direction.

Not one to waste time, Joe came straight to the point. "I've called you together because we have a problem on our hands," he said gravely. "Guido has been indicted on a drug charge. Now before anyone jumps to conclusions, I want to make it quite clear that Frankie and I have spoken to him and we are satisfied that he is innocent. He may do some stupid things, but doing drugs is not one of them."

"Oh Jesus!" cried Vinnie. "That's all this family needs. What happened?"

"Tell 'em, Franco."

With their attention focused on him, Frankie cleared his throat. "He was on his way home from a singles bar when he was stopped by the police and he and some young guy who was with him were then ordered out of the car while they searched it. They found a large packet of cocaine hidden in the glove compartment," he said with a glance at Vinnie.

"I don't believe it! He doesn't do drugs, so how come drugs get into his glove compartment?"

"I'm only telling you what they told me," said Frankie.

"Did they have a search warrant?"

"They did. They said they were acting on a tip."

"A tip? From who?"

"They wouldn't say."

"Who was this guy with Guido?"

"Someone he met at the bar. They got into a conversation and he asked Guido for a lift uptown."

"Does he have a name?"

"Brian! That is all we know about him."

"Was he charged?"

"It seems the police were satisfied with his explanation, and you know Guido; he was quick to confirm everything he said."

"But they had to check him out, right? They had to get a full name and address."

"The way I see it they had who they wanted and that was good enough for them."

Vinnie shook his head. "It smells. Had to be a setup or else how did they know the route he would be taking? What's the betting that this Brian, or whatever his name is, is in with the cops?"

"It smells all right," cried Johnny, "the bastards!"

"Maybe," said Frankie, "but we can't go around accusing the police without proof."

"Then get it!"

"Not so easy. This Brian has disappeared into thin air; no one knows him, and no one remembers him being at the bar."

"So what are you saying, we give up?" snarled Johnny.

"No one is saying anything of the kind," snapped Joe. "Now listen: Frankie and me, we've discussed the matter and he has a plan. You see, it's not Guido they're after; they want me to testify against some of the Mob and they think this is the way to get me to talk." He paused, and a look of pain crossed his face. "You know I can't do it. It would be signing our death warrant. They believe that by threatening to prosecute Guido, they hold an ace in their hands, so what we now have to do is trump that ace."

"It's my boy we're talking about, Papa, not some game of cards."

"Don't you think it's killing me? Why do you think I called this meeting? But to rat on the Mob, no way!"

"Papa's right," said Vinnie. "Once a part of 'em, always a part of 'em, and the only way out is in a pine box."

"That's right, and don't let anyone forget we have been lucky to get this far on our own," said Joe. "We mustn't push our luck by going against them."

"What I say is, let's take the problem to them," said Aldo, suddenly waking up. "It's no secret the Mob have pull in the Justice Department, so why not take advantage of it and let them settle the matter; after all, it's as much their problem as ours."

"They may not see it that way," said Frankie.

"Franco's right," said Joe, "and how many times must I tell you, if you ask a favor, you're expected to do a favor; that's how the system works, and after all these years I don't want they should have one single marker on me or my family. We paid our dues and so far we've kept their respect. I'm too old to go back to that way of life, and none of you should want to unless you are prepared to look over your shoulder for the rest of your days." Suddenly Joe fell away, and his voice shook as he continued. "I cannot—I will not allow anything or any one person to destroy what we have built. Have you forgotten the sweat that went into this business? It's ours, we earned it; it's for our children and their children after them. Now I know how much you trust Franco, so finish with the questions and listen to what he has to say."

Every eye shifted to Frankie in anticipation, and as he glanced from one anxious face to the next, he was all too aware of the burden their faith placed upon him. What he hoped was that he would be able to live up to their expectations. "I know how you feel," he said, "and what your fears are. I wish I could tell you it was only a matter of slipping someone a few bucks, but I can't.

4

"The person who will be prosecuting Guido is a deputy district attorney named Archie Bingham, and from what I've gathered, he is also the one responsible for the re-opening of an investigation against a certain Mob boss. He is after the job of D.A. when it comes up, which should be some time next year. He's ruthless and will stop at nothing to get what he wants."

"I get the picture," said Vinnie. "He thinks that by getting Papa to talk, he'll get the conviction he's after, and the nomination will be his for the asking."

"That's what I figured. Obviously, he's made himself familiar with our family background and is putting his money on Joe talking."

"Huh! If he believes that then he still has a lot to learn!"

"Maybe," said Frankie, "but I wouldn't bet on anything where this guy is concerned. He's bright; very bright as I recall."

"You know him?" asked Johnny.

"Oh yeah! He was in his final year when I was a freshman at Harvard. I never spoke to him, but I was well aware of his reputation for knowing his law; in fact, he was so knowledgeable that it led to some speculation."

"Such as?" asked Vinnie.

"Let me put it this way. By the time you leave Harvard you may have a pretty sound understanding of the law and how it works, but you don't know everything—the important stuff you gain while practicing. This guy knew it all, so the question arose, how come? There was something else that made us wonder about him. Apart from being British and a good ten years older than any of his contemporaries, his father was none other than Sir Archibald Bingham, a famous British barrister with a brilliant reputation. So why would a son of his want to take a law degree in America when he already had an LL.B. from Cambridge, which, by the way, he earned ten years prior to his immigrating."

"So what are you saying?"

"That it doesn't make sense; and add the fact that there are those ten years unaccounted for on his immigration file, then I would say that is where the focus has to be."

"Where is this leading?" asked Johnny.

"I'm leaving for England this evening with an introduction to a British colleague who was at Cambridge with Bingham. I intend to find out as much as I can about those ten missing years, and if my instincts are right, there is more to Archie Bingham than meets the eye."

5

"Instincts are not good enough; what if you come up empty-handed?"

"Sometimes, all you have to go on is a gut feeling, so let me tell you what I found out about him. He's bumptious, has a magnetic personality, really riveting in the courtroom, but outside he allows no one to get near him, as though he has something to hide. He also has an ego as big as an elephant, yet he never mentions his famous father. Neither does he ever talk about England and his days at Cambridge. Now I find that odd. Who wouldn't want to talk about their country of origin? Or that they went to a famous college such as Cambridge? And this guy likes to boast; so what is the story here?"

"So there's a story. But what if he isn't the one who framed Guido?"

"It doesn't matter who framed Guido. He is the one prosecuting, so he's the one we deal with. You have to trust me on this."

"Frankie's right," said Vinnie. "Who do you deal with but the dealer?"

"It's all too much in the air," said Johnny.

"Then if you can come up with a better idea, let's hear it," snapped Joe.

He shook his head. "You know I can't, Papa. I'm so devastated I can't think straight. I'm sorry, Frankie, if I seem to be questioning every-thing."

"Hey, no sweat, Johnny. I understand," he replied.

"By the way, where is Guido?" asked Vinnie. "Why isn't he out on bail?"

"It's set for today," said Frankie. "I'll be going there as soon as I leave here. I expect bail to be set high, so Papa and I had to liquidate some assets yesterday. He should be home with Johnny this afternoon."

"How long before this business comes to trial?"

"That depends on the caseload of the judge appointed. Usually there is a backlog, so I doubt it will come on before September."

"That gives you three months. Is it enough?"

"Has to be. I'll work round-the-clock if necessary."

Johnny was alarmed. "But what if it isn't?"

"Then we'll find cause for delay; but it won't come to that. Relax, Johnny, this isn't my first investigation. I know what I'm doing. I'll leave nothing to chance."

"It's the waiting that gets me. I want it to be over."

"It will be," said Joe. "Now if that's it, let us adjourn so that Frankie can get on with what he has to do."

Aldo was the first to hurry from the room. Full of anguish, Johnny was somewhat slower to rise, and moving over to Frankie, he took his hands in his. "Me and Guido," he said, "we're counting on you."

"I know, and I make you a promise: he will not go to prison."

Johnny nodded sorrowfully, and then, letting go of Frankie's hands, he trudged out of the room.

"I feel sorry for him," said Vinnie as he watched his brother's heavy steps.

"We all do," said Joe.

"Hey Papa, need a ride home?"

"No Vinnie, I have my car downstairs. Anyhow, I want a few words with Franco before I leave."

"I could wait?"

"I'm not a child. I can manage on my own."

"Okay, you win; but to please me, drive carefully."

Joe sighed with impatience, then turned to Frankie when he was gone. "I feel sorry for him as well," he said. "He should have someone other than me to worry about."

"You love someone, you worry about them," said Frankie.

Joe nodded "True," he said, "that's why I wanted a word with you. If anything should happen to me, Franco, look out for the family. Not one of them has your brain or ability. They need you more than they know."

"I don't want to hear talk like that; nothing is going to happen to you, not for a long time."

"Let's not kid ourselves. I'm no spring chicken, and this last year, with your grandmother so ill before she died, it took it out of me. I'm not the man I once was."

"You are still more man than anyone I know. Anyhow, no need to ask; you know how much I love this family."

"I do, and that is why I'm talking to you like this. Now I want you to be honest. Do you think maybe Aldo was right? I should take this matter to certain friends I still have in the Mob?"

"It's the last thing you need to do at your time of life. Anyhow, with their contacts, don't you think they already know what's going on? At some stage they will come to you, and when they do, make sure they know the favor you are doing them for giving you their trust."

"That's good advice, Franco, and speaking of good advice, did I ever tell you how Myer Lansky helped me to leave the organization and start up on my own?"

Frankie smiled to himself. He had heard the story a dozen times or more, but knew nothing could stop his grandfather from telling it once again, so he said, "I'm listening."

Joe heaved a sigh of nostalgia and his eyes appeared distant. "In a way, they were exciting days back then—bootlegging, illegal gambling. It was the Depression and those who could afford to, wanted to enjoy themselves, and those stupid laws made a lot of people very rich. Anyway, I was this raw kid from the Old Country, and more than a little afraid of what I was getting myself into.

"Lansky wasn't a true member of the 'family,' being Jewish and all that, but was still the most trusted man in the organization. He was the brains behind many of their schemes and everyone knew he was a man to be reckoned with. Well, he noticed how worried I was, and one day he took me aside and said, 'You want to make sure you die a natural death, kid? Just be smarter than the next guy and never, never get greedy. Don't even think about it. Don't give them a reason to mistrust you. Remember that, and you'll do okay.'" Once again, Joe sighed. "I know good advice when I hear it; that is why I sleep easy in bed at night, and that is why Myer spoke up for me when I wanted to get out. One thing that separated the Jewish Mob from the Italians, they never wanted their children in the organization, so he understood my concerns. He knew they would listen to him—everyone did. Even Lucky Luciano, who listened to no one, listened to him. I was fortunate, Franco, the family was fortunate, and I want to keep it that way. You don't split on the Mob and get away with it!"

"I understand; but don't worry, we'll work it out ourselves," said Frankie.

"You know, it was a lucky day for this family when you came into our lives. I may have regrets about my past, but you could never be one of them. Now your mother, that is a different story. I feel so helpless where she is concerned. It kills me to see the way she drinks, and it kills me to hear how that husband of hers plays around. The worst fear is it might be my fault."

"That's nonsense; they're two grown people and their lives are what they have made of them, not because of anything you did or didn't do."

"You say that because you don't know everything. I warned her not to marry him. What she needed was a nice Catholic boy from a good Italian family, one who was familiar with our ways; but she never listened to me, and now she blames me for everything, and in a way she is right. You see, she expected her husband to be taken into the family business, and in the normal course of events, he would have been. Unfortunately, in those days, we still had connections to the Mob and I was afraid he might cause trouble for us. He had no idea, nor did he take an interest in our Sicilian ways or particular code of honor. They meant nothing to him, so I gave them a large allowance to help keep him at a safe distance, especially from doing us harm with the Mob.

"I didn't think it would cause a problem. Now I realize it can't do much for a man's pride to be kept by his wife's family."

"You can't blame yourself. They are who they are, and no matter what, chances are things would have turned out the same."

"I don't know that!"

"Then know this: she doesn't really hold you responsible for anything. It's just easier than blaming herself for all her woes. She loves you, Papa, and needs you more than she is ready to admit."

"She loves you most of all, Franco; she couldn't love you more if you were flesh of her flesh, and neither could I. I'm sorry if you are disappointed in her. I did what I thought best for you when your parents died."

"I'm unhappy for her, not disappointed. When this mess with Guido is cleared up, I'm going to get her to go to one of those clinics. She has your strength, Papa; she'll lick this problem."

"You know, I don't deserve a grandson like you, but for some reason, God saw fit to give you to me."

"Well, I for one am glad He did."

Joe's eyes lit up. "I'm glad we had this little talk, but now I think we better leave. You have a lot to do before this evening."

The private elevator took them straight to the garage. Frankie walked Joe to his car, reminded him to buckle up, then waited for him to put it into gear and drive off before going to his own.

It was almost nine o'clock and a steady stream of traffic was driving into the garage as he drove out. He waved to one or two of the staff members as they passed, then swung onto the road and made for the courthouse.

CHAPTER TWO

Frankie took his seat on the British Airways flight, settled in, and watched from the window as the craft backed away from the gate before taxiing to the runway.

As they waited for takeoff, the captain's voice came over the speaker. "We are second in line, so it shouldn't be long before we are in the air, and as soon as we are out over the Atlantic, we will be flying at an altitude of 33,000 feet."

Frankie's thoughts returned to the day's events. Apart from the meeting that morning, nothing went right. First the D.A.'s office put forth a strong argument and bail was set even higher than expected. Then, when he finally left the courthouse with Guido, the car wouldn't start and he had to get it towed to a garage; and to cap it all, there was a very unpleasant scene at his parents' house before he left for the airport.

His parents' behavior was nothing new to him, but that evening it got to him more than it usually did; perhaps because he wouldn't be seeing them for some time and he wanted to take away a much happier picture than the one presented.

With so much to attend to before leaving, he had arrived late at their home, and the argument was already in progress. His mother, who had been drinking heavily, was shouting obscenities at her husband, while he called her a drunk, a rotten excuse for a wife, as well as a few other choice names.

Suddenly it got even uglier when his mother, calling him a whoring bastard, slapped him across the face, but before his father had an opportunity to retaliate Frankie stepped between them and pleaded with them to stop. This didn't prevent them from continuing their verbal abuse, however, and it continued until his father walked out of the house, leaving him to attend to his distraught mother.

The horrible spectacle left him feeling sick at heart. With an unhappy sigh, Frankie looked down from the plane into the sea below, deceptively calm and peaceful from that height, like his parents' marriage, he thought, composed from afar, turbulent up close. How did they come to such a sorry stage in their relationship? It wasn't always like that, so what went wrong?

Most of his memories, before he was adopted, were vague. His life seemed to begin the day he first met his adoptive mother. He had arrived in America with Joe, a scared and confused little boy, not understanding how or why his parents had died and left him alone. They went straight to Joe's house from the airport, where his wife, a gentle, warm person, helped to console him by holding him to her soft bosom while she muttered soothing words to him in Italian. But it was the next day, when Joe took him to his daughter's home, that a deep and lasting impression was made upon him. From the moment she opened the door, it seemed that a miracle had taken place, and his little heart began to pound with excitement. The smile, the long black hair, the large dark eyes that appeared to fill her face—they were so like his mother's that he believed he had found her again.

When Joe saw the look of wonder in his eyes, he pushed him into her arms, and from that moment on he clung to her side for fear she might suddenly disappear and leave him alone again.

There was so much joy and laughter in the house in those early years, so much love between the three of them, even though his father's nature was more reserved than his mother's. What happened? Was it her drinking? His womanizing? Whatever it was that set them off, it certainly turned his world upside down and left him feeling guilty that somehow it was his fault.

As the situation grew worse at home, he spent more and more time with his grandparents, drawing comfort from the stability of their relationship. It was during that time that he learned about the family business and how his grandfather built it up from nothing to the huge corporation it had become. It was also during that time that he discovered disturbing facts about its origin.

It was around his twelfth birthday and his uncle Vinnie had come to see his grandfather. They were in the library speaking in low tones so that Frankie, who was in the hall playing with one of Joe's model ships, couldn't hear what was being said. Suddenly, his grandfather's voice rose sharply. "Forget it!" he cried. "I am not letting you make that run!"

Taken by surprise, Frankie moved closer to the door to hear his uncle's reply. "If I don't do it, who will? It's much too risky for Aldo or Johnny; they have families to think of. Things are heating up at the border like you wouldn't believe."

"All the more reason for me to go," said Joe. "No one is more familiar with the guards than I am. I know who can be bribed and who can't."

"Not anymore you don't," cried Vinnie. "It's been a long time since you made a run on your own. I'm telling you, Papa, things are changing fast; it's not like the old days. If anything should go wrong, think what it would do to Mama."

"It doesn't scare me. Greed is one thing that never changes, and I have a nose for rooting it out. You have to trust my judgment the way you used to. Anyhow, it will be the last trip; after this, we don't owe them a thing. I have kept my end of the bargain, and I know they will keep theirs. Now, that is my final word!"

Without warning, the door opened and his grandfather was looking down at him. "Franco! What are you doing outside the door?" Frozen in terror, he heard his grandfather's stern accusation, "You were listening!" he said. "That is not a nice thing to do, Frankie!"

Whenever his grandfather called him Frankie, he knew he was upset with him, and he felt ashamed to have been caught like that; nevertheless, his fear for his safety far outweighed his fear of him, and he cried, "You have to listen to Uncle Vinnie; don't make that run, Grandfather, please?"

He looked cautiously at him. "What are you talking about child?"

Frankie resented being called a child and lifted his chin in defiance. "I'm not some stupid child. I know what I heard."

"I didn't say you were stupid," said his grandfather, "but you are still a child, and I would like to know how much you heard."

"Enough to know there is danger involved."

"Then you misunderstood. There is no danger; nevertheless, I want you to forget this nonsense. I do not want to hear as much as a whisper about it again, especially in front of your grandmother. Is that clear?"

He nodded, but he wasn't satisfied. He was nobody's fool, even at that age, and he had a very good idea what the conversation was about and feared for both his grandfather and the family.

It took two years before he felt confident enough to bring the subject up again. He and his grandfather had grown extremely close and spent many hours together in the library, when his grandfather would reminisce over the past, relating stories about Sicily and what it was like on the streets of New York for a poor immigrant boy in the old days. They were stories he could never tire of listening to, and his grandfather's gift for telling a tale helped to bring those days alive for Frankie so that he could imagine being there himself.

It was during one of these conversations that he suddenly asked, "Do you think I am old enough to know everything about those days?"

"Everything? What do you mean?"

"The run you and Uncle Vinnie were discussing two years ago, what was that about?"

His grandfather regarded him with surprise. "I thought I told you to forget it?"

"I tried. But how could I if it involved who I think it did?"

"And who did you think that was?'

Frankie swallowed. "Must I say it out loud?" he asked hesitantly.

His grandfather drew a deep breath. "I see, and how long have you held this suspicion?"

He had spent two years struggling with the thought, and now that it seemed to be confirmed, he felt neither shock nor horror. "A long time," he said.

"Then I guess you are old enough to know everything about this family, including the business we are in. But before I try to explain, I must go back to the beginning so you will understand how and why I took the risk that I did."

"Before you do, I would like you to know, Grandfather, that whatever the reason was, my feelings for you will never change. I will love you always."

He smiled. "That is very reassuring, very! But I have to say that I make no excuses for what I did. I did what I felt I had to. You see, it was a tough life for a child in Sicily in the old days. I was eight years old when I worked, like a man, beside my father in the fields. My mother was always pregnant, it seemed, and with each new mouth to feed, the burden upon the family income became heavier and heavier; and as I was the only one to survive past my fourth birthday, it was to me that my father looked for help.

"I had no choice but to grow up quickly, and before long I realized that if we were to survive, I would have to know more about the finances of running a farm than my father did. He was content to live from hand to mouth, but not me. I wanted more, so I worked beside him by day and studied at night, teaching myself enough bookkeeping to know what I was doing.

"I found that I had a good head for figures; not that I was able to turn a profit, but I did keep us in the black, and that was more than my father ever did.

"He was proud of me and treated me with the respect reserved for an equal, and I was proud to have earned the respect of a man I both loved and honored. One day—I was about fourteen at the time, your age—we were sharing a lunch that my mother had packed for us, and, for the first time, I really looked at him. His back was bent from toiling in the fields from the age of six, his hair was white, and his eyes were dull. He was only thirty-four or -five. I can't remember exactly, but he looked like an old man, and I thought, I don't want a child of mine to have to work the way I was working. So I read and read and educated myself from books, and discovered that there was another kind of world out there, one that I never dreamed existed, and I was determined to be a part of it.

"America was all people talked about back then. It was looked on as the land of opportunity. 'The streets were paved with gold!' they said. You could become as rich as a king in America! In America, you were somebody! I listened to these stories and dreamed along with everyone else. The difference was that I knew I was going to make my dreams come true.

"What I found, when I arrived in America three years later, shook me to the core. The streets of New York weren't paved with gold; they were paved with garbage. The poor, and there were so many of them, were crowded into tenements. Whole families lived in one room, and if a man was lucky enough to have found a job, they had two rooms, with cold water and a heating system that never worked.

"It was the time of the Depression and there were no jobs for Americans, let alone immigrants; and if I had had my fare, I would have turned around and gone back home. I didn't, so I had to make the best of it.

"I was used to clean air and clean living, but I had to put all that behind me and become streetwise. I ran numbers for the bookies. I sold bad fruit from a barrow. I scrounged leftover pieces of material from the dress manufacturers and sold them to the shop girls at half the price they would have to pay in a store. I sold newspapers on street corners. Anything to make a buck, and through it all I managed to hold on to my dreams.

"When we start out in life, Franco, the world is so full of promise. We are certain of who we are and what we are about, and that nothing can stop us from doing what we were put on this earth to do; nothing, that is, except hunger, and we soon learn that having high ideals doesn't put food on the table.

"I was at my lowest ebb when I ran into a young Sicilian boy who came over on the boat with me. We talked for a while and when he heard how I was making out, he said that I should go and see his uncle who was big in the Mafia. Coming from Sicily, I knew all about the Mafia, so I said 'No thank you.'

"'Hey look,' he said. 'My uncle is always on the lookout for fresh faces, especially anyone good with figures and who has never been in trouble with the law. Just listen to what he has to say, and if you don't like what you hear, you can walk.'

"I thought to myself, what's to lose? Hadn't I already run numbers? So what if I do a little running for them? Well, I went, and I must have looked like I just came off the onion boat, because when he saw me, the first thing he said was, 'Here's some dough, kid, go get yourself a decent suit of clothes, then come back and we'll talk.'

"I hesitated, and he said, 'My nephew tells me you're good with figures, is that right?'

"I was as nervous as a kitten and barely whispered, 'I suppose so.'

"He banged the table with his fist and cried, 'No, no. You don't suppose anything. If you wanna get ahead in this town, you got to be more positive. Let everyone know who's in control. Now, tell me again, are you good with figures?'

"He scared the life out of me, but I wasn't about to let him know it. So I looked him straight in the eye and said loud and clear, 'Yes, sir, I'm very good with figures.'

"He smiled. 'There!' he said. 'Now that was good and I have more confidence in you, so take the money and get going.'

"I took the money and ran. I couldn't believe how much there was, more than I had earned in a year. Well, I bought what I thought was a good suit, teamed it with a shirt and tie and new shoes, then topped it off with one of those fancy fedora hats and pulled it down over my eyes the way some men did.

"I thought I looked the cat's whiskers, but when I walked into his office the next day, he just stared in disbelief, and after a while he said, 'The suit will pass, the tie is a bit flashy, but we can do something about that. It's the hat that really gets me. If I had wanted another hood on the payroll, I would have got myself one. Now take if off and let me get a good look at you.'

"I did as he said; then waited nervously for him to say something. Eventually, he spoke. 'You got honest eyes, kid, that's good; don't ever cover 'em up. They're your passport to a fortune. People will trust you. You're gonna make a lot of money for us and yourself. Just make sure you don't touch what's not yours, okay?'

"I didn't know what to say, so I nodded. 'You do wanna make money?' he asked.

"Well, I had no idea what I was getting myself into, but he was right about one thing. I wanted to make money, so I answered, 'What do you want me to do?'

"'Now that's what I call positive,' he said. 'I knew we'd get along the moment I laid eyes on you. Now what we want you to do is run a club—a gambling club. Any problem with that? D'you think you could do it?'

"I was a farm boy. What did I know about running a club? But I knew the answer he was waiting for, so I gave it to him. 'I don't think; I *know* I can do it.' And believe me, I looked more confident than I felt. I was a bit wary at first, but when he explained the position, and that I was to run a clean house, no funny business, everything strictly above board, and that that was to be my only job—it didn't seem all that terrible. Sure, gambling was illegal in the state; but people wanted it, and what people want, someone will give them. So I thought, why not me?

"Just as I was about to leave, he asked, 'How come you speak English so good?' I learn fast, I said. He seemed to like that and nodded.

"Well, they taught me a few things and the rest I figured out for myself. They were happy with the result: the people were happy. I paid off the police and kept them happy. And for the first time I was making more money than I ever dreamed of, and when the time was right to leave them, I got out and went into business for myself. That's it Franco, that's everything."

"Not everything, Grandfather; there is still that run to explain."

Joe laughed. "You don't give up, do you?"

"I learned that from you, Papa," he replied proudly.

"It was part of the deal worked out. They weren't about to let me go just like that, not the Mob. Fortunately, they liked the idea that I was buying a road haulage business and saw opportunities for themselves. I was to transport certain contraband items across the border from Canada. No heavy drugs, nothing like that; only pharmaceutical stuff that hadn't been approved yet in America. A friend I had in the organization helped me to cut a deal that was to be for a limited period only; then I was free and clear to go my own way, as long as I kept my mouth shut about what I knew. That day, when you overheard my conversation with Vinnie, was the last run. So what do you think, Franco? Was what I did so terrible?"

"I never lived through those times, Grandfather, so I can't really say. But I think that if I had, I might have done exactly the same as you did. They were stupid laws anyhow; you can't order people not to drink or gamble. Under the circumstances, I think you were absolutely right to do what you did!"

"But it was still illegal, Franco. Never forget that. I am not proud of what I did. I simply did what I had to do to survive. But that was my past, and there is nothing I can do to change it. You are lucky; you live in different times and your opportunities are far greater than mine were. So, good laws or stupid laws, the law is meant to be kept. Always remember that, Franco."

"I will, Grandfather. I will!"

"I beg your pardon, sir?"

Frankie opened his eyes with a start. A flight attendant was looking at him, a tray of hot towels in her hand. "Did you say something?" he asked.

"I thought you were speaking," she replied.

"I was dreaming. What time is it?"

"Six o'clock. We are getting ready to serve breakfast. We land at Heathrow in two hours."

Immigration, baggage, customs—then the rush for a taxi. If he had been stiff and tired from the journey, he was now fully awake.

London was one of the great cities of the world—huge and exciting, with a throb that sent the blood racing through your veins. New York was like that, quickening the pulse with its vibrancy; but London had an added ingredient—a history unmatched by any city in the New World.

Winding its way through the elegant streets of the West End, the taxi entered Park Lane and came to halt outside the Dorchester Hotel.

This wasn't his first visit to London, nor his first stay at the Dorchester. The first time was with his grandparents as a special treat for having passed the entrance examination into Harvard Law School. The second was with a friend after graduating; but it was a city he could never tire of no matter how many times he visited.

After signing in at the desk, he followed the porter and his luggage to his suite overlooking the park. Placing the bags in the dressing area, the porter then hovered expectantly. Frankie dug his hand into his pocket and came up with a ten-pound note and some small change. After a moment's deliberation, he pressed the note into the young man's hand. His face broke into a huge smile. "Thank you, *sir*! If there should be anything else, please let me know."

Frankie smiled back. "I most certainly will," he said, and closed the door.

It was a beautiful suite, much like the accommodations his grandparents shared on that first visit. His quarters had been far less grand. He unpacked, arranged the bathroom to suit his needs, then returned to the bedroom and threw open the window. The roar of the traffic below was deafening; he closed it, and the sound became a whisper once again.

Glancing at the comfortable-appearing bed, he regretted that he had an appointment for that afternoon, but nothing could be done at such a late hour. He rang the office of Phillip Peel to confirm the meeting, took a shower, and changed into a fresh suit before making his way to Wigmore Street.

The hotel's head porter was very helpful with the directions. He also told him where he could get a quick snack on the way there. "The Brass Rail at Selfridges," he said. "You won't get anything quicker than that, and it's a short distance from Wigmore Street."

It was quick, but the porter failed to tell him that he would have to eat standing at a bar. Still, it was good food as well as convenient for his appointment, and he arrived at Peel's office with ten minutes to spare.

Peel was ready for him, and he was ushered into his luxurious office by a rather prim secretary. Peel thanked her, then came from behind his enormous partners desk, a podgy hand with stubby fingers extended in welcome. "Mr. Leeman," he said shaking hands, "a pleasure. Manfred had nothing but the nicest things to say about you when he telephoned."

"That's a pleasant surprise," laughed Frankie. "Did he mention that he was my tutor at Harvard?"

"No, but I assumed that was how he knew you. He always did prefer teaching to practicing. Is he still doing his best to upset the establishment?" An amused twinkle came to his eye.

"I think he derives a great deal of pleasure from the discomfort of others over his extreme left-wing views."

"Indeed, that sounds very much like the Manfred I knew! So when did you arrive?" Peel asked when they were seated.

"This morning."

"And already at it? You impress me. I assume you had a good flight?"

"Very good, thank you."

"And where are you staying?"

"The Dorchester."

Peel gave an approving little nod and, without further small talk, came right to the point. "What exactly is your interest in Bingham?" he asked, his eyes narrowing with curiosity.

"Manfred said you and he were at Cambridge together. How well did you know him?"

"Not well," he said, "but you haven't answered my question."

"I will come to that, Mr. Peel; but first, did you know that he is an assistant district attorney in New York?"

"I have been kept informed."

Frankie found his reply a bit odd. Why would he want to be kept informed if he didn't know him well? He shrugged it off as a figure of speech. "What did Manfred tell you over the phone?" he asked.

"Nothing beyond that you were interested in Bingham's Cambridge days. Why do you ask?"

"Well, the fact is, he is the prosecuting council in a case against a client of mine, and while doing some investigating, I realized that I knew very little about Bingham prior to his immigrating. I have always found it wise to know as much as I can about my opponent; wouldn't you say so, too?"

Peel looked doubtful. "I still can't help you," he said. "You see, we didn't mix in the same circles at university. The most I can say is that he was a brilliant student, and I have no doubt he makes an excellent lawyer."

"That's what I have heard; so you can appreciate why I am anxious to know more about him. It would give me an edge. His father is Sir Archibald Bingham, isn't he?'

"Was! He died many years ago."

"I didn't know that. Did he die before or after his son immigrated?"

Sounding impatient, he said, "I really have no idea, Mr. Leeman. I know nothing about Bingham, his family, or why he did whatever he did."

"I'm sorry if I am upsetting you with my questions, but you did say you were kept informed."

Peel's face reddened. "This really won't do, Mr. Leeman; you are questioning me as if I were a hostile witness!"

"I sincerely apologize; my training I suppose."

"Then kindly leave your training to the courtroom. Now if that is all, I have a very full schedule ahead of me."

It was the brush off, but Frankie wasn't finished yet, so he dug in. "Just bear with me a little longer and I promise to leave you alone," he said.

Peel huffed. "Very well, but make it quick. I am a busy man."

"Did you know any of Bingham's friends?"

"I never concerned myself with anything about him."

"Not even one name, Mr. Peel?"

"Not even one name!"

Frankie had his doubts. Three years at the same university and the very same college. That was hard to believe, he thought. "Then there is only one thing I can do," he said. "And that is to make a trip to Cambridge and see what I can find out for myself. There have to be records, names, etc., of those in his year."

He had him, and Peel knew it. "Well, er—" he began awkwardly. "There is someone. I just wasn't sure I should mention his name. You see, he and Archie had a particularly nasty falling out; before that, they were quite close. I cannot guarantee that he will want to speak to you, of course."

"I can but try," said Frankie. "If you would be good enough to let me have his name and phone number."

"I'll do better than that. I'll get my secretary to put a call through right away. Jack … Jack Williams, that is, has a small country practice," he said, and buzzed his secretary to give her instructions.

"I really do appreciate this," said Frankie as they waited for the call to come through.

"Not at all," replied Peel. "He should still be in the office; he usually leaves around four o'clock. You know what country folk are like: don't believe in overdoing it. Can't blame him really! Sometimes you have to wonder whether it's all worth it."

"It's a lucky person who knows what they want out of life."

"Indeed! Have you visited our countryside?"

"Afraid not," replied Frankie.

"If you want to get the real feel of England, then that's what you should do. London has become a bit too cosmopolitan these days."

Frankie was about to respond when Williams was put through. "Jack?" cried Peel. "How are you, dear fellow?" Williams must have been well because Peel said, "Glad to hear it, old chap." Then, after a brief pause, "Jack, I have a young man with me from America, a lawyer named Leeman. Frankie Leeman.…" They went on talking, and, from his end of the conversation, Frankie gathered that Williams was being difficult. But, surprisingly, Peel could be persuasive and he soon handed the phone over to him, whispering, with his hand covering the mouthpiece, "I've got him this far; now it's up to you."

Williams was pleasant enough over the phone, if somewhat hesitant. "Mr. Leeman, I have spent the best part of the last twenty years trying to forget that Archie Bingham ever existed; now you come along and expect me to discuss him with you? Give me one good reason why I should?"

"In truth, Mr. Williams, I can think of no good reason other than my personal interest in him," he replied.

"Honest enough, but you still haven't convinced me."

"If my intention was to convince you, I would have provided a more convincing response. But then I had hoped the truth would be as compelling as any fabrication."

"Now you intrigue me!"

"Then you will meet with me?"

"My first instinct is to say no; but then, why not? The Savoy Grill, Monday, one o'clock for lunch. Can you make it?"

"I'll be there," he said, and handed the phone back to Peel with a nod.

"That's settled then," said Peel with a sigh of relief. "You will like Jack; everyone does. Well, as much as I would like to prolong this visit, I really do have a busy afternoon," he said rising to his feet with his hand extended.

As they shook hands, Peel said, "I will mention to Manfred, when I next write, what a pleasant meeting we had."

"Please do," said Frankie, then thanked him for his time and left.

Peel gazed after him for a moment or two, then returned to his desk. He had worried about meeting Leeman ever since he spoke to Manfred. Now he was relieved it was over. It hadn't gone all that badly, he thought, and putting him in touch with Jack was the best thing he could have done, under the circumstances. Of everyone he knew from his Cambridge days, he was the most discreet, and felt comfortable with his choice.

For years, he had tried to put his past behind him; it hadn't always been easy. Now this Leeman fellow had forced him to face it once again, and, painfully, he realized that it had lost none of its power to hurt. Archie had put him through one of the most devastating times of his life, and just thinking about it made him shake all over.

His years at Cambridge were not all that they should have been; but then, nothing about his life was ever what it should have been. His mother had never married, and in her scatterbrain way, the idea that she didn't know who was his father was a source of amusement to her; to him, it was a source of humiliation and regret that he had to bear in silence for fear of offending the moral code of society.

His mother's questionable conduct, which was erratic at best, always managed to provoke gossip of one kind or another, but it was her loose behavior that caused him the most embarrassment. Perhaps today she would be referred to as a woman before her time, but he had come to understand that her indiscretions were more a result of insecurity than immorality; nevertheless, it was a fine line that separated the two, and it was his feelings that bore the brunt of what she said and did.

She was a strange combination of childish petulance, amiability, and attractive femininity, which made her very desirable to men, and there was never a lack of them, married or otherwise, who were ready, able, and willing to take on the task of looking after her. Indeed, it was a task with her queer notions and peculiar fears. Unfortunately, it was those same things that first attracted men to her that they eventually tired of.

It was an unhappy state of affairs, but to give her her due, she always tried to do her best for him, sending him to some of the finest boarding schools when money was available, which wasn't too often. So his life was a series of ups and downs and changing schools as often as she changed lovers.

There was no permanence in his life; no figure to whom he could confide or take his problems; and as for friends, he feared getting too close to anyone, dreading the questions that might arise. As a consequence, he withdrew into himself.

It was a very lonely existence for one so young, and his hunger for companionship finally drove him into the arms of an unscrupulous schoolmaster who took advantage of his situation and seduced him.

He may have been naïve, but not blind. He knew what went on between some of the boys at boarding school. The very idea was repugnant to him, but fate can be cruel, and fear can make a person do things that were otherwise against their nature, and his fear of losing the one human being who had shown him more warmth than he had ever known forced him into a relationship that lasted until he left for university.

He saw Cambridge as being a new start, a new beginning, with new hopes and aspirations. Unfortunately, it was not to be, and he found himself in the same situation as at boarding school, with the same fears and the same sense of inferiority that had beset him for as long as he could remember. He was driven toward the only set he felt at all relaxed with, the so-called "gays," and this quickly established him as one of their number.

He sought no relationship among his newfound friends; however, he did gain their respect, and in a strange way, he knew more peace of mind than he had ever known before. That is not to say it stopped him from dreaming; far from it, and when he first set eyes on Archie Bingham, with his exceptional good looks and magnetic personality that drew people to him like flies to flypaper, his dreams revolved around him and what it would be like to actually be him. Even talk of his shocking behavior and total disregard for the feelings of others couldn't make him feel any differently. Archie was his idol, representing everything he had ever wanted to be like, especially his ease with the opposite sex.

The very last thing he expected was that this glamorous figure would actually seek his companionship, and had he not been so overawed at the prospect, he might have questioned his motive. As it was, it never entered his head for one moment that Archie was only using him for his own purposes, and when the penny finally dropped, the damage was already done.

Of course, no one could figure out Archie's motives; they were as complex as his personality and often as degraded. He thought nothing of playing with people's feelings. It was a game to him, a bit of fun; and when rumors started to fly, as they inevitably did around Archie, that they were having a homosexual affair, the shock knocked the ground from under him and he beseeched him to put an end to the gossip.

Amused by the whole idea, Archie had responded, "Lighten up. Let them have their fun; after all, it isn't really that absurd. It wouldn't be your first time, would it? But true or false, it is mine, and I must admit it gives me a kind of kick."

It was then that he realized their friendship had been nothing more than a sport to Archie, and he felt sick and humiliated. When he told him so, his reply was, "Well, I have had enough anyway; you really are a bit of a bore."

He might have gotten over the incident if his mother hadn't taken it into her head to pay him an unexpected visit. She arrived looking as pretty and youthful as ever with her baby blue eyes and blonde hair that fell in curls about her face. Archie was the first to notice her and immediately came over and insisted on an introduction.

It was most embarrassing for Peel. His mother, who loved being paid attention by the male species, quickly succumbed to his charm, smiling and giggling like a young girl and lapping up his compliments like a cat with cream. Before Peel knew what was happening, she and Archie were going off together.

It was the worst nightmare that he could ever have imagined. The gossip that followed was bad enough, but the next day, the word all over the campus was that Archie "had it off" with Peel's mother and what a great lay she was for her age.

The sniggers, the whispers behind his back, were intolerable. If Archie had plunged a knife into his heart, it could not have been more painful. He had robbed him of all pride once; now he had robbed him of his dignity, and he couldn't hold his head up for all the shame.

If it had not been for Jack, he was certain he would have taken his own life. He was wonderful to him; he knew what it was to be humiliated by Archie, and understood his pain. He also got him through the worst time of his life; and more than that, he helped him to regain his self-respect. Because of him, he was able to go out into the world and make a place for himself.

His greatest fear now was that Leeman, through his investigation of Archie, might uncover his past and so rob him of his dignity once again. He trusted Jack, and knew his secret would be safe with him. Without a doubt, he thought, he had made a wise choice in giving Leeman his name.

Frankie emerged from Peel's office feeling that he had missed something, not so much from what he had said, but from what he chose not to say. He could actually feel him holding back, but why? *Strange fellow,* he thought.

Black clouds had been gathering all afternoon; now the sky looked positively threatening. He quickened his pace when he heard thunder in the distance, and then it started to spit. As he turned the corner into Park Lane, the sky darkened further, the thunder grew louder, and the rain came down in torrents.

Taxi after taxi swished by, all occupied. He made for a doorway and waited for the rain to subside before making a dash for the hotel. He entered the lobby, his trousers clinging to his legs, his jacket soaked through, and his hair dripping into his eyes. "Got caught," he said to the doorman who eyed him with amusement.

"Indeed, sir!"

Tea was being served in the lounge, but all he wanted was to get to his room, take off his clothes, and soak his tired limbs in a hot tub. After the bath, he crawled into bed to take a rest before dinner. During the night, the thunder returned; heavy rain lashed against the window, and through it all, he slept, not stirring until the first light came creeping over the sky.

As the room grew brighter, it suddenly dawned on him that it was a new day. He looked at his wristwatch and couldn't believe that he had slept the clock around. Pushing back the cover, he got out of bed, went to the window, and threw it open. There was no rumble of traffic in the street as yet, and the sun was filtering through a mist that covered the park. He put on his tracksuit and headed for one of London's best-known open spaces—Hyde Park.

The air was sweet with the smell of earth after rain; the grass was wet; the trees still dripping; and, feeling invigorated, his feet flew over the grass as though they had wings on their heels, and he didn't stop until he reached the Serpentine, whose still waters sparkled with reflected sunlight.

He stood at the edge of the lake, his heart pounding, his pulse racing, and he felt wonderful. By now, a few early risers began to appear—jogging, walking, running. One elderly gentleman had brought some bread to feed the ducks, and their noisy quacking drew the birds from the trees ready to share in the morning feast. It reminded him that he, too, was hungry and he turned back to the hotel for breakfast.

It wasn't until he finished breakfast that he realized he had two whole days of leisure ahead of him. He didn't like being alone, but this was London and, like it or not, he was determined to make the most of it. Furthermore, it offered freedom with none of the pressures to please others, none of the arguments in deciding when and where to go. You ate when you were hungry; slept when you were tired. You pleased yourself.

He had never wandered aimlessly. Everything had always been planned down to the last detail; but not that day. The sky was blue, the air warm, and to wander was exactly what he felt like doing. He followed the flow of traffic down Park Lane and turned west at Hyde Park Corner. By then, the roads were full and the pavement bustling with the Saturday morning crowds. He ambled along, admiring the pretty girls in their light summer frocks, some down to their ankles, others baring their legs to the top of their shapely thighs. It was one of the nice things about European girls, he thought with pleasure: they didn't mind being stared at, and, taking it as a compliment, they would even smile back at you. At home, one had to be careful for fear of being misunderstood.

His wandering took him to Knightsbridge, behind which was Belgravia, a fashionable area where the well-heeled and up-and-coming executives had their flats. Back again on the main road, there was the Royal Albert Hall, the home of the famous Promenade concerts and main boxing events. Further along, the expensive shops of Knightsbridge began, and in their midst was Harrods, one of the most famous department stores in the world.

He browsed, bought gifts to take home, even chatted to a pretty young assistant who was giving him the eye. He contemplated asking her out, but thought better of it. He expected to be busy over the next few weeks and didn't want any distractions.

Time flew. The lunch hour came and went, and by the time he felt like something to eat, all that was available was tea. The British had their set hours for meals, and if you missed one, you had to make do till the next.

He found a pleasant little café close by on Sloane Street and sat at a table by the window so that he could continue to enjoy the view of one of London's fashionable streets. He filled his empty stomach with toasted teacakes, then settled back, sipped his tea leisurely, and simply enjoyed his liberty.

The day had filled him with more satisfaction than he thought possible when he set out; but when the sun dipped and night fell, he was lonely.

He spent Sunday much as he did Saturday, ambling along the streets of Mayfair this time. There was Curzon Street, where Disraeli once lived. Park Street, South Audley Street, Bond Street, where the rich and famous did their shopping; and then there were the squares such as Berkley and Grosvenor, where the American Embassy is housed.

Unlike New York, where the streets could fit into a square box, London was a fascinating maze of streets, seemingly undisciplined in its planning, yet interwoven to bring together the best in a harmony that pays tribute to the architects who created this splendid city down through the years. Once again, Frankie became so engrossed that he lost track of time, and when he returned to the hotel, tea was already being served in the foyer.

It was crowded, and if not for an elderly gentleman who beckoned him, he would not have found a table. "If you wouldn't mind sharing," said the man, "I would be only too glad of your company."

Frankie thanked him and sat down. "I didn't expect the lounge to be this full."

"It's always like this on a Sunday," he replied. "I suppose that is why I come here every week. At least I can see life around me if I can no longer take part in it."

"Oh, come on! You're not that old."

"Would you like to bet?" he asked with a grin.

"Somehow I think I better not," he replied, smiling back at him.

"Turned ninety last week," said the man. "Lonely affair. All my friends have gone to greener pastures."

"What about family?"

"No family; I never married. You looked lonely when you walked in; that's why I beckoned you. An American, right?"

"Right."

"I like Americans. I find them very open. You have a good face, a kind face; intelligent as well. You will make some lucky girl a good husband."

"Don't tell me you are clairvoyant?" chuckled Frankie.

"Not clairvoyant, just a gift for reading faces."

"I have heard of many things, but never a gift for reading faces."

"Since I was six years old. I was at my aunt's engagement party when I saw her fiancé for the first time. I was horrified by what I saw in his face and immediately told my mother to tell her sister that she mustn't marry him … he is a wicked man! Of course, she took no notice. A few months after the wedding, my aunt left him because he would beat her."

"And you saw all that in just one glance at his face?" asked Frankie.

"That's right, and it is a gift that has served me well over the years. Right now, your face tells me that you are hungry," he said, smiling kindly at him, and he called over the waiter. "My young friend here would like the full tea, and make it snappy; he probably hasn't eaten since breakfast."

Frankie was hungry, and ate heartily when tea arrived, bringing more smiles to the man's pleasant face. He was almost finished when a sudden babble of voices broke the relative quiet of the lounge. Looking up in surprise, Frankie saw a large company of elegantly attired men and women descending the stairs on their way to one of the banqueting suites. "What's going on?" he asked.

"A wedding," replied the man.

"On a Sunday?"

"A Jewish wedding."

"Ah!" he said knowingly; then he looked up again, and suddenly his heart stood still. If he had been hit by a bolt of lightning, he couldn't have been more stunned; for there, standing out like a goddess among them, was the most beautiful woman he had ever seen. Large, almond-shaped eyes; silky black hair worn back in a coil that accentuated her shapely head and slender neck; an exquisite nose; and a wide mouth with full lips that looked as though they were made to kiss. She was gorgeous.

"Wow!" exclaimed Frankie when she passed by.

"Indeed!" agreed the man. "That was a breathtaking woman."

"Indeed!" said Frankie.

"Pity we couldn't manage an introduction for you."

"A woman like that must have hundreds of men after her. What chance would I have?"

"Oh, I don't know about that! A lovely woman such as she would choose her men carefully."

"Don't tell me you read that in her face?" grinned Frankie.

"I did, and a lot more beside. There is nothing bad in her face. If I had been fortunate enough to meet a woman like that, I would have followed her to the ends of the earth."

"After one glance? I don't believe it."

"A man can fall helplessly in love at a glance."

"Don't they call it sexual attraction?"

"Is there a difference? Isn't what it turns into what matters in the end?"

"That's taking a big chance, isn't it?"

"Taking a chance is what life is about."

"How come you never took one?"

"Because I was a fool. Now I am left repeating to myself the two saddest words in the English language: 'if only.' Having regrets is the hardest part of getting old; you haven't the time to set things right. Trust an old salt, young man; you don't want any part of those two words."

Frankie could hear his grandfather saying the same thing, and glancing at the elderly man sitting on his own, save for a stranger for company, he felt sad. "No!" he said. "I don't want any part of them."

"Then don't let life slip through your fingers for fear of taking a chance; and with that thought," he said, sighing heavily, "I must take my leave of you. My landlady goes into a fit if I am late for Sunday dinner." Then, placing his bony hands with their swollen joints firmly on the arms of his chair, he struggled to rise.

Seeing the difficulty he was having, Frankie was quick to offer help. The man waved him aside. "Have to do it on my own. You know what they say: 'God helps those who help themselves,' and most of the time, there is only God and me."

His words touched Frankie, and he said, "In that case, may He always be with you."

The man studied him for a moment, and then said, "Don't be sad for me. I have had a longer time on this earth than most, and on the whole, life has been good."

Having risen, he drew himself up to his full height. He was taller than Frankie imagined, and broader. He must have cut quite a figure in his youth, he thought.

"Well, goodbye, young man," he said. "It has been a pleasure talking to you." Then he turned slowly and walked, stiff kneed, across the floor to the exit.

Frankie watched him, his eyes fixing on the revolving door he just passed through. All at once, a great loneliness engulfed him. The last thing he wanted was to end up like that old man, and it made him wonder how life could begin with such bright expectations, and then end with nothing more than the promise of the grave.

CHAPTER THREE

Walking down Piccadilly Monday morning, his stride light and easy as he went, Frankie was reminded of what his grandmother used to say to him when he was a boy. "You have a bounce in your step just like your grandfather." He smiled to himself; how he loved to hear things like that. Anything she said that likened him to his grandfather, he would lap up. He adored him, and as far back as he could remember he wanted to be just like him.

At Piccadilly Circus, he turned into Lower Regent Street, and when he came to Trafalgar Square, with its fountains and Nelson's Column, there was the Strand, and the Savoy Hotel stood less than a stone's throw away.

With half an hour to spare, he wandered down a side street to the Embankment and took a short stroll beside the River Thames. Upstream could be seen the House of Commons, a great Gothic structure dating back hundreds of years, with a tall tower at one end and Big Ben—that huge clock with the world-famous chime—towering at the other.

At Cleopatra's Needle, he turned back and his glance fell on the Tower of London—a medieval fortress that once served as a prison to many a royal personage incarcerated for life or until their execution. It was an area full of history. Even the Savoy Hotel stood on the historic site of the original Palace of Savoy that was built by Count Peter of Savoy on land given him by King Henry III in the year 1246.

As he entered the hotel, he glanced at the lobby clock and found that he had a few minutes for the men's room, then find the Grill Room to meet Jack Williams. He pushed open the door in a hurry and almost knocked aside a man who was on his way out. "I am so sorry!" he cried, seeing his dazed expression. The man straightened his glasses, setting them firmly on the bridge of his nose again, ran a hand through his thinning hair, and with the ghost of a smile murmured, "No harm done." Then, giving Frankie a wide berth, he attempted a more dignified exit.

After freshening up, Frankie entered the Grill Room. The headwaiter immediately escorted him to a table by the window where a clean-shaven gentleman of medium build was already seated. He was more taken by surprise than was Williams, whose pleasant, very recognizable face broke into smiles the moment he saw him. "I had a strong feeling it might be you," he said as he rose to greet him.

Frankie laughed. "Am I forgiven?"

"But of course!" he exclaimed, a twinkle in his eye. "After all, you are my guest."

There was a natural warmth about him that made Frankie take to him immediately. In fact, everything about him was natural and unaffected—from his mismatched shirt and tie to his sports jacket with its well-worn leather cuffs. Yet he managed to look the perfect English gentleman. He could see why his old chum from school, Peel, said he would like him.

"Would you mind if we ordered right away?" Williams asked when they were seated. "They are very busy for a Monday and we may have to wait a while before being served."

Frankie agreed, and having made their choice, they placed the order with the waiter; and then Williams perused the wine list. "Not for me," said Frankie. "I never have anything stronger than water before dinner."

"Are you sure? They keep an excellent cellar here."

"I am, but please, don't let that stop you."

"I think I will indulge myself," said Williams. "I don't get up to London all that often, and when I do, the Savoy is one of my favorite haunts." He ordered a Riesling to go with his fish; then settled back, pondering for a moment before asking, point-blank, "Now tell me, why the interest in Bingham?"

Frankie was beginning to appreciate the blunt manner of the British, so the direct question came as no surprise. "Curiosity," he replied.

Williams looked skeptical. "Forgive me, but I hardly believe you would travel three thousand miles across the ocean out of mere curiosity."

"Would you accept inquisitive?"

Williams chuckled. "Now we are splitting hairs."

"Perhaps," he replied. "Nevertheless, that is exactly what I am. I will be arguing against him in court when I return to America, and I want to know more about him. You see, it's important to me to get an impression of what the man behind the lawyer is really like. Professionally, one can never know enough of one's opponent."

"I agree. So you want me to fill in?"

31

"Yes!"

"That puts me in a very awkward position. I find discussing a colleague, on any level, unethical."

"Then explain why you are here. You knew what I was after; you could have decided not to come."

"I nearly did."

"But you didn't. Why?"

Williams smiled. "Curiosity," he said.

Frankie grinned. "Then we have something in common."

Williams eyed him closely for a moment, then asked, "Why don't we start with the real reason for your interest in him. It isn't quite as simple as you state, is it?"

Frankie smiled to himself. Williams was more astute than he gave him credit for, as were most of the British. "All right," he said, "perhaps openness is the best way to go. I have reason to believe that a client of mine has been framed in a criminal action, and the finger points to Bingham. Is that truthful enough, Mr. Williams?"

"I would say so, Mr. Leeman. At least now I understand what it is that you are after, and if Archie hasn't changed his ways since I knew him, then I would have to say that, in all probability, your assumption is correct."

"Then help me; tell me whatever you can about him."

If lunch hadn't arrived just then, Frankie was certain that Williams would have opened up; but as it happened, he looked relieved to be let off the hook.

The conversation was general during the meal, with both avoiding mention of Archie. Frankie learned that Williams was married, had no children, loved the country, fished, played tennis, and enjoyed a good glass of wine, which was obvious by the way he was savoring it with his lunch. Frankie told him as little as he could about his own life, merely saying that he was not married, but, like his host, did enjoy a good game of tennis.

It was over coffee that, with his tongue considerably loosened by the wine, Williams suddenly opened up about Archie. "When I first met him," he said, "I could not help but fall under his spell. He was the most charismatic figure I had ever known; in fact, I was so taken with him that I completely overlooked his faults. I mean, who is without fault? But then I began to notice little irritating things about him; then bigger things like the way he treated women and the way he could turn vicious at the drop of a hat for no apparent reason, and very soon his charm wore thin.

"I don't know why, or what made him choose me as a friend. We were completely opposite in every way. Perhaps it was because of that very fact; and for some time I basked in his light. He wouldn't accept an invitation unless I received one. It was a sort of joke around the campus. 'Archie's sidekick,' they called me. I didn't mind. I was enjoying all the privileges that went with being his friend.

"There were times, however, when I thought of ending our friendship, especially when I realized that he was completely without conscience. It not only upset me, it also sickened me to see some of the wicked things he was capable of. I am ashamed to say I stood by him, even when he did the most vicious thing to poor Hamish, one of our set. If I had any sense, that is when I should have protested and put an end to our friendship; but it's all very well in hindsight, isn't it?"

"What did he do?" asked Frankie.

"Well, you see, Archie was a heavy gambler, and when he was barred from most of the betting shops for not paying his debts, he found someone who didn't know him by sight and used Hamish's name to get credit. You can't mess with bookies; one way or another, they collect—so I leave the rest to your imagination."

"You mean he set this fellow up? Did he admit it?"

"He had no choice. But with Archie, guilt was like water running off a duck's back. I don't think he was capable of feeling guilt."

"What happened to Hamish?"

"He had his leg broken—as a warning."

"My God! What did he do about it?"

"He didn't. To cut a long story short, the matter was taken to Archie's father, and he settled it with a capital sum of money for Hamish as well, of course, as seeing that the bookie was paid."

"So he got away with it, but why? Why didn't Hamish go to the police?"

"What would he have gained by going to the police? With Sir Archibald Bingham's name behind him, I am sure Archie would have got off with a warning. At least Hamish got something out of it."

"And you remained friends with him after that? How could you?"

"Everyone else deserted him. I might have done the same if he hadn't made me feel so guilty about leaving him. He had, after all, given me a social life that I would never have had otherwise. Because of him, I got to mix with some of the elite of Cambridge society. So I took the easy way and stayed by him, much to my regret."

"What was his relationship with his father after that?"

"Archie never spoke of his father. I got the impression that he didn't care for him, maybe was even afraid of him somewhat. He never did come to Cambridge to see his son. Strange, really. Archie was very clever; you would have thought it would make his father proud. Then it's possible he knew his son better than most fathers."

"Fathers are usually blind when it comes to their children."

"Yes. But then no one could be that blind to someone like Archie; not all the time, that is."

"So what did cause the rift between you?"

Williams swallowed and his eyes wandered to the far side of the room, and when they returned, they were filled with pain. "It's so much easier to talk about others, isn't it?" he said sadly. "I knew that if I came here today, I would end up talking about myself. You asked before why I came; perhaps that is the reason, to get something off my chest that has been eating away at me for years and years.

"Archie destroyed my life once, and I feel that if I remain silent much longer, he just may destroy it again. I need to confide, and to whom better than a total stranger, one that I may never see after this day.

"Everyone thought Archie loved women; nothing was further from the truth. He hated them and used them whenever the opportunity arose, and it arose often. They loved him, couldn't get enough of him; then he was a handsome bugger. It was a very different story with me. Women never gave me a second glance. Of course I minded, but then I was used to it. I am no Don Juan, as you can see.

"One day, the unthinkable happened. I met a girl, and she had eyes for no one but me. She may not have been as attractive as the girls Archie went out with, but I found her pretty and I fell in love. When he found out he went berserk, even accused me of betraying him. I mean it was ridiculous, and I just couldn't understand his behavior. It was as though he considered me his property and that I wasn't entitled to a life of my own, let alone a love of my own.

"Anyhow, he treated her badly. He thought of her as the enemy. I couldn't talk to him, although I tried to explain that my relationship with Penelope had nothing to do with my friendship with him, but he wouldn't listen. Everything was black and white in his mind; a tortured mind, if you ask me, but I couldn't see it back then.

"For a while, I thought that I had got through to him, but I was fooling myself. I should have known better. I had seen enough of his shocking behavior to have understood that Archie did what Archie wanted, and Archie's demands had to be met. Whatever I had to say made no difference, no matter how I tried. Penelope tried as well, because I asked her to, and eventually I paid the price."

Williams looked away, and Frankie could tell he was struggling with himself. He waited for a few minutes, and when he didn't continue, Frankie asked gently, "What did he do?"

Williams turned his eyes to him, haunted eyes that were moist with tears. "He added my girl to his list of conquests," he said, a tremor in his voice.

Frankie had half expected it; still, when he heard it from his lips, he felt sick. "How did you find out?" he asked.

"I heard it from everyone except them, and that was the hardest part."

"She said nothing?"

"She vanished, disappeared. I couldn't find her."

"And you never saw her again?"

Williams opened his mouth to say something; then closed it again without a word.

"Then you don't know if the rumors were true or false?"

"What was I to believe? She left Cambridge without leaving a forwarding address. Not even a note for me, as if we had never meant anything to each other."

"Then you were inclined to believe the rumors?"

"I don't know what I believed," said Williams. "All I know is that I still have a hard time coming to grips with it."

"Then you never considered that she might not have been the one to blame?"

"Of course, I have agonized over it a thousand times or more, but I always come back to the question, why would she leave without trying to explain what happened?"

"If you could have found her, she would have been able to tell you. Why didn't you try? What were you afraid of?"

"What makes you think I was afraid?"

"Because it's still torturing you, and that is what fear does to people."

"You seem to know a lot about fear. So what is your advice? Forget about it, just like that?"

"No! My advice is to do exactly what you are doing now: confide, get it off your chest, but not to a stranger; to someone close, like your wife.

Also, a woman's point of view might shed some light on why someone would run away like that."

Williams appeared reflective. "Relationships should be about sharing, trusting," he said slowly as though speaking to himself. "What is a marriage worth if you cannot trust in someone you love."

Seeing the agonizing look in Williams's eyes, Frankie thought it time to change the subject. "What happened to Bingham after he left university?"

Coming to himself, he said, "He took articles with a firm of solicitors."

"Isn't it strange that he didn't follow in his father's footsteps?"

"One would have thought so; but then who could figure out Archie?"

"Do you know who the firm of solicitors were?"

"Haley & Son. Old man Haley is dead, so the son now runs the practice."

"You wouldn't happen to know their address or phone number?"

"They are listed in the directory. Actually, their offices are close by, just off the Strand."

"When I get in touch with them, may I mention your name?"

"Certainly. Alfred Haley knows me well."

"I am really grateful to you for seeing me. I know talking about the past hasn't been easy for you."

"No, it hasn't," replied Williams, "but what it has done for me is to make it easier to talk about in the future. Things must be resolved, one way or another, before they can be put behind you, don't you think?"

It was a strange reply, and it made Frankie wonder, but he made no comment.

"Well," said Williams with a sigh, "I really must be going," and with that he signaled to the waiter.

Frankie wanted to take the bill when it arrived, but Williams wouldn't hear of it. "Should I ever run into you again," he said, "it will be your pleasure; today, it is mine."

He didn't argue, and as soon as it was taken care of, they left.

Standing on the pavement outside the hotel, Williams said, "The Royal Courts of Justice are close by; it might be interesting for you to see them, if you have the time."

"I think I would like that," he replied.

"I would accompany you if I didn't have a train to catch, so this is where we part. You go east to the Strand, and I go in the opposite direction."

Frankie thanked him as they said goodbye, and walked toward the Law Courts. Williams watched him disappear into the crowd, then went his way. He was dejected; he hadn't been completely honest with Leeman, and he felt that in not being so, he had been disloyal to Penelope, and it weighed heavily upon his heart.

Why hadn't he told him that he had found her again, and that she was now his wife? What was he afraid of? That he might have thought him a fool after what he had told him? What did it matter? The truth was she was the best thing that ever happened to him. It was by a miracle that they met again, a miracle that should not be denied, and in a way, he had denied it.

He was a coward, and increasingly so every time he stopped her from telling him the truth about that day back then. She needed to speak, and he feared hearing what she had to say. How could he? How could he have wronged her so? She was no more capable of deception than Archie was capable of the truth.

God, how he loved her! But how often had he told her? Almost never. He didn't deserve her, he thought. He didn't deserve her love. Love is to trust, and he had never trusted her enough to hear her side of the story. It had to change. They would talk. They would tell each other their worst fears and their best hopes, and finally, there would be understanding between them, the sort of understanding that would overcome all.

He had made a decision, and a cloud dissipated from over his head. He hadn't felt so good in years, and he could hardly wait to see her sweet face and tell her how sorry he was for any pain he might have caused her. She would understand and forgive because she was a forgiving person.

Suddenly, a car hooted furiously, and he almost jumped out of his skin with fright when it missed him by inches. He had stepped off the curb without looking to see if the lights were in his favor, and, catching his breath, he stepped back onto the pavement and waited for them to change.

"Frankie? Hey, Frankie!"

Frankie looked around. *It couldn't be,* he thought.

"Frankie!" came the cry again, and sure enough there, halfway across the road, dodging the traffic like a footballer dodges the tackle, was his buddy Bill.

Frankie's face beamed. "Of all places! What are you doing over here?"

"I was about to ask you the same question," replied Bill. "How long has it been?"

"Too long. So what are you doing here?"

"I've been here a month having the time of my life before leaving for Paris tomorrow morning."

"Postpone it."

"I would do anything for you, Frankie, except postpone Paris. Do you know how long I have been planning for this?"

"Are you saying that you are going to do it? You're gonna write?"

"You bet your sweet life I am! What are you doing right now? Can you spend the rest of the day with me?"

"I was on my way to the Law Courts, but that can wait. Where are you staying?"

"The Grosvenor, and you?"

"The Dorchester. If only I knew; I have just spent the whole weekend on my own. So where are you going now?"

"I am going to introduce you to a gal that you wouldn't believe. She's waiting for me at the Savoy. Come on, we have to hurry. This gal has one great big fault; she's always on time."

"You haven't changed," laughed Frankie, "still playing the clown."

"Isn't everyone supposed to love a clown?" he said grinning widely at his friend.

"So tell me," asked Frankie as they rushed along the pavement, "where did you meet this girl of yours?"

"Last year at a party in Boston. We saw each other for a bit, and before she left for home, she gave me her phone number; and as soon as I arrived in London, I got in touch with her. We have been seeing each other four, five times a week for the past month, and today, as a going away present, she has promised to show me a few of her favorite places."

"Is it serious?"

"If only it were. We are just friends. She is special, very special! You'll see what I mean when you meet her."

"Are you sure you want me along. I mean this being your last day together?"

"Actually, I would appreciate your company. It will stop me from making a fool of myself. You see, I'm crazy about her; she's just not crazy about me—and here we are," he said, whizzing around the revolving door of the Savoy Hotel.

Frankie followed him and trailed behind as they crossed the floor of the foyer. "There she is!" cried Bill, quickening his pace.

Frankie couldn't believe his eyes. It was her, the girl from the wedding party, looking as beautiful as he remembered. What happened after that, he wasn't too sure. He knew that Bill introduced them, because he heard him call her Cynthia; beyond that, his heart was pounding too loudly for him to make sense of anything.

What he did feel like was a fool, tagging along while they talked non-stop. Suddenly, she turned to him and said, "Didn't I see you at the Dorchester yesterday?"

He couldn't believe that she had noticed him, and his heart missed a beat. "Um … yes."

She smiled at him, and it was the warmest, sweetest smile he had ever seen. "I thought so the moment I saw you walk in with Bill."

"What's this all about?" asked Bill.

"That wedding I went to yesterday—we were both at the Dorchester. Isn't it amazing?" she cried with delight.

"Amazing!" exclaimed Bill, looking from one to the other with uncertainty.

They had just crossed Trafalgar Square and were standing at the foot of the steps to the National Art Gallery. "I thought we would start here," she said. "It's one of my best-loved places."

It was a wonderful afternoon. She knew her London and they saw a part of it they would never have seen if it were not for her: cobbled passageways where dusty old bookshops thrived, tiny antique shops, French patisseries with the most delicious concoctions, more art galleries, quaint pubs tucked away in the corner of one mews or another, art shops and more art shops. "By now, you must have gathered that Cynthia loves art," laughed Bill.

Frankie guessed that from the first moment they entered the National Art Gallery. Her face had glowed with pleasure as they went from one painting to the next, her eyes alight with wonder and excitement as she tried to explain to them the purpose of the artist. "They are simply expressing emotion, experience, and ideas that are beyond the reach of language. Notice how each new generation of artists interprets their ideas onto the canvas. They immortalize their own particular era and we get a glimpse of their perspective on what was. It's like seeing into a person's mind," she said, the light never leaving her eyes.

He smiled to himself as he thought back. "Yes!" he said. "Not very difficult to figure it out."

"She studied at the Royal Academy," said Bill.

"D'you paint?" Frankie asked her.

Her eyes dropped. "I used to dabble," she said with embarrassment.

39

"What made you give it up?"

"It's a long story. Anyhow, I now design for my father's shoe business."

"And that satisfies you?"

"It's more a question of knowing my limitations than being satisfied."

"That is nonsense and you know it," said Bill. "You forget I have seen some of your work, and you should be painting as a career."

"Can we have done with this conversation? I really don't like discussing it. Anyhow," she said, "we are at the Selfridges Hotel, and a good strong cup of tea would be very welcome. How about the two of you?"

It was five in the afternoon and the lounge on the first floor was almost empty. They chose a comfortable couch in a corner, sank their weary bones into it, and ordered tea, scones, and whatever cake was available at that late hour. Then Cynthia left to freshen up.

"So what do you think of her?" asked Bill when they were alone.

"She's nice."

"Just nice? Come on, Frankie, I saw the way you were looking at her."

"Okay, so I like her very much."

"I knew you would. She likes you as well, I can tell." He paused then asked, "So what's going on? Why are you over here?"

"Family business. Remember my cousin Guido? Well, the police say they found a large stash of cocaine in his car."

"Cocaine? Guido?" exclaimed Bill. "That kid was afraid to smoke a joint! I find it hard to believe he's doing coke."

"He isn't. It was a plant, but go prove it!"

"Has it got something to do with Joe?"

"They haven't approached Joe yet, but it's only a question of time. The prosecutor, in this case, is a man named Archie Bingham. Ring a bell?"

"Bingham! Wasn't there someone at Harvard named Bingham?"

"That's him. He's after making a name for himself at our expense, but not if I have anything to do with it!"

"I'm beginning to get the picture."

At that point, Cynthia returned. "What?" she asked. "No tea yet? I'm starving!"

After tea, she marched them down Baker Street to Regents Park. "Can't let you leave without seeing Queen Mary's rose garden."

The entire park was worth every moment. Much smaller but more manicured than Hyde Park, Regents Park was a picturesque combination of flower beds, lawns, and a tiny lake with a rustic bridge spanning it. From there, a path edged with a fine display of summer blooms led to the inner park and Queen Mary's rose garden.

Passing through a circle of tall hedges with benches inset, a wonderful profusion of roses meets the eye, their scent intoxicating like a potent wine that goes straight to the head.

"Well?" she asked eagerly when they were seated. "What do you think?"

"Beautiful!" replied Bill, smiling at her enthusiasm.

She looked to Frankie for his comment. "Lovely!" she heard.

Content, she sighed with pleasure. "I knew you both would love it." Pointing to a huge cabbage rose, its red velvet petals curling one on top of another with a romantic softness, she said, "That one is my favorite."

"I would never have guessed!" teased Bill.

She smiled. "It has been a perfect day, hasn't it?"

"Perfectly perfect," replied Bill, his eyes lingering on her face. He had never seen her look more radiant. Then suddenly he realized what he would be missing, and a sadness crept into his eyes.

"What is it?" she asked, her voice betraying concern.

"It's nothing!" he replied. "I always feel sad when something this perfect comes to an end."

Understanding, she touched his hand. "Nothing ends, Bill," she murmured, "not if you keep a memory of it."

"You're right," he said brightening. "Anyhow, we still have this evening. Let's do something special."

"Why not dinner at the Hilton's rooftop restaurant? It has a lovely view over the city. Music, good food, and it's Monday! It won't be crowded and we will be treated like royalty."

"I like the idea!"

She turned to Frankie. "What about you?" she asked.

He glanced at Bill, wondering how he would feel about him going along. His face gave no indication either way, and feeling uncomfortable, he said, "I think the evening should belong to the two of you."

Her face fell. "No!" she cried. "I mean … tell him, Bill, tell him he has to come with us."

Bill met her anxious gaze and in a subdued voice said, "Of course, he must."

If it were anyone else, it might have put him off, but Frankie knew his friend too well. Whatever his feelings about it were, his invitation to

41

him was genuine. "It seems I have no choice," he said. He was glad. After spending the afternoon in Cynthia's company, he didn't want it to end there. She also looked pleased, and it made him feel good. Only Bill looked a trifle put out.

It was getting late, and they decided not to bother with changing for dinner and went straight for the hotel. She was right; the restaurant was half empty, and the service excellent. Bill had placed all gloom aside and kept them amused throughout the meal with tales of their escapades at university. "Frankie and I shared everything," he said, "our secrets, our clothes, even the girls! And boy … did we have some fun! Eh, Frankie?"

"We sure did."

"You must have been very close," she said.

"Like brothers. One wouldn't move without the other. I miss those days," said Bill.

"What happened to them?" she asked.

"His home is in Boston, mine in New York," said Frankie.

"But you keep in touch?"

"Sure, we do—birthdays, Christmas, and once a year we get to meet. That's what happens to college friends, close or otherwise," said Bill.

There was a pause while they reflected upon their friendship, then Frankie suddenly said, "So you are finally going to make it to Paris. What happened? Did your father relent and accept the fact you wanted to be a writer?"

"You must be joking," said Bill. "My father relent? It's not in his nature. The fact is he had no say in it this time. For five long years, I worked my butt off in his law office, trying to be the lawyer he expected of me, but I was dying inside, and he didn't even notice. He was so wrapped up in himself and what he wanted. Well, I saved enough to be independent, and for as long as the money lasts, Paris is where I am going to be."

"I'll say this for you—you have always been persistent, and that's what it takes, not to mention talent, of course, and you have plenty of that."

"Talent on its own isn't always enough; let us hope I have luck as well!"

"You're the luckiest bastard I know!" laughed Frankie. "But explain why it has to be Paris. America has produced many good writers without them having to take off."

"Part of the reason is the romance, I suppose. Like Hemmingway and Fitzgerald and so many others, I feel that Paris is the place to be. Only there, in that cosmopolitan atmosphere, can a starving artist be socially acceptable. There is also the advantage of being as far away as possible from my father's influence."

"I agree about Paris," said Cynthia. "The rest of the world merely tolerates the impoverished artist. They know nothing of the sacrifices that are entailed, nor wish to know, but the French understand. It's what makes Paris, Paris."

"Then come with me," said Bill. "Paint again."

"That's the problem. I am not prepared to make the kind of sacrifices that are needed; nor can I imagine myself roughing it for the sake of being considered an artist."

"Then who is Cynthia Gould? What is she ready to commit to?" asked Frankie.

"Why would you want to know?" she asked.

"Because you don't strike me as being a shallow person."

"You have asked me the one question that I am still unable to answer. But then, I have heard it said that it takes a lifetime to get to know yourself. The only two things that I am certain of are: one, my family, and two, my Jewish background."

"So now I have discovered that you are religious."

"Not at all. You don't have to be religious to be Jewish. You simply have to have a deep sense of who you are and where you came from in the first place."

"Then where does God figure in your life?"

"I'm not sure that he does. On the other hand, I don't believe that the world came about in a haphazard fashion. So there must be an all-powerful being. A creator."

"So in reality, you do have faith."

"To an extent. When science fails to provide me with an answer, like most people, I turn to God. When he fails, as he often does in this unjust world, who is left? It either has to be science or God, or a combination of both."

"Combination my foot!" cried Bill. "You might as well believe in voodoo as believe in some mythical being. The truth is, the world is nothing but a tiny speck in a vast ocean of space—a tiny ball that broke off from the sun, billions and billions of years ago. What took place, from then on, was evolution, plain and simple. What we are now is more of our own making than a creator's, not that we can be proud of what we have achieved. If there were such a God as the scriptures tell us there is, then I certainly hope he would have made a far better job of things than we have."

43

Frankie smiled. "Same old Bill," he said. "It seems your beliefs haven't changed much since university."

"Why would they? Nothing else in the world has changed, except the division between the rich and poor nations is greater than ever. While we indulge ourselves with too much, there are those who suffer from not having enough. As for the belief that there is a better life after death for those who suffer, they are nothing more than words to placate the poor and make the rich feel more comfortable about their obscene wealth in the face of such tragic poverty. Where is the equality the preachers preach about? Where is the humanity we are supposed to exercise?"

"No one has said the world is perfect," said Frankie, "and that is why it is important to have faith. Without it, there is no hope, and without hope, we might as well be dead. If God chose to let us have direction over our own lives, then what we have created is not his fault, but ours. If we want a better world, a more equal one, then faith is what is needed to implement it."

"Humanity is what is needed to implement it." Bill suddenly lightened up and grinned. "But then, what can I expect from you?" he said. "You are Italian, and religion to you is as much a cultural thing as Michelangelo, Caruso, and Ferrari!"

Frankie laughed. "But you must agree," he said, "that they are all top of the line."

"I had no idea you were Italian," said Cynthia.

"Don't let his fair skin and blue eyes fool you," said Bill. "He's as Italian as they make 'em."

"My father was from northern Italy," explained Frankie, "my mother from Sicily. I hardly remember them; they died when I was still a child. I'm adopted, and apart from my adoptive father, who is of British descent, the rest of the family is of Sicilian origin."

"I'm sorry about your parents," she said, her eyes soft and sympathetic.

"So am I, but then I was adopted into a wonderful, generous family who have more than made up for what I lost when my parents died. We are all very close."

"I can vouch for that," said Bill. "You would need a crowbar to pry them apart."

"I think that's nice," said Cynthia. "I know what it is to come from a close-knit family. I cannot imagine what my life would be like without mine."

"I can imagine what my life is going to be like without my family—peaceful!" declared Bill. "Not that we aren't close, but sometimes that very closeness can inhibit a person's potential. If I want to be a writer of any worth, then I have to be allowed to grow on my own terms."

The conversation moved from one subject to another. They laughed, bantered, and turned serious, their emotions running according to the mood of the argument. Slowly, all the words, the passion, and the excitement came to an end, each of them retreating into themselves to ponder over the events of the day—their thoughts, their feelings.

Frankie would have liked to know more about Cynthia, but he could detect a sudden tension in his friend that made him feel awkward, as though he was intruding.

Bill suddenly glanced at his watch. "Almost midnight," he said, breaking the silence.

"I suppose we better be going," said Cynthia.

No one wanted the evening to end; least of all Frankie, who feared it might be the last he would see of Cynthia.

There was some argument over who would pay for dinner. Bill won, and as soon as the bill was paid, they left.

It was a short distance from the hotel to Cynthia's flat on Park Street. So much had already been expressed; so many views exchanged. There seemed little left to talk about, and so they walked in silence, still in a reflective mood.

At the entrance to her building, Cynthia bade Bill goodbye. "I'll miss you," she said.

"No, you won't," he replied, "but it's a nice thought to take away with me."

"Will you write? Let me know how things are going?"

"I'm not much of a letter writer, strange as it may seem. I'll send you a Christmas card."

She laughed. "I thought you didn't believe in Christmas?"

"I don't," he said, "but then neither do you."

"Oh Bill! You're such a fool. Just be the best damn writer in the world, okay?" And throwing her arms around his neck, she kissed him; not slow and passionate like a lover might, but gently as a friend.

Frankie felt uncomfortable as he watched, and took a step back. He was the intruder, the outsider, once again. She glanced at him, her expression one of sympathy, as if she sensed what he was feeling.

"Well, this is it!" said Bill, and with a last, lingering look at Cynthia's lovely face, he turned to leave.

Expectantly, her eyes met Frankie's. He hesitated for a moment; then, in a somewhat stiff slow manner, said, "Goodbye," and they shook hands.

Disappointed, she whispered, "Goodbye!" and rushed into the building as if she couldn't get away fast enough.

With an unspoken question between them, the two friends began to walk toward the Dorchester Hotel. Suddenly, the sound of a woman's hurried steps made them stop and turn to see who it was; and there, in the dusky light of the street lamps, was Cynthia running toward them, coat open and whirling.

Frankie glanced at Bill. If he was surprised, he didn't show it; in fact, he said nothing when she caught up to them. She looked from one to the other, uncertain of herself, then pressed a piece of paper into Frankie's hand. "My phone number," she gasped. "I'm not in the directory." And with an apologetic glance at Bill, she turned and ran back.

Frankie didn't know what to say to his friend. There had been a strained silence; now it seemed deeper. When they reached the Dorchester, Bill said, "Don't do it. Don't get in touch with her."

Embarrassed, Frankie felt the need to defend himself. "Look, I'm sorry," he said. "I had no idea she was going to do something like that."

"I suppose you think I must be jealous?"

"No, of course not," he replied quickly.

"Of course you do, and of course I am, but that isn't the reason I don't want you to see her. Neither of you are casual people. You have strong feelings about everything, strong ties. You heard her say how committed she was to her people, and I know how committed you are to yours. Only pain can follow an affair between the two of you."

"For heaven's sake! A few dates, that's all we are talking about."

"Don't you think I noticed the strong attraction between you right from the first minute? That woman is ready to give herself, and she doesn't give herself lightly. Let it be, Frankie. She'll get over you soon enough, if you just leave her alone."

"If it really means that much to you, all right, I'll forget about her."

"You would be doing the right thing."

"Perhaps."

"Look, I'll let you know as soon as I'm fixed up with an apartment, and maybe you can come over to Paris. We can spend some time together; have a great time the way we used to. Remember how good it was?"

"Yeah, I remember, but a lot has happened since then. It isn't easy to recapture something that has gone forever."

"It's always worth a try?"

"It's too sad when it fails."

"You're right as usual, buddy," said Bill.

"Don't lose touch; that is important now."

"Yeah, true friends are hard to come by."

There was a brief hug and a slap on the back, then they parted.

Somewhat nostalgic, Frankie watched him disappear down the road to the Grosvenor Hotel; then, with a relief that follows a deep breath, he entered his hotel.

CHAPTER FOUR

The first thing that caught Frankie's attention when he awoke in the morning was the slip of paper with Cynthia's phone number that he had placed on the bedside table the night before. What was he thinking? he wondered. He had made a promise to Bill; he should have destroyed it the moment he reached the room.

Suddenly angry, he snatched the paper, tore it in two, and threw it in the wastepaper basket. There were more important matters to attend to before getting involved with a woman he had only just met.

Keeping himself busy, he rang room service and ordered breakfast. He looked up the phone number for Haley & Son solicitors, put a note of it beside the telephone, and went to take a shower. By the time he finished dressing the order had arrived.

One glance at the bacon and eggs, the croissants, and his appetite vanished. It was impossible. He felt like some lovesick fool who had just discovered the attraction of a woman. Damn, he thought and rushed over to the wastepaper basket, fished through it until he found what he was looking for, and without giving it a second thought, telephoned Cynthia.

The moment she answered, he felt an even bigger fool. "I—I hope I haven't wakened you," he stammered. "I—I want to apologize for last night."

"For what?" she asked.

"I—I should have asked for your phone number. I wanted to, but I felt awkward in front of Bill."

"I thought that might be the reason. I felt a bit silly myself, running after you like that," she said hesitantly.

He breathed a sigh of relief. He no longer felt like an idiot. "When can I see you?"

Her reply was instant. "When would you like to?"

"Tonight," he said, and held his breath in anticipation.

"Is seven too early?"

Never had he met a woman who didn't play games to begin with, and it felt refreshing as a cool breeze on a hot summer's day. "I'll pick you up at seven," he said.

"Flat nine. You know the building. I'll make the arrangements. There is an old pub down by the river that I know you'll love. Must go, see you later."

He now tucked into the bacon and eggs with relish, and at nine thirty telephoned the offices of Haley & Son. "Whom shall I say is calling?" asked the young voice on the switchboard.

"Frank Leeman. Tell Mr. Haley that I have an introduction from Mr. Jack Williams."

"I'll see if he's in," she replied chirpily, and returned almost immediately. "Mr. Alfred would like to know in what connection you wish to speak to him?"

"Tell him that I am a lawyer from New York and that the matter is of a private nature."

Moments later, Haley was on the line. "Mr. Leeman, how may I be of assistance?" he asked in a clipped English accent.

"I am making inquiries about a lawyer named Archie Bingham, and Jack Williams mentioned that he took articles with your firm."

"That is correct, although my father had more to do with him than I. Unfortunately, he is no longer with us."

"But you do remember him?"

"Er—what is the nature of your inquiry?"

"May I have half an hour of your time? You need only say where and when."

"I don't know! I'm really very busy, and, as I said, I had little to do with him."

"He must have made some impression on you."

"I fail to see what that has to do with you."

"Mr. Haley, please say you will have lunch or dinner with me, and then I will explain."

"I never take a lunch hour, and dinner is out of the question."

"Please, Mr. Haley, you would be doing an American colleague a big favor."

"You make it difficult to refuse." He paused then said, "I'll tell you what. Every Friday, I spend a quiet hour at my club before going home. Do you know St. James?"

"No, but I could find it."

"Good! Write this down," he said, and gave him the address. "Five thirty for drinks. Ask for me at the porter's desk."

"Thank you, Mr. Haley. I'll be there five thirty on the dot."

Frankie replaced the phone, and then sat back and thought. Three days! There had to be something he could do in the meantime, and then it occurred to him, if Archie had practiced in England, there had to be a record of it somewhere—of course, the Law Society. Where else?

Upon making inquiries, he discovered that the Law Society was situated in Chancery Lane, in the City of London. He could make a phone call, but decided he might do better if he went there in person.

The cab driver knew it immediately. "'Op in, guv," he cried. "I know the city like the back o' me 'and."

He did, indeed. All the little side streets and back doubles, and before Frankie knew it they were there.

"Want me to wait, guv?" asked the cabby.

"I don't know how long I will be."

"It's gonna rain."

"I'll take my chances," said Frankie, and after thanking him, paid him off.

He already knew that the British were sticklers for rules and regulations, but he didn't realize just how stuffy they could be until he came up against the receptionist at the Law Society. "Yes," she said, "they did have a legal journal with past and present members listed, but that information was for members only."

"I am a lawyer!" explained Frankie.

"An American lawyer!" she said, looking down her nose.

"Look, Miss. I am not asking for the crown jewels—just some information!"

"You might as well be asking for the crown jewels," she said in that haughty tone of hers.

"Well, how is anyone to get information about a lawyer?" he cried in exasperation.

She huffed in annoyance. "That is your business, sir," she said. "Now, if you will excuse me, I have work to do."

It was the polite British "kiss off," and he went away feeling frustrated and sorely defeated. And to top it all, it had started to rain. Normally when it rained in London, the taxis either seemed to disappear or were taken. Fortunately for Frankie, one rolled up minutes after he emerged from the Law Society and dropped off a city gentleman in his bowler hat and rolled umbrella at the ready. "The Dorchester," said Frankie getting in.

That particular taxi driver either didn't know the back routes or was out to take Frankie for a ride. As it happened, it turned out well, and as they neared Selfridges, he tapped on the partition and asked to be dropped off. He paid him and went inside the huge department store. It was lunchtime and, in no hurry to return to the hotel, he thought he would grab a bite to eat and look for an umbrella.

If time passes quickly, it didn't pass quick enough for Frankie and it seemed an age before he was ringing Cynthia's doorbell. He thought he knew what to expect, but when she answered, he was stunned by her loveliness all over again.

Her face lit up when she saw him. "Hello," she said, giving a nervous smile.

This was a different side to her: shy, uncertain, and he found it appealing. "Hi," he said, and stepped over the threshold into the hall. She closed the door after him and took him through to the lounge.

"Make yourself comfortable. Whisky is on the side table. I shan't be long," she said and left him alone.

He glanced around the room; it was well furnished in traditional style: warm colors, a few choice antiques beautifully inlaid, an Adam fireplace in white marble, crystal chandelier and sconces, but what really caught his eye was the painting over the mantelpiece. It was a pastoral scene with a stream meandering through the lush countryside with two young boys asleep beneath the boughs of an old gnarled tree. The artist had caught the sun shining through the leaves in broken beams, lighting the figures of the two boys in an amber glow.

He was still staring at it when she returned to the living room. "What do you think?" she asked.

He hadn't heard her come in and turned with a start. "Yours?" he asked.

"One of the few that I finished."

He turned to look at it again. "Bill was right," he said, "you are good."

"Not good enough. Now if you are ready, we ought to be leaving. I booked a table for nine."

"I thought you said we are going to a pub?"

"We are. There is a restaurant upstairs." Then, lowering her eyes, she asked shyly, "Would you help me on with my jacket?"

He went to her side. He could feel her trembling as he placed the jacket over her shoulders, and all at once, he had her in his arms. Her body melted against his and their lips met in a passion that neither of them could have anticipated. Suddenly, he drew away. "I'm sorry," he said, "I shouldn't have done that."

"Please!" she whispered, "don't spoil it by apologizing." And the next moment, they were together again in a heated embrace, their lips caressing, their hands exploring, their emotions running away with them.

Afterwards, when he looked down into her eyes, tears glistened. He kissed her lids. "Regretting it already?" he asked gently.

"How could I? It felt so right."

"I know," he whispered. "That was how I felt."

"Then why does my heart hurt so much?"

"I don't know," he said and touched her lips with his. "You tell me."

"I suppose because, even while you were holding me, I knew that it couldn't last. It isn't fair, is it? We should never have fallen in love."

"I should never have gotten in touch with you. Bill warned me not to, but I didn't listen. I didn't want to listen. All I could think of was being with you, and what it would be like to hold you in my arms."

"I feel like saying to hell with everything I have ever believed in, everything I have expected of myself, and just surrender to what I have found in you," she said.

"Could you do that, in all honesty?"

"Could you?" she asked.

"I don't know. I didn't expect this to happen. How can you give up a lifetime of believing in something important in a just a moment?"

"Then we have a problem. Let's just take what we have now and let tomorrow take care of itself."

"It might be painful!"

"I don't care."

He kissed her, and they clung for a while. Suddenly she asked, "What shall we do?"

"Perhaps we should go," he said, "or we may run the risk of starving to death in each other's arms."

The pub known as the Prospect of Whitby was situated on the Thames, close to one of the city's roughest neighborhoods, the East India Docks, which is part of the greater London Docks. This portion of the river was once the busiest thoroughfare in the world, at a time when England not only ruled the waves, but most of the trade. Although its glory was now diminished, it still had an importance as well as a certain aura that was built upon the reputation of the sailors, men of commerce, and ladies of the night from that bygone age.

After the taxi had taken them through some of the oldest and seediest backwaters of the city, including some streets that dated back to the Elizabethan era, they entered a world of boarded-up buildings and narrow-terraced cottages that looked ready to be condemned. And here, flanked by derelict warehouses, was the famous pub, a tiny beacon of light in that rundown area.

"This is it," said Cynthia when the taxi came to a stop.

"This is it?" he asked in disbelief.

"Wait until you get inside."

History oozed out of every corner of the small, crowded room; even the well-polished bar spoke of long ago, while the clinking of glasses and the loud chatter of the well-heeled patrons brought it back to the present.

"Well?" she asked.

"Fabulous!"

"There is a verandah over the river at the back. If you can manage to push your way through to the bar, we could take our drinks out there."

"What will you have?" he asked.

"Let's try ale from the wood."

She watched him maneuver his way through to the bar; then return, a glass in each hand, trying not to spill the contents as he made his way back through the tight crowd. She took one of the glasses and they stepped out onto the verandah.

The last rays of the dying sun shimmered like gold upon the surface of the water. A barge slipped silently by, much as they did in the reign of Elizabeth I. The rhythmic sound of the tide as it lapped against the wooden posts of the verandah had a soothing effect. Resting her head against his shoulder, Cynthia put a hand in Frankie's.

Caught in a tide of emotion, they neither spoke nor moved. They had discovered love, and love needs no words, only the touch of a hand, a tender glance, a sigh.

Once the sun had disappeared, Cynthia murmured. "I suppose we better go in or they may not keep our table."

He followed her up the narrow staircase to the dining room. The chatter in the restaurant was more restrained than the hubbub in the bar downstairs. A fresh-faced waiter, with green hair standing up in spikes, saw them to their table.

"Got a couple of Dover Soles," he said. "That's if they haven't gone yet."

She ordered the sole; Frankie went for a fillet steak—rare. Over coffee, their eyes met and lingered, both suddenly aware that their love was impossible. It was an emotional moment; their feelings and their particular devotions left no room for anyone outside of their faith. Heartbroken, Cynthia looked away and said, "I think we better leave."

On the ride back in the taxi, he could feel the tension in her hand as he held it. He made no comment. When they reached home, she whispered, "Stay the night."

He wanted to but how could he? Their affair had barely begun, and already he could see that she was suffering. Bill was right; there was nothing casual about them or their love, and to prolong the agony would be unfair to her.

"Perhaps we are going a little too fast," he said.

"Have we time to go slow?" she asked.

"No!"

"Then what does it matter?"

"It matters. If not now, then later."

"What are you saying?" she asked, a note of fear in her voice.

"I'm not sure," he replied.

Suddenly she was angry, and opening the door of the taxi, she cried. "Then let me know when you are," and getting out, she slammed the door behind her.

The taxi took him on to his hotel. He felt bad. He had done the very thing he didn't want to do: he had hurt her. He had been selfish, thoughtless, but however late in the day, wasn't it better to do the right thing now? Of all the women in the world, he thought, why did he have to fall in love with her?

Wednesday morning found him depressed and tired from a sleepless night. He needed to get her off his mind or he would go crazy. He went for a run in the park; it didn't work. He took a cold shower; all it did was leave him feeling cold and more depressed. Breakfast was a cup of coffee. How was he going to fill the day? he wondered. Then an idea came to him. Why not go up to Cambridge? It would help fill the time and there had to be someone, even one person on staff, who still remembered Archie. He discovered a train was leaving at ten thirty. If he hurried, he could catch it.

At eleven thirty, the train rolled into the town station. He had no plan of approach, no idea whom to ask for. The Master of Bingham's old college, he thought—that would be a good place to start. The stationmaster pointed him in the right direction and he set off.

Cambridge is the main town in the county of Cambridge and stands on the River Cam. It is an ancient place that was once a Roman station, but now its importance is mainly due to the university, which dates back to the thirteenth century. The various colleges encompass the town with their lovely gardens, on both sides of the river, and as soon as Frankie found the college Bingham had attended, he went in search of the Master's office.

He was in luck. The Master of the college ,Geoffrey Price, happened to be free that hour, and his secretary showed Frankie to his room. "Always happy to welcome a graduate of Harvard to Cambridge," he said, shaking his hand warmly. "Are you here simply to tour the university, or is there another purpose to your visit?"

While searching for the college, he had given some thought to what he would say. "I am writing an article on British law and its influence on the American system and the name Sir Archibald Bingham keeps cropping up. I believe he graduated from this college, is that correct?"

"Yes, it is. Are you writing for a specific journal?"

"A new journal not out yet. Of course, I would like the piece to be riveting, and I thought you might be able to help me there."

"Well, I am flattered, of course. As a matter of fact, Bingham and I graduated from this college together."

"So you knew him well?"

"Quite well! He had a brilliant mind even then, and it was obvious to all of us that he had a distinguished career ahead of him."

"His reputation is well known in the law circles of America, so I thought a piece written on a more personal level might be of interest to the American public."

"Beyond these ancient walls, I knew nothing about the private life of Archibald Bingham I'm afraid."

"He had a son, I believe?"

"Yes, he did. In fact, he also graduated from this college. I wasn't his professor, but I do recall him quite well; he looked very much like his father. Brilliant as well, I was told."

"Who was his professor?"

"I don't recall."

"Is there anyone who might remember?"

"Professor Gates. He and young Archie were reading law at the same time. I feel certain he would remember the name of their professor."

"I would love to speak to him."

"I think that can be arranged," he said, glancing at the time. "Lunch is in half an hour. If you will be my guest, I could introduce you."

Professor Gates was a very amiable fellow who enjoyed talking, especially when it came to Archie Bingham. "Yes indeed!" he exclaimed, his eyes alight with interest. "We did have the same law professor, but, unfortunately, he is no longer at the university. Now if it is Archie you want to know about, I think I knew him as well as most, which isn't saying much."

"What impression did he make on you?"

"The same impression he made on everyone, I would say. He could be charming when the mood took him, but you would have been wise to beware of those charms; he could turn nasty at the bat of an eye, which he did more often than not."

"Then you didn't like him?"

"Didn't like him, didn't trust him. But then, who did?

"He did have friends, I gather?"

"None that lasted."

"Are you saying that he was a loner?

"Archie was an enigma. No one really understood what he was about. One thing I do know, however, he wasn't a loner."

"Sounds a fascinating character!"

"Hypnotic, some would have said. Not that I ever found him that riveting, but certainly interesting."

"Tell me as much as you can about him."

"Good or bad, he aroused a passion in people. He was the sort of man everyone loved to hate; and guilty or not, when something shocking happened, it invariably was attributed to him. Perhaps because we were never really friends, I saw him more objectively than most. Don't misunderstand; I held no brief for him. He was a rotter, no doubt about it; but there were occasions, one in particular, when he didn't deserve the accusations against him."

"Such as...?"

"He was in his final year at Cambridge. For one reason or another, all his friends had deserted him, and he began to mix with an undesirable element that used to frequent a particular café in town. There was a girl, fifteen she was, who used to work there after school. Very shy but pretty; unusual type of girl, really. Never could understand how she came to be there.

"Anyhow, it used to amuse Archie and his friends to tease her. You could see she didn't like it, was even a little afraid of them, which only made their game more exciting.

"I don't know all the details. Some say it was for a bet; others that he simply fancied her. The next thing I heard was that Archie was going out with her, which did surprise me."

"With a minor?" exclaimed Frankie. "A bit dangerous, wasn't it?"

"As it turned out, very! You see, not long after Archie left Cambridge, the rumor spread that she was pregnant, and that her father, who held Archie responsible, was seeing a lawyer about bringing charges of statutory rape against him."

"Good God! That must have been a nasty shock for him."

"I'm sure it was—as well for his father. Anyhow, the whole thing suddenly died down and not a word was heard about it again, and that was after someone said that he saw Sir Archibald leaving her father's house one evening."

"Pay off?"

"No comment!" replied Gates.

"So he must have been guilty."

"I believed so at first; but then she had the baby and, according to my calculations, it would have had to be a seven-month baby or Archie wasn't in the picture. I saw that infant a week after its birth, and I can tell you that was no seven-month baby. It was full term."

"How could you be sure?"

"My sister had five of them, so I know babies, and that one was nothing less than nine pounds."

"So whose do you think it was?

"Not Archie's. The whole incident was very strange. Nothing seemed to add up, including what happened afterwards."

"Afterwards?"

"Well, not a month after the birth, the girl was found in an alley, beaten to death."

"Good Lord!" cried Frankie.

"Indeed! It shook us all. I mean, something like that just doesn't happen in Cambridge."

"Was the person responsible found?"

"No. The police eventually wrote it off as an unsolved murder. It was established, however, that she hadn't been killed in the alley, but moved there afterwards to make it look like a mugging."

"Then whoever did it must have known her."

"Her father accused Archie. Said he saw him in the vicinity the very day she was found. Personally, I doubt her death was intentional, and that whoever was responsible, panicked and moved her body to avert suspicion."

"What drew you to that conclusion?"

"If you want to kill someone, wouldn't you strike them on the head? Her body took the beating. That's not the work of a killer. That was the deadly assault of an extremely angry person."

"So who? And why?" asked Frankie.

"I gave my thoughts to the police, but they didn't follow through."

"They must have questioned Archie about it. What did he have to say?"

"I'm not sure they did. You see, her father suddenly withdrew the accusation. Said he had made a mistake, and that the person he saw couldn't have been Bingham because he was far too short and plump. Then, as soon as it all died down, he picks up his family and moves to London where, it was said, he had bought a house in Tottenham. Now the question arose, where did all that money come from?"

"Savings? An inheritance?" asked Frankie.

"He had been on the dole for years, and what he collected from the government he drank away in the pub. His wife had to clean floors, and his daughter had to support herself—by waiting tables, while at school. As for his two sons, they were as bad as the father. And an inheritance? He didn't come from that sort of family."

"So what was your guess?"

"Not for me to say, but why? That is anyone's guess."

"But I thought you believed Archie was innocent," said Frankie.

"Still do! More went on in that girl's family than met the eye. If I were into speculation, that is where my thoughts would run."

"That's heavy stuff!"

"Very heavy; but then I am not into speculation."

"And the child? What happened to it?"

"It was a girl. As far as I know, she is still living with the family in London. She is the man's granddaughter after all," he said with a cynical lift of his brow.

"So Archie's reputation, or what was left of it, was still intact."

"As you said, what was left of it." Professor Gates heaved a sigh. "Well now, I have a class in a few minutes. Of course, when you write your article, you won't print a word of what was said, I trust?"

"I think I know enough law not to seek a libel suit."

"Funny," mused Gates. "I had almost forgotten about Bingham. I wonder what has happened to him? No good, I would think."

Frankie smiled to himself. "Goodbye, Professor Gates," he said. "And thank you for your time."

Frankie caught the five o'clock back to London by the skin of his teeth. He barely had time to close the carriage door when the whistle blew and the train chugged out of the station. Being alone in the first-class compartment, he put his feet up on the bench opposite him and sank back with a sigh of relief. He wouldn't have wanted to wait around for another hour.

The door to the corridor suddenly slid open and an elderly woman, with a dog in her arms, entered the carriage. Frankie put his feet down immediately and sat up straight. "Would you mind?" asked the woman as she struggled to close the window. "Poopy hates a draft—don't you, Poopy?" she said, snuggling her nose against the dog's tiny face.

"Allow me," said Frankie, and closed the window. The woman made a few appreciative little noises. Whether they were meant for him or the dog, he wasn't sure, but she was smiling at the dog at the time.

Throughout the journey back to London, he couldn't get the story of the dead girl out of his head. Gates was right; nothing seemed to add up, and you were left wondering if Bingham was, indeed, vile enough to commit such a vicious act against the girl and then try to cover it up. You would have to be crazed out of your mind to do such a thing. Vicious he was, but that crazy? He couldn't believe it even after everything he had heard about him.

He had caught the slow train and he didn't get back to his hotel until seven in the evening. He wondered what Cynthia was doing or if she was thinking about him, and to help get his mind off her, he made a call to his grandfather.

"Franco!" he cried. "Thank God you phoned. Johnny has been breathing down my neck since Monday. What is there to report?"

"It's much too soon, but I have been getting down to it—seeing people who knew him well—and I still have more to see. Tell him not to worry; everything is going according to plan."

"The truth, Franco?"

"Things are beginning to build up against him. Nothing that we can use yet, but it's early."

"You sound different, Franco. Is something the matter?"

"I'm not used to being on my own this long, that's all."

"Have you phoned your mother?"

"I will phone tomorrow, promise."

"Why not today? Something is wrong, isn't it? Don't lie to me, Franco. I can hear it in your voice."

"I'm tired. I have just returned from Cambridge, where I met someone who told me a tragic story about a girl and her affair with Bingham; it has taken a toll on me. Also, I have a lot to think about. Is Mother all right?"

"What can I say? The same as usual."

"Then I will telephone tomorrow."

"I understand. Don't forget to let me know as soon as you have news."

"Don't worry, Papa, I will."

The moment he replaced the phone, he felt guilty about his mother. He knew that she must be anxious to hear from him, but he wasn't in the best of moods, and certainly not up to her problems. Anyhow, she was probably too drunk to speak to him at that hour of the day.

He glanced around the room and heaved a sigh. It had a lonely feel about it, and was smaller, as though the walls were closing in on him. He had to get out of there or go mad, he thought, and went down into the dining room for something to eat. His thoughts kept returning to Cynthia, and the food tasted like straw in his mouth. *Damn her! Damn her!* cried the little voice inside his head.

By the time he returned to his room, he was more of a wreck than when he left. He knew what was right, but carrying it out was another matter, and throwing caution to the wind, he telephoned her.

"When can I see you?" he asked.

"Now!" she cried.

"Now?" he laughed. "It's late."

"I don't care," she replied.

"I'll be right over," he said, and replaced the receiver.

***

The moment he stepped inside her flat, they fell into each other's arms. Nothing had ever felt so good to him, and taking her by the hand, he led her to the bedroom.

Later, his arms still holding her, she asked, "You weren't going to phone, were you?"

"I believed it was for the best," he said.

"I sat by the telephone all evening, and when I thought I would never see you again, I wanted to die."

His arms tightened around her. "Don't ever say something like that again. Don't even think it," and he kissed her tenderly.

Tears were running down her cheeks. "I can't help it," she whispered. "I have never felt like this before, and it hurts."

"I know. That is why I was afraid to phone you. I can't bear hurting you and I can't bear the thought of not seeing you. We really do have a problem."

"Didn't we realize it from the beginning? Oh, Frankie!" she cried. "I just want what we have for as long as possible, and after that, whatever will be, will be."

"But—"

"No buts, my darling! Just stay with me tonight."

He drew her closer. "Yes!" he whispered.

CHAPTER FIVE

For the next twenty-four hours, Frankie put all thoughts of Bingham on hold. There was time enough for obligations. He and Cynthia needed space for themselves. They knew how painful their love could be; now they needed to know how wonderful it was.

They awoke Thursday morning to a cloudless sky. She cooked breakfast, telephoned her office to say that she wouldn't be coming in that day, and then devoted herself to Frankie.

They wandered through the park the rest of the morning, had lunch at a café in Shepherds Market, returned home and made love, and talked a lot and laughed, as lovers will do.

She insisted on making scones for tea. They were a disaster; still he ate them, and she laughed when he called them stones instead of scones. They were having fun—no thought of the future, for there was no future, only the present—and they were intent upon making the most of it.

"I know just what we should do this evening," she said, her eyes lighting up. "How would you like to picnic in one of London's most beautiful settings?"

"As long as I am with you, every setting is beautiful."

Her face beamed. "Give me two hours and we will have a picnic fit for a king."

"Then while you are busy, I'll return to my hotel, change, and return at six. That okay?"

"Perfect," she replied.

Humming happily to himself back at the hotel, he decided to telephone his mother before taking a shower. Within seconds, she managed to change his mood.

"Oh darling!" she cried. "I'm glad you phoned. I've been feeling wretched all morning. Aldo came to see me earlier and I was nasty to him. He only comes by when he wants something from me, and so I just let fly."

"I'm sure he understood, Mother. What did he want?"

"I don't know. I didn't give him a chance to say anything and he left in a huff. Now I feel bad about it; as if he hasn't enough to put up with from that wife of his!"

"Now, Mother, you know how happy they are."

"I know no such thing. He's changed since he married her. He used to be such a good-looking boy. Now look at him—fat and miserable! I swear that woman uses food as a substitute for sex! Poor Aldo."

"Well, I wouldn't brood over it if I were you. He'll soon forget about it."

"No, he won't, and it will be months before he visits me again. It's bad enough Johnny stays away, but then he feels guilty because I know how he killed his wife."

"Mother, she died of cancer; no one killed her."

"How do you think she got cancer in the first place? Johnny used to fool around just like your father, and that's how she got cancer. It aggravated her. Oh, Frankie, I'm so scared—I don't want to get cancer."

"For heaven's sake, Mother, it doesn't happen just like that. It was one of those tragic and unfortunate things, and it doesn't mean that it will happen to you."

"A lot of unfortunate things happen in this family—there is a curse on all of us. Do you really think that Vinnie is as happy-go-lucky as he pretends? Well, he is not. He puts a happy face on for Papa's sake because he doesn't want him to find out."

"Find out what?"

"That he has a mistress!"

"He's a bachelor. He has had many mistresses."

"Not like this one. She's not only Jewish but she's black as well, and she has been the only one for the past ten years. What do you think of your uncle Vinnie now?"

"If what you say is true, then it is his business, Mother, and I don't see what's so terrible."

"I'll tell you what's so terrible," she said. "We are, all of us, doomed to love the wrong person!"

It was the last thing he needed to hear. "That's enough!" he snapped. "What has gotten into you?"

She started to weep, her words almost incoherent. "It—it—it's your father! He will kill me, just as Johnny killed his wife. I don't want to die the way she did. Oh Frankie! Come home, please!"

It wasn't just her rambling that got to him; it was the sound of fear in her voice. She had come to depend upon him in the last few years, and suddenly he resented that dependency. He wanted his life back, and more than anything he wanted to be free to love whomever he wished. He knew that Cynthia was at the root of these feelings, and he felt ashamed. "Look," he said gently, "you need rest. Tell your maid to make you an ice pack. That always helps to clear your head, and I will phone again in a few days."

"Promise, my darling?"

"Of course, I promise."

He was so drained when he came off the phone that it took an immense effort just to take a shower and put on fresh clothes, when what he really wanted to do was crawl into bed, pull the covers over his head the way he did when he was a child, and sleep away all his fears and doubts. But he was no longer a child, and he had to face up to the facts, no matter how painful they were.

He must have looked pretty awful when he arrived at Cynthia's place, because the first thing she asked when she saw him was "Are you all right?"

No, he wasn't all right! But the sight of her standing there—an apron around her waist, her hair falling in wisps about her face, her cheeks shining as if she had just polished them—made him realize how much she meant to him, and a cloud lifted from over his head. He took her in his arms and kissed her passionately. "I'm fine," he said, "now that I'm here with you."

She smiled happily. "I didn't expect you so early. I had planned to look my best when you arrived."

"You look very good to me just as you are!"

"In these old things?"

"In anything, especially without anything!" he said with a cheeky grin.

She blushed like a schoolgirl. "I might have known you would say something like that."

He laughed. She had the face that made a man happy just to look at it, and for the moment, he forgot all about his mother and his feelings of hopelessness.

He waited while she changed, then they took the picnic she had prepared to the car and placed it on the back seat. "She's a beauty," he gasped when he saw the red Mercedes sports car. "New?"

"A few months old. It was a twenty-fifth birthday present from my parents," she said as she got in behind the wheel.

"Mine was a Porsche," he said as he got in the passenger's side. "I would have preferred a Ferrari."

"Who wouldn't!" she replied and switched on the engine.

"So where is this beautiful place of yours?" he asked as they drove up Baker Street.

"In Hampstead Lane. It's called Kenwood, and it was once the home of the Rothschild's. They donated it to the people. You'll love it. The grounds are superb, and there is a lake with an island on which an orchestra plays, and this evening it's Gershwin."

"And who doesn't like Gershwin."

After Baker Street, one road looked much as another to him until they reached Hampstead High Street, which had more of a village atmosphere. They climbed the hill to the Heath, passed Stone Pond, then went down by the side of the Heath to the Spaniards Inn, a pub made famous by Dick Turpin—the most notorious highwayman of the eighteenth century. Passing through a narrow passageway, they were in Hampstead Lane, with its grand houses one side of the road, and Kenwood on the other.

"This is some area!" said Frankie.

"Isn't it? My grandparents used to live in that lovely block of flats opposite the pond we passed. I spent many happy hours there."

They found a parking spot, took the picnic basket and a blanket from the back of the car, and went through the gate into the park.

To one side of the path, rolling lawns unfurled and a profusion of color filled flowerbed after flowerbed, while a host of trees provided shade from the evening sun. On the other side of the path, the lawns swept down to the lake, and there in the center, beneath a shell-like canopy, was the orchestra, its music filling the air.

Cynthia chose a spot on top of a hill, and with matching strides they climbed to where a tree stood, its branches spreading out like a giant umbrella. They laid the blanket beneath it, placed a linen cloth on top, and unpacked the treat.

China plates, cut glass, silverware, and then salmon pate, lamb chops in aspic, green salad, stilton cheese, strawberries, and a bottle of Bollinger champagne packed in ice.

Frankie looked on in disbelief. "This isn't a picnic! It's a banquet. How did you manage it in such a short time?"

She smiled, beckoned him closer, and like a conspirator whispered, "With one call to Fortnum & Mason."

They exchanged thoughts and ideas while they ate, wanting to know as much as possible about one another, the scenery and the music a romantic background as they gazed into each other's eyes. When they finished, they lie back on the blanket, fingers entwined, eyes closed, each taking pleasure from the nearness of the other; and thus, a perfect evening passed all too quickly.

A sudden breeze stirred the air, and they opened their eyes to a sky that had deepened to shades of night.

The orchestra played on. A full moon shone down, and a myriad of stars twinkled like diamonds against a dark velvet heaven. Frankie bent over Cynthia and kissed her parted lips, and overwhelmed by emotion, their mouths sought one another's over and over again.

All at once, the music came to an end, but not the magic. Slowly, they rose, collected their things, and hand in hand walked back down the hill and along the path to the gate.

"Do you think you could find your way back?" she asked.

"I think so," he replied.

She handed him the car keys, then got in the passenger's side as he got behind the wheel. He could feel her eyes on his face as he drove, and his heart soared with love.

When they reached her place, he parked the car and, taking the picnic basket from the back seat, followed her up to the flat.

Once inside, he lifted her in his arms and carried her to the bedroom—and there, somewhat self-consciously, she undressed. And so began a night of love neither would ever forget.

He awoke the next morning to find her watching him from a chair across the room. "You were restless as you slept," she said. "Something is bothering you. What is it? Is it us?"

"No. I was having a bad dream, that's all."

"Do you want to talk about it?"

"If it were one simple thing, perhaps I could, but it's many things; mostly to do with my family and their expectations of me, my mother especially."

"Why she especially?"

"My mother is an alcoholic," he said with a sigh. "Sometimes just thinking about it drains me. I spoke to her before I came here last night. She was in a strange mood and it upset me."

"I knew something was wrong the moment I saw you. It must be awful for both you and your father."

"He is part of the reason she drinks. He plays around. Their life is one big mess, and I am bang in the middle of it. Does that shock you?"

"It doesn't shock me; it upsets me to see you suffer because of it. What about your mother's family, what are they doing to help?"

"What can they do?"

A sudden flicker of pain crossed her face.

Concerned, he asked, "What is it?"

"How long have we, Frankie? When must you return?"

He had been expecting the question for some time. It wasn't going to be easy telling her the truth, but what alternative did he have? "I'm here investigating another lawyer on behalf of my family. It's one of those obligations I feel I have to fulfill. Six weeks. It will probably take another six weeks."

"Then it's back to America," her voice strained with anguish.

There was a brief pause, then a hushed, "Yes."

She stared at him and the unhappy look on her face almost broke Frankie's heart. Suddenly she rose, mumbled something about breakfast, and rushed to the kitchen before he had a chance to see the tears that were beginning to gather.

Damn! he thought. *Why must it be like this?* and he sprang from the bed, went after her, and held her close. "No regrets, my darling, no matter what." Through her dressing gown, he could feel the pounding of her heart. "Say it!" he whispered. "No matter what!"

She lifted her face to his. "No matter what!" and brushed away a tear.

After breakfast, he asked, "Must you go to the office today?"

"It's Friday. There is always a lot to do before the weekend, but I might be able to take the morning off. I'll phone my father and see if he can manage without me for a few more hours."

"Will he ask why?"

"No! He knows that I wouldn't ask for anything unless it was important."

"Then he trusts you; that's good. There has always been a lot of trust among us in my family. I suppose that is why I sometimes feel bad about having doubts."

67

"We all have doubts at one time or another; it's only natural."

"Not in my family; it's one for all and all for one. Look, I don't want to bother you with my problems. I have to work them out for myself."

"It's not good to keep too much locked up inside you; it's better to share."

"I doubt you would understand, so let's forget about it and you now make that call to your father."

She turned to go. He pulled her around and kissed her. "Now you can go."

When she returned, she was all smiles. "We have until two in the afternoon," she said, "then I have to leave, but I will be back by five to make dinner. We can just relax afterwards, listen to music, or do whatever you want."

"Actually, it works out well. I have an appointment at five and I shan't be back until around seven. That should give you plenty of time to concoct something special."

"I don't know how special the meal will be, but just sharing it with you will make it special for me."

"And for me," he said, and brushed her cheek with his lips.

Frankie returned to his hotel as soon as she left. He changed into a suit, looked over last-minute notes, and then ordered a taxi.

On the dot of five the taxi pulled up in front of an impressive gray-stoned building in posh St. James. He paid the cabbie, then glanced up at the building before mounting the steps to one of London's most prestigious men's clubs. As he entered the main hall he was approached by an elderly porter who looked as though he came with the original fixtures. At the mention of Haley's name, his dull eyes became alive. "Right this way, sir," he muttered in a quivering voice, and shuffling his feet along the marble floor, he escorted Frankie to the smoking room.

"The gentleman by the window," he whispered discreetly and, having performed his duty, returned along the corridor to his desk.

The moment Haley saw Frankie walking toward him, he placed his cigar in an ashtray and rose to greet him. "Glad to see you found us," he said as they shook hands.

"Thanks to your wonderful taxis!"

"They are, indeed, a wonder. I'm drinking whisky. What will you have?" he asked when they were seated.

"The same, but with ice."

"Of course!" he exclaimed with a grin, and summoned an elderly waiter who might have doubled as the porter who escorted Frankie.

"Do you smoke?" asked Haley.

"Never acquired the habit."

"Good for you!" he said, lifting his cigar from the ashtray and puffing rings of smoke into the air. "My wife won't allow me this simple pleasure in the house, so I come here most evenings and indulge myself before going home."

"With all the new information on tobacco and its effects, life must be quite a trial for the seasoned smoker."

"It certainly is," agreed Haley. Then after a curious glance, he asked, "Tell me something about yourself."

"What would you like to know?"

"You appear to be very young. How long have you been qualified?"

"Five years now."

"From Harvard?"

"Yes, as a matter of fact. How did you know?"

"A good guess. Didn't Bingham go to Harvard after he left England?"

"He qualified while I was in my first year. But somehow I get the impression you already knew that."

Haley gave a secretive smile.

Frankie's drink arrived, and after the usual toast, Haley asked, "So what has Archie been up to these days?"

"Why would you assume that he has been up to anything?"

"Because I knew him. Isn't that the reason we are here? To discuss him?"

"You were reluctant over the telephone. What changed your mind?"

"You did, for one; curiosity for another. He has been up to something, if I know him."

"Then it would seem we both share an interest in him."

"A dislike would be more correct; then, given your family background, I can understand that."

"If I read you right, you have run a check on me."

"I don't discuss a fellow lawyer with just anyone. I like to know with whom I am speaking."

"Then I take it you are comfortable with what you discovered."

"You may take it that I detested the man enough to be honest with you."

"Good enough, Mr. Haley."

"So, what is it you want to know?"

"As much as possible; but first tell me, what did he do to make you so bitter toward him?"

Haley raised his glass to sip then slowly put it down again. "Did I say that I was bitter? Anyhow, what does it matter? He was completely without principle. Made a fool of my father. Made a fool of all of us and I will never forgive him for that, not as long as I live. I suppose I am bitter. You see, I saw right through him from the beginning, but not my father. He was blinded by the fact he was the son of Sir Archibald Bingham, an idol of his."

"You must have expressed your doubts to him."

"I warned him, but he wouldn't listen to a bad word against him. My father could be very naïve when it came to people in general. He was completely immersed in trust work, considered an authority on the subject. So you see, he never came into contact with some of the seedy characters you meet in practice, and believed most to be honest and trustworthy like himself."

"So what did Archie do to confirm your suspicions?"

"For starters, he persuaded my father to take him under his wing. Said he'd always had an interest in trusts. Ha! The only interest he had in the work was to get a good look at some of those documents. I will say this for him, though: he proved to be very good at the work and was a big help to my father, at first."

"At first?"

"He was so good, in fact, that my father made the mistake of allowing him full access to some of the most sensitive documents such as the Nesbitt Trust. Poor Patricia didn't stand a chance once he made up his mind to marry her."

"He was married?" asked Frankie in surprise.

"Almost, but didn't quite make it to the altar. He eventually showed his true colors, and not a day too soon, I might add."

"What happened?"

"Let me start at the beginning. The Nesbitt Trust, of which Patricia is the life tenant, was, and still is, worth untold millions, and my father was the sole trustee, with full discretionary power. He took his duties very seriously, especially so in the case of Patricia, whose parents were his dearest friends before they died in a plane crash; and with no other family to fall back on, she looked to my father for guidance.

"Well, Archie must have had a good look at that trust and decided that he wanted a piece of it. Now there was only one sure way to get it, and she, poor idiot that she was, fell hook, line, and sinker for the bugger."

"But you said he didn't marry her in the end."

He laughed. "Well, Archie had one big problem—infidelity. He just couldn't keep his trousers zipped up long enough to get to the altar. Just a day before the wedding, Patricia came home early from one of her charities and found him stretched out on the library floor with another woman."

"You mean, in her house?" exclaimed Frankie in disbelief.

"He had been living there since the engagement, at her insistence, so he said. Had his own apartment, in that mansion of hers; his own butler, plus an Aston Martin, which she bought for him as an engagement present; and he threw it all away!" said Haley, his eyes glistening.

"What possessed him?"

"I learned never to second-guess Archie. He was as unpredictable as he was loathsome. Would you believe he even dipped his hand into the petty cash while they were engaged? Let one of the secretaries take the blame for it. I knew he had to be involved, with all that money he was spending to keep up with those who suddenly wanted to become Patricia's friend, but I couldn't prove it, so the girl was fired and we were left with Archie."

"But he came from a wealthy family!"

"Whatever he had was never enough for him."

"How did your father take it?"

"You mean Archie's indiscretion?"

"Yes!"

"It destroyed his faith in his own judgment. He found it difficult to believe how wrong he had been to trust someone he liked so much. And worse, he felt bad about having given his blessing to the union between his best friend's daughter and the son of a man he had idolized for so many years. That is what really pained him."

"Did anyone know who the woman found with Archie was? I mean, was it someone he picked up, or knew well?"

Haley took a sip of whisky and followed it with a puff at the cigar. "I have no idea," he said. "What does it matter anyway? The man behaved despicably, but that was Archie."

"And so she ended it?"

"What else could she do? She might have been stupid in the first place, but she couldn't ignore what she saw with her own eyes."

"How awful!"

"You can't imagine how awful. She was always shy and uncomfortable in the presence of people, and now she is a complete recluse. Of course, I see her, and so does my wife, who has been a friend of hers since school days."

"Who is the trustee now that your father is dead?"

"The court appointed me."

"What happened after that? Surely, Archie didn't continue to work with your father."

"Heavens, no! My father felt betrayed; couldn't bear to look at him. His first instinct was to throw him out; but then, he always did have a soft streak. Also, out of respect for Sir Archibald, he let him stay to finish his articles. There were only a few months left, you see. However, it was left for me to deal with him, and I can tell you, it wasn't pleasant. The swine didn't have an ounce of remorse in him; in fact, he behaved as if he were the one wronged."

"How did his parents receive the news?"

"According to my father, his mother took it calmly. Sir Archibald was a different matter. He was filled with indignation over his son's behavior; couldn't apologize enough. Wouldn't have liked to be in Archie's shoes when he confronted him; but then, I doubt there was much love between them anyhow."

"I have heard that said before, but what makes you say it?"

"Just a feeling you got when you saw the two of them together."

"What was his father like? The man, not the lawyer."

"He was of striking appearance. Not quite as arrogant as his son, but I suspect he could be a bit overpowering at times. But then, I never really socialized with him, except for a short period when Archie was engaged to Patricia."

"After he finished his articles, to whom did he go?"

"He didn't. He went straight into practice for himself."

"Immediately?"

"Bought a going concern. Tried to take some of our clients with him, but they wouldn't have it. Few liked him."

"I don't understand. If he had his own practice, what made him leave England?"

"Ah!" exclaimed Haley, with a glint in his eye. "Now we come down to the bottom line, but I am afraid you will hear no gossip from me. Ethics— all that nonsense! On the other hand, there is nothing to stop you from digging deeper," he said with a wink.

"I would have to know where to start."

"Use your imagination, Mr. Leeman. He ran an office, and an office doesn't run without a chief clerk. Now, his father had a clerk by the name of Thomas Phipps, and he had a son who bore the same name."

"I appreciate the input," said Frankie.

"Oh please! What have I told you that you couldn't have found out for yourself?"

"And of course, the telephone directory is the place to look."

"If a phone number is what you are looking for," he replied.

He was a strange combination, thought Frankie: congenial with an edge of mischief. He certainly wouldn't like to cross him. "Well," he said, "it has been a pleasure to meet you, Mr. Haley. My one regret is that I didn't have the privilege of knowing your father. He must have been a wonderful man, being of such high moral standards."

He had said the right thing, and Haley's face beamed. "He was indeed." Rising to his feet he asked, "May I give you a lift anywhere?"

"My hotel is reasonably close by and I do need to stretch my legs, but thank you for asking."

Passing the porter's desk on their way out, Haley called, "Good night, Boswell." The elderly porter bent his head and peered over the top of his glasses. "Oh, it's you, Mr. Haley! Good night, sir."

Once outside, Haley said, "My car is parked just over there," and pointed to a maroon Rolls Royce on the other side of the road, "so good-bye, Mr. Leeman."

"Goodbye, Mr. Haley, and thank you once again."

A smug smile crossed Haley's face as he got behind the wheel of his car. For years, the thought of Bingham had bothered him. Perhaps now, with that fellow Leeman on his back, he would get what he deserved. It was about time someone took him to task.

He turned on the engine, listened to it purr for a while, then put the car in gear and slowly pressed his foot down on the accelerator. The Rolls slipped smoothly out of its parking spot, into the center of the road.

He glanced at the clock on the dashboard as he drove. It was past seven. Abigail would be furious with him for being late; but then, she was always furious with him about something or other. There was no pleasing her, no matter how he tried. The problem was she was bored. Not that she said as much, but he knew her well, and it frightened him to think that she might take it into her head to leave him one day; so he did what any man in love might do and gave in to her every whim.

She'd had an affair with Archie and was always throwing him in his face. Archie would do this. Archie would do that. Archie knew how to keep

her amused. Archie was a bastard, he thought, who used to beat her whenever the mood took him, and she loved it, so she told him, with a gleam of
excitement, while they were on honeymoon. God, how he hated him!

He did try to be a bit bolder when making love, but it just wasn't him,
and he failed to please her anyhow, so what was the point? But the worst
part was the contempt with which she looked at him, and he knew that she
was comparing him to that swine.

If only he didn't love her so much! But then, how could he not? He had
loved her since they were children, playing together in the back garden.
He had made up his mind, even then, to marry her. That rotter Bingham
nearly upset his plans. Might have done if his intention hadn't been to gain
an introduction to Patricia all along.

Then he had his own little secrets. To that day, Abigail had no idea he
was aware that she was the woman Patricia found with Archie. Knowing
her as he did, she must have planned the whole thing from the moment he
dropped her in favor of her friend. No one takes advantage of Abigail and
gets away with it. When she had vengeance on her mind, heaven help her
victims. God knows what her explanation to Patricia was. But then, she
could make anyone believe what suited her.

He heaved a sigh. His father would turn in his grave if he knew what he
was doing to keep her happy. The mansion in Wildwood Road, the Rolls,
the flat in Cannes, the boat—not to mention the jewels, the Dior gowns—
all paid for out of Patricia's trust.

"We are only borrowing the money," she would say when he questioned their conduct. "You will pay it all back someday." She knew very
well it was nigh impossible to repay the sums they were stealing. Stealing!
The word sent shivers down his spine. He never dreamed that he could be
capable of such a crime.

Without having noticed the drive home, he suddenly found himself
pulling into the garage of their house, which faced the Heath extension in
one of London's most prestigious suburbs. She had always been jealous of
the way Patricia lived, ever since her father lost his money in a bad deal
and they had to move to more modest accommodations, and the moment
she saw the large house, she knew that she had to have it.

Haley entered the garden through the side door. There she was on the
terrace, swaying backwards and forwards on the hammock, a drink in
her hand, looking as ravishing as ever with her flaming red hair tumbling
about her pale shoulders, much as it did when she was in her twenties. Her
skirt was pulled up above her knees, showing off her long brown legs and

shapely thighs. Her nipples strained against the bodice of her dress in a provocative manner. She had wonderful breasts, full and firm with never the need of a brassier. How they excited him, and his heart missed a beat just thinking about them.

Hearing his footsteps, she turned. "You're late," she said. "I was about to have dinner without you."

"I had a meeting."

"Oh! Who with?"

"You don't know him—an American lawyer from New York."

"You didn't go to the club then?"

"It was at the club."

"A business meeting at the club? That's not like you."

"It wasn't a business meeting. He wanted to know about Archie," he said, watching her closely for a reaction.

There was none. She was a master at hiding her feelings when she wanted to. "What did you tell him?" she asked casually.

"Nothing you need worry about."

Her green eyes regarded him with caution. "And what is that supposed to mean?" she asked.

"Make of it what you like, but there is no need to get your knickers in a twist over it!"

"You're full of strange remarks this evening. What has got into you?"

For a brief second, he actually hated her. "I took a long, hard look at myself on the way home, and I didn't like what I saw."

"Oh I see!" she said with a contemptuous grin. "We are on about that again, are we? It's a bit late for a conscience, wouldn't you say?"

"Well, one of us ought to have one, my dear," he said tartly.

Her lovely face suddenly turned dark and ugly. "You fool!" she cried. "You work and work, investing and managing that woman's money for the best part of your life, and for what? We deserve more than the pittance we get out of it. Now, let us have no more of this nonsense and go in for dinner. Mavis had been very patient while trying to keep it hot for the past hour."

What was the use, he thought, and followed her in to the dining room.

"You're smiling," said Cynthia when she opened the door to Frankie. "Does that mean your meeting went well?"

"Sort of. I think I am on to something. I have the name of Bingham's chief clerk when he practiced law in England. He certainly forgot to mention that on his visa."

"Bingham? Is that the lawyer you're investigating?" she asked.

"Yes, and I feel very hopeful."

Her face clouded. "Then the investigation will soon be over."

He understood her fears, and taking her sad face in his hands, he said, "I promise, whatever happens, we shall have our six weeks together."

"Six weeks!" she sighed. "And when they have gone, what then?"

Her words were torture to his soul. "So what do you want me to say?"

"I don't know! Love shouldn't be like this. There shouldn't be any boundaries, no chains. We should be able to love freely without thought of race or religion."

"You need to share more than just feelings if love is to survive. I thought we both understood that from the beginning. Are you changing your mind? Are you saying that you could give up everything you believe in for the sake of love? How long do you think it would last, if we did? There would be regrets at some point, and I don't ever want to regret having loved you. This way, I will never stop loving you. No matter how far apart we may be, you will remain a part of me forever."

Tears gushed down her cheeks. "You're right," she said. "If only we weren't so damned sensible about everything, life would be so much simpler. I am scared, my love, because I know that if I never see you again, or never touch you or feel your arms around me, I will surely shrivel and die."

"Not if our love goes on," he whispered, and took her in his arms and kissed her tears away.

He realized that he needed to devote the entire weekend to her, with no outside distractions. What little time they had was too precious to spoil. Monday would be soon enough to get back to work and get in touch with Phipps.

Their days were a mix of joy, tears, and passion. They were growing close, and bit by bit, he began to confide more about himself and his family and what their connections were, and the reason for his investigation of Bingham. She listened without judging. "That's what I love about you," he said, "you don't condemn out of hand."

"Do I have the right to condemn another?'

"Mafia connections? It would shock most people."

"Crooked politicians, crooked police, the abuse of power—those are the things that shock me. What your grandfather did didn't hurt anyone."

"I understand that; you seem to understand it, but some people can only see things in black and white."

"Then they are color-blind. My great grandfather had a similar problem when he first arrived in England. Not too many doors were open to Jewish immigrants in the early 1900s. Perhaps if there had been a Jewish Mafia, or its equivalent, in this country, they might have been forced to join them to make a living. But there wasn't, so the immigrants did what they had to and set up their own industries to employ their people. It was how my family got started in the shoe trade. My great grandfather was a cobbler back in Poland, so what else could he do? If things had been more equal back then, my father would probably be a cobbler today, instead of the successful businessman that he is."

"At least there are no skeletons in your family," said Frankie.

"No family is without its skeletons, and for my father, it is my brother."

"What's wrong with your brother?'

"Nothing, as far as I am concerned, but my father would disagree. My brother is 'gay' and my father can't come to terms with it."

"It takes a man time to adjust to something like that."

"That is because they tend to see their sons as an extension of themselves. They are not; they are individuals in their own right, with their own personalities and needs, and until my father learns to let go of his image of what Paul is supposed to be, he will never be able to accept him as he is."

"How does your mother react to all this?"

"As she always does—with love, understanding, and the hope for Paul's happiness. That is all that concerns her."

"And you find it easy to accept the way he is?"

"What way is he except the way God made him? I always knew he was different, even before he realized it. I never loved him less or more because of it. He is my brother, and we will always be close, no matter what."

"What does he do?"

"He is in Israel at the moment, trying to sort out his life. At least there, he can live it in peace, and my father can feel comfortable. Of course, my mother and I are working on Dad, hoping for the day when he will be able to accept Paul unconditionally. It's slow, but we are getting there. You see, he has never stopped loving Paul; he simply fails to understand him for now."

"Your brother is lucky to have you for a sister."

"No more family talk," she pleaded. "Let's just concentrate on us." And taking his arms, she pulled them around her and kissed him.

All too quickly, Monday arrived and Cynthia had to be in the office. Frankie returned to his hotel, sent clothes to the laundry, and packed others to take to her place in the evening. He also had that important phone call to make and got out the directory to look up Thomas Phipps.

There were two Thomas Phippses in the phone book. It had to be one or the other. He tried the first one. A little girl answered. "He's my grand-dad," she said. "I'll call him."

There was a growl in the background. "Who's on the blower, Jeannie?"

"A man, Granddad; he wants to speak to you."

"Does the man have a name?"

"Forgot to ask."

"You always forget."

"Sorry, Granddad!"

"Oh, never mind. I've got to do everything else for myself, I might as well find out who it is for myself. Yes!" he huffed impatiently into the receiver. "Who wants to talk to me?"

Frankie realized he had to be Phipps Sr.; nevertheless, he asked, "Is this the same Thomas Phipps who used to work for Archie Bingham the solicitor?"

There was a pause, then the man asked cautiously, "Who wants to know?"

"My name is Frank Leeman, Mr. Phipps, and I am an American law-yer."

"So?"

"So are you the Mr. Phipps I am looking for?"

"That depends on why you are looking."

Cagey old so-and-so, thought Frankie, smiling to himself. "I have a feeling that I am speaking to the wrong Mr. Phipps," he said.

"Then I'll thank you to stop bothering an old man," he replied sharply and replaced the receiver with a bang.

That certainly didn't go down well, he thought, and dialed the next number in the book. It was engaged. He tried again five minutes later. A woman answered.

"Here!" she exclaimed when he told her his name. "Aren't you the gent who spoke to Dad a few minutes ago?"

"If you mean the gruff old man with the temper, yes."

She laughed. "That's Dad all right! He told me not to say anything to you. Anyway, my husband isn't home; he's at work."

"Have you a number where I can reach him?"

"Don't know as I should give it to you. Dad would be real mad with me if I did." There was a pause while she thought; then she asked, "Is it Archie you want to know about?"

"Yes. Did you know him?"

"Only met him once, but that was enough to leave a lasting impression. Handsome devil, he was. Didn't like his eyes, though; they looked right through me. Made me feel all undressed."

"So you didn't like him?"

"Wouldn't say that! My husband didn't care for him much, though."

"Why not?"

"I think I've said enough. Don't want Dad mad with me."

"I really would like a word with your husband, Mrs. Phipps. It would be to our mutual benefit, I can promise you."

"Umm ... well, that puts a different complexion on it, it does. Can't do no harm in you having a word with Tom. Got a pencil and paper, have you?"

"Yes. Go ahead."

"Just a minute, love, got it written down somewhere. Ah ... ready?" she asked.

"Just one thing," she said, when she had given him the number. "Don't say I said anything. He wouldn't like that."

"Not a single word," he whispered.

She giggled like a young girl, then replaced the phone.

Phipps was with the senior partner of his law firm when Frankie phoned. "I could ask him to phone you," said the girl on the switchboard.

He didn't like leaving messages. "I'll try again later," he said. "How long before he is available?"

"About an hour," she replied.

One hour thirty minutes later, Frankie was speaking to Phipps. "You're Leeman. Right?" he asked.

"That's right. Your wife mentioned that I phoned, then?"

"She did, and so did Dad."

"And he told you not to speak to me?"

Phipps laughed. "You got that right."

"Not an easy man to talk to, your father."

"You've got that right too. Likes to keep things to himself, he does."

"What about you, Mr. Phipps? Are you better disposed toward strangers asking questions?"

"If there is a good enough reason."

"Having a reason is important, Mr. Phipps. I am also a very reasonable man."

"Go on, Mr. Leeman. I'm listening."

"I don't like wasting a person's time, especially when time is money."

"You sound like a man after my own heart. Who would have thought that I would agree with a Yank?"

"You don't like Americans, Mr. Phipps?"

"You're okay. Just don't like the way you do things."

"Well, agree to meet me, and perhaps I may alter your mind."

"My father would skin me alive if he ever found out. Of course, it's all right for him. Sir Archibald rewarded him very nicely for his years of service. All I received from that bugger of a son of his was a thin 'thank you.' Can't do much at the bank with a 'thank you,' can you?"

"Let me say that I am a man who believes in rewarding those who help me."

"I think we could get along very nicely with that kind of philosophy. Do you know Harley Street?"

"I've heard of it."

"There is a mews just off. Nice little pub there—quiet, not too many people around. Can't make it tonight, but I can tomorrow. Is six o'clock all right for you?"

"Perfect. How will I know you?"

"I'll know you. I can spot a Yank a mile off."

Frankie chuckled. "Tomorrow at six then," he said, and hung up.

Frankie felt excited. He was certain this was going to get results. It was just a question, now, of how much. He glanced at the time. It was too early to phone his grandfather, not that he needed his okay on the money side of it; he had already given him carte blanche but he wanted to keep him up-to-date, with the family being so anxious.

Somewhat anxious and restless himself, he went for a run in the park, and by the time he returned, he was ready to make the call. His grandfather was very pleased to hear what he had to say. "You are right, it does sound positive. Johnny will be pleased. There's no problem with the line of credit, is there?"

"None. So what do you think, Papa?"

"Whatever it takes. Don't stint."

"That's what I thought." He hesitated for a moment and said, "Papa, don't say anything to Johnny just yet. I don't want to get his hopes up, then let him down for an unforeseen reason."

"You sounded positive a few moments ago. What changed your mind?"

"Nothing is certain, Papa, you know that. I just want to be absolutely sure, that's all."

"All right, I'll keep it to myself, but let me know as soon as you find anything more."

"Give me a week. I may need to do a lot more checking first."

"Sure," he said, then after a pause, "I get the feeling you're holding something back, Franco. What is it?"

"Nothing. I have just been a bit uptight lately. It's nothing, nothing at all."

"The investigation has been getting to you. Is that it?"

"A bit. The man is unscrupulous and I am hearing things I don't like. Anyhow, it will be over soon. Give my love to mother when you next speak to her. She needs your reassurance, Papa. She is uncertain of herself. Her mind seems to be going off in a strange direction."

"What do you mean?"

"She has a fixed idea in her head that she is going to die of cancer, and that is all she thinks about."

"She probably has Mama and Johnny's wife on her mind. She'll be all right. I'll go by and talk to her this afternoon."

"Bye, Papa. I'll phone again in about a week's time."

The moment he put the phone down, he hated himself. He knew why he was delaying, and it had nothing to do with checking on Phipps's story, and he felt unsettled about it. The least he could have done was to be honest.

Cynthia picked up on his mood when he arrived. "You look troubled, again," she said. "Weren't you able to reach the person you wanted?"

"I'm meeting him tomorrow night, but how I feel has nothing to do with that. I spoke to my grandfather after I spoke to the man in question.

I wasn't completely truthful with him, and I have never done that before. I made an excuse for not phoning to let him know how it goes with Phipps, and that is after knowing how anxious the family are about this affair."

"Because of us?"

"That was only part of the reason."

"And the other part?" she asked.

"I don't know how to explain it, but as soon as I made the appointment with Phipps, an excitement took hold of me. Getting to know and understand Bingham is like watching one of those old 'cliff-hangers' in the cinema: you can't wait for the next episode. I hate what I am doing. I am horrified by what I hear, but at the same time, I'm intrigued."

"Sounds as though you are becoming obsessed."

"Exactly! What kind of person is intrigued by another's wickedness?"

"The human kind."

"What if I should get what I want, and still can't stop digging? Why is he getting to me like this? It scares me."

"As soon as it's over, you'll feel more like yourself again."

"Will I? The truth is I'm getting to know more about him than I know about myself."

"I don't understand what you are trying to say."

He sighed, "I don't either. Look, forget what I said. Right now, all that matters is that we are together, and to hell with Bingham and everything and everyone to do with him!"

Frankie found Harley Street easily the next day, and, just as Phipps said, the mews was just off the street. It was a quaint mews, with a mix of cottages, shops, and a small block of flats with the pub immediately opposite. It was a tiny place, almost indistinguishable from the other shops except for that distinct aroma of a pub. There couldn't have been more than half a dozen people sitting at the bar, or at one of the marble-topped tables that were scattered around. It took a few seconds before he noticed the middle-aged man with the graying hair and thin mustache, raising a hand to beckon him. Then, using a foot to push a chair out from the table as Frankie approached, he said, "Take a seat, Mr. Leeman."

Frankie smiled as he sat down. "What gave me away?" he asked.

"The tie," he said. "No English gent would wear a tie like that with an expensive suit."

At a glance, Frankie sized up Phipps. Blue shirt, stiff white collar, sober tie, and an ill-fitting jacket in charcoal gray. The typical uniform of your underpaid clerk, he thought. Phipps noticed the glance and his lips curled cynically. "So what's your pleasure?" he asked, keeping a steady eye on Frankie's face.

"If that's ale you're drinking, I'll join you," he replied.

He rose and went to the bar, and Frankie noticed how his trousers rode up as he walked, to show a good deal of black sock. He returned with two glasses, placed one in front of Frankie, and the other beside his first drink. "A chaser," he said with a grin, and sat down.

Frankie raised his glass to Phipps, then took a sip. Phipps raised his half-finished glass, then finished it off in one go. Putting the glass down again, he wiped the froth from his upper lip with the back of his hand and asked, "So what's this all about?"

Frankie eyed his craggy face with interest, took another sip of ale, and then said, "I thought the agreement was for me to ask the questions and you to answer them."

"Just as soon as you have given me reason enough," came his impudent reply.

Frankie raised an amused eyebrow and, placing a hand into his inside jacket pocket, withdrew an envelope, placed it on the table, and slid it across to Phipps without taking an eye off his face.

Phipps looked at it for a moment, then slowly picked it up and looked inside, counting the contents without removing them; then, poker-faced, he slid it back across the table to Frankie, his eyes fixed on his face. "My wife just got laid off work," he said. "Now, I don't have to tell an intelligent gent like yourself what hard times these are. It could be anyone next, even me. There is no loyalty between employer and employee these days. It's everyone for themselves and to hell with the next guy. But then, I don't suppose you know too much about that."

"I'm all too aware of the difficult times, Mr. Phipps," he replied and withdrew a second envelope from his pocket and, placing it with the first, pushed them back to Phipps, who then picked them up and weighed the contents of the second envelope in his hand.

Phipps declared, "That's more like it," and put them in his pocket.

"Now," said Frankie, "if your information can match the sum, I would say we have struck a good deal."

"You'll be pleased," he replied with confidence.

"In that case, the ball is in your court."

"I'm not going back on anything, but I would like to know what you intend to do with the information I give you."

"Have no fear; whatever is said remains between us."

"And Bingham?"

"If what you have to say is as good as you think, I doubt he will want to publish any of it."

"As I thought," he said, "you intend to confront him with what you learn."

"Does that bother you?"

"Not really. Didn't like him that much. Now if his father were still alive, I wouldn't be talking to you. He was a bit of all right. Didn't look after me when Archie left the practice, but did look after my father, and in my book, that made him a toff."

"If you disliked Archie so much, how come you worked for him?"

"It was my dad's idea. Sir Archibald needed someone he could trust to keep an eye on his son and report to him if anything was amiss. I wasn't thrilled with the thought, but the money was good, and that's what it's all about, isn't it? Money!"

"You can't do much without it, that's for sure," Frankie replied. "That was when Archie first went into practice, right?"

"Right! He bought a going concern, old, established but underdeveloped. Archie knew his stuff. I'll say that for him, and with Sir Archibald's name behind him, it wasn't long before he doubled the clientele.

"But it was easy come, easy go for him—didn't look after his clients— and soon began to lose some of them. I suppose I should have reported it to his father, but then I thought he was young and still had to find his feet. Well, things got worse, and that's when I discovered he was doing some shady deals with an unscrupulous estate agent, which helped to fill Archie's coffers very nicely."

"What kind of deals?"

"He kept it very hush-hush. Wouldn't let me in on any of it. It was nothing criminal, just to do with buying and selling property. It was unethical, though, so I mentioned it to my father. If he told Sir Archibald about it, I wouldn't know. All I do know is that it didn't stop until the property market slowed down. Still, it was none of my business, so I said no more."

"So you don't know how Sir Archibald took the information?"

"He never came near the firm, except for once, and that was a couple of years later. It had nothing to do with the business between Archie and the estate agent, but it was bad—very bad, from what I gathered. The staff had gone for the day and I was on my own in the office when he came in. Didn't see me, but I saw him; he looked like death itself. He went straight into Archie's office without knocking. Left the door wide open behind him, so I heard a bit of what was said."

"What did he say?"

"Some girl was killed right outside Sir Archibald's house the Saturday before. Funny thing is I read about it in the papers that morning. She was run over. It was only a few lines, but it drew my attention when I noticed the name of the street. Coincidence, I thought, but not from what I overheard. Not that I heard much, mind you. Archie was very quiet, which was unusual for him. His father did all the talking. He was very upset, I gathered that much. I did hear him say that he never wanted to see him again, and when he left, Archie called out to him that he also loved her and didn't mean her any harm, and that was it."

"Who was the girl?"

"Obviously someone close to Sir Archibald."

"A mistress?"

"I knew from my father that he had a mistress, but this girl was young. No, she wasn't his mistress."

"You must have had some idea of whom he was speaking?"

"I don't speculate about other people's lives, Mr. Leeman. It was a private matter. The man is dead; he deserves some privacy, even in death."

"You do have an idea, though?"

"Ideas are worth nothing."

"Who did your father say she was?"

"How do you know I asked him?"

"A guess."

"Then I will tell you what he told me. It was none of my business, and that I was to keep my nose out of it."

"Did Archie ever see his father again?"

"Archie was a gambler. Until the incident with the girl, it was small stuff. He was making plenty of money and he could handle the losses, but all that changed pretty quickly after the girl's death, and so did his personality. He became more morose, solitary, and sometimes you just couldn't talk to him. He would just bypass everything you said as if he didn't hear you. Pretty snappy, too; he would bite your head off for nothing.

"I had no idea that he was losing big until he sold his beloved Aston Martin. That's when I should have been warned, but I didn't think he would do anything as stupid as he did. By the time I found out, it was too late."

"What did he do?"

"In short, Mr. Leeman, he embezzled funds from our clients' account to pay off his gambling debts."

Just what he needed, thought Frankie with satisfaction, and asked excitedly, "So what happened? Did he do time?"

"Might have done, if it were not for his father. He repaid the money. Archie would have gotten away with it completely if someone hadn't split on him to the Law Society. Of course, he was disbarred when they found out."

"Who split on him?"

"There were only four of us who knew about it, so your guess is as good as mine."

"You, Archie, his father. Who was the fourth?"

"The client his father paid off. But I can't see that he did it. Sir Archibald was very generous to him."

"So if it wasn't you, could it have been his father?"

"A scandal was the last thing Sir Archibald wanted; that's why he coughed up. No, he was too proud to have his name dragged through the mud. It shook him to the core when the story was made public. Was never the same after that."

"Is that when Archie left for America?"

"Had no choice, did he? Even if the Law Society hadn't found out about it, his father would have seen to it that he never practiced again. The long and short of it was he couldn't trust his son any longer."

"It must have made him a very bitter man."

"Bitter isn't the word. It was because of Archie that he didn't get the judgeship that should have been his."

"I have heard a lot about Sir Archibald, but nothing about his wife. How did all this affect her?"

"You couldn't tell what affected Lady Bingham and what didn't. She was a true lady in every sense of the word. Held her head high no matter what."

"Was she aware that her husband kept a mistress?"

"If she was, she never let on. Came from good stock, she did. Lawyers, high court judges—all the way back to Elizabeth I. I would imagine Archie was the first black sheep in the family."

"Is she still alive?"

"Oh, yes! Lives in a home for the aged on the South Coast. Fancy place. My father goes down to see her a couple of times a year. He really liked her, he did. She always had a moment for him, even through some of the most trying times. Yes indeed, a real lady."

"I would love to meet her."

"That's out of the question. I wouldn't want her upset in any way. What's more, my father would kill me if I were to give you her address.

"Why would he have to know?"

"Now look here, isn't it enough that I've gone this far? You have what you want. Leave the woman in peace. She deserves it after everything she's been through. Anyhow, my father tells me she's not with it any longer. Her mind goes in and out of the present. Can't seem to distinguish between what was and what is."

"I'm not insensitive. I would tread carefully; make it more like an interview about her past life with her husband and son. She would do all the talking. I would simply listen. No digging about Archie."

"Then what would be the point? No, leave her alone."

"The point is there was a great lawyer and his great lady, as you pointed out, so how can they produce a son like Archie? Something must have happened in his childhood, and I would like to know what and why."

"And that is none of your business, Mr. Leeman, is it?"

"No, but I have never liked leaving a story unfinished."

Phipps gave it some thought. "No," he said, "I can't."

Frankie pulled out his wallet and placed it on the table between them. "I have no idea how much money is in it, but I never carry less than five hundred pounds. Just say the word and it's all yours."

Phipps stared greedily at the wallet. Frankie could almost hear him thinking. "All right!" he said suddenly. "Got a piece of paper?"

Frankie searched his pockets and came up with a card. "You can write the address on the back of this."

"Oh no, I can't!" exclaimed Phipps. "Now, you write down what I tell you," he said and dictated the address in Branksome on the Dorset Coast where Lady Bingham was living. "Now if anyone asks, you didn't get it from me. Okay?"

"I have never even met you, Mr. Phipps," he replied.

He nodded solemnly. "Good," he said. "Well, I best be on my way. Don't want to keep my wife waiting tea." He finished off his beer then got to his feet and after a furtive glance around, picked up the wallet and stuffed it in his pocket, leaving Frankie to finish off his beer.

***

87

Phipps tapped his breast pocket as he stood in the queue for the bus to Hammersmith. He could feel the bulge, and looked around suspiciously, afraid someone might have noticed. He would breathe easier when he got home, he thought.

A smile deepened the lines of his craggy face as he walked down his street. Hilda would be tickled pink when he gave her the money, he thought. He could picture her crying out with delight. He had only done it for her. She needed a holiday. Now, he could give her one, the very best, with no expense spared. It was what they both deserved. That bastard Archie, he owed him; well, now they were quits!

Hilda was more than tickled pink when he arrived home and threw the envelope on the kitchen table. "Go on," he said with a gleam in his eye, "count it."

She looked from him to the envelope; then, in a rush of excitement, emptied it on to the table. Her mouth dropped open. "Ooh!" she cried and began to count. "It's a bleeding fortune!"

"Now you can have that washer and dryer you've been on about."

"And don't forget, two weeks in Majorca. You did promise."

He smiled. "What would you say to three weeks? And you can buy yourself some new dresses while you're at it."

"I'd say I've died and gone to heaven."

"You're such a silly bitch!" he laughed.

Her face suddenly became serious. "What will we tell Dad?" she asked. "He's gonna suspect something."

"Leave that to me."

"Well, it better be good. He's smart, he is!"

"Well, maybe I can be just as smart," he said, coming up behind her to squeeze her breasts. "We haven't done it for a long time. What about going upstairs right now?"

"That's all you ever think about," she teased, and taking one of his hands led him up to the bedroom.

CHAPTER SIX

Frankie waited until Phipps was out of sight, drained his glass, then left the pub. He had what he wanted, but instead of feeling satisfied, he felt hollow inside. He hadn't expected things to move as fast as they did and now he was torn between what was right, in his mind, and what he felt in his heart.

He could see the strain around Cynthia's eyes when she opened the door to him.

"Well?" she asked anxiously.

How could he tell her that the investigation was as good as over and that there was no reason for him to stay on? He couldn't. "Do you know a place on the South Coast called Branksome?" he asked.

"Very well! My parents had a house nearby in Sand Banks. We used to spend our summer holidays down there when Paul and I were children. Why?"

"How far is it from London?"

"It's close to a seaside town called Bournemouth, which is about a hundred and twenty miles from here. Who is in Branksome?"

"Archie's mother, Lady Bingham. Do you think you could go down there with me for a few days?"

"Yes, but why do you want to see her? Didn't you get what you wanted?"

He met her anxious gaze and he knew there was no putting it off. "Yes," he replied. Her face fell, and immediately he followed with "but there are still some questions that I need answers to."

"Need or want?"

"Want, I suppose. Also, it will give us more time to be together."

"You would delay telling your grandfather what you have discovered just for us?"

"You sound disapproving. I thought it was what we both wanted?"

89

"It is, but not this way, Frankie. Can you honestly tell me that you will be able to live with yourself if you keep such an important piece of information from the family you have lived with and loved all these years?"

"You have a hard way of hitting home!"

"Sometimes the truth is hard."

"So what do you suggest?"

"You said there was trust between you and your family. Trust your grandfather now. Tell him what you have."

"What about us?"

"Why don't we wait and see what he says first."

"You haven't asked what Archie did."

"I was waiting for you to tell me."

"He was disbarred for embezzlement. It doesn't get much worse than that for a lawyer."

"So you have him where you want him, so to speak."

"Hopefully. But he is a strange character, and from everything I have been hearing, I would say nothing is certain where he is concerned."

"But you could get him disbarred in New York, couldn't you?" Frankie lowered his eyes, and immediately she suspected something. "That isn't the intention, is it?"

"Let's not talk about it," he said. "If my grandfather goes along with what I want, will you come with me to Branksome?"

"I said that I would. But why do you need to speak to his mother if you already have what you need? Why cause her pain by bringing up the matter of her son?"

"I just want to hear what she has to say about the relationship between Archie and his father. I will tread carefully; I have no wish to cause her further distress."

"Why is their relationship so important to you?

"Because I believe it has a bearing on everything, and if I don't find out for myself, I will be left hanging in midair."

"Then it is for no other reason than your obsession with Archie Bingham."

"Look, what harm is there in knowing more about their relationship? I know practically everything else about him."

"I just don't think it is healthy being consumed like this, that's all."

"Let me worry about that. All you have to worry about is…," and he whispered the rest of the sentence in her ear.

She blushed and said, "Only if you allow me to plan the trip."

***

Frankie telephoned his grandfather later that evening. He was overjoyed by the news. "Johnny will be relieved," he said.

"I know he will, but there is something I have to ask first. I need more time, if that's all right with you."

"Why?" he asked.

"To know more about Bingham wouldn't hurt. There is something else; I would like to spend a few more weeks over here."

There was a pause while Frankie waited anxiously.

At last, Joe said, "All right. There is no rush; anyhow, we didn't expect it to be over this soon."

He sighed with relief. How could he have had any doubts? he wondered. His grandfather always came through for him no matter what, and he was somewhat ashamed for his lack of trust in him.

Cynthia was excited as she planned the trip. It had been a long time since she visited the South Coast, and to spend a whole weekend there with Frankie sounded like heaven.

The plan was to leave early Friday morning and make for Bournemouth, where they would stay at the Royal Bath Hotel, a favorite of hers. From there, everything was within easy reach including Branksome.

"You will love the hotel," she said. "It stands on the cliff right over the sea."

"I have always loved the sea; it's the only thing I recall about my birthplace."

"Where's that?"

"In a little village on the Amalfi Coast called Positano. I gather it is now a very fashionable resort."

"I've heard of it. They say it's lovely, but surely you must have been back there since you were a child."

"Afraid not. For years, my grandfather has promised to take me but has never found the time."

"Why couldn't you go on your own?"

"He wants to be with me when I first set eyes on the house where I lived. He also wants to take me to see my parents' grave. I can't remember what they looked like."

"You must have seen photographs."

"There are none."

"Not even one?" she asked in astonishment.

"When my grandfather came over to bury them and take me back with him to America, he didn't think to look for photographs, and then it was too late. Who knows what happened to them. I have no living relatives, so there is no one to ask."

"That is terrible. I can't imagine how it must feel not to know what your parents looked like."

"Very frustrating!" he said. "But I try not to think about it. My grandfather says that I am the spitting image of my father, so I have some idea of what he must have looked like."

"What does he say about your mother?"

"That she was musical, gentle, kind, and very beautiful, with black hair, dark eyes, and a smile that could light up a whole city. Sometimes when I look at you, I think that is what she must have looked like."

"You should go, Frankie. Don't wait too long. Who knows, there could still be someone living there who remembers your family, or even has a little snapshot of them."

"I have often wondered about that. I will go with Granddad—the very first opportunity."

He didn't sleep over on Thursday night. Soon after dinner, he returned to his hotel to prepare for the weekend. They had arranged for Cynthia to pick him up early the next morning, and when she arrived, he was already packed and waiting for her in the lobby.

She was determined that he see something of the English countryside, and so she took the old route instead of the fast motorway. The first town they came to was Staines—a pleasant place not far from Runnymede—where the historic Magna Carta was signed, bringing democracy to all, regardless of birth. Windsor, with its royal castle, was also close by. From there they went on to Basingstoke, a stepping-stone to some of England's glorious country.

It was June, and as far as the eye could see, everything was clothed in green: the trees, the meadows, the gently rolling hills.

After two hours of traveling, they came to Winchester, an ancient city that was once the capital of old England, and there they stopped for lunch.

It was a city of contrasts—the old side-by-side with the new. It was the old that fascinated Frankie. The cobbled streets, the little traffic-free passageways, shops with their bow windows and dark beams that looked as though they were straight out of a Dickens novel.

They took a tour of the cathedral, built in the eleventh century in the shape of a cross, and Winchester College—that famous public school for boys built in the year 1387. There were numerous tea shops, old and quaint as well as the more modern, each tempting with their homemade cakes and cream teas. Then there was that other British institution, Marks & Spencer.

Frankie couldn't believe it. "A bit out of place, isn't it?"

"I disagree. We can't stand still, and what we have here is a marriage of convenience."

"Don't you think that a place like this should stand still as a reminder of how good life was back then?"

"Was it so good? In the early centuries, only the wealthy were able to enjoy what England had to offer. At the other end of the scale, there was extreme poverty, hunger, fear of the wicked landowners; disease was rife, as was crime, most of it petty, for which the punishment was excessive by far. It was immorality at its worst, so you would have to say that this is a better world. Then, you take a look at what is happening today: high pollution, related cancer, the decline in standards, the atomic threat to civilization, greed at all levels of society including the politicians and large corporations, whose hunger for wealth goes beyond the bounds of moral decency; and let's not forget mounting crime for which the punishment is now inadequate. So tell me, which is the better world?"

Frankie shrugged. "There is no answer to anything, is there?"

"When you are dealing with human nature, only one thing is certain—it never was and never will be an equal world. No matter what we do to try and make it so, it is an impossible task."

"So what are you saying? Give up on the hungry of the world and the poor?"

"What I say is stop the greed; then there will be enough to go around."

"That is no solution. If you stop people from getting rich, then the wealth of a country suffers, and the poor are dependent upon the wealth of their country."

"Heaven forbid I should want to stop people from getting rich, but there is a big difference between what is rich enough and what is obscenely rich in this struggling society."

Frankie smiled. "Now you sound just like Bill," he said.

She laughed. "I'm not far left enough for Bill," she replied, "but you must admit he is right when he says there is not enough conscience out there. It's all self-interest and to hell with the next person."

He laughed. "Have you ever thought of getting up on a soapbox at Speakers Corner?"

She grinned. "Funny you should say that; it's what my father often says."

After lunching on fresh farm eggs, Hovis bread and butter, tea, and homemade Victoria sponge, they set out for Bournemouth, passing through the New Forest, whose little villages with names such as Romsey, Cadenham, Brochenhurst, and Lyndhurst seemed to be dozing beneath the glare of the afternoon sun.

Some of the lanes in the forest were so narrow that the overhanging boughs whipped furiously against the windscreen, slowing them to a crawl. Then there were the New Forest ponies who leisurely crossed their path bringing them to a complete halt—magnificent creatures whose symmetry was a living testament to the immortal hand that shapes all things wild and wonderful.

The car windows were open, the sunroof pulled back, and the breeze fanned them as they traveled through the unusual heat of that summer's day. Suddenly, the quiet of the country lane gave way to the noise of traffic flying along the tarred surface of the motorway, and coming to the end of the narrow road, they were confronted by this modern piece of engineering where car after car whizzed by in what seemed like a frantic race against time. It was a rude awakening after the slow, peaceful pace of the country. More alert now, they joined the unholy masses with their secular taste for the fast and the furious.

In no time at all, they were driving along Bournemouth's East Cliff, at the end of which was the Royal Bath Hotel with its Victorian elegance and lovely gardens. They entered the narrow slip road and pulled up in front of the entrance. Immediately a porter appeared to take their bags inside, while another parked the car.

They registered at the desk and were then taken up to their suite on the top floor of the three-story building. It was a large room tastefully furnished in period style, with a panoramic view over the garden and sea beyond. The first thing Frankie did was lift the window and let in the fresh breeze, and with it came the roar of the sea as wave after wave crashed upon the shore below.

Moving to his side, Cynthia looked out over the ocean. "Doesn't it make you wonder why we choose to live in the city?" she asked. Then looking up at him she said, "How would you like to go for a swim before tea?"

He put his arms around her and drew her close. "I have a better idea," he whispered.

The warmth of his breath on her ear was tantalizing and, her pulse quickening, she replied, "Yes!"

They were too late for tea and too early for dinner. "What would you like to do now?" she asked as she unpacked for both of them.

He was still in bed, his hands clasped behind his head, watching her through half-closed lids, as she busily moved about the room. "Go on looking at you," he said.

She laughed. "You'll get hungry eventually."

"You are all the food I need. Come here."

Their eyes met, and hesitantly she whispered. "But—!"

"Just be quiet and come here."

Without another word, she went. He pulled her down on top of him and kissed her, undid her dressing gown, and drew her naked body against his. It felt warm and exciting, and once again, they yielded to passion.

Lying quietly in his arms afterwards, she suddenly reminded him of Lady Bingham and the purpose of their visit. "Oh Lord!" he exclaimed. "I almost forgot." Sitting up, he grabbed the phone and got through to directory inquiry. He glanced at the time; when he had the number, it was close to six. "What do you think?" he asked. "Is it too late to phone?"

"I wouldn't have thought so," replied Cynthia, and he immediately dialed the number he was given.

The young lady at the other end put him through the third degree before she would place the call through to Lady Bingham. The only thing she didn't ask for was his date of birth. "And what did you say your name was again?" she asked.

"Latimer! Frank Latimer, and I am a freelance journalist. Did you get that?"

"Yes, sir. If you wait a moment, I'll see if she will talk to you."

"Latimer?" exclaimed Cynthia.

"I thought it best not to give my own name," he whispered.

She wasn't satisfied with his reply, but before she could express her feelings, Lady Bingham came on the line.

She was pleasant, but reluctant to see Frankie at first; then she softened. "What magazine are you with?" she asked.

"I'm freelance, but I assure you the article will only be published in the very best."

"And you say you want to write an in-depth article on my husband's career? How in-depth?"

"That is entirely up to you, Lady Bingham. There is a great thirst in America, especially in law circles, for anything on the British justice system, and who understood it better than your husband?"

"How right you are, Mr.—er—Latimer, is it not?"

"That's right, Lady Bingham."

"Well, I suppose there is no harm in giving you an interview. Heaven knows there is little enough excitement around here. Three o'clock tomorrow. We can have our little chat before tea. You do like tea?"

"I have grown quite a taste for it in the past week."

"Well done!" she cried. "It's about time we British civilized you Americans."

Frankie laughed. "If the Boston Tea Party is anything to go by, you did try once and failed."

"Failure, Mr. Latimer, is often the prelude to success."

"I bow to that! Would you mind if I bring a friend along?"

"Another journalist?"

"Just a friend. An English lady."

"Oh!" she cried with delight. "It's getting better and better. Of course I don't mind; in fact, I welcome it. Life gets so boring at one of these so-called genteel establishments. Everything is so organized, leaving no room for a little surprise now and then. Is there anyone else you would like to bring along?" she asked with a wisp of humor.

He laughed. "Afraid not, ma'am," he said, "just the two of us."

"Then it will have to suffice. I look forward to it with great pleasure. Now don't be late. With the limited time left to me, I am inclined to impatience."

"You may rely on us being there precisely, Lady Bingham."

"Just make sure that you are!" she laughed and hung up.

"Are you certain you want me with you?" asked Cynthia when he had replaced the receiver.

"I think that a woman present would help to make her feel more comfortable."

"She may feel more comfortable, but I doubt I shall. I can't say that I approve of all this cloak-and-dagger."

"Apart from giving a false name, there is no cloak-and-dagger. I am not about to ask for the most intimate details of her life with her husband; in fact, I will let her do most of the talking. She may say whatever she pleases. Now, if that upsets you, then I can't force you to go with me."

She thought for a moment. "What did she sound like?"

"Pleasant, with a sense of humor. Not what I expected."

"I'll go with you, but if you should get out of line—"

"I know," he said, "you'll kick my leg under the table."

"And don't think that I won't," she replied, and jumped off the bed before he had an opportunity to pull her to him again.

They had a quick swim in the pool, showered, dressed, and went down for dinner. The elegant restaurant overlooked the garden, and the head-waiter, dressed in formal tails, escorted them to a table by the window. After presenting them with the menu, he left them to make their choice.

They went for the Table D'hote, a five-course meal that included veal scaloppini sautéed in a cream and brandy sauce. The food was excellent, perhaps too good, and after dinner, it was as much as they could do to make their way to the winter garden for coffee.

As soon as they felt more comfortable, they took a stroll through the grounds. Evening had fallen while they were still in the dining room, and the garden, filled with warm, friendly sunshine earlier, was now full of shadow and mystery. Even the trees had taken on a ghostly quality in the dark.

A light breeze helped to freshen the hot, sticky air, while the sound of the surf drew them to the edge of the cliff. The water was dark; only the white tips of the waves could be seen as they came riding in to the shore. It was a night made for lovers: a silver moon, an ocean of stars, and the rhythmic beat, beat of the sea. Suddenly of one mind, they turned and, hand in hand, went straight to their room.

Such were the moments of lovers: the consuming passion, the fulfill-ment, the sheer joy of being together; but nothing compares with that first moment in the morning when you awaken to find your partner beside you, and you know that you still love and are loved. Then the wonder of the night becomes the wonder of the day.

"Did you know that you are as beautiful asleep as you are awake?" asked Frankie.

She smiled contentedly. "You are beautiful," she said.

"Men aren't beautiful."

"You are to me."

He laughed. "God, how I love you! I want to know everything about you—what you feel, what you think, what you want. Especially who you want."

"You already know who I want."

He kissed her and, leaning on his elbow, looked down into her eyes. "I want to know more. I want to know why you stopped painting."

She looked away, eyes misting. "Why did you have to bring that up at a time like this?"

"Because you made it sound mysterious, and I get the impression that it had something to do with your art teacher. I don't want to go on wondering about it. I want to know!"

"But he is no longer important to me. Can we just leave it there?"

"Did you love him? Is that it?"

"It was infatuation not love, and I am not proud of that part of my life. I really don't want to talk about it!"

"No one is proud of everything they do. I know I'm not. Yet if you were to ask me, I would tell you whatever you want to know because I trust your love. Why can't you trust mine?"

"I do! I was young and foolish back then, and it's not something that I care to remember. I prefer to put it behind me and get on with my life."

"But you haven't. You stopped painting, and anyone who can paint as well as you do should never stop."

She gave a helpless little shrug and said, "You don't give up, do you?"

"Not when it's important, and don't tell me that painting isn't important to you, because I won't believe it."

Little lines appeared around her eyes and he could see that she was struggling with herself, and he took pity. "Look," he said, "if it's going to be that difficult for you, then forget it."

"No, you are right; it is time I brought it out into the open, but I am afraid."

"Of what?"

"Of what you will think of me afterwards."

"Don't you understand what I have been trying to tell you? There is nothing you can say that would make me change the way I feel. I told you to trust in my love."

"You will see me differently!"

"Never!"

There was a pause. She swallowed, and then began to speak, uncertainly at first, then with more confidence. "I was eighteen and very impressionable when I entered art school. My teacher was in his forties. He was a very romantic figure with long black hair tied in a ponytail, a small pointed beard, and dark, piercing eyes that seemed able to see right through you. Like every other female student, I had a crush on him. I worked hard, as much for him as myself, in the hope that he would notice me. He never appeared to, but I didn't mind—just to be near him was enough.

"A year went by. I didn't think he even knew my name when suddenly he asked if I would like to go on a painting trip with him up to a friend's cottage in the country. I couldn't believe that, out of all the students, he had chosen me, and I was beside myself, so much so that without thinking, I said yes.

"It took some persuading before my parents would agree to let me go, and when they finally did, I was in heaven. We drove down in his car and, all the way, he talked of nothing but art and I hung on every word.

"It was late afternoon when we reached our destination, and much to my surprise, there were no friends to be seen. When he saw the look of concern on my face, he laughed. 'I'm sorry if you misunderstood,' he said, 'but the only reason I have the cottage is because they are away.' I felt stupid. He was a mature man, I thought; not some eager teenager. Of course I could trust him, and I tried to act more grown-up myself, even relaxed, believing I was in good hands. I soon discovered how naïve I was.

"It was after dinner; we had taken the wine and sat down on the couch in front of the fire. He had already put on some music and turned down the lights, and we talked mostly about me and the hopes I had for myself. Oh … he was smooth! I didn't even notice him inching closer to me until he put an arm around my shoulder. I was embarrassed and didn't quite know what to do, then I didn't want to make a fool of myself again so I did nothing. After all, I didn't think it meant much to a man of his mature years; it was simply a friendly gesture.

"When the kiss came, I was taken aback at first. But it was what I had dreamed about so I didn't object, and he took that as an invitation to go further. I have to admit that a part of me wanted him, too, but there was that other part of me that didn't. I was so scared. I had never been touched in that way before, and it awoke all sorts of feelings inside me that I had no idea existed. Also at that moment, I realized that what was happening had nothing to do with love, and when he suddenly went too far, I knew that I had to stop him. So, using all the will and strength that I could find, I pushed him away.

"It was a bad moment for him and the abuse that followed makes me cringe to this day. I know I deserved it. You don't let things go that far unless you intend to go all the way. At least he was gentleman enough not to force himself on me afterwards.

"As soon as he calmed down, I asked him to take me home. It was after midnight so, of course, he wouldn't. He said, 'If you think I'm going to bother you, you are wrong. I don't make the same mistake twice.' So I had no choice but to stay. I locked myself in one bedroom and he took the other. Next morning just before sunup as we had planned, he knocked on the door as if nothing had happened, and called me down for breakfast. I thought, if he could do it then so could I, and soon after breakfast, we went with our canvas and paints to a spot we had selected on the way to the cottage the day before, and set them up ready to catch the first light of day.

"It began well enough, but all too soon, he started to criticize my work: it was amateurish; it had no perspective, no dimension; I had learned nothing about colors; and he went on and on without stopping. I began to cry, and that is when he snatched the brush out of my hand, dipped it in the white paint, and with vicious strokes, blotted out all that I had done.

"I watched in horror, and when he had finished, I turned and ran back to the cottage, gathered my things, and waited in the car for him to return. Neither of us said a word on the journey home. Needless to say, I didn't return to art school; nor have I painted since...." She sat very quietly. "Now you know," she said.

Frankie looked away, and just when she began to wonder what he was thinking, he said, "I still can't understand why you let him destroy your faith in yourself. The man was unscrupulous; he should never have taken advantage of one of his young students in the way he did. That was bad enough, but to destroy your work, that doesn't sound like a very balanced person to me—that or he was jealous of your talent."

"I don't know about that. As for the other, I put myself in that position—I should have known better. I made a vow afterwards that I would never let anything like that happen again, not until I was certain it was right."

He turned her face toward him and searched her eyes. He didn't say a word. He didn't have to—the question was there in his silence. "It never did happen again," she whispered, "until you came into my life."

He knew—he knew even before she said it, but sometimes you just need to hear it, and his heart leaped with joy. Never again would it be like that; never again would he be so desperately in love, and he kissed her over and over again; he couldn't stop. It was as though he was trying to make up for all those days, months, years, when they would no longer be together.

They had a late breakfast in their room, went to the beach for a little sun and swim, and returned to the hotel for a light lunch around the pool. They showered, dressed, and made their way to Branksome.

The nurse, who escorted them to the terrace where Lady Bingham was waiting, had the fixed eye and set mouth of the long suffering. "You have caught her in one of her more lucid moments," she said, "but a word of advice: don't let her give you any of her nonsense; she can be quite the actress when it suits her."

"She sounded very pleasant over the phone," said Frankie.

"Huh!" she exclaimed with cynicism.

Lady Bingham was sitting at the far end of the terrace, staring into space, and didn't appear to hear them approach. "Your guests are here," announced the nurse. Lady Bingham continued to stare ahead of her and, with a sigh of exasperation, the nurse repeated, "Your guests are here. Now I know you heard me, so there is no need for pretense."

Slowly, Lady Bingham's eyes glanced up at her. "Are you talking to me?" she asked in a haughty manner.

"I don't see anyone else around!"

"Then kindly address me properly," she said, and lifted her chin in defiance.

After eyeing her contemptuously, the nurse said, "If I must ... your guests have arrived—Lady Bingham." Then, having said it, she marched off without waiting for a response.

A look of satisfaction spread across Lady Bingham's face, then her attention turned to her guests. The second she saw Cynthia, a startled look came into her eyes and she whispered, "Sophie!"

"I beg your pardon!" said Cynthia.

Lady Bingham shook her head as if to clear it. "I'm sorry, you took me by surprise. What is your name, child?"

"Cynthia, Cynthia Gould. Why did I take you by surprise?"

"You are the living image of a friend of mine, Sophie Levine. Is she a relative of yours?"

"I don't even know anyone named Levine."

Her face fell with disappointment. This frail woman, with cheekbones protruding through her stretched, opaque skin, which gave her a sharp appearance, then turned to Frankie. "And you, of course, are Mr. Latimer. Have you a first name?"

"Frank, and I have no relatives named Levine either," he said with a saucy grin.

She laughed. "No! Neither do you look as though you should have."

There was nothing offensive about the way she said it; nevertheless, he stole a quick glance at Cynthia to see how she took it. He needn't have worried.

"Have you two known each other long?" asked Lady Bingham.

Cynthia didn't know what to say. Frankie said, "Not nearly long enough," and his face softened.

Lady Bingham heaved a sigh and said, as though to herself. "Sophie was so beautiful. Men were always falling in love with her." Then to Cynthia, "You are fortunate. No one ever looked at me the way he just looked at you and when Sophie was around, no one even noticed me."

"Where is she now?"

"I don't know," she replied sadly. "Once I was married, things were never the same between us. Ah … well, I mustn't brood. They don't like us to brood here, and if you do, they think there is something wrong with you." She sighed, then suddenly her eyes began to dart all over the place, and she whispered to Cynthia, "Has she gone?"

Somewhat confused, she asked "Who, Lady Bingham?"

"Why, the nurse of course!" she said sharply.

"Yes, she has."

She looked relieved. "Good. You have to be very careful with everything you say. Only last week, they put a poor old girl away in a mental institution, and all because she couldn't remember who she was. I can't remember everything; who can at my age? That bitch of a nurse would have me put away if she could. She doesn't like me because I stand up for myself, but I don't care. I don't like her either."

"She does seem to try to please you," said Frankie.

"That's what she wants you to think, but I know better. There's no fooling me!"

"How long have you been here, Lady Bingham?" asked Cynthia.

"It feels like forever." Then her eyes became distant and she said, "Nothing is ever as it seems in this world. There is so much pretense going on and always has been, yet despite everything, what I wouldn't give to go back to yesterday. You are somebody when you are a wife; you are nobody when you are left alone. Sad, isn't it? We should all be someone in our own right."

"But you are someone in your own right, Lady Bingham. You must never forget that."

"Oh my dear! What do you know of life—you are so young and innocent of the ways of the world."

"You were unhappy in your marriage?" asked Frankie.

Cynthia gave him a stern glance. Lady Bingham's eyes widened in astonishment. "What made you say that?" she cried. "Don't you know that I was married to a great man? If I had to make sacrifices, it was for us both, and how many women can boast they were loved by such an outstanding figure?"

"Not too many, Lady Bingham, and it is the reason I am here talking to you. No one could have known him better. The world knew him as a great lawyer. I would like to tell the public what he was like as a husband and father."

"I don't see what that has to do with anyone; it was private, but what you may tell your readers is that he was a good man, a good husband, and a good father."

"Then he and his son were close?"

She appeared somewhat uncertain at first, and then said, "Why would you ask that? My husband was a very famous man, and famous men are in great demand. The law is demanding; it leaves you little time for relationships. People don't understand men like my husband. He lived for his work and that is why he was the best there was."

"Didn't that make life difficult for you and your son?"

"Yes! No! Oh, I don't know!" she cried in confusion. "Archie loved his father. You should have seen him when he was a baby. His little eyes would follow him everywhere; he adored him. It wasn't anyone's fault if his father had no time for him; that's how it was. But Archie never understood; he saw everything in black and white, but life isn't like that. Is it? Oh! How my heart used to bleed for him. Why is it that people don't always love those they should?"

"Then your son did find life with his father difficult?"

She looked close to tears. "What difference does it make? My husband was a good provider. We weren't short of anything; isn't that what is most important in a marriage?"

Lady Bingham was becoming more and more agitated, and, feeling sorry for her, Cynthia gave Frankie's leg a kick. He was quick to respond and, softening his voice, said, "Indeed, Lady Bingham, it certainly is."

She looked relieved for a second, but just as swiftly, her face clouded and she said as if to herself, "Why did he have to find out about her? If only he hadn't known, things might have been different."

Cynthia and Frankie exchanged glances, and from the look in her eyes, he was left in no doubt as to how she felt about his line of questioning. Fortunately, at that moment, tea arrived and saved the situation. Immediately, Lady Bingham perked up; she was in her element while playing the gracious hostess.

As she and Cynthia were talking, Frankie, in thought, only half listened, giving an appropriate nod now and then. His mind was sifting through the information, not that it had been much, but it was enough to confirm his suspicion that the relationship between father and son was not all it should have been. Life is not an easy matter for the young growing up in the shadow of a successful father, but it still didn't explain his complex personality or his vicious nature. There were more demons at work in that relationship than met the eye, but whatever, there was no denying Archie was one very sad and sorry human being.

Frankie's thoughts were suddenly interrupted by the harsh voice of the nurse as she asked, "Have we finished our tea?"

Lady Bingham glared at her. "I was not aware that you were an invited member of this party!"

The nurse glared back, then without a word, she turned and marched away.

Lady Bingham gave a self-satisfied nod. "She needs to be put in her place once in a while. If only she didn't treat me like some backward child; or if only her manner was more pleasant; if only...." She paused. "How many times do we say that and how many lives could be summed up by those two little words?" Suddenly, she became pensive. "If only his father had shown him more affection, who knows what might have been." Then her gaze wandered to the distance and rested there.

Turning to Frankie, Cynthia whispered, "I think we should leave." He nodded.

As though she had read her lips, the nurse came over once again, and addressing Lady Bingham, said, "I believe your guests are ready to leave. If you will bid them goodbye, I will see them out."

Lady Bingham's head jerked to attention. "They are my guests. I will see them out myself."

"As you wish," she replied, and watched with detachment as she maneuvered her rheumatic fingers, with their swollen joints, down against the table top and with great determination rose to her feet. The effort left her breathless, and after a short rest, she grabbed her cane and, leaning on it, straightened her back. "There!" she said with a triumphant smile.

She was much shorter than they realized and appeared even frailer, and Cynthia held her arm as she placed one painful foot in front of the other and walked with them to the end of the terrace. When they reached the door, she stopped and said, "I'm afraid this is as far as I can go. I used to walk for miles before this wretched arthritis set in."

"Would you like me to see you to your room?" asked Cynthia.

"No, you run along, the nurse will do that; it is her job after all."

On impulse, Cynthia kissed her cheek. "I'll not forget this afternoon," she said.

Lady Bingham's lined face broke into a sweet smile. "Neither shall I, my dear. You have brought back so many good memories of dear Sophie. Such is life!" she finished with, and waved them goodbye.

When they had gone, the nurse asked, "Are we ready?"

Lady Bingham nodded. The fight had gone out of her and she allowed the nurse to help her to her room.

Before leaving her, the nurse asked, "Will you be all right now?"

She nodded again, then as an afterthought said, "Do you really care?"

Their eyes locked for a second before the nurse replied, "I am paid to care, Lady Bingham."

"That is the nurse speaking. I want to know how Nelly feels."

"You want the truth?"

"I wouldn't have asked if I didn't."

The ghost of a smile replaced the grim set of her mouth, and she said, "You are a pain in the neck and if the job didn't pay so well, I wouldn't put up with your nonsense for one single moment."

There was an uncertain pause while the two women eyed one another, then suddenly Lady Bingham's face softened. "Believe it or not, Nelly, I think a whole lot more of you now."

There was that ghost of a smile again, and with an uncharacteristic gentleness, the nurse said, "I'll see you downstairs in the dining room. Meanwhile, get some rest; you have had a big day."

When the door closed and she was alone, Lady Bingham put down her cane and, clinging to the edge of the furniture, made her way over to the dressing table and took a good look at herself in the mirror. *Whatever happened to that young girl?* she wondered. *When did her features become so sharp? He would barely recognize me if he were to see me now.* She sighed and, opening a drawer, took out a photograph of her husband that was taken shortly after they were married, and stared at it for a long while.

All at once she spoke out aloud. "Your mistress was there at your grave again this week. I know when she has been because she always leaves a single yellow rose. Was that her favorite color or yours? I didn't even know if you had a favorite color; in fact, I am beginning to realize how little I did know about your likes and dislikes.

"We never talked much, did we? Did you talk to her? Did you listen when she spoke to you? Or did you ignore her the way you used to ignore me? I am not even sure if you ever loved me, or what your real feelings were. I can hear you saying, 'After all this time, does it really matter?' Oh yes, it still matters. You see, I have never stopped loving you.

"It hurt when I found out about your mistress, more deeply than you could have imagined. I think it was even worse for Archie when he discovered your affair. He never spoke about it, but I could see it destroying him. He was just a boy and didn't understand, and he felt as if you had betrayed him and he never got over it. You must have noticed that something was upsetting him, but you never said a word. Didn't you care? Or were you so taken up with your own selfish needs? It made you seem so callous. If only it was possible to turn back the clock, I think that I would leave you for his sake, but who knew what was best at the time?

"Funny, after all the years of hating your mistress, I now feel sorry for her. It was no more her fault than mine; we were both your victims in a sense. It must have hurt her to know that you would never marry her, not even when she bore you a daughter. You weren't aware that I knew about your daughter, and, like everything else, it hurt terribly.

"It was tragic the way she died; the irony of it, right on your doorstep. Despite everything, it upset me to think of an innocent life wasted like that, but what shook me was the way you handled yourself. Oh, you shed your tears, but only in private. You had to think of your position and it would never have done to acknowledge that she was your daughter, would it? After all, what might it have done to the Bingham name? That name that you were more protective of than your children. You couldn't even bring yourself to go to her funeral in case the world would guess who she really was. I found it despicable!

"I know that you blamed Archie for her death, and perhaps it was partly his fault, but the blame was also yours. You can't hide something like that and not expect someone to get hurt in the end. Well, you made the choice and you paid the price. You see, you were incapable of giving; you could only take, and the sad truth is that you never really belonged to anyone but yourself—not to her, not to me! So, in the end, there were no winners, only losers, and the children were the biggest losers of all. At least Archie bore your name; your daughter never had that advantage. Oh well, it's all water under the bridge now, and in the end, it is all the same."

It was almost two minutes before she spoke again. "I had visitors today—a young man and a woman. She was remarkably like Sophie. You remember Sophie, don't you? My friend from boarding school! Of course you do; who could forget Sophie with her beautiful looks and wild temperament. You used to refer to her as 'that Jewish bitch' but I knew that was only to mask your true feelings. You were very attracted to her. Did you honestly think that I didn't notice the way you looked at Sophie? I was so jealous I couldn't think straight; she was very upset when I told her that I didn't want to see her again. She wanted to know why, and I lied. I told her it was you who didn't want me to go on seeing her because of the things she said about you. You didn't know that she saw right through you; that was because I never told you, but I told her that I did. Of course, I had no idea about your mistress then.

"I think of Sophie more and more these days and wonder how differently life might have turned out if we had kept on seeing each other. For all her airy-fairy notions, she was a realist deep down, and I think she could have helped Archie to overcome his feelings about you and your mistress. I do hope she found the love she always dreamed about.

"Ah, there is the dinner bell. It's steak this evening, or is it lamb? Let me see; if it's Saturday, it's lamb, at least I think it is. Oh, if only I could remember the present as well as I remember the past. What happens to us when we get old? At least I am glad, in a way, that you never lived long enough to find out for yourself. You were always such a vigorous man; I doubt getting old would have suited you at all. It's hard when you look back at yourself and see someone who is almost alien to you now.

"Well, back in the drawer you go with the rest of my past," she said, and pulling at the handle, she placed his photograph among the other treasures of long ago.

Cynthia passed the car keys to Frankie, then took the passenger seat. For the first five minutes neither spoke. He could see out of the corner of his eye that she was deep in thought and knew that she was thinking about Lady Bingham. "So what did you make of her?" he asked.

She didn't reply immediately and continued to stare at the road ahead. Then all at once, she turned to him and said, "There was something so sad in the way she spoke of her husband and son, as though the memories were too painful."

"He had a mistress and I realized, as she spoke, that she knew about it."

"Poor woman!" she said, shaking her head sadly.

"There is more. A girl was killed right outside the Bingham home, and somehow her son was involved. I believe the girl might have been a daughter of her husband by his mistress. Could it be possible that she was aware of that as well?"

"Whatever, it seems she had a lot to put up with, what with her husband's infidelity and her son's behavior."

"Yes! Yet I got the impression of a woman still in love with the memory of her husband," said Frankie.

"I can't understand any woman who goes on loving a man who has deceived her. I know I couldn't."

"It takes all kinds! Sometimes, I wonder why my mother stays with my father. He's such a terrible womanizer; no one special, just many. Perhaps that is the reason they are still together: his affairs don't mean much to him."

"It still has to be an unhappy situation for her."

"It is. Separately, they are two decent people, but together...!"

"Sad!"

He nodded. "I believe my father's philandering has little to do with love; it's purely a sexual thing. Not that I like it, but I can deal with it."

"But what if Archie Bingham couldn't? Wouldn't it have made him a very bitter person?"

"Bitter, disappointed, unhappy, but that man was vicious, wicked. He had a big problem, and I think that problem stemmed from a lack of love from his father as well as selfishness. But then, who knows why people do what they do."

"Some people have a very mixed-up life. It's sad all around."

"Yes! Anyhow, I have something more important on my mind right now. While I was listening to Lady Bingham, I made the decision to not wait any longer. I am going to Italy to visit the place of my birth. I want to know more about my roots. Will you come with me?"

"Yes," she replied without a moment's hesitation. "More than anything, I want to be there with you."

"Good," he said with a sigh of relief. "Then all that is left is to decide when, and I would like to go as soon as possible, if that's all right with you."

"I can see no problem. It's the slow season at the factory and I'm due for a holiday. How will you explain it to your grandfather?" asked Cynthia.

"I'll think of something. Can you manage two weeks? We can make it a real holiday."

"Yes, I can. How soon is as soon as possible?"

"You tell me."

"All I need is a few days to get ready."

"Okay, we leave here tomorrow morning for London and for Italy on Wednesday."

She laughed. "You are in a hurry, and yes, Wednesday will be perfect."

When they reached the hotel, he switched off the engine and turned to her. "We will make it a wonderful holiday," he said. "Absolutely wonderful. God, I love you so much!"

Her eyes met his tender gaze and she said, "I know it will be wonderful." Then she cast her eyes down and said softly, "But how will we deal with what comes afterwards?"

"Look at me," he said, and she looked at him, and he saw her suffering and his heart went out to her. "Every time you feel sad or lonely, just remember that wherever I am, no matter how far away, I will be thinking of you and loving you for the rest of my life."

A tear fell and she said, "I will remember every touch, every kiss, and every word you have spoken until my dying day."

CHAPTER SEVEN

'High up in the north in the land called Svithjod, there stands a rock. It is a hundred miles high and a hundred miles wide. Once every thousand years, a little bird comes to this rock to sharpen its beak. When the rock has thus been worn away, then a single day of eternity will have gone by.'

Cynthia was gazing out of the window of the plane. Frankie took hold of her hand. She turned and smiled at him. "What were you thinking?" he asked.

She had become wistful. "I was thinking—if I could spend but one day of eternity with you."

A lump rose in his throat, and his hand tightened over hers.

The plane landed at Naples Airport, and a taxi took them the rest of the way to Sorrento. Frankie had a room booked at the Hotel Michelangelo, which was perched on a cliff high over the Bay of Naples. "It's where my grandparents spent their honeymoon," he said. "I hope it lives up to expectation!"

Behind the unimposing entrance was an elegant marble hall with giant pillars, a vaulted ceiling, and small sitting areas placed in alcoves for privacy. Along the main wall hung original paintings from the Renaissance era. Facing the wall was the grand dining room, and further along the lift took them to their suite overlooking the bay.

The huge suite had an Italian tile floor, traditional furniture, and a pair of shuttered doors, which led to a narrow, wrought-iron balcony that overhung a sheer drop to the sea. Cynthia caught her breath at the grandeur of it.

Behind, Frankie folded his arms around her. "My grandfather didn't exaggerate when he said the view from the hotel was superb," he said.

110

"He most certainly didn't. Just look at that sea!" Its still water was alive with a fiery glow from the intense Italian sun, and Cynthia sighed with contentment.

"Are you glad you came?" he asked.

"Oh yes!" she said and rested the back of her head against his shoulder, and they stood, wrapped in their happiness.

When they were able to tear themselves away, they unpacked and left to explore the rest of the hotel and grounds. Nothing disappointed them—elegance and tradition abounded inside, while outside the garden was an Eden to behold. Shady paths meandered through banks of flowers; rockeries, nooks for quiet reflection guarded by bushes whose tiny white blossoms perfumed the air. The pool with a wall of glass surrounding it enabled you to enjoy an unbroken and spectacular view while swimming or sunbathing.

A few guests, lounging by the pool, glanced up as they passed. Cynthia smiled at them; they smiled back. She slipped a hand in Frankie's and whispered in his ear, "Thank you."

"For what?"

"For taking me with you. For letting me share a part of your life for however briefly."

"It is I who thank you. There is no one in the world I would rather share this with."

She had never been so happy. "I can't wait to see the place where you were born."

"I thought we would go to Positano tomorrow."

"Oh yes!" she cried. "I am as excited about it as if I was the one born there."

"I hope the house is still standing. It will be awful if it isn't."

"I know, but if it isn't everything else will still be there—the beach, the sea, the streets—they were all a part of your world."

"What an optimist!" he laughed.

"It's as easy to be an optimist as it is to be a pessimist!" she retorted in mock anger.

He gave her hand a warm squeeze.

They had an early dinner, then sauntered slowly down the hill to the square. It was full of people strolling as they were, or at the cafés eating, drinking, laughing, or just enjoying themselves and the Neapolitan songs that rang out of every restaurant. They bought an ice cream, which they shared, then went down to the water's edge and sat gazing before returning to the suite.

It had been a long, tiring day, and content, they fell asleep in each other's arms.

When Cynthia awoke in the morning and found Frankie gone, she suffered a moment of panic, until she heard the key in the lock; and when the door opened, there he was, looking young and boyish in a pair of shorts. It brought a smile to her lips. "I was worried for a second, where were you?"

"I couldn't sleep any longer so I went for a walk. I also rented a car and ordered breakfast; it should be here in half an hour."

"Good, that will give me time to shower," she said and threw back the cover, got off the bed, and stepped barefooted to the bathroom.

"What car did you get?" she called out to him when the shower stopped.

"It's a surprise."

"Not even one little hint?" she asked as she came out of the bathroom wrapped in a large towel.

His eyes swept over her and with a devilish grin, he said, "Drop the towel and I'll think about it."

In a flash it came off, and at that very second, there was a knock at the door and she made a dash for the bathroom.

"Saved by breakfast!" he laughed.

The fresh air had made them hungry and in no time the mountain of freshly baked rolls disappeared along with the contents of a huge pot of coffee. Almost as soon as they finished, the desk rang through to tell them the car had arrived and was parked at the front of the hotel.

Full of excitement, Cynthia dressed in a pair of shorts, a T-shirt, and sandals. She tied her hair back in a ponytail, grabbed a shoulder bag, and they were ready to leave.

Her eyes widened in wonder when she saw the dark green Ferrari standing in the driveway. "Oh!" she gasped. "How did you manage it?"

He looked pleased with himself. "All I had to do was mention my grandfather *et voila.* It seems he is well-known in these parts and, as the manager said, nothing is impossible for a member of the Bocacci family."

The top was down and the keys already in the ignition waiting for them.

Frankie got behind the wheel and examined the instrument panel. She got in beside him and ran her fingers over the pale leather seats. They felt soft and warm against her bare thighs and she whispered, "She's beautiful."

"She is. Got your seat belt on?" he asked, and the moment she said yes, he started the engine.

He took a turn around the block first, putting the car through her paces before attempting the hazardous drive to Positano. It handled like a dream, and as soon as he felt comfortable with her, he took off along the narrow road that was cut high into the cliffs above the sea.

It was a road filled with dangerous twists and turns as it followed the glorious coastline on the way to Amalfi. Cynthia stared in wonder as wave after wave of awe-inspiring beauty met the eye at every bend. Sculptured cliffs descended into the sea below. Rocks, like huge monuments, rose up out of the azure waters forming arches and passageways for the waves to rush through. In that little corner of Italy, nature had produced a work of art finer than any mortal hand could ever hope to achieve and it drew gasps of delight time after time. Poor Frankie had to keep his eyes on the road and could only spare an occasional brief glance.

Between Sorrento and Amalfi was Positano, an age-old fishing village with its flat-roofed houses and hotels cut into the face of the tall cliffs that surrounded a small cove with a sandy beach. The streets were narrow alleys with steps or winding paths down to the sea. Boutiques displayed their wares along the cliff face. Terraces burgeoned with blossoms and pink-washed walls reflected the sun.

Cynthia and Frankie took their first look down at the village from the cliff top. It was even more lovely than either of them could have imagined. "How did I forget a place like this?" asked Frankie.

"You were too young to remember when you left. Did you never see a picture of it?"

"A painting, but it didn't do it justice."

"Have you any idea where your house might be?"

"According to my grandfather, it's at the end of a private road. The house can also be seen from the beach, where it stands at the north end of the cliff."

Her eyes wandered along the cliff top. "There is nothing to see but foliage from here."

"Then let us walk along the road and see what we can find."

They set out and soon came to a side road that displayed a sign saying Private. "This has to be it," said Frankie. "Let's take a look."

The road was no more than a narrow lane with room for only one car at a time. It twisted and turned, and the further they walked, the more rough the road became as though it hadn't been traveled for a long time. The gravel had been eroded, leaving large stones that bit through the thin soles of their sandals. Potholes were everywhere, and they walked carefully for fear of twisting an ankle on the uneven surface.

Suddenly, the road turned again and there was the house standing well back from a pair of six-foot-high wrought-iron gates. They immediately ran up to them and peered through the bars. The desolation that confronted them was unbelievable: knee-high grass, overgrown bushes, fallen branches, rotting leaves that hadn't been cleared since the autumn. Weeds had taken root everywhere including the path that led up to the house.

The house itself was in a shocking state. Tiles were either missing from the roof or hanging precariously. Doors leaned open on broken hinges. Windows were shattered, the paint was peeling, and a layer of slimy moss was creeping up the outside walls where damp existed.

The gates were padlocked and rusted with age. Frankie tried them; rattling them back and forth, they held fast. "No one can have lived here for years!"

"Are you certain this is the house?" asked Cynthia.

"As certain as I can be; but what I don't understand is why it isn't occupied?"

"It has to belong to someone. Perhaps they know who in the village."

He shrugged. "I suppose it is worth a try," and they started back along the lane.

He was disappointed; nevertheless, Cynthia's optimism kept him going and when they reached the path down to the beach where the boutiques were situated, they tried the first shop. The owner hadn't lived in Positano very long and knew nothing about a derelict house on the cliff.

They fared no better at the second or the shop after that. At the next, they were directed to the boutique with hats displayed on the cliff wall. "It belongs to a mother and daughter," said the owner, a slight woman of about fifty. "As far as I am aware, they have lived here all their lives. In fact, that's the mother sitting outside the shop crocheting."

Frankie thanked her in Italian, and he and Cynthia proceeded down the path to where the old woman was sitting.

"It's good that you speak the language so fluently," remarked Cynthia.

"My grandfather has never allowed me to forget."

The old woman, skin a leathery brown, looked up as they came close. "Good morning!" said Frankie. The woman gave a brief nod, then continued with her crocheting. "The derelict house on the cliff, the one at the end of a private road, do you know how long it has been empty?"

"A long time," she said without lifting her eyes.

He glanced at Cynthia, with a glimmer of hope, then turned back to the woman. "Would you say as much as twenty-six years?"

Immediately, her hands stopped still and a pair of frightened eyes looked up at him. "Why do you ask?" she whispered.

"Is it possible that it once belonged to the Bertolli family?"

If he had placed a bomb in her lap, her reaction could not have been faster. With a gasp, she dropped her work and ran inside the shop, crossing herself and muttering as she went.

Astonished, Frankie stared after her.

"What was that all about?" asked Cynthia.

"I don't know!" he exclaimed in bewilderment.

Almost immediately, a younger woman came to the door and asked curtly, "What do you want here?"

"All I wanted to know was if the house on the cliff once belonged to the Bertolli family, and it seemed to frighten the life out of the old woman!"

Her eyes narrowed with caution, and after a keen glance at him, she asked, "Why does it matter to you?"

"Because," he replied, "if it is the Bertolli house, then that is where I was born."

Startled, she took a step back; then recovering somewhat, she came closer and peered into his face. Slowly, a sign of recognition lit her eyes and she cried, "Francesco! Is it really you?"

"You know me?" he asked with excitement; then speaking in English, he said to Cynthia, "She knows me!"

She was all smiles at his happiness.

The woman looked from one to the other, and Frankie noticed the same look of fear in her eyes that he saw in her mother's. Suddenly, she drew him closer to her and whispered, "What are you doing here? You shouldn't have come. Don't you know it's not safe for you?"

"What are you talking about?" he asked in confusion. "Not safe from what?"

Her eyes darted to Cynthia, then back to him. "Who is she?" she asked.

"A friend. Why?"

"I don't like strangers; you never know with them."

"She's all right; anyhow, she doesn't understand Italian."

She appeared uncertain; then all at once she said, "You must leave immediately. If word should get out that you are here—!"

"Look," he asked with exasperation, "just tell me what this is about, because I'm a bit bewildered at the moment."

"The man who took you back to America with him when you were a child; surely he must have explained everything to you."

"If you mean my grandfather—of course, he told me about the accident."

"Accident? Murder is no accident," she cried.

The word murder pierced his heart like a stake. "What?" he gasped.

"Alida, tell him to go away," cried her mother from the back of the shop.

"He's going. Don't worry so much," she called out. Then to Frankie, she whispered, "We can't talk now; you have frightened her. Come back at one o'clock; that's when she takes a nap. The shutters will be closed, but I will leave the door unlocked. First, make sure no one sees you; then come straight in." After a cautious glance at Cynthia, she said, "Don't bring her with you."

"First tell me who you are."

"Later," she said with impatience. "Now, please leave." And before he could say another word, she disappeared into the shop and quickly closed the door.

His face was troubled when he turned to Cynthia, and filled with concern she asked, "What is it?"

"I don't know."

"Well, what did she say?"

"That I'm in some danger!"

"Danger! What kind of danger?"

"She couldn't talk. She wants me to return at one o'clock when the shop will be closed. She wants me to come alone. Do you mind?"

"Of course not! Was it the house where you were born?"

"It would seem so. She certainly knew the name Bertolli. Look, there's a café on the beach. Let's go down and have some coffee. You can have lunch if you like, but I couldn't right now. Perhaps after I have seen the woman again, I might feel more like eating."

Cynthia didn't feel like eating either, and they ordered two espresso coffees when they reached the café, and then sat at one of the tables on the beach quietly sipping and reflecting on the strange reaction of the women.

Frankie's head was in a whirl. The word murder kept repeating itself over and over in his mind, filling him with a sickening fear. There had to be a mistake, he thought, but deep down, he wasn't sure of anything. Whoever the younger woman was, she seemed very certain of what she was saying.

He glanced at Cynthia. He could see that she was also concerned but trying hard not to show it, and when their eyes met, she smiled at him with reassurance. His hand touched hers in a gesture of gratitude, then his gaze turned to the house on the cliff. His grandfather had been right; it could be seen clearly from the beach. It didn't appear as dilapidated from that distance, and he could imagine what it must have looked like when he lived there with his parents.

His attention turned to the sea. It didn't have the calming effect upon him that it usually had, and he wished to God that they hadn't come. There was something terribly foreboding about the place; perhaps it was just him, he thought. Perhaps he was imagining things and attaching too much importance to what the woman had to tell him. He hoped so.

He glanced at the time; it was almost one o'clock. "I suppose I had better make my way back up the cliff. Will you be all right on your own?"

"Don't worry about me. I'll be fine."

"Perhaps you should eat something. I don't expect to be long, but you never know."

"Should I get hungry, I will have something."

He hovered for a moment, obviously not willing to leave.

"Go!" she said. "I promise I will be all right."

He turned and trudged across the sand to the winding path where the shops were located. It was the hottest time of the day and there wasn't another living soul about. No wonder, he thought, as the sun beat relentlessly down on his head. Beads of perspiration trickled from his forehead into his eyes. He stopped to wipe them away then continued. Every shop was closed and shuttered against the heat of the day, and when he came to the one with the hats, he looked around first before trying the door. It was open, as she said it would be, and he stepped inside. It was dark and cool. "Quick, close the door," whispered a voice from deep within. He closed it immediately.

As his eyes became accustomed to the darkness, he saw the younger woman sitting at a small round table, pouring something into a glass. "You must be thirsty," she said, and handed it to him when he came near. It was lemonade made from fresh lemons, and he drank thirstily. "Slowly, slowly," she whispered. "I didn't think that I would still have to remind you."

There was something very familiar about the way in which she said it. He stopped drinking and stared at her in astonishment. "You have said that to me before, haven't you? Who are you?"

Her face softened and her eyes filled with nostalgia. "You would always drink too fast, eat too fast, and I had to keep telling you to slow down. You were such an impatient child. You couldn't even stand still long enough for me to wash your hands and face after we had been on the beach. You were like a live wire. You had to be on the go from the moment you opened your eyes in the morning until you were put to bed at night."

"The house on the cliff, you were there with us, right?"

"You used to call me Alli; you couldn't say Alida. Do you remember that?"

He tried to think back for a moment. "No," he said in frustration. "I only remember someone telling me to slow down; the rest is blank. I can't even remember my parents."

"That's a pity. They were good times when the three of you were together. Your parents were wonderful people, especially your mother. She was an angel. I worked for your family from the age of fourteen, and when you were born, I helped to look after you. It was my job to take you down to the beach after your nap in the afternoon. Your father would be working on an article and needed quiet in the house. I also used to feed you and help put you to bed after your mother had bathed you. She wouldn't let anyone else do that for her. It was one of her greatest pleasures to watch you play with the rubber ducks and fish in the bath. Sometimes your father would join you, and the sound of your laughter would ring through the house," she said, and a tear ran down her cheek.

"What did you mean earlier when you said, 'Murder is no accident'?"

"Is that how your grandfather explained it—as an accident? And how come you call him grandfather?"

"His daughter adopted me. He has been very good to me; they all have. We are a very close family. It was lucky for me that he was a good friend of my parents or I might have ended up in an orphanage after the car crash."

"What?" she cried in disbelief. "What car crash? They were murdered in cold blood, and as for the man you call grandfather, he didn't know your parents!"

The sudden impact of what she said made his head reel and it took a while before he could find his voice. "What are you saying?" he asked in alarm.

She realized that she may have said too much. "Oh dear God!" she gasped, "I am so sorry. You should never have learned the truth like that. He should have been the one to tell you. A child has the right to know how his parents died."

"Forget all that!" said Frankie. "Just tell me."

"Oh! Francesco," she said, shaking her head sadly. "It's not a very pleasant story. But I have gone this far. I fear I must finish what I started."

His head was hammering and his heart filled with dread. He swallowed. "I'm listening," he said. "Just don't spare me anything."

She poured herself a glass of lemonade, took a sip, then looking directly at him, she said, "These eyes, that you are looking at, saw your mother fall to her death from the cliff. We were on the beach, as usual; you were busy playing with your pail and shovel. I don't know what made me look up just then—a premonition perhaps, who knows. I only remember the horror I felt as I watched her fall. When I looked up again, there was a man standing there looking down."

Frankie felt his blood drain as the shock of what he heard went through him like a bolt of electricity. He felt sick. He closed his eyes against the vision of his mother's body lying at the bottom of the cliff, but the vision only intensified.

The pressure of a hand on his arm made him open his eyes again. Alida was staring at him with concern. "Are you all right?"

He nodded, not trusting himself to speak. When he had sufficiently recovered, he asked, in a voice quivering with emotion, "Who was the man?"

"I don't know, but when I gave my father a description of him—all dressed in black with a hat that was pulled well down so that you couldn't see his face—he said that such a man was in the village earlier that day asking questions about the house and who lived in it, and that from the way he spoke, he thought he might be Sicilian."

"Where was my father when it happened?"

She sighed sadly. "He was already dead. I didn't know it at the time; nevertheless, I was too frightened to go back to the house so I gathered you up in my arms and ran with you to my home. That is when I told my father about the man and what happened to your mother. He told me to stay put and went to the house himself. He found your father's body on the study floor—a bullet through the back of his head. The police said that your mother must have witnessed the shooting, and that is why she ran, and when there was no more ground beneath her feet—!" Again, Alida

119

sighed, and wiped a tear from her eye. "That is as much as I know about their death."

"Where does my grandfather fit into all this?"

"That was strange. I only remember him from the beach. I would see him there every year for two weeks, and then he was gone until the next year. When the police came to ask me questions about what I saw, they told me to keep you with me and not let you out of my sight until I heard from a man who would be coming over to take care of the funeral, and then take you back home with him. I asked them who he was, and they said it was better I didn't know his name or anything about him, for my own safety as well as yours. That man was the same man from the beach—the one you now call grandfather."

He shook his head in disbelief. "None of what you say makes sense. First, you tell me that he didn't know my parents; and then you say he came over to bury them and take me back to America with him! How is it that the police knew him? And why would they tell him about my parents' death if he didn't know them? You are either lying or imagining things, and either way, I don't want to hear anymore." He rose to go.

She grabbed his arm with one of her large peasant hands and forced him to remain. "As God is my witness," she whispered vehemently, "I am telling the truth. It is your grandfather who has been lying to you all these years. Not two days after he received the news of their death, he was in Positano. He knew very well how they died; perhaps he even knew why. I certainly didn't. All I knew was that two good people were dead, and you were left an orphan and in his care."

He sank back into the chair, confused and not knowing what to believe. "How does he know so much about my parents—where they were born, how they met, that my mother's name was Valentina and my father's Amando. He even knew my mother's parents. How does he know all that if he never knew them? He must have said something to you about them when he arrived. What did he say?"

"Nothing at all; he just thanked me for looking after you. Then he asked me to keep you with me for another few days while he attended to some important business. I agreed. When he returned, he buried your parents and took you away with him."

"Where did he go when he left me with you?"

"I was told not to ask questions and simply do as he said. Before he left with you, he gave me some money. I didn't want to take it, but he insisted. He said that I was to think of it as a gift from your parents for taking such good care of you, and that they would have wanted me to have it. It was with that money that I bought this shop."

"I would like to talk to the policeman who knew my grandfather."

"He died a few years ago. I don't know what the connection was between them, but I knew from a cousin who used to work for a bank in Sorrento that for years, ever since your parents bought the house in Positano, a large sum of money would be deposited each month into the account of the chief of police, and it continued until his death."

"Did he say where the money came from?"

"A New York bank. I can't recall exactly, but it sounded like the name of a man."

"Morgan Guarantee?"

"Yes, I think that was it!"

"My grandfather's personal bank. But why would he pay him? What did he do for him other than tell him when my parents died?"

"I don't know, and I certainly didn't ask."

"Who owns the house now, Alida?"

"As far as I know, no one has bought it. It just stands there rotting away."

"Someone has to own it. I would like to take a look inside. Who can arrange it for me?"

"You don't want to go inside that house, Francesco. No one in the village must know who you are. If you had been with your parents that day—! Who knows?" she said shaking her head sadly. "Leave, Francesco, and forget you were ever born here. Believe me, it is better."

"Alida!" cried out the old woman. "Who are you talking to?"

"She is up already," whispered Alida. "You must go now. She gets frightened at the mention of the name Bertolli."

"I'll leave, but first, are there any photographs of my parents?"

"I never went back to the house. Whatever there was must be long gone. Young hoodlums are always climbing over the gate to see what they can find or destroy."

"Well, thank you for everything, Alida. I'll not forget you this time."

Her eyes were awash with tears. "Goodbye, Francesco," she wept. "May God bless you," and she kissed the back of his hand. "If your parents could see what a fine young man you are, they would be so proud."

"Thank you for that," he said, and kissed her cheek before leaving.

***

Cynthia was sitting on the sand, her knees drawn up to her chest, intent on the small islands lying off the coast. It wasn't until his shadow fell across her that she looked up and saw Frankie standing there. He appeared completely shattered, and fearing for him, she asked anxiously, "What is it? What did she tell you?"

His eyes seemed to be staring straight through her, as though she were invisible. She held her breath for what felt like an eternity before he spoke. "Not now. Let's go," he said and helped her to her feet.

Without another word, she followed him up the cliff to where the car was parked. She had never seen him like this before and it worried her; nevertheless, she kept her thoughts to herself. She knew that in his own time, he would confide in her.

It was a solemn drive back to the hotel. The silence was heavy, the sun fierce, and the air suffocating. Even the slight breeze did little to temper the heat. Every few minutes, Cynthia would steal a glance at Frankie. His eyes were strangely expressionless and his jaw had a grim set to it. He was driving too fast, even taking the dangerous curves without slowing down, and more than once, she had to cry out in fear.

When they pulled up in front of the hotel, he switched off the engine and turned to face her. "I have a phone call to make. I need to be alone when I make it. Would you mind?"

"Of course not. I'll be in the garden when you come downstairs."

"Thanks for being so understanding, and for not asking questions." Before she could reply, he was out of the car and rushing into the hotel with that determined step of his.

The moment he entered his room, he went to the phone and put a call through to his grandfather in New York. The housekeeper answered. "Is he there?" he asked without formality.

His grandfather's voice in the background gave him the answer. "Who is it, Rosa?" he asked.

"Mr. Frank," she called out.

Within seconds, he was on the line. "Franco," he cried in his usual bustling manner. "Thank heaven it's you. Johnny has been driving me mad and I am running out of excuses why you are not home yet. When will you be back?"

He took a deep breath. Anger had been building up inside him ever since he left Positano; now, hearing his grandfather's voice, a good part of that anger disintegrated, and he felt more confused than ever. They had always meant so much to each other—how could he put that aside on the word of a comparative stranger? Still he had to know, and so he hardened himself. "I'm in Italy, you remember, the place where I was born—the place where my parents died so tragically."

From the tone of his voice, it didn't take much imagination for his grandfather to know what he was referring to. "I see," he said quietly. "Why didn't you tell me you were going to Italy?"

"What were you afraid of, Joe, that I would learn the truth?" he cried, and the bitter edge to his voice sounded alien even to himself. But what was he supposed to say? How was he supposed to respond to the lies he was brought up to believe?

"I'm sorry!" apologized his grandfather. "But what did you expect me to do? Tell a young child that his parents had been murdered? It was difficult enough for you to understand that they were dead and that you would never see them again."

"I can't accept that as an excuse. I have been a man for some time now. Didn't you think I deserved the truth? They were my parents, my own flesh and blood. You had no right to keep it from me."

"I made a mistake, and I admit it. Go ahead and punish me if it will make you feel any better. I can't hurt more than I already do."

They were both suffering. Perhaps if his grandfather had been angrier, it might have been easier for Frankie to express his own anger. It wasn't just one lie that he had to deal with; it was a whole pack of lies. "Why did you tell me that you were a friend of theirs when the truth is you didn't even know them?"

There was a deep sigh followed by a pause. "Who have you been talking to?" he asked.

"What does it matter? The truth is the truth, and a lie a lie whomever it comes from."

"The truth!" exclaimed his grandfather in an unexpected burst of anger. "No one knows the truth but me. No one knows anything about who I am or what your parents were to me. That is why I wanted to be with you when you first visited Positano; so that you would hear what happened from me and no one else. Now please, Franco, come home so that we can talk."

"Not until I know who murdered them and why, and who you really are."

"It cannot be discussed over the phone. Return home, Franco, and I will tell you everything you want to know. Please? It's important."

"So that you can lie to me again?"

"No more lies, I promise."

"There are things I must attend to first. I am going to Sicily. Whoever they were to you, they were my parents first, and a son has to do what he must."

"You are talking like a fool. There is nothing to be gained by going to Sicily. All you will do is attract attention to yourself, and that is the last thing you need, believe me."

"Why should I believe you now?"

"Because whatever had to be done was done. Do you understand what I am saying? It was done!"

He felt as though he had been stunned by a blunt instrument. Did he hear right? Had he understood what he was saying? Alida said he didn't know them, so why would he avenge their death? He was more confused than ever. "I don't believe you," he said.

"That is why we have to talk. When you hear everything, you will understand. Come home, Franco, please?"

"I can't. I need to know everything first."

"Then if you won't come to me, I will have to come to you. Just promise me that you won't do anything rash until we have had a chance to talk."

The last thing he expected was for his grandfather to come to him in Italy. It had to be important. Whatever he had to say had to be big or he wouldn't make the journey. What could he say except, "All right, I'm staying at the Michelangelo in Sorrento. I believe you know it!"

There was a pause; then sadly he murmured, "I know it well.… If you phone my secretary later today, she will be able to give you details of my flight. No need to meet the plane. I will get a taxi to Sorrento." There was another pause, and then his grandfather asked, "Are you alone?"

"I'm with someone."

"I thought so. Who is she?"

"A friend."

"I understand. I will see you in a couple of days."

Frankie found Cynthia sitting in one of the little nooks in the garden. She didn't say anything when she saw him, but there was a question in her eyes. He sat down beside her. "My grandfather is coming here," he said. "I'll know when after I've telephoned his secretary."

"I see," she said quietly.

He stared at her. She had been very good, he thought, never pressing him with awkward questions and he appreciated it. "Look," he said, "you will know sooner or later so I'll tell you now. I heard some disturbing things this morning. My parents didn't die in a car crash; they were murdered."

"Oh no!" she cried. "From the look on your face when you returned from seeing that woman, I knew it had to be something terrible, but I never imagined anything like this."

"It seems my grandfather has known all along and never said a word to me about it; he just let me go on believing a lie."

"You sound bitter. Surely, you don't think he did so on purpose? He must have had good reason."

"You don't think a son has a right to know how his parents died?"

"Of course I do, but you don't know what the circumstances were, do you?"

"What have circumstances got to do with anything? He lied to me."

"Does he know how you feel?"

"I made it very clear."

"Is that why he is coming?"

"I suppose."

"Then he must love you very much."

"All the more reason for the truth."

"Sounds to me as if you are judging him before he's had an opportunity to explain."

"I can't help feeling that he has failed me. I thought we were very, very close. I thought there was nothing that we couldn't discuss between us. I was wrong, and that's what makes it so hard to bear."

"Loving someone and being close to them doesn't necessarily ensure that you do the right thing by them. Have you never done the wrong thing for the right reason?"

"I can't believe this," he scowled. "You're taking his side."

"I am not taking either side, but I do know you. If you allow whatever it was that your grandfather did to come between you and spoil the special relationship you share, then you will regret it for the rest of your life. No one is perfect, Frankie; so if you cannot forgive him, how can you ever forgive yourself for things you should or shouldn't have done?"

"So you are asking me to give him the benefit of a doubt."

"That is up to you."

"I suppose it's the least I can do for a man I have loved for the better part of my life." He heaved a sigh. "The truth is, I would like to," he said.

***

125

After dinner, Frankie telephoned his grandfather's secretary and was given details of his flight, and what time he was expected to arrive in Sorrento the following afternoon.

"Does he know about me?" asked Cynthia.

"He knows that I am here with a woman. You have nothing to worry about; he is quite understanding in that matter. Anyhow, I know he will like you."

"That isn't what is worrying me. He will want you to return with him right away, won't he?"

"In all likelihood, but the final word is still mine. I'll not run off and leave you, if that is what's worrying you. There is no need for me to return to New York for another few weeks yet."

"A few weeks!" she whispered, and her eyes filled with pain.

He knew what she was going through. His own heart ached at the thought of leaving her, but it was their decision—they understood what was right for them. "Look," he said, brightening up for her sake, "tomorrow is a day just for you and me. What would you like to do?"

"Spend it with you."

"I know, but there must be something special we could do together?"

"Well, they do say, 'See Capri and die'!"

He laughed. "It's see Naples and die!"

"In that case," she replied, "we will have to make do with Capri."

When time is limited, everything becomes urgent: what you do, what you say, and especially your love. They needed to make everything perfect for each other, and when they awoke next morning, they knew whatever they did was going to be special.

They ambled down to the jetty after breakfast. For one complete day, the wonders of the world would be theirs. The rude awakening came when they reached the ferry. It seemed every tourist in Sorrento was of one mind—to go and see Capri. By the time they boarded, there wasn't a seat to be had and they had to stand by the rail for the entire crossing.

Once they left land behind, it wasn't that unpleasant. The ferry ploughed steadily through the calm waters. The light breeze was refreshing and the sun, not yet at its height, was still cool enough to enjoy. Cynthia placed an arm through Frankie's and drew closer to him. He smiled at her. She looked happy and he was grateful.

His feelings were still adrift; he was unable to make sense of anything that had happened in the last twenty-four hours. Now Bingham entered his head. It was ironic that after all the shocking things he had discovered about his past, it seemed that his own beginnings might not bear close scrutiny. What did his grandfather have to tell him? How much worse could it get?

Cynthia glanced up at him and smiled, and the dark thoughts disappeared.

The sudden, shrill voice of an English Cockney woman rose above the drone of the boat's engine. "'Ere Fred?" she cried. "Are you sure you know where our Gracie used to live? I mean, I wouldn't want to go 'ome without 'aving seen it. What would I tell the neighbors?"

"Oh, come off it, Mable!" exclaimed Fred. "No one bloody cares!"

"I do!" cried an indignant Mable.

Cynthia smiled to herself. Frankie whispered, "Fred doesn't seem to like our Gracie."

"Can't say that I blame him. She was a popular singer in the '30s. According to my mother, she was a great fan of both Hitler and Mussolini. She used to run a café in Capri with her Italian husband. The British, bless them, tend to forgive and forget very quickly."

The ferry docked, the gangway went down, and all at once the well-ordered crowd became an unruly mob, pushing and shoving as they surged forward in their hurry to be the first off the boat and onto the cable cars that would carry them up to the little town of Capri.

Cynthia and Frankie were poked and dug in the ribs as they were carried along with them. "This is awful," cried Cynthia. "I never dreamed it would be anything like this. If it were not so difficult to get through this lot, I would go back immediately."

"As we are here, we might as well take a quick glance around," he said.

The cable car stopped when it reached the town; the door opened and in a more orderly fashion, it was vacated. They waited until the last person had gone; then they left.

The crowd filled the sleepy little square; and then, all at once, they dispersed in every direction, leaving it quiet and peaceful once again. There were cafés—their tables spilling across the wide pavements. Narrow alleyways fanned out from the center, leading to different parts of the island. A church stood at one end of the square, while at the other end a wider road, where all the expensive tourist shops were located, led deeper into the town.

"This is more like it!" said Cynthia with a sigh of relief.

"Come on," said Frankie, "let's explore."

They started out down the most interesting alley, which was little more than a narrow passageway, tightly packed with small shops and restaurants, and followed it up hill until it came out to the country perched on the cliff over the sea below. They wandered along the top, admiring the spectacular rocks that stood out in the sea forming arch after arch where the waves had spent their energy over the centuries. They found steps cut into the cliff, and like a couple of excited children, they descended eager to see what lay at the bottom. It was a tiny beach strewn with huge boulders, and they climbed over them, dipping their feet in the tide pools.

When they had had enough, they traced their steps back to the narrow little alley and bought rolls, cheese, little plum tomatoes, and a bunch of yellow Muscat grapes and went in search of a quiet spot where they could enjoy their picnic.

They found such a place along one of the coast roads. It was a small cove without another soul. It was no wonder: the sea here was wild with waves a mountain high as they rolled in and crashed upon the sandy beach, and the only way to get down to it was by a ladder, which stopped short of the beach by at least four feet. Only the brave would attempt such a steep descent, or foolhardy lovers seeking solitude. It couldn't have been more ideal if Cynthia and Frankie had dreamed up such a place.

The sand felt warm and soft beneath their feet, and the roar of the sea drowned all other sounds so that they could make believe they were alone in the world. They were Adam and Eve in the Garden of Eden.

They ate their picnic; nothing had ever tasted so good. They paddled at the water's edge and laughed with delight when being chased back by the waves. It was a day of those little things that gave the greatest pleasure; the best things in life, you might say, and the best of all was just being there together.

When the day grew hotter and the sun too fierce for comfort, they made their way back to the ferry. It was early afternoon, and with the crowds still reluctant to return to the mainland, they had the ferry to themselves. They sat forward, enjoying the little breeze there was coming off the water. They sat close, their arms, their thighs touching, their hands clasped, filled with an inner peace. Even Frankie, who was anything but calm when they set out, was feeling tranquil. Indeed, the day had been special. He glanced at Cynthia; her eyes were glowing, her lips parted in a faint smile. Whatever happens after today, he thought, they will have shared an unforgettable moment in time.

As if she had seen into his thoughts, she looked up at him and whispered, "I will remember this day forever."

He swallowed. *How long is forever?* he wondered. How long would he have to live without the woman he loved beside him?

Night fell with no change in the heat; in fact, without a breeze, the air only became heavier. After dinner, they took their usual stroll down to the water's edge. It was as balmy by the water as it was in the town, making everything an effort. Even words seemed to die before they had a chance to leave their lips, so they sat quietly, content to simply gaze out over the bay, empty of all thought.

All at once, the same Cockney voice they heard on the ferry cut through the air. "Oh, look Fred! There's a seat next to that young couple over there."

"Oh no!" whispered Cynthia. "I think we are about to be invaded."

"Shall we go?" asked Frankie, but before she had a chance to reply, Mable and Fred had taken possession of the other half of the bench.

"Don't mind, do you?" asked Mable as she inched closer to Cynthia to leave more room for Fred.

"No! We were about to leave anyhow," she answered.

Mable's mouth fell open in amazement. "'Ere," she cried, "you're British like us! Aren't you the same couple from the ferry this morning?"

Oh, Lord! thought Cynthia, and nodded half-heartedly.

"Thought so! Small world, isn't it? So, 'ow did you like Capri?"

"Very much."

"Yeah!" she said dreamily. "It were nice, weren't it? So romantic. I said to Fred, if only we'd spent our 'oneymoon there. Are you two on 'oneymoon?"

Uncertain what to say, Cynthia looked to Frankie. He raised an amused eyebrow, and quick to catch the look between them, Mable said with a familiar nudge and a wink at Cynthia, "I see! Trying it out before you tie the knot. Well, I can't say that I blame you. I mean, you don't know these days, do you? You think a person is one thing, then you find out they're another; then it's too late to do anything."

"Cor blimey, Mable!" exclaimed Fred. "What will you say next?"

"Well, what 'ave I said?" responded an indignant Mable. "It's not like it was when we were young, Fred. They're all doin' it, aren't you, love?" she said, addressing Cynthia. "I mean, you only 'ave to watch tele to know that."

"Come on, old girl," said Fred. "We 'ad better go before you take it into your 'ead to say something worse. Sorry about that," he said to Frankie. "She gets a bit carried away at times."

Frankie gave Fred an understanding smile. Fred then rose and Mable toddled after him, but only under sufferance. "Well, I never!" she could be heard saying. "I was just being friendly. After all, us Brits 'ave to stick together, what with all these foreigners over 'ere!"

Frankie laughed. "Thank God for Fred."

Cynthia smiled. "I'm not sure who I feel more sorry for—Fred or Mable."

The air had become more humid, the stars had fled, and the sliver of a moon was slowly retreating behind a thick cloud. Frankie looked up at the sky. "I think we are in for a storm," he said. "We should leave."

They crossed the crowded square and made their way up to the hotel. Lightning streaked across the sky, followed by a loud clap of thunder, and then came the rain. A few more steps and they reached the hotel before it really came down.

"This should clear the air," said Frankie, and opened the shutters to their balcony to allow in the breeze that had blown up. It was still hot, and they undressed and lay naked on top of the bed covers to listen to the rain.

After a while, Cynthia asked, "Are you worried about tomorrow?"

"Anxious, not worried."

"Me too."

"You? Why?"

"Meeting your grandfather for one, and wondering what he will think when he meets me."

"Why would you worry about what he thinks?"

"How many Jewish girlfriends have you introduced to him?"

"What kind of a question is that? If I didn't know you better, I would take it as an insult. My grandfather hasn't a biased bone in his body; neither has anyone in my family."

"Perhaps, but you are his grandson, and whatever you may think, it does make a difference in what a person feels about a situation."

"Why do I get the feeling that your being anxious has nothing to do with your being Jewish and what my grandfather may or may not feel about it?"

She didn't reply right away, and then it came blurting out. "It's coming to an end too fast," she cried. "I'm scared Frankie, scared of facing life without you."

He understood only too well, but he was a man, and men were supposed to be in control of their emotions. Supposed to be, but he felt as devastated at the thought as she was. "I know," he whispered and took her in his arms.

CHAPTER EIGHT

Joe was struggling for breath. *It must be the heat,* he thought. He had forgotten how hot it could be in Naples at that time of the year. "Haven't you got air-conditioning?" he gasped.

"Sure," said the taxi driver, "but why would you want air-conditioning? All the windows are open."

"Don't argue, just turn the damn thing on!" he cried.

"That's all you know in America—air-conditioning! Maybe you think fresh air is gonna kill you, huh?"

"The way I feel it will kill you if you don't do as I ask." *The impudence!* thought Joe. *Who does he think he is talking to me like that!*

The driver swore under his breath, closed the windows, and put on the air.

Joe's breathing fared no better. "Angina," said the doctor when he went to see him to complain of shortness of breath. "Angina? No way!" he replied. "I have no pain. I can walk up a flight of stairs with no trouble at all; in fact, I can walk up two flights of stairs. It's impossible! An allergy, maybe."

The doctor shook his head and sent him for tests. Some tests! They put him on a treadmill, hooked him up to a cardiogram machine, and told him to start walking. So he walked and walked while they kept taking his blood pressure. Okay, so he had a little high blood pressure; who wouldn't with everything that had been going on in his life lately? Anyhow, he did well; he walked for fifteen minutes, non-stop, and surprised the lot of them, doctors and nurses alike. No way did he have angina.

"Are you satisfied?" he asked somewhat smugly when, a few days later, he went to see the doctor.

"I'm satisfied," he replied, "you've got angina."

What a year it had been. First, his wife dies. After fifty happy years, you would have thought God might have spared them and let them live out their lives together; after all, it was He who brought them together in the first place.

Then, there was the mess with Guido, and he had the D.A.'s office breathing down his neck. Now, there was Frankie. That was his fault; he should have confided in him a long time ago.

As they neared the outskirts of Sorrento, memories came flooding back—some good, some bad. But it was the bad that dominated his thoughts that afternoon, and tore at his heart. *Damn heat...,* he thought, and cried, "Can't you make that lousy air-conditioning go higher?"

The taxi driver glared at him through the mirror. "Hey! You grumble too much. You ask for air-conditioning, I give it to you; now it's not good enough. You know what I think? I think you live in America too long."

What was the use, thought Joe. "Okay," he said, "just keep your eyes on the road and shut up."

"A pleasure!"

Frankie was waiting inside the front entrance when Joe's taxi pulled up. He looked tired and frail, he thought, and it stabbed at his conscience. "You go in and register," said Frankie. "I'll look after the taxi driver and attend to the luggage."

Joe wasn't feeling well enough to argue, and went inside without a word. Moments later, Frankie was at his side. "I'll see you to your room," he said. "The luggage is already on its way."

Joe's suite was at the other end of the corridor from his. He opened the door for him and asked, "Can you manage on your own or would you like me to unpack for you?"

Joe shook his head, and then looked around, remembering the last time he was in a room just like that one with his wife; nothing had changed much, he thought.

"Are you all right?" asked Frankie.

"I'm fine, just a little tired. If only planes had sleepers like trains."

Frankie smiled. "I know what you mean. Why don't you take a rest before dinner? You will be joining us, won't you?"

"What time is dinner?"

"Eight. If you would prefer it earlier or later, just say so."

"Eight will be fine. What of the woman you are with?"

"You will meet her then." Somewhat uncomfortable, Frankie hovered for a moment, then said, "Well, if there is nothing you want, I'll leave you. We'll be waiting in the hall outside the dining room when you come down."

He nodded. "Good," he said, "and Franco, can we leave our talk until the morning?"

"Of course," he answered, then left him to himself.

Cynthia was on the balcony of their room gazing out over the bay. She turned when she heard Frankie enter. "Well?" she asked with concern.

"The journey has taken it out of him. I was wrong to have allowed him to come all this way; he's not up to it."

"Could you have stopped him?"

"Not Joe! Nothing can stop him once he has made up his mind to do something."

"Then you have your answer. Did he say anything about...?"

"Only that we will talk in the morning."

"Then what is making you so miserable?"

"All the time I was with him, I couldn't help thinking about the lies he let me go on believing. I felt as if I had never really known him and it upset me."

"I thought you agreed not to judge him before hearing him out."

"I wasn't judging him. It was just that after what I heard from Alida, I don't know what he can say that will alter how I feel."

"Isn't that the point—that you don't know? I cannot see him having come all this way only to confirm Alida's version of what happened."

"How do I know he won't lie to me again? That's what makes it so hard; it pains me to go on doubting him like this."

"Then give him a chance. Go to him tomorrow with an open mind."

"If it were just that easy; but I will try," he said.

Cynthia was somewhat apprehensive when the lift doors parted and Frankie's grandfather got off and came toward them. She needn't have been; his smile put her at ease even before Frankie introduced them. "My friend Cynthia Gould," he said.

The lines on Joe's tired old face deepened as his smile broadened. "Joseph Bocacci," he said and extended his hand. As she placed her hand in his, she couldn't help wondering how this slight man with the warm smile and gentle manner could possibly have been connected to the Mafia. It intrigued her, and she couldn't stop glancing at him out of the corner of her eye as they moved to the dining room.

He looked at her and smiled as if he had read her thoughts, and if it wasn't for that smile, she might have been embarrassed. She liked him more and more; in fact, she was quite taken with him.

The headwaiter saw them to their table, presented them with the menu, then left them to make their choice. "If there is nothing you fancy, they will make you a steak," said Frankie.

"Everything looks good to me; you know what I am for pasta!"

"Yes," he said and smiled for the first time that evening.

With their order taken, Joe's attention turned to Cynthia. "So, Miss Gould, what part of England are you from?"

"London. Frankie tells me that his first visit to the city was with you. How did you like it?"

"It is exactly what you would expect a great city to be—old and historic. In New York, if someone tells you that a building is over a hundred years old, you marvel that it still stands. In London, when you hear that something is over a thousand years old, you accept it as commonplace. The old and the new, Miss Gould, an ocean apart, and yet in a working relationship that is of benefit to both parties…. Your Shakespeare had it wrong when he wrote 'Crabbed age and youth cannot live together.'"

"In other words, you believe that youth and age have a lot to learn from one another?"

"Don't you? I have lived to see great and small in all things, and that is what makes life so rich."

"It would seem we agree, Mr. Bocacci."

Joe laughed. "I am never sure if it is a good sign or not when the young agree with the old. What do you do, Miss Gould?"

"I design shoes for my father's business."

"Cynthia is really an artist," said Frankie, "and a very good one, I might add."

"I thought there was an artistic look about you!" commented Joe. "I have always admired artists' dedication to their work. One of my many regrets is that I have no artistic talent."

"Talent is the key word, Mr. Bocacci, and few are without one kind or another. I very much doubt you are the exception."

"Doubt is a word I have never liked; it conjures up confusion, mistrust, skepticism, so let me leave you in no doubt whatsoever. If I have a talent, it is for reading into a situation; of course, it stops there. I never take it upon myself to interfere in what is right or wrong; I leave the good sense to the people concerned."

135

It was a message, nicely put; nevertheless, the meaning behind his words had a sting to them. "Fortunately, or unfortunately," she said, "both your grandson and I are full of good sense."

Joe's hand went out and briefly touched hers. She understood that it was meant as a gesture of compassion, but it held little comfort for her. She knew, only too well, how hopeless their situation was. All Frankie's grandfather had done was to reaffirm it.

The conversation was light after that, as though they had reached an understanding and all was well. Frankie was relieved, and as he watched his grandfather's face come alive when speaking to Cynthia, he was reminded of something his grandmother had said to him—"Your grandfather seems to flourish in the company of a beautiful woman." It surprised him and he asked, "Doesn't it make you jealous?" And she replied, "If a man is incapable of enjoying a beautiful woman, then he is incapable of enjoying any woman, and heaven forbid he shouldn't enjoy me." He didn't understand what she meant back then—now he did.

Joe suddenly looked exhausted, so they were not surprised when he announced that he was ready to retire. "I'll see you to your room," said Frankie.

"I would appreciate it," he said, then turning to Cynthia, "I won't keep him long. I remember what it was like to be young and impatient."

"Please don't hurry on my account," she said. "My grandfather used to say that if only the young had the patience that comes with age, how much sweeter their lives would be."

"He was right. Everything tastes sweeter for the waiting. Well, I will bid you good night, Miss Gould, and may I say what a pleasure it has been talking to you."

Frankie eyed his grandfather as they rode up in the lift and asked, "What was that Miss Gould bit all about?"

"Your Miss Gould is very bright. She understood; in fact, we understood each other. I like her."

"Nevertheless, you made your feelings about our relationship quite obvious at one point!"

"That was the grandfather in me speaking, not the man."

"Then you know we are in love."

"I'm not blind. The looks that passed between you could have started a brush fire in the wet season."

"And you are not concerned?"

"Your Miss Gould laid those concerns to rest; at least I thought she had. Are you telling me that you feel differently?"

The lift reached their floor and Frankie walked his grandfather to his room. Joe opened the door, then turned to his grandson. Frankie knew he was waiting for an answer, but the words seemed to stick in his throat. Did he feel differently? He wondered. He couldn't meet his grandfather's gaze for fear of giving himself away. He half turned, whispering, "I don't feel differently," and walked back down the corridor.

His grandfather called after him. "Let's have breakfast together in the morning; then we can have that talk."

He stopped and turned. "I would prefer to have breakfast with Cynthia," he said.

"Then come afterwards—at ten."

"All right," he said, then continued to the lift.

With her head to one side, Cynthia was examining one of the paintings in the hall, when he returned. "Who is the artist?" he asked.

"It's unsigned. I can't recognize the brush strokes, but it is very good. Notice the treatment of light—that marvelous glow. It could well be an early Caravaggio, but if it isn't, whoever did paint it copied his style."

Frankie's mind had already wandered away from the painting. "So what do you think of my grandfather?"

She gave him the same searching glance she had given the painting moments before.... "I liked him," she said, having given the matter some thought. "In some ways your grandfather reminded me of mine. He also was amazingly eloquent for someone whose first language wasn't English."

"Joe has always been a great reader of the classics."

She chuckled. "Every time he called me Miss Gould, I could hear my grandfather calling you Mr. Leeman."

"I thought it might have offended you."

"He was making a point, and I understood. Why? Did he say something to you?"

"Only that he liked you and that you understood each other. Seems he was right."

"What are your feelings about him now?"

Lines appeared around his eyes, and he said abruptly, "I would rather not talk about it. I need some fresh air. Shall we visit the square?"

Without another word, she placed her hand in his, and they strolled down the hill and sat on their favorite bench by the water's edge. The night was less humid than it had been. The sky was alive with a million stars, not that they noticed. Their minds were full of unspoken questions, spawned by the arrival of Frankie's grandfather, and their hearts were heavy for the lack of hope.

Having slept fairly well, Joe awoke to a red sky that was slowly fading to pink, as dawn gave way to a perfect day. He stepped out onto the balcony and breathed in the fresh sea air. His mind, never still, was going over his life; where he had gone wrong, where he had done right. On the whole, he decided, there had been more right than wrong. There had been his wife, Lucia, the best thing that ever happened to him, and, by a twist of fate, there was Franco, the next best thing. Now, he worried that because of a mistake he made all those years ago, he might lose him.

Of course, he deserved to know the truth, but the truth wasn't always simple; it had many facets. His only hope was to make him understand how and why it happened, and pray that he had it in him to forgive.

At ten sharp, there was an impatient knock on the door. He had been expecting it. Punctuality was important to him, and his grandson took after him in that respect. "It's open!" he called out, and Frankie entered.

"Did you sleep well?" Frankie asked with concern.

"Well enough. The coffee is still warm. Would you like a cup?"

"Thanks, but I've just finished breakfast."

"Then don't stand there looking like a lost sheep; sit down."

Frankie pulled out a chair from the breakfast table and sat opposite his grandfather. "How is mother?"

"I was wondering when you would ask."

"I know I should have asked before, but there has been so much on my mind."

"I can imagine! Well, there is nothing new to report. She seems bent on destroying herself. It's hard to watch, but then you know all about that, don't you?"

He nodded then looked away. He felt uneasy and he didn't want his grandfather's probing eyes to see into his thoughts. They had always been so close; he couldn't imagine what life would be like without his love and support. Now he didn't know what to think or feel; it was as though a stranger was sitting opposite him.

It wasn't an easy moment for Joe either. For over fifty years, he had kept a secret, and now, to suddenly bring it out into the open was more difficult than he could have anticipated. But it had to be done, and the only way he knew how was to tackle it head-on—the way he did everything in life.

It also pained him to see the injured look in his grandson's eyes. All he did was follow his conscience. How could he have foreseen the problem he was now faced with? Instinctively, his hand went out and touched Frankie's arm. He didn't respond, and Joe silently prayed that after he heard what he had to say, he wouldn't judge him too harshly.

"When you lost your parents," he began, "I lost a daughter and son-in-law." It was the first time he had ever uttered those words, and the painful memory of that day was as sharp as it was then, and in his grief, he failed to notice the shattering effect it had upon his grandson.

"It was the worst day of my life. I shall never forget the horror I felt when I was given the details of their death. What made it even more unbearable was that I couldn't share my feelings with the family. I couldn't even confide in your grandmother; I had to bear the pain alone and in silence. You cannot keep a secret like that for so long and then suddenly come out with it and expect everyone to understand, least of all the woman you have loved and been married to all those years."

Frankie's head reeled as the significance of what he had just heard hit him, and he stared at his grandfather in disbelief.

Still unaware of the impact his story was having upon his grandson, Joe continued. "How often we wish we could turn back the clock and start afresh; then, who can say we wouldn't make the same mistakes all over again? Regret is a terrible thing, Franco, and I have so many." He sighed and looked his grandson in the face for the first time since he began speaking. "I know this must have come as a shock to you, and I wish I could have confided sooner, but at the time I thought I was doing the right thing. How are we to judge but after the fact? I suppose I should start at the beginning; but before I do, I ask one favor—that you do not judge me until you have heard it all."

Frankie could barely contain his anger. He had been lied to from beginning to end. Now, he was expected to reserve judgment and he burst out, "How could you keep something as important as this from me all these years? I'm your grandson, for heaven's sake, and you let me go on believing I was an outsider. To think I was grateful to you and the family for taking me in as though I was some poor waif in need; it was indefensible, do you hear me? Indefensible."

Shocked by the outburst, Joe struck back, "You are not being fair. No one ever thought of you as an outsider. The whole family loved you and considered you one of their own from the first day you came into their lives. You should be ashamed to have had such thoughts."

He knew his grandfather was right. He had never been made to feel anything less than family; but in his anger he said the first thing that rose to his lips, and now he was sorry…. "The truth is you are the one I cannot forgive, not them."

"I am not asking for forgiveness, only understanding," said Joe.

"Really!" exclaimed Frankie. "And what am I supposed to feel about that?"

"How you feel afterwards is something you will have to deal with. I made a mistake, and I have had to live with it. If you think you are incapable of making mistakes, then that is your first big one. Even the most perfect among us err. When I have finished, you are free then to hate me, never see me again, if that is what you want, but don't hate the family or lay my sin upon their head. They love you as much as I do."

What was he doing to him? wondered Frankie. He couldn't hate him if he tried, but he was hurting and he wanted to hurt him—only in doing so, he was hurting himself even more. "Go on," he said quietly, "I'll not interrupt you again."

Joe searched his grandson's eyes. "It's painful, isn't it, Franco? To hurt someone you love?" He shook his head sadly. "How well I know that feeling…. Francesca, that was your maternal grandmother's name. I didn't want to hurt her; we didn't want to hurt each other, it just happened. We grew up together, sweethearts even in first grade at school. Little did we realize how sweet those days of innocence were. We knew nothing of the world or how cruel it could be. Our pleasures were simple; our life was simple. We were in love and believed that love conquers all. That is how naïve we were.

"The first obstacle was her parents. As you know, my family were poor farmers; hers were better off, if only enough to make them dream of better than the little ragged boy who called on their daughter, and they made life difficult for us, but we managed to keep our dreams. We also realized that I would have to make something of myself if they were to ever give their consent to our betrothal. I had already decided that America was for us, so I went ahead to seek my fortune before returning to claim her as my bride.

"Just when I was beginning to make some real money, the Second World War came along and I couldn't return, neither could she come out to me. We couldn't even exchange letters, so we lost contact for the duration.

"It was tough on both of us, and as soon as the end of the war was in sight, I made plans to return. Unfortunately, I was so caught up in what I was doing that I made the mistake of not writing to let her know when I would be returning. When she didn't hear from me during those first few months of peace, she assumed that I had forgotten about her and let her parents talk her into marrying a local boy who had a very prosperous business at the time.

"Of course, I imagined her waiting for me and didn't send her a telegram, letting her know that I was coming, until the last moment. A friend met me at the dockside, and when I asked about Francesca, he told me that she was already married. I was devastated; I couldn't believe that she could have forgotten all about me just like that. Under the circumstances, I didn't try to see her. It was over, and hurt and bewildered, I decided to leave as soon as I wound up my parents' affairs. You see, my father died in a farming accident during the war, and my mother died soon after, so there was nothing to keep me in Sicily.

"The day before I was to return to America, I received a note from her. She wanted to see me that afternoon at the old cave in the cliff where we used to play as children. The best thing I could have done would have been to ignore it, but I couldn't. I wanted to see her, and I wanted to know why she hadn't waited for me.

"I arrived early and I sat there, barely able to breath at the thought of her. Soon I saw her walking along the cliff toward me, and my heart stood still. She was a shadow of her old self, so thin that she looked as if the wind would blow her away. Then, as she came closer, I saw how hollow her cheeks were, and how sunken her eyes—those eyes that had danced with life had disappeared, and my stomach turned with fear for her. She looked like a dying woman. My first thought was that her husband was ill treating her, but she assured me that he was a good man and would never do anything to harm her. It was the war, she said; they didn't have enough to eat. But I knew it had to be more than that.

"We talked for a while. I told her about America and how well I was doing, and her eyes shone with pride the way they used to. Of course, I made no mention of the Mafia. I didn't want her to remember me with shame.

"Suddenly, while we were still talking, she took hold of my hand and pressed it against her breast. I could feel her heart pounding as she told me how much she loved me, and that she would never have married if she knew that I would be returning. It was a moving moment. There were tears in her eyes and passion in my heart, and before either of us knew what was happening, she was in my arms, and we were clinging to one another.

"I didn't intend for anything to happen, but when I felt her body against mine, I lost control, and all I could think of was how much I wanted her. I still remember the wonderful look on her face after we had been together."

Joe was choking on the last few words and couldn't go on. Frankie watched him, unable to sympathize, but at the same time understanding what he must have gone through. He knew, only too well, the overwhelming power of passion and what it could make you do.

When Joe had collected himself, he went on. "For the second time that day, I received a shock. While making love, I found her to be a virgin. Oh, I know that it sounds impossible, but she confirmed it later. You see, Georgio, her husband, was impotent. They discovered it on their wedding night, and although he sought help, there was nothing the doctors could do about it. It seemed he was born with a defect.

"There was talk of an annulment, but he couldn't accept it. He said that he would commit suicide rather than let the world know he wasn't the man he should be, so she couldn't go through with it for fear of what he might do.

"I told her that I would stay on and support her if she should decide to go ahead and leave him, I even begged her to. She only smiled sadly, and said that I would always be her one and only love, and that what we had shared that day would help sustain her through the lonely years without me. She said it was enough for her to know what it was like to lie in my arms and be a part of me. Then she kissed me, not passionately as before, but gently, and I knew then that I would never see her again. I did, however, give her my address in America, 'Just in case,' I said."

Joe wiped the tears from his eyes. Frankie asked, "Was that when my mother was conceived?"

"Yes!" he replied. "If I had known, I would never have returned to America. As it happened, a few months before I left for Sicily, I was introduced to a fine young woman whom I was attracted to. But I had Francesca on my mind and knew that I would be returning to Sicily to make her my bride, so I did nothing about it. However, when I got back, I called on her and we started to go out together. Before long, I was in love as I had never been in love. A few months later, we were married."

"Grandmother...! Did you tell her about Francesca?"

"It was all over before I started courting her, and to tell her that I had an affair, however briefly, with a married woman—well, I didn't know what her reaction might be. Neither did I want her to think that I had married her on the rebound. She was special, and if I had to choose all over again, I would choose her. I knew from the beginning what a treasure I had, and we loved each other until the day she died, and I still love her." He heaved a sigh, then said, "Love is never without pain, Franco; if it's not there at the beginning, it's there at the end when one leaves the other behind. There is no fairy-tale ending."

Frankie's thoughts turned to Cynthia, and he understood what he was talking about; but then, his grandfather never had to choose in the same way that he had to, and he wondered if in the end he would be able to say, as his grandfather did, that if he had to choose all over again, he would make the same choice. Life was so simple for some; why did his have to be so complicated? "What happened when my mother was born?" he asked.

"Not three months into our marriage and your grandmother already pregnant with our daughter, I received a telegram from a friend Francesca had confided in. It said that she had given birth to a girl and was now fighting for her life. It was septicemia. I knew that I had to go to Sicily to see her—I owed her that. I also had to make arrangements for the child, should it have been necessary.

"Fortunately, your grandmother was out when the telegram arrived, and in the delicate condition she was in, I feared telling her about Francesca and the baby. I thought there would be enough time later when our child was born, so I made an excuse about family business, and left for Sicily the next day.

"By the time I arrived, Francesca was dead and the child, Valentina, was in the care of Francesca's mother and Georgio, who had acknowledged the baby as his from the moment he discovered that his wife was with child. I don't want you to think I gave her up that easily. I was fully prepared to fight for custody, but Francesca's mother pointed out that I would only bring shame on her daughter's good name and the child would be branded a bastard. It was not a pleasant thought. Anyhow, Georgio was a good man and I had no doubt that he would provide a good home for the baby. I also knew her grandmother could be relied upon to do what was best for her.

"I cannot deny that I was relieved. I didn't know my wife well enough yet to understand how she would react to my bringing an illegitimate daughter into her house to live. I know now I need not have worried, and if

I'd had the courage to do what I should have done, things might have been different, and that is a burden I have to bear."

"So you never told grandmother the truth?" asked Frankie.

"To my shame, no!"

"Then you lived a lie your whole married life. How could you?" demanded Frankie. "I always thought of you and grandmother as the perfect couple, but you did to her what you did to me. How does it make you feel now?"

"How do you think it makes me feel? But that's what happens when you allow a deception to go on for as long as I did. One lie follows another, and you begin to fear the truth coming out. Then, when your parents were killed and I brought you back to America with me, I had to add another lie."

"Why were they murdered? Did it have anything to do with you?"

"It was vendetta!"

"Vendetta? But why?"

"Another of my burdens," said Joe. "You see, when your mother was born, I made a deal with Georgio. If he allowed me to have a say in how she was brought up, I would never attempt to see her or let her know who I was. I thought it would be best for her sake. Anyhow, when she turned eighteen, I sent her to finishing school in Lugano, Switzerland. Georgio was against it; he was afraid it would spoil her, but I didn't want her growing up some little peasant girl from Sicily. I had big ideas for her, and so I persuaded him to let her go. He didn't tell me that she had become betrothed to a local boy whose family were among the wealthiest landowners in Sicily, and that they had lent him money for his failing business, and that the debt was to be forgiven upon the marriage of his daughter to their son.

"Meanwhile, while she was away in Switzerland, she met Amando, your father. He was a tall, fair-headed young man from Milan with a good future as a journalist, and they fell in love. By then, she was no longer the little girl from Sicily, but a free-thinking woman of the world with a strong mind of her own, and she decided that she didn't want to marry the boy back home.

"She had no idea about the loan to her father, or the conditions attached. The Sicilian ways of betrayal and revenge were something from the past, not the world she now lived in, and so she wrote to Roberto, breaking off their engagement; then, to avoid an argument with her father, she married Amando before returning home with him.

"Disaster followed. The loan to Georgio was called in and he went bankrupt. He lost his home and was forced to go looking for work, but even that was denied him; no one would hire someone who had crossed an important Sicilian family. As soon as I heard what happened, I arranged to send him a monthly check through a friend of mine in Rome. Georgio thought it wise that there should be no connection between us. He also asked me to keep a watchful eye on Valentina and her husband. He was always worried about Roberto and what he might do, and as it turned out, he was right."

"He killed them?" asked Frankie in disbelief.

"His family was connected to the Sicilian Mafia. They have their spies everywhere, and when they discovered where they lived…!" he said with a helpless shrug.

"The house in Positano," said Frankie.

"I should have got them to come over to America; Georgio could have managed it. They needn't have known who was behind the decision. Instead, when I heard that they were looking for a house in Positano, and that they had found one they loved but couldn't afford, I bought it; then I got the bank to sell it to them at a greatly reduced price. I also arranged for the bank to grant them a mortgage, which I held, at a monthly sum that was well within their budget. I then went there to make a deal with the police to look out for them and let me know how they were doing. I was told that they couldn't believe their good fortune. So much for good fortune!

"Barely nine months later, you were born. I couldn't contain myself when I heard, and had to go and see you, so I booked into the same hospital on the grounds that I needed a checkup. Every morning I would walk up the corridor to the nursery and see you lying there, peaceful and quiet, looking like a little blonde angel among all those dark-haired babies. You were so perfect, with your blue eyes and long lashes that swept your little pink cheeks. The nurses said that they had never seen such a lovely baby. Best of all was the look on your mother's face when she came to take a peep at you while you slept. The love in her eyes made her look even more beautiful, and to this day, I can picture her face as she stood there.

"I only spoke to her once. I asked her what she was going to name you, and she said that, had you been a girl, she would have named you after her mother, Francesca; so now, they were going to name you Francesco. I thought I would choke on the lump in my throat when she mentioned her mother, and it was all I could do to stop myself from taking her in my arms and telling her who I was. I did manage to say that it was a beautiful name for a beautiful baby. She smiled happily and I could see my mother in her smile. I had to turn and walk away before she saw the tears in my eyes."

Tears were spilling down Frankie's cheeks. "If only I had known all this before," he said.

Joe's eyes were also awash. "I'm sorry," he whispered. "So sorry!"

"Was that when you began to take those yearly vacations in Positano?"

"Yes."

"To see her?"

"I wanted to see you grow up."

"And while I was playing on the beach, Roberto killed my parents."

Joe sighed, "Yes.… After five years had passed, I thought he had forgotten about them. I should have known better; we Sicilians never forget."

"Was he ever caught and tried?"

"Even if he had been caught, it would never have come to trial. His family would have made certain of that, so I took his punishment into my own hands."

"Oh my God!" cried Frankie. "That is where you went when you left me with Alida for a few days; you went to Sicily in search of Roberto!"

"I thought it had to be Alida who told you. Yes, yes … that is where I went, and when I found him, I killed him with my bare hands. I had never done anything like that before, but I was so full of pain and anger that all I could think of was to avenge my daughter and her husband's death. The tragedy was that his family thought it had to be Georgio who did it, and when I went to see him later that evening, I found him dead—a bullet through the back of his head, just like your father. I must have missed the assassins by minutes; his body was still warm."

"I wish that I had been old enough to have done it!"

"No matter what the provocation, it is no easy thing to kill another human being; it haunts you for the rest of your life. Never will I forget the look on Roberto's face as I was strangling him. His eyes bulged as they looked into mine with fear. It was horrible. I am not saying that he didn't deserve to die; what I am saying is that it is better to leave punishment to a higher authority."

"I can't believe I am hearing this!" cried Frankie. "Didn't you say, only seconds ago, that he would never have been brought to trial? There is no justice in this world except for the rich, and if it is God you are speaking of, then it gets even worse. When has He ever taken care of the innocent? Wickedness is rewarded more often than goodness. The Bible is right. An eye for an eye: that is the only satisfaction!"

146

His grandfather threw his hands up in horror. "Don't talk like that! It's not the way you were brought up, Franco. Your grandmother would be devastated. She trusted in the Lord and His right to dispense punishment as He sees fit; if not in this world, then in the next. She was a staunch believer and had great peace of mind because of it. I should have had more faith. Hate destroys, Franco, and so does revenge when you take it into your own hands."

Religion had always played an important part in his life, and Frankie knew his grandfather was right. He would be lost without it, but sometimes your faith is tested in the most cruel way and it makes it hard to come to terms with it. "I'm sorry," he said, "it's just that there are times when you need to see punishment take place in this world. It isn't easy to relate to the next, no matter how strong your belief."

"Then just remember what your grandmother used to say: 'Love gives us a reason to live. Not hate.' Only when we love, Franco, are we whole. If I had my time over again, I would not have killed him. We pay a heavy price when we take it upon ourselves to avenge those we love. I have often wondered, if I'd had the chance to ask them what they wanted me to do about their death, what they would have said. I doubt revenge would have been a part of their answer."

"Is faith the only answer?"

"In most cases, yes!"

"Then I suppose my faith isn't strong enough yet. How are you supposed to know when it is? What magic formula can make it happen?"

"Only your heart can answer that. When you put your mind to it, you can find all sorts of reasons to believe or not to believe, but when you embrace God with your heart, then He is strong within you."

"I feel as though I am in a halfway house. I used to be so sure. I wish that I could go back to those days. I wish you had told me about my parents sooner."

"I thought it was for the best, not only for you but for my wife as well. I couldn't bear the thought of hurting her."

Frankie suddenly recalled some of the things she used to say to him. "You wouldn't have done," he said. "She knew!"

Joe was taken aback. "That's impossible! She would have said something to me."

"Maybe she was waiting for you to say something first?"

"Your grandmother never played those games. If she had something on her mind, she would say it. That's what I loved most about her; she never left you in doubt."

147

He was more certain than ever that she knew, but looking at his grand-father's face, the pain in his eyes at the mention of his wife, he couldn't bring himself to tell him everything she used to say to him especially about how alike they were in their ways. "True flesh and blood," she would say..., "Flesh and blood!"

"You are right," Frankie said. "There is no way that she could have known."

"It would kill me if I thought that she knew and didn't say anything to me," he said.

"She loved you very much."

"That she did. We loved each other very much."

"So who owns the house in Positano now?"

"You do," said Joe. "When your adoption was finalized, I wrote the deeds over to you, Frankie Leeman. I thought it wiser than Francesco Bertolli. No one would connect the two. We could go there after lunch if you wish; at the same time, we can stop by your parents' grave."

"I would like that. I have seen the house, but only from the road. One question still nags at me, though—what if you had died before I learned the truth?"

"There is a letter to you which is held by my bank, along with the deeds to the house, to be opened after my death. In it, I explain everything, as I have explained to you now. I have also left you more than enough funds to do whatever you want with the house. You can restore it or sell it; it will be up to you."

"And photographs? Do you have any? Or were they really lost?"

Joe took out his wallet, withdrew an old, worn photo, and handed it to him. It was a picture of his mother and father taken soon after they were married. "Georgio sent it to me," he said.

Frankie stared at it in disbelief. "I don't understand!"

"I know. They might have been twins, they looked so alike. Both my daughters were the image of my mother. Now you know why I could never show it to you or anyone. There would have been questions that I didn't want to answer."

"I thought I had forgotten her, because every time I tried to remember, all I could see was mother's face before my eyes."

"It was easy to mix them up in your mind. I remember the day I first brought you to her home; the look on your face said it all, and I knew then that I had done the right thing by bringing you back with me. Anyhow, there was nowhere else for you to go."

"I've just realized something! Mother and I really are related. We are bonded by blood."

"Yes, you are," said Joe.

"I've got to tell her as soon as I can. She will be so happy."

"Not so fast, Franco. I know that it will make her happy, but it will have to wait until I have gone to join your grandmother. I don't want her to be angrier with me than she already is. Then there is the rest of the family; they will expect an explanation and I am not ready to repeat what I have told you. Call me a coward, if you like, but the family has an image of me, and I don't want to destroy it."

"You are no coward, Papa. We build our own image from the day we first think for ourselves. In effect, we are who we want to be, and we would not want what we had built destroyed by anyone."

"You know, that is the first time you have called me Papa since I arrived. Does that mean I am forgiven?"

"I am not sure. I suppose after everything I have heard, there isn't much to forgive. The strange thing is that in reality, nothing has changed between us, and yet everything has changed. I feel different for one!"

"You may feel different, even think differently, but you are no different. As you said, you are who you have always been and always will be." He smiled, "Your image of yourself has changed a little, that's all."

"It's more than that. Everyone is an extension of someone else. I have never been able to relate to that feeling before."

"I'm sorry if I let you down, Franco, I really am."

"Wasn't it grandmother who used to say, 'Don't waste time on being sorry; just go forward'?"

"Can we go forward, Franco?"

He looked at his grandfather's face, so anxious to hear what he would say. How could he have doubted him? He had always loved him; he loved him now, maybe more than ever. "It would be a sad day for me if you and I couldn't," he said.

It was an emotional moment. Their feelings were rising to the surface, and tears glistened in their eyes. All at once, their arms were around each other.

When the moment passed, Joe dried his eyes and said, as if nothing important had passed between them, "Now, what about this new development you mentioned over the phone before you left for Italy? Are you certain you have what we need on Archie Bingham? The family is very anxious, as you know."

It took Frankie by surprise and he had to laugh. This was the Joseph Bocacci he knew and understood well, right to the point, not wasting any time. "We have it in the bag!" he assured.

"The family wants it resolved as quickly as possible. I don't need to tell you the toll it has taken on us."

"I know. As soon as I return I will get onto it immediately."

"That brings me to the next question. When will you be returning home?"

He pursed his lips and asked, "Can you hold the family at bay for another couple of weeks?"

"Has it something to do with Miss Gould?"

"Almost everything!"

Joe eyed his grandson. "All right," he said, "I'll do what I can, but Franco, for her sake as well as your own, don't drag it out any longer."

"Don't worry, we both know what the score is and have come to terms with it."

"She does strike me as being sensible." Again, he eyed his grandson. "How much have you told her?" he asked.

"I was in shock when I heard about my parents' murder. I had to confide in someone and she was there for me."

"I understand!"

The two men stared at one another. It had been quite a morning; now it was time to digest what had been said, what had been discovered. For Joe, it had been a matter of getting it off his chest. For Frankie, it would take time before he could mentally adjust to such an astounding revelation.

Suddenly, Joe said, "Shall we go in search of your Miss Gould? I feel that she has been patient with us long enough."

They found Cynthia reading in her favorite nook in the garden. She closed the book when she saw them and glanced, anxiously, from one face to the other. The tight little lines around Frankie's eyes had disappeared, and there was an ease between him and his grandfather that had been absent during dinner last night, which left her relieved.

They told her of their plans to visit the house in Positano that afternoon. Frankie seemed to take it for granted that she was included, but in effect she was a stranger, and knew that she had no place to be with them at such a sensitive time, so after lunch, she made her excuses. "I think I will take this opportunity to do some sketching. This is a beautiful coastline and I don't know if I shall ever be back again."

They were all aware of the sadness to those words, and for a moment there was silence.

"Are you certain you will be all right on your own?" asked Frankie.

"I have been on my own before and I will be again. Don't worry about me; of course I will be all right."

He pressed her hand in gratitude. "We shouldn't be too long."

Joe's piercing eyes held hers for a moment. "Thank you," he said.

She understood and smiled warmly.

When Joe saw the Ferrari, he grinned. "I should have known! How does she handle?"

"Like you wouldn't believe," replied Frankie.

"I believe! Nevertheless, take it easy on the road. This old heart isn't what it used to be."

Frankie glanced at him with concern. "Is there something I should know?" he asked.

"You know I am getting older … what do you expect, the heart to remain young?"

He chuckled with relief, "That would be nice," he said.

The day was hot, but not as hot as it had been in the past few days, and with the sun drifting in and out of the clouds, it provided a welcome relief from its ferocious glare. Frankie was filled with thoughts as they drove along the cliff road. Drained after the morning, Joe was glad of the silence. Suddenly, Frankie asked, "Will we be going to the grave before or after the house?"

"Before. It's on the way to Positano. I'll warn you when to turn off."

Frankie was strangely apprehensive; he didn't know why he should be, but somehow the thought of seeing his parents' grave for the first time was daunting. What would he feel? he wondered.

All of a sudden Joe called out, "Here, here on your left, turn." And as he turned, Frankie's heart lurched.

He parked the car in front of the church and they made their way to the cemetery. There was row after row of graves, and Joe appeared uncertain as he glanced around. "It wasn't this full when I was last here." Then he saw what he was looking for—a huge tree whose branches gave shade to the grave beneath. "That's it," he said.

Frankie felt numb as he followed his grandfather up the path to the graveside. Suddenly, he was beside it, looking down at the granite slab that covered his parents' remains. Apart from the inscription that gave their names and the dates of birth and death, strangers might have been lying there. He wanted to feel something; they were his parents and they deserved some feeling from him, but he couldn't remember them, and that hurt more than anything else.

Tears came to Joe's eyes as he read the inscription aloud, and Frankie wished that he could shed them as easily. He read the inscription over and over to himself until it finally sank in that they were his parents, his flesh and blood, and that he would never be able to see or know them as he should have, and the pain he was searching for came to life. "I never had a chance to mourn them," he said sadly.

"That's not so," replied Joe. "You did mourn them. You carried your grief inside you for a long time. I recall grandma saying, about a year after their death, 'He has stopped grieving at last.' I asked her how she knew, and she said, 'His eyes are no longer sad.'"

"I miss her so much," said Frankie. "She was such a good woman. I wish I could miss my parents in the same way, but all I can feel is regret at the thought of a great loss."

"That's understandable." Then, after a few more minutes of silence at the grave, Joe said, "Come, let's go to the house now."

The house was in a worse state of repair than had been seen from the road, especially the inside. It seemed that everything had either been smashed or ripped out and taken away. The tiled floors were cracked and thick with grime. Hand basins were broken or missing. Taps were rusted, toilet bowls had gaping holes in them, wallpaper was hanging in strips, and the oak stairs were splintered with large chunks missing. Only the ceilings showed remnants of a former glory. Even through the mould that had gathered, the beautifully carved cornices still bore signs of a certain splendor.

"My God!" cried Joe as his eyes swept room after room. "I had no idea it was in this state."

"Has no one looked after it?" asked Frankie.

"The police were supposed to keep me informed of the condition, but from the look of things, I seriously doubt they ever came near the place."

"Alida said that vandals were continually climbing over the gate to see what they could steal."

"I wouldn't be surprised if some of those vandals were the police themselves. Let's go upstairs and see how that has fared."

It was the same story all over again: a few broken pieces of furniture, tattered curtains hanging from broken windows; there was a thick layer of dust everywhere, and dried brush that had blown in through the windows was scattered around. Disturbed by their footsteps, a mouse scurried across the floor and disappeared into a hole in the skirting.

The rooms were large, and one in particular had a connecting door. They pushed it open. It creaked with age and lack of use, and one of the rusted hinges came away, leaving the door hanging. They went through into the next room; the condition was similar except the wallpaper, or what was left of it, had little bunnies printed all over it. Frankie stared in surprise.

"This must have been your room," said Joe. Then, seeing the look on his grandson's face, he asked, "What is it?"

"I remember these bunnies. For years, I have been seeing them in my mind's eye. There should be a cot as well," he said looking around, but there was no cot—only a broken wicker chair and a chest of drawers without the drawers.

"What else did you see?" asked Joe.

"A woman standing over me as I lie in a cot. She was always smiling, and then she would kiss me and leave. I had assumed that what I was seeing was my room back home in America, and that the woman was Mother coming in to wish me good night, but it couldn't have been. I never had bunnies on my wallpaper, and I slept in a proper bed from the beginning." He looked around again; suddenly he cried in excitement. "My God, this is what I have been seeing. This room ... and the woman ... she must have been my mother. I mean, it was her—it was really her!"

There were tears in Joe's eyes. "Oh, I am so glad, so glad that you can remember something."

Frankie was walking around the room, getting the feel of it. He went to the window. "I can remember my father coming up the path and waving to me as I looked out of this very window." Suddenly, he turned to Joe, and his eyes were moist. "I haven't lost them," he wept. "They are here with me; they are still a part of me. You know what I want to do now. I want to return to the cemetery and stand by their grave for a while. I feel a closeness to them that I didn't feel before, and I want them to know."

"Let's go," said Joe.

***

Cynthia was waiting for Frankie in their room. She had just taken a shower and was toweling her hair dry, and when she saw the look of excitement in his eyes, she said, "It went well?"

"Yes, I remembered my mother. I remembered them both. I wish I could explain how wonderful it makes me feel."

"I know," she said. "It makes you feel like a whole person, as though you have found a part of yourself that you thought you had lost forever."

"How did you know?" he asked in astonishment.

"My mother lost hers when she was only a few weeks old, and when I asked her how it felt not to have a mother, she said, 'Incomplete, as though an important part of yourself is missing.'"

"Amazing, I have always had this strange lost feeling inside me, and until today, I didn't know why, and there is more. You will never believe this, but my grandfather really is my grandfather—he really, really is!"

He anticipated surprise—a look of disbelief. Instead, she smiled and said, "Oh, but I can believe it."

He stared at her. "How...? I mean, there is no way that you could have known before I did."

"All I had to do was look at you both. You have the same expression in your eyes when you speak. The same stubborn chin, and although your coloring is different, there is no mistaking the resemblance."

"Why didn't you say something to me?"

"It had to come from him. What is amazing is that no one in your family noticed it."

He smiled to himself, and there was a faraway look in his eyes as he spoke. "I think someone did. Anyhow, it is all part of an incredible story that I have to tell you, but not just yet. I am still in a dream; nothing seems real, and I feel as if I will wake up to find that nothing really did happen. I hope not, dear God ... I hope not!"

"If you think about it, life is like a dream. Some have a good one, while for others it can be a nightmare. In the end, that is all that life amounts to—a dream."

He drew her close and kissed her. "If that's all there is," he said, "let's make our dream a good one."

They found Joe in an exuberant mood when they came down for dinner. "Come on," he cried, and ushered them into the dining room. "I haven't been this hungry in years." His face was glowing, and they laughed to see him so happy.

He was astonishing for his age, and his quick wit kept them amused all through the meal. Frankie was particularly happy, and kept glancing at his grandfather with eyes full of wonder and love. It had been a meaningful day for both of them, and loving Frankie as much as she did, Cynthia basked in the glow of their happiness. There was no room for despair that evening, and their joy became her joy.

As dinner came to an end, so did conversation and the good-humored banter that had been going on during the meal, leaving a feeling of satisfaction all around. Suddenly, Joe sighed and his face showed signs of exhaustion. "Why must all good things come to an end?" he said. "You have been very patient with us, Cynthia, you are a remarkable young woman. It is no wonder that my grandson is so taken with you."

She smiled and thanked him. Her thanks were for more than the compliment; it pleased her to hear him call her by her given name at last.

He refused Frankie's offer to see him to his room when they left the dining room. "The evening is still young," he said. "Enjoy it."

Frankie and Cynthia took their usual stroll down through the square and sat by the bay. So much had already been said between them that there was little more to add; only questions remained, but neither wanted to bring up the big one and spoil the evening.

Eventually, Frankie felt that he had to mention it. "He wanted to know when I would be returning to New York."

She held her breath, and waited for him to tell her what he had said.

"I told him not for another two weeks."

Her heart sank, and she tightened her grip on his hand. "Two weeks!" she whispered sadly.

They sat in strained silence for a while; then suddenly he asked, "What do you want to do? Stay on, or go back to London?"

She was afraid that if she spoke, she would lose control of herself. He didn't press her; he knew the kind of emotion she was going through. He was having a difficult time with it himself. All at once she said, "London. Will you stay with me at the flat?"

"If that's what you want."

"It is," she murmured.

"Then we can leave tomorrow. There should be no problem with airline tickets."

"What about your grandfather?"

"He wants to visit some old friends in Rome. I will arrange for a private car to take him."

She nodded, then cast her eyes out over the bay. Her heart was bleeding, but she didn't want him to know. They had two whole weeks to spend together, and she made up her mind that she wasn't going to spoil them for him. Putting on a brave face, she turned to him and smiled.

He understood her more than she realized, and after giving her hand a comforting squeeze, he said gently, "Come on, let's go back to the hotel."

His arms around her in bed, she snuggled closer to him and whispered, "What does it matter if our dream lasts two weeks or a lifetime. We will have had our time together and that is all that matters."

"That's all that matters," he whispered, and his arms tightened about her.

CHAPTER NINE

How different the journey returning to England was from the one leaving, thought Frankie; there was no expectation, no excitement. It was an anticlimax and his heart felt like a sinking ship. He glanced at Cynthia, who was staring out of the window, as they flew over Europe. Mostly, he could tell at a glance what she was thinking, but that afternoon her face was a mask hiding her innermost thoughts and feelings.

Wasn't he doing the same? All he could think of was the two weeks they had left and how little it was when compared to the lifetime he wanted to spend with her; then, how long was a lifetime? He glanced down at her hands lying limp in her lap as though expressing her hopelessness, and taking one of them, he put it to his lips. She turned to him and smiled.

"Glad to be going home?" he asked.

With a sigh, she turned back to the window. He felt stupid. Why had he asked a question to which he already knew the answer? Of course, she wasn't looking forward to it; it marked the beginning of the end. What was left except kisses that gave no hope, and a love that was full of desperation?

Perhaps he should have spared her further agony and returned to America right away, but that wasn't what either of them wanted. Another week, another day, another hour—time that would belong to them and remain a part of their lives for as long as they lived. He sat back and closed his eyes, and his grip on her hand tightened.

The streets of London appeared drab and gray after the sunny climate of Italy. Frankie glanced up at the sky. "Looks like rain," he said as he paid the taxi driver.

"Sure does, guv," he replied. "It's been raining for days, and there's a lot more where that came from." Then, seeing the large tip in his hand, he thanked Frankie profusely.

The porter helped them up with their bags, and as soon as they were inside the flat, Cynthia went around turning on all the lights while he took the luggage into the bedroom.

"Do you want to go out for something to eat before or after we unpack?" he asked.

She was standing by the door staring at him. He had never seen her look so forlorn and it broke his heart. "Come here," he said.

Being together, making love was the only thing that made any sense out of their relationship. That's all there was for them—that's all there would ever be.... Two weeks, two whole weeks to look back on forever, and forever would be a long, empty time without each other.

The next morning, a choice loomed before them: they could be either happy with what they had or wallow in self-pity, and the latter would be a terrible waste of precious time. "I'll tell you what we are going to do," he said. "We will take each day and live it as though it will never end. No tears, no heartbreak, just the joy of being together. Do you think we can do that?"

"Yes, because we have to, or we will have nothing good to remember."

"Do you recall the day we met?"

"How could I forget? That was the day I lost my heart."

"I lost mine the day before when I saw you coming down the stairs in the Dorchester Hotel. How strange and wonderful life can be. If I hadn't been on my way to the Law Courts, I would have missed Bill and then I would never have seen you again."

"I think that is what we should do today, visit the Law Courts."

"Would you mind?"

"Somehow, it seems fitting," she replied.

Although she had passed by on many occasions, Cynthia had never seen inside the Law Courts, and was as struck by its magnificent, age-old structure as Frankie. So many beautiful Gothic arches, cloisters, numerous courts, both large and small, and stairs leading to more courts or down into a labyrinth of stone corridors and alcoves where the barristers would meet to discuss a case.

Naturally, being a lawyer, Frankie wanted to know more about it, and discovered that the Courts were actually made up of three separate divisions, namely: The Queen's Bench, Probate Divorce and Admiralty, and

Chancery. This meant little to Cynthia, but just to walk through those hallowed halls gave her a sense of a glorious past and an illustrious present that filled her with awe.

Behind the Courts, they wandered through Lincoln's Inn Fields, as ancient and historic as the Courts themselves, and they watched, fascinated, as the bewigged barristers, their black robes billowing out behind them, crossed the green in their hurry to wherever. The whole area was a place of history made and still being made. The renowned Laws of England, entrusted to the lawyers, down through the ages, and followed by many countries, both new and old.

With obvious pleasure, Frankie glanced around. "You get a feeling of timelessness in this place. You don't get that in an American court of law."

"Being a part of this country gives you a feeling of timelessness. That is what's so reassuring about having a long history; you feel that the earth is solid beneath your feet. Countless others have trodden it before you, and countless others will follow. It's inspiring!"

"I would think it is the same for the whole of Europe."

"I suppose so," she said, "but somehow, that little stretch of water that separates us from them makes you feel more special, more individual. We are, in reality, an island people, and therefore an entity unto ourselves."

He laughed. "You are very proud of being British, aren't you?"

"Does it show that much?" she asked.

They turned into Fleet Street and lunched at one of the many pubs frequented by the lawyers—some of whom were still in their wigs and gowns—racing through the usual fare of steak and kidney pudding, roast beef, or bangers and mash in their hurry to get back to court for the afternoon sessions.

The food, as in most pubs, was good and satisfying, not to mention the beer that was dark, rich, and delicious, as only the Irish and the British can make it. "Guinness," said Frankie. "I must remember that name."

From Fleet Street, they walked back along the Strand to Trafalgar Square, and then up the Mall. It was early July, yet another glorious month, and the flowers in the park were in full bloom, the trees were heavy with leaves, and the grass was as green as you could ever see. The ducks on the lake were quacking noisily; the swans, their regal heads held high, were gliding gracefully through the water. It was as perfect a day as they could have hoped for. Even the rain stayed away as they walked hand in hand along the bank of the lake, glowing with happiness.

Thus, the days slipped by—with trips up the Thames to Henley, walks in Windsor Great Park, climbing Box Hill in Surrey. Of course, there were visits to the art galleries, where Frankie would watch with pleasure as her face came alive while describing the different eras, and how each one had changed the face of art to portray the history of the times. How he loved to listen to her and see the ever-changing expression in her eyes as she spoke. It was at times like these that he wanted to take her in his arms, and never let go.

Speaker's Corner, in Hyde Park, was a must on Sunday morning. It was fun to listen to the hecklers shout down one speaker or another. Most were spouting their own brand of politics, which was either to the extreme left or far right. One, in particular, a skinny little man with a big voice, who had the attention of a large crowd, was trying to rile the people against industry, the banks, and especially the computer giants. "They have it all neatly tied up," he cried, "and they are selling us, the workers, down the river for their own greedy ends. Money! That's all they care about. There is no human factor built into their calculations. We are dispensable, unnecessary, unwanted, redundant, and we are expected to accept it graciously.

"Well, not bloody likely! We, the workers, created their wealth. Are we going to let them get away with it? Are we…? I can't hear you."

"No!" shouted one of the crowd, and soon everyone took up the cry. "No! No! No!"

"Louder!" demanded the speaker. "Let the whole world hear you."

The cry grew louder; the speaker was still inciting them. "The politicians, the conglomerates, they're all in it together, and I am getting tired of it. How about you?"

"Yes! Yes! Yes!" they roared as one.

"Let us unite and rise up. Why should they be the only ones in the boat while we flounder in the water, doing our best to survive? We deserve more. We deserve what is rightly ours!"

"So what do you suggest?" called out a bystander. "Reinstate the Tyburn Gallows and hang the lot of them like common criminals?"

"That is the best suggestion anyone has had yet!" claimed the speaker.

The crowd tittered; the speaker grew angry. "That's right!" he shouted. "Laugh! Well, if you don't hear the wakeup call, you'll all be laughing out of the other side of your face."

The mob became unruly. A few punches were exchanged.

"I think I've had enough," said Frankie. "How about you?"

"I think so," she said, "but it was fun. I thought that bit about the Tyburn Gallows was very appropriate."

"What was the significance?"

"The Tyburn Gallows used to stand right there at Speakers Corner over a century ago. It was where they used to hang the wicked highwaymen who roamed the park, in those days, looking for unsuspecting travelers to rob. There was a great division between the rich and poor back then. It seems those days are returning once more."

"That sounds more like Bill's platform."

"Bill," she said wistfully. "I wonder how he is doing."

Most evenings, they were too tired to go out and stayed home listening to music or simply talking and talking until the early hours of the morning. They had a great thirst for knowledge of each other. What were they like as children? Who was their favorite film star? What was their favorite food? Their hopes, their fears, their dreams. They spoke about everything under the sun. They needed to know it all, from the smallest detail to that which most shaped their lives.

She took him to Quaglino's for dinner. "It's where my parents used to go when they were courting," she said. There was a trio playing and they danced, cheek against cheek, thigh against thigh, until the music stopped and the restaurant closed.

They were putting so much into so short a space that neither noticed time passing until they awoke, one morning, to find it was their last day together, and from that moment on, nothing was the same again.

The closed little world they had created for themselves was coming to an end, and it was time to face the truth. There is only one truth in life, one certainty, and that is that all things come to an end. Nothing can be saved, nothing is sacred, nothing is worth more than what it amounts to in the end, and the end is final. They tried, how they tried to make those last few hours mean something, but it was useless, and they walked through the day like a sleepwalker walks through the night, without hope, without thought, and without feeling; they were numb, afraid to feel for fear of the pain.

Darkness fell and the night passed, like a train rushing toward the end of a tunnel. *It's time to get off*, thought Frankie as he watched the first light of morning come chasing the shadows away. He turned to look at Cynthia; sometime in the night, she had fallen asleep in his arms. As though she could feel his eyes on her face, she awoke. He kissed her. "Have you any idea how lovely you are?" he whispered.

She stared at him for a moment. "Just tell me how long we have. How many hours, how many minutes to go on saying I love you, I want you?"

"However long, it would never be long enough to tell you what I feel."

"Then tell me you love me enough times to last me my whole life."

"Listen to me," he said gently, "what we have had is more than what some have in a lifetime. So don't make too much of this lifetime thing, my darling, because it can be as long as the longest living person or as short as the life of a butterfly."

"Like our love?"

"No, our love will go on until the end of my days, and if those days are long, then so will be my love for you."

"How will I know? That's what scares me more than anything. I won't know what is happening to you or where you will be, or what you are doing at any given moment."

"Just know that you will always be in my heart; that's all you need to know, that's all I need."

Her eyes brimmed with tears, and she clung to him. After a while, she pulled away and said, "I better go and make breakfast; we leave for the airport in a couple of hours."

"Not we, just I. I think it would be for the best if we said goodbye here."

"No!" she cried in panic. "I have to go with you. If we say goodbye here, it will be as though you are walking out on me. I need to have people around; I need there to be noise, not deathly silence, as there would be if you left me behind. Don't you understand?"

He couldn't bear to see the pain in her eyes, or hear the panic in her voice as she pleaded with him. "All right," he said, "but no tears; neither of us could take that, and when I say go, you go, no fuss, no last-minute stay. Is that a promise?"

"Yes," she whispered, "I promise."

It was lunch hour and traffic was heavy along the Great West Road. Frankie glanced at Cynthia as she drove; her eyes had a fixed look about them. What were her thoughts? he wondered. How would she react when it came time to part? Would she be able to keep her promise? Would he?

His emotions were balancing on a tightrope, and it was all he could do to keep them steady. He swallowed and looked away.

Heathrow came into view, and very shortly they were turning and on their final journey together through the tunnel; then they followed the signs to international departures and Cynthia drew up in front of the terminal.

"No need for you to come inside," he said.

"You need help with the luggage," and before he could stop her, she was out of the car and beckoning a porter.

It was useless, he thought, and followed her, the porter, and his luggage into the terminal. She stood aside and waited while he checked in. "Well, this is it!" he said trying to sound casual when he returned to her side. Suddenly their eyes met, and they were in each other's arms.

Neither wanted to let go, and when they did, the wrench was terrible; it was as if they were giving up a part of themselves, and the pain was excruciating. Barely able to speak, he whispered, "You better go, before we break down completely."

She couldn't bring herself to leave, and they continued to stare at each other for a few seconds more. Seconds—that was all that was left. Steeling himself, he gave a nod. She understood; they were going through hell and he had left it up to her to make the first move. She braced herself, and without a word turned and walked out of his life.

How she managed to make it to the car, get behind the wheel, and drive off, she would never know. Her eyes were swimming with tears, her heart breaking. She was driving blindly and didn't realize it. Cars were hooting as they passed her on the road; she neither saw nor heard them. Apart from her own pain, she was oblivious to the world around her.

All at once, everything seemed to be happening; horns were honking, breaks were screeching, wheels were skidding as cars veered all over the place. She was driving on the wrong side of the road, and suddenly, struck with terror, she slammed her foot on the brake pedal and skidded into the guardrail.

The seatbelt saved her; nevertheless, the jolt to her neck was very painful. Drivers were shaking their fists at her as they passed. One stopped his car and came over to see if she was all right. She stared at him in a daze; then, coming to herself, she said, "I'm fine. Thank you for asking, but I will be all right now."

He looked concerned, but when she showed him that she could move her neck freely, he returned to his car, but not before offering a word of caution.

The shock had helped bring her to her senses, and her tears dried; all she could think of was how lucky she was to be in one piece.

Frankie watched Cynthia disappear through the terminal door. People were milling all around, but all he could see was the emptiness she had left behind. How long he stood there, he had no idea, but suddenly someone with a cartload of suitcases bumped into him and brought him back to himself. He picked up his hand luggage from the floor and went through into the VIP lounge, where he waited for the call to board.

It was going to be a long journey, but at least he was going home, back to the people he had known and loved for most of his life. It was the only permanence he could count on, and right then, he needed that permanence more than ever.

The pain was still there, wringing his heart like a wet rag being wrung of the last drop of water. It was excruciating. *Please God,* he prayed silently, *let it pass. Let it pass.*

CHAPTER TEN

Frankie stacked his bags onto a trolley and wheeled them out of the airport. The lineup for a taxi stretched as far as the eye could see. *Damn,* he thought with irritation, and proceeded to walk to the end of it, when a hand grabbed his arm. "Hey, Vinnie," he cried with relief, "what are you doing here?"

"Papa sent me. Now, come on. I'm in a no-parking zone."

Sure enough, there was a ticket on the windshield. "That's gonna cost you," said Frankie.

"So I'll put it on the business."

"You're asking to be audited!"

"Let them. I'll tie 'em up with so many bits of paper they'll wish they hadn't. I'm a big taxpayer, Frankie. I'm entitled to the occasional business expense!" Frankie raised an eyebrow. Vinnie laughed. "So let them call me a liar!"

The traffic was a nightmare, as usual, and the flow constantly interrupted. It was stop, start, stop, start, practically all the way into town.

"So what's the story?" asked Vinnie.

"What story are you talking about?"

"The chick—there has to be a chick or Papa wouldn't have asked me to collect you."

"Yeah, the chick," sighed Frankie. "What can I tell you? I fell in love. Right girl, wrong religion."

"Oh, that bug religion," he said with a shake of his head. "If anything can mess things up for a fellow, that can. So tell me about it."

"You remember my pal Billy? Well, I ran into him in London and he introduced me to this wonderful Jewish girl, and that was it—love at first sight! Funny thing is, I never believed there was such a thing before that."

"Is it over?"

"It's over, but it wasn't an easy decision for either of us."

"Maybe not, but it was a wise one. You'll get over it Frankie. We always do, and I know what I'm talking about."

"Do you? Not according to mother."

"Ah, my sister! So what has she been telling you? That I am seeing a black Jewish girl and it has been going on for some time?"

"Is it true?"

"Partly. She had a black grandmother and a Jewish grandfather so I guess that makes her partly black and partly Jewish. She is some gal, Frankie, and we have a great thing going between us."

"How long has it been going on?"

"I can hardly believe it myself—fifteen years with one gal!"

"Fifteen years, but I always thought—"

"That I have been playing the field all this time? I put that out to please the family. Can you imagine what my brothers would say if they knew—not to mention Papa?"

"I know. Mother sounded pretty upset; it's a wonder she hasn't told anyone else."

"It surprises me, too."

"How does the girl feel about you not wanting to marry her?"

"Get this: she won't marry me because I am Catholic; it might upset her father, who is Protestant, so what can I tell you—the world is one huge bigoted place! Still, it suits me. An affair is one thing, and marriage another. I have witnessed it so many times. You can live with a person for years and years, but the moment you have that little piece of paper that says it's all tied up and legal, something happens, and it's never the same again."

"It's hard, though, isn't it? You love someone, and you know they are so right for you, yet you are afraid to marry them because of one unimportant difference."

"Sometimes, those unimportant differences can grow into a very important factor later on in life."

"I suppose! I suppose even if you have never thought of yourself as bigoted, there are always reservations."

"Welcome to the real world, Nephew."

"Sometimes I don't much like the real world. How is Papa by the way?"

"I don't know; he seems remote since he returned from Italy. What went on over there?"

"Has he said anything?"

"No. He won't even talk about it when I ask him. I have never known him this secretive and it worries me."

"Well, it needn't worry you. There were a few things that had to be cleared up between us, that's all."

"And are they?"

"Yes. It had nothing to do with the family or business, so you can rest easy."

"I can't rest easy when something affects Papa, but if you don't want to talk about it, I can't make you."

"I will tell you all about it one day, but for now, I can only say this much—it was personal, to do with my natural parents, something that I couldn't understand, and Papa put me right. Okay?"

"It will have to be! Now, what about Bingham? Papa said we've got him. Is that right?"

"I would say so. Of course, he may not be as predictable as I believe he is. I'll know that when I present him with the information I've gathered."

"So what have you got?"

"It's a long story, and I'm tired Vinnie. Also, I would like to get things clear in my mind before I discuss it with the family. I'll phone Papa as soon as I get home and see if he can set up a meeting for the morning."

"Same time as usual?"

"Same time as usual."

"Good! The only one with a complaint will be Aldo," he said with a chuckle.

Vinnie swung the car around into the drive when they reached Frankie's condominium, and stopped in front of the entrance. "Need help?" he asked.

"The porter will bring out the trolley and help me up."

"Okay, then I'll be off. You might want to ring your mother before you phone Papa; I know how anxious she is to see you. Actually, I spent a lot of time with her in the last two weeks, and I think she is ready to take the pledge. She admitted to me that she had a problem, and, as they say, that's the first step. You know, I don't know who is really to blame for all your parents' troubles, but I do know what a shame it is. Why can't people just get on with each other?"

"I know! The rows are terrible and they go on getting worse and worse."

"Yeah! It's such a waste. Well, who knows, miracles do happen. Perhaps, there is one waiting to happen for them."

"Perhaps! Anyhow, thanks for being there for me, Vinnie."

"Hey! What's family for, right?"

"Right," said Frankie.

He telephoned his mother even before he unpacked. She was overjoyed to hear his voice, but the best news was that she was sober, and he promised to go over for dinner that evening.

Joe was also happy when he phoned. "Franco! Thank goodness you're home safe and sound. Vinnie met you?"

"He was there at the airport, waiting."

"So what did he have to say?"

"You know Vinnie! He worries about you. Are you all right?"

"Of course, I am all right; well, generally speaking. Vinnie is the one we have to worry about; he needs to get married. Oh, how I would like to see it before I die."

"Marriage isn't the beginning and end of everything. As long as he is contented, that's all that matters."

"So, now that you're back, when shall we meet? The family is anxious."

"I thought tomorrow morning, the usual time."

"It's done! Franco, it's good to have you home; I miss you when you're not around."

"I love you too, Papa."

As always, Frankie arrived first at the office next morning, and settled down to wait for his uncles. He was going over a few last-minute notes when Aldo entered the boardroom. He nodded briefly to Frankie, as though he had only seen him yesterday, then took his usual seat. Vinnie came bouncing in moments later. "So, how goes it, Nephew? Feeling better than yesterday?"

Aldo's head popped up. "What's this?" he asked anxiously. "Aren't you well?"

"Just tired after a long journey," replied Frankie.

"Oh, is that all! The last thing we need right now is you getting ill, and we have to deal with this mess ourselves."

"My, my!" said Vinnie somewhat facetiously, "such concern. You really have outdone yourself this time, Aldo."

Aldo huffed.

Johnny arrived on Vinnie's heels. "Glad to see you at last, Frankie," he said. "Boy what a time I've had with Guido, but that is over now. Papa says you have good news for us."

"I hope so!"

"Hope so? What are you telling me?" he asked in alarm.

"I didn't mean it that way. It is good news, but you still have to realize that nothing is a certainty."

"I don't like the sound of this. I thought Papa said it was over, in the bag."

"What Papa said is neither here nor there," said Joe as he came through the door. "Now, give Franco a chance to tell it his way."

Their attention turned to Joe, who looked pale. Vinnie asked, "You tired, Papa? Didn't you sleep well?"

"Sleep? Who needs sleep at my age; what I need is more life. Where is Guido?"

"He was out late last night," said Johnny. "I told him he could stay in bed. I can tell him whatever is discussed."

Joe shook his head. "You treat him like he was still a school boy. He's twenty-seven, for heaven's sake, treat him like a man! Uh!" he exclaimed in frustration. "What's the use?"

Aldo gave Johnny a smug look. Johnny hung his head. "Sorry, Papa," he said, "I don't know what to do for the best; it's so difficult bringing up a boy on your own."

"That's the problem; he's not a boy any longer!"

When it came to Guido, they were all exasperated with Johnny. They looked at one another and shrugged.

"Franco," said Joe, "let us hear what you have for us."

Frankie took them through everything, from his first meeting with Philip Peel to his last meeting with Thomas Phipps, Bingham's chief clerk. He kept to the relevant facts; they certainly wouldn't have understood his strange curiosity and obsession with the character of Bingham, and would have considered it a terrible waste of time. The "nitty-gritty" was all they were interested in.

They were satisfied. "Embezzlement and lying on his entry permit! If that doesn't do it, nothing will!" said Vinnie. "You've done good, kid."

"Maybe so, but he is a strange and unpredictable fellow, and you can't really gauge what someone like that will do in certain circumstances."

"So where would that leave us?" asked Johnny uneasily.

"In the shit!" said Vinnie.

"Vinnie!" snapped Joe. "You know I don't like to hear that kind of language."

"Sorry, Papa, it just popped out."

"It's no good trying to outguess this man," said Joe. "All we can do is wait and see his reaction when Franco confronts him with his findings."

"What's the next step if it doesn't work?" asked Johnny.

"Then we fight it in court," said Frankie. "I've been giving a lot of thought to the evidence they have, also to the young man to whom Guido gave a lift that day, and I think I could make a good case for collusion. At the very worst, we would have a fifty-fifty chance of clearing Guido, but I don't think it will come to that, not with Bingham's history. He's been a loser for most of his life, but that was because he was so screwed up; he couldn't think straight. He is no longer screwed up, not since his father died. He'll comply."

"That's not what you said before. You said nothing is a foregone conclusion."

"That was to prepare you for the worst, just in case."

"So when will this meeting take place?"

"I'll be in touch with him later today. I think a luncheon appointment will be good. I want him away from the office."

"If all else fails, do you think he can be bought?"

"I have known people who cheat, lie, and steal; yet when it comes to a bribe, they get all moral about it, as if you have insulted their integrity. I wouldn't be surprised if he is one of them."

"Why is everything so complicated in this world? You can steal but you can't take a bribe. What's the difference? At least it isn't stealing."

"I'm only telling you the way I see it. Trust me, if I get the impression that he is open to taking money, then I will offer it, but for what my opinion is worth, money is not what drives him—it's ambition."

"Just my luck," said Johnny, shaking his head in frustration.

"Well, I think we have heard it all," said Joe, "so if everyone agrees, we can adjourn and let Franco do whatever he considers necessary."

"Fine with me!" said Aldo, and he made a beeline for the door.

Johnny, his shoulders bent with worry, trudged over to Frankie. "You really think it will work?" he asked with concern.

"Look, I told you before I left for England that I would take care of things, and that is exactly what I intend to do, so don't worry so much."

"You're a good boy, Frankie; I know you mean well. Thanks."

"Hey! What's family for!" he said with a glance across at Vinnie, who grinned at Frankie.

Vinnie made the usual offer of a lift to Joe, and he, as usual, declined. "You go. Frankie will take me home. I need to talk to him."

***

It was early Saturday morning and the roads were still relatively quiet. Frankie stole a glance at his grandfather, who was deep in thought. "What is it?" he asked.

"Oh, I was just thinking about things. My heart has been playing up a bit lately, nothing to worry about. I'm taking pills for my blood pressure and the doctor says that they will also take care of the heart."

"How long has this been going on?"

"A little while, but that isn't what I want to talk to you about. I think it is time that I stepped down and let someone else take control of the company. I am naming you as the next president."

"Me? Is this because of your heart? Is it worse than you say?" he asked in alarm.

"No. I just realized that there is more to life than work. There are a few dear friends I would like to see before I pass on, but mostly I want to spend more time with my daughter. My whole life, I put work and the company before her. I thought I was doing what was best for my children, but not all children are alike—some need you more than others—and I wasn't there for her when she needed me most. Hopefully, it is not too late to correct that mistake.

"This past year, ever since your grandmother died, I have been walking around as if I am already dead—not feeling, not seeing what is under my nose. It was like I had buried myself along with her. The truth is, I wanted to die; I wanted to be with her. I feel differently now, and I think the trip to Italy had something to do with it; it reminded me of how precious life is, and that what God has given is not to be wasted."

I'm glad," said Frankie. "I'm glad for all of us, but mostly I am glad for you and Mother. It will make a difference, and that is what it's about—people, and doing right by them. That is why you can't make me president. You have three sons and each of them has worked hard in the company since the beginning. I am a newcomer; it wouldn't be fair to them."

"That is where you're wrong; it is them that I am thinking of. They need someone like you; they need your strength, your will. We are so alike—you and I—and they recognize it, even though they don't know the reason. It has to be you, Franco, for the family's sake. You are more than a lawyer; you are a born businessman."

"You're placing a big responsibility upon my shoulders. Are you sure that I am up to it?"

"Even when you were a mere boy, I could see the man in you. I could feel your strength. Your grandmother saw it as well, and said to me once, 'When you and I are gone, the family will be all the better for Franco.' It's what I want. With you taking care of everyone, I will be able to rest in peace when I go to my grave."

"I don't know what to say," said Frankie. "I suppose I can't refuse."

"No, you can't. Don't worry; I won't just spring it on the others. We will discuss it as we always discuss something important, and they will agree with me, not because I say they should, but because they will be relieved to hand the responsibility over to you. Johnny's head is too full of Guido. Vinnie takes too many chances; he is a gambler and he knows it. Aldo! Well, we won't talk about Aldo. We all know where his heart lies. Then there is your mother and father. What you do about your father will be up to you, and I know you will make the right decision. I think that with you at the helm—their marriage has a chance."

"How soon?"

"As soon as this business with Bingham is over and done with. Do I have your okay?"

He nodded.

"Good," said Joe. "I feel better already."

Frankie's eyes softened. "You really are something—you know that, Grandfather? Grandma was lucky to have you for a husband, and my maternal grandmother was lucky in her choice of you for a lover. She must have been something, too, to have earned your love. Thank you from all of us."

There was a glint of a tear at the corner of Joe's eye. "I was the lucky one to have known two wonderful women, and I will be forever grateful that my sweet Francesca let me make love to her, that day, for something very special came from that brief union—you."

CHAPTER ELEVEN

Bingham replaced the phone, and with a smug grin sat back and let his mind go over the conversation he had just had with Leeman. He was feeling good about himself. He always felt good when he knew that he had the upper hand. So old man Bocacci was sending his "boy" to handle the affair, he thought. Well, if he believed that a fat lunch on a fat business account was all it would take to get him off the hook, then he had better think again.

He knew quite a bit about the adopted grandson of Bocacci—that he was smart, quick thinking, with a sound knowledge of the law, but he had a long way to go before he could catch up on him. No one was a match for the son of Sir Archibald Bingham Q.C. No one could have had a better education in the fine art of negotiation. Lies, cunning, and deception were what it was all about; he had that much to thank his father for. He wanted Bocacci's testimony against certain Mob members, and he was going to get it one way or another.

He glanced at the time; it was almost five o'clock. He smiled to himself, cleared his desk for the night, and summoned his secretary. "Cancel all my appointments for tomorrow afternoon," he said. "I shall be out to lunch, and I don't know when I shall be returning."

Bingham made certain that he was ten minutes late arriving at the restaurant the next day. He glanced around when he got there, expecting to see Leeman waiting. He was nowhere to be seen and it irked him. *Snotty nose,* he thought with annoyance.

The headwaiter was expecting him, and immediately showed him to a discreet table in a corner of the room. "What shall I fetch you to drink while you wait for Mr. Leeman?" he asked in that haughty manner some waiters adopt.

"Nothing!" snapped Bingham. "But you may bring me the menu. I will order for both of us. Unlike my host, I haven't time to waste," he said curtly.

"Indeed, sir!" replied the waiter, looking down his nose at him. It niggled Bingham, but then, he was niggled to begin with. Leeman had started out on the wrong foot if he thought he could keep him waiting.

Ten long minutes and still he hadn't shown. His right knee began to twitch—up and down, up and down—a nervous habit he had when agitated. *Damn the bastard!* he thought. He was about to get up and walk out when Leeman suddenly appeared.

Although he hadn't set eyes on him since Harvard, he recognized him at once. He hadn't changed one bit since university; but then, he was still a young man and the years had yet to take their toll. He watched him approach. Long strides, self-assured, and immediately he despised him as he always despised those who seemed so secure and self-possessed. As a deliberate slight, he remained seated until Leeman was practically standing over him. "Ah!" he exclaimed, with a smirk. "So you decided to show up. I was about to leave."

Leeman smiled. "Oh dear! Did I keep you waiting?"

He knew damn well that he had kept him waiting, but he was not about to let him see how irritated he was. "Not at all," he replied. "It is rare that I have time to myself these days, and your late arrival offered me just such an opportunity."

"Then all is well," said Leeman, and sat down. Looking across at Bingham, he noticed that he wasn't drinking. "I gave strict instructions that you were to be well taken care of. The waiter should have offered you something to drink."

"Indeed he did, and I declined. This is hardly a social event, Mr. Leeman; it is a working lunch, and I never drink when working. Neither do I like wasting my time on trivialities."

"In that case, you will be assured to know that I never waste anyone's time, Mr. Bingham, especially my own. I am certain that the outcome of our meeting will be to our mutual advantage."

"I sincerely hope so. I wouldn't want either of us to go away empty-handed, and by the way, I have already ordered lunch for both of us. As I said, I don't like wasting time, and you were late!"

"Then I hope you ordered the lobster. It is always excellent."

"The Dover Sole," he said with an air of authority, "although they never manage to prepare it quite as well as they do in England. But then, what can you expect?"

"I have just returned from England, so I know exactly what you mean. That is why I shall change my order. Why don't you do the same if you are unhappy with the way they prepare the sole over here? After all, Mr. Bingham, this is the New World and our tastes differ from yours, much as our ways do, especially when it comes to morality. Wouldn't you agree?"

It wasn't so much what he said as the suggestive manner in which he said it, and taking exception, Bingham spoke brusquely. "Those who speak of morality, Mr. Leeman, are usually those with the least. Now, if you don't mind, can we dispense with the small talk and get down to what matters?"

"Absolutely, as soon as I have ordered my lobster."

Bingham was bristling and his knee began to shake, once again, as he waited, with impatience, for Leeman to order his lobster. He stayed with the sole. It had become a matter of principle; he never liked being undermined, and he wasn't going to be now over a bit of fish. As soon as the waiter left with Leeman's order, Bingham let his irritation out on him. "It was a big mistake for your grandfather not to be here today, but if that is the way he wants it, then so be it as long as you have his authority to make a deal."

"Deal?" questioned Leeman. "Nothing is further from my mind. You are the one who has made a mistake if you think that I, or any member of my family, would make a deal with you. The charge is false in the first place."

"False?" he snorted. "Whatever gave you that idea? I have the evidence and the testimony of the arresting officer. I would say that is quite conclusive."

"You can't pull that one on us. We both know that it was a plant, and if I had to, I could make you look a fool in court."

"Could you now! Then, what are you doing here speaking to me if you are so certain of your case?" He gave a cynical little chuckle. "I'll tell you what you are doing here," he said. "You know that I hold all the cards, and whether false or otherwise, evidence is evidence, and neither you nor anyone else can argue against that. Your cousin will go down for a long time; I will see to it unless.... Do I have to spell it out for you?"

"You don't have to spell it out. We know exactly what you are angling for, and that is another mistake of yours. We do not give in to blackmail, period! As for you holding all the cards, I have a few choice ones of my own."

It was becoming a game of cat and mouse, and nothing suited Bingham's conniving character more, and he smiled smugly in the belief that he had him. "Then by all means, place them on the table. Let's take a close look at what you think you have."

It didn't take Leeman long to wipe the grin off Bingham's face. "Embezzlement!" he said with satisfaction. "I would say that is a pretty strong hand."

It knocked the wind out of Bingham's sails. Where did he get that information from? he wondered. But if he had learned anything from living with his father, it was never to let your concern show. Recovering somewhat, he said, "You better have proof to back up such an accusation, or I wouldn't want to be in your shoes!"

Their eyes fixed on one another, Leeman replied, "I'm not a fool. I've done my homework; otherwise, I wouldn't be here speaking to you now. You know, if I were you, I would think very carefully before going ahead with this prosecution."

"Well, you are not me," he said angrily. "Anyhow, it's out of my hands. The case is neatly tied up and packaged, and I couldn't stop the process if I wanted to, and I don't want to."

"That's the pity, Bingham, because you have more to lose if you go ahead than we have. You're a good lawyer; you didn't have to resort to these tactics. You could easily make it to the top through your ability, but that's not you, is it? It's not the way you play. You have a warped mind like a common criminal, and you wouldn't know how to play it straight if you tried."

Bingham saw red. No one could talk to him like that and get away with it; he was still someone to be reckoned with. "Common criminal?" he exploded. "Then you and your kind would know all about the common criminal. Do you really think that in one generation, you could wipe the dirt out from under your fingernails? It sticks to you like mud. It was your family who had a profitable association with the Mob, not mine, and a law degree doesn't make you any cleaner than the rest of them. If I go down, I promise you will go down with me. Now, you think about that!"

Unruffled, Leeman said, "I have, and it is not necessary for either of us to go down if you just stop and think about the situation."

"You think you are damned smart, don't you? Well, you think about it. I have you and your family where I want you, so forget about your little games."

"They are not games, Bingham. I am giving you a chance to back away before it's too late. It's as simple as that."

"Nothing in the world is as simple as that!"

176

"It is we who choose to complicate matters. All you have to do to unravel this mess is to see that the so-called evidence is mislaid and cannot be traced; then we are both off the hook."

"I thought you didn't like blackmail?"

"Nothing distresses me more, but you set the rules; I am merely playing by them."

Leeman had all the answers, and it was an uncomfortable feeling. He had never been in a corner like that before. Bingham took a deep breath. "I need time to think," he said.

At that moment, the waiter arrived with lunch. Leeman waited until it was served, then took a card from his jacket pocket and pushed it across the table to Bingham. "My private number. You have until nine tomorrow morning."

Bingham stared at it, then after a moment's hesitation, picked it up, put it in his pocket, and without so much as a glance in Leeman's direction, he rose and walked out of the restaurant, leaving the food untouched.

The air was hot and humid outside, and with the pollution, and one thing and another, he was finding it difficult to breathe. He could hardly go back to the office, he thought. With everything he had on his mind, he wouldn't be able to concentrate on his work. His apartment was barely a block away, so Bingham loosened his tie, removed his jacket, and proceeded to plod along the steamy sidewalk.

In the short time it took him to reach his building, his shirt was wet through and beads of perspiration stood out on his forehead.

"Power's out," greeted the porter. "Always happens when it's needed most!"

"Elevator?" asked Bingham.

He shook his head. "'Fraid not, sir."

Bingham clenched his teeth in exasperation. Ten floors up, he thought, and began the climb. The stairwell was stifling and the sweat from his forehead kept trickling into his eyes, and he had to stop every flight to catch his breath and mop his brow.

What a rotten day it turned out to be; nothing had gone his way. That bastard Leeman! What right had he to pry into his private affairs?

By the time he reached his floor, he was gasping, and had to wait until he had recovered sufficiently before going out into the hall and on to his suite. Automatically, his hand went to the light switch when he entered the apartment; they were still out, so was the air-conditioning, and the place was as hot and stuffy as a Turkish bath.

He went to the bathroom, stripped to the waist, turned on the cold water—the faucet was dry—"Damn!" he moaned—and glanced at his reflection in the mirror. It had been some time since he really took a good look at himself, and what he saw wasn't a pretty sight. Thinning hair, puffy eyes that appeared to be embedded in a mound of flab, and a chin that disappeared into a second chin that hung down his neck like a deflated balloon.

He stared at himself in horror. How come he didn't notice it happening? Didn't seem right. It never happened to his father; he only grew more handsome and distinguished with age. It wasn't fair; then, he wondered, when was life ever fair to him? His father never had to fight for everything the way he did; it just came to him like gifts from the gods—wealth, power, and position. As a lawyer, he glittered like a star and won the loyalty of his peers, but if the truth be told, he was never loyal to anyone or anything in his entire life—except himself.

It pained him to think about his father. God, how it hurt! Why couldn't there have been love between them as there was in other families? Why was life such a struggle for him?

Archie sighed; there were so many unpleasant memories. What might he have achieved if it were not for him? What might he have been without his dominating presence following him around like a ghost? He had made such a mess of his life, not that he could hold his father accountable for everything that happened to him. But then he never had the pressure of being the son of a famous father; he came from simple stock. The road ahead, for him, was clear.

All he ever looked for was his father's approval, so why was it so difficult for him to give it? Did he really dislike him that much? Even now, the thought that he might have done tormented him.

Leeman! How he hated him. He never had to fight for acceptance; it was handed to him on a silver platter by that doting grandfather of his, and they were not even of the same blood. Why him and not me?

Then, if his burden wasn't hard enough, there was Belinda—that is what upset him most. He had set out to punish his father, and ended up punishing himself along with him. What had he done to her? When will the anguish cease? How long must he go on paying for what he did?

A tear wet his cheek. It surprised him; he hadn't shed a tear since he received that letter from his mother, not long after he arrived in America, telling him of his father's death. Funny; with everything he had ever felt about him, it was still a bitter moment to hear how he had died a broken man. He hadn't meant it to go that far, but once he started out on the road to destruction, there was no turning back.

He turned from the mirror in disgust, grabbed a towel, and wiped away the sweat and tears, then went to the kitchen. What he needed was a comforting cup of tea. He sighed with frustration—neither electricity nor water.

It was ironic. He had run out of the bottled variety that morning, and had intended to buy some on the way home from the office.... Even a glass of that most humble of refreshments was denied him, and in a fit of rage, he smashed his fist through the glass door. It shattered into a thousand pieces, and as he watched them spread across the floor, it seemed to him to symbolize his entire life.

He glanced at his hand: it was bleeding. He tied it with a towel, then moved into the living room. It was hot in there, and he drew the blinds against the heat of the midday sun, went to the sideboard, and poured himself a stiff whiskey. He took it with him to an armchair, placed it on the wine table beside it, sat down, and let his thoughts wander back over his life and how he came to be in the position he was now in.

CHAPTER TWELVE

"Napoleon, the little Corsican who grew up fighting against the French occupation of his beloved country, became a Frenchman himself when the French Revolution unexpectedly recognized the Corsican's claim to independence from the Genoese; and having been trained as a soldier at the military school of Brienne in France, what could have been more natural than for him to drift into the service of his adopted country.

"In his twenty years as a soldier, he fought more wars, won more victories, and killed more people, in that short span, than Alexander the Great or Genghis Khan. He wasn't very impressive to look at, neither did he enjoy the advantages of breeding or birth, but what he did have was an unshakable belief in his own destiny, and ambition was the engine that drove his life.

"He knew instinctively what attitude to adopt to impress a crowd, and how to use words to his advantage; and at all times he was master of the situation, and managed to hold center stage even when sick and in exile after his defeat by Wellington at Waterloo."

Archie's mind began to wander as he listened to his history teacher expound the virtues of Napoleon. Here was a man you could believe in, who could excite the imagination, he thought, a man to follow to the death, and in his impressionable mind, he likened him to his own father. How many times had he read an article, by one journalist or another, on a case his father either was defending or prosecuting; such words as magnetic, brilliant, and great would be used to describe him, and indeed, he had a following among his peers, just as Napoleon did.

"Archie Bingham, you are not paying attention!" shouted the teacher. "Have you heard one word of what I have been saying?"

He snapped to attention. "Yessir!" he said quickly as if it was one word.

"Then tell us, of whom have I been speaking?"

"My fa—er, I mean Napoleon, sir," he said and went a bright red.

The class tittered; the teacher grinned. "Would you care to share some of your thoughts about him with us? Napoleon, that is, not your father!"

Again, the class tittered, and again Archie turned red. "Well, sir," he stammered, "he was a fearless soldier, a genius who did great things for France."

"Yes he did, but let us not forget his darker side," said the teacher. "He was also indifferent to human suffering, leaving his men to rot in agony on the battlefield when wounded and no longer of any use to him; neither did he ever keep his word when it was to his advantage to break it; and as for gratitude, he was completely devoid of any such maudlin emotion. Why men chose to follow and die for him will always be a mystery to me."

He knew why, thought Archie. He inspired the kind of allegiance that set men apart from the humdrum, the ordinary, and placed them on the same plane as the great heroes of history, but he didn't contribute his thoughts. They were his and his alone about Napoleon Bonaparte, and in his wild imagination, Napoleon and his father were one and the same.

At dinner that evening, Archie stole a glance at his father. Yes indeed, he was a most impressive figure, the Napoleon of the legal profession, he thought, and his chest puffed up with pride.

Conversation was usually sparing at the dinner table. His mother never had much to say, his father always seemed preoccupied, and he would be deep in his own fancies, so when his mother suddenly said, "It's Archie's birthday in a few days," his father stopped chewing and looked up at her in surprise.

"Oh! When?"

"June the twentieth" replied Archie smartly.

His father's attention turned to him. "Twelve?" he asked.

"Thirteen," he replied proudly.

"And have you thought about what you would like for your birthday?"

He didn't have to think; he knew exactly. "Long trousers," he said.

His father was taken aback. "Long trousers? Then what are you wearing now?"

"Shorts, sir, but all the boys at school have been in long trousers for over a year, and they keep making fun of me."

"Well, we can't have that! We'll do something about it."

"Yes, sir, when?" he asked anxiously, wanting to tie him down.

"Soon. Whenever I can find the time."

Archie knew better than to press him. It was his father's stock reply, and somewhat despondent, he said "Yes, sir, thank you."

***

After school the next day, he asked his mother, "Do you think he might keep his promise this time?"

She knew his father as well as he did, and smiled kindly at him. "Who can say?" she replied. "But not to worry; if he does forget, I shall go with you. One way or another, you will have those long trousers."

He nodded and hung his head. He would rather go with his father, he thought miserably; not that he didn't care for his mother, but she was a woman, and at his age, it was embarrassing to be seen shopping with your mother, and feeling both discouraged and irritated, he announced tersely, "I'm going out. I'll be back before Father gets home."

"Where are you going?" she asked.

He shrugged and walked out of the house without giving her the courtesy of a reply.

They lived in a fashionable townhouse just off the Bayswater Road, with Hyde Park close by. He often went walking through the park after school, going down to the lake to feast his eyes on the girls in their light summer frocks, so light that you could see their legs through the flimsy material, but that day he wasn't in the mood for girl-watching. His thoughts were taken up elsewhere, so he entered the park and sat on a bench just inside the gates, with the Bayswater Road running behind.

He wasn't supposed to be there. His father had strictly forbidden it. "All those prostitutes coming and going," he'd said. "It's not a place for a young boy." The fact was it intrigued him to watch the comings and goings of the prostitutes along that part of the park. It fired his imagination to see them being picked up by some randy old man in a fancy car.

Some of the prostitutes weren't much to look at, showing that they had seen better days. Then there were the newer ones, still in their prime and eager to go, with their full breasts spilling over the top of a tight bodice, and long legs that appeared even longer with the platform shoes and six-inch heels that they wore.

One of the prostitutes came and sat down next to him. He glanced at her out of the corner of his eye, and noticed that she was a lot older than any of the others and looked more like a clown with the two blobs of rouge painted on her cheeks.

She noticed him looking and smiled. "Sweet ducky?" she asked, and offered him one from a crumpled paper bag. He glanced inside and declined.

"So what's a young man like you doing in this part of the park?"

He gave a careless shrug. "It's a free world, isn't it?"

She grimaced. "Not that you'd notice!" she said, then smiled and asked, "Fancy one of the girls, do you?"

He blushed. "Not really."

"Go on!" she said with a nudge of the elbow. "You don't have to be ashamed to admit it. Men and boys have fancied girls since Adam and Eve. It's natural."

Again, he shrugged.

A passing car pulled into the curb and stopped. The baldheaded driver, with a moon-shaped face, leaned across the passenger's side and wound down the window. One of the girls went over and spoke to him. A few seconds later, the car door opened and she got in. As she drew her legs in after her, Archie noticed that she wasn't wearing any underwear; his eyes nearly popped out of his head.

The woman beside him chuckled. "Bit of a shock, was it? Not hard to tell you haven't had it before! Well, any time you want to do something about it, come by and I'll fix you up with one of the girls; only wear long trousers. Wouldn't want any of them to be brought up before a magistrate for kidnapping, among other things."

Archie looked at her with disgust, and without so much as a nod, he abruptly rose and walked away. It wasn't the thought of sex that repelled him. Indeed, he wanted it badly every time he looked at a picture of a nude woman, every time he saw a pair of bare thighs, or the talk among his friends became crudely explicit; but the thought of having it with a common prostitute was distasteful to him. When he was ready, he would do it with someone of his own class. After all, didn't they all want it? Didn't he overhear his father's best friend, a big, ruddy-faced fellow with a handlebar mustache and a lusty laugh, say that all women were whores at heart? The high born, the low born—it made no difference; none of them gave it away for free. Even his wife was more amenable after he had bought her an expensive gift.

Then, he and his father chuckled as if it were a big joke. However, it made a lasting impression upon him and, ever since, when he looked at a woman he fancied, he saw her in the light of that conversation.

It was still early, and he wandered out of the park and down the Edgeware Road to George Street. It was a long time since he visited that part of the West End, and it was as though he was discovering it anew. He loved the old streets of London, especially the squares such as Bryanston and Montague with their private gardens surrounded by large Victorian houses that had been converted into fashionable flats for the well-to-do. He had always liked Montague best and took a stroll around the perimeter of the garden, while peering inside at the children at play. One little girl pricked herself trying to pluck a rose from a bush and went crying to her mother, who consoled her by giving her a sweet. Another child, a little boy, was rolling around on the lawn, his white shirt gathering grass stains, which made his nanny very cross. She demanded that he get up, but he ignored her and continued to roll about.

It brought back memories of his own childhood, and it amused him to see the boy flouting authority with such indifference. Archie was still smiling to himself, when to his astonishment, he caught sight of his father, sitting on a bench, in conversation with a young woman. His initial reaction was to call out to him, but there was something about the intimate manner in which they were conversing that made him hold back. More curious than alarmed, he continued to watch them when, suddenly, he saw his father bend down and lift a little girl, who had been playing at his feet, and give her a kiss and a hug, and the child clung to his neck as if she belonged there.

Somewhat bewildered, Archie wondered who they were, and what his father was doing there with them. Moments later, he saw his father rise from the bench, and with the woman at his side and the child still clinging to him, he left the garden, crossed the road to one of the houses, and went inside with them.

Puzzled by what he had witnessed, he was still standing there when a girl of about seven came tripping down the front steps of the house, crossed the road, and entered the garden. He watched her bounce a ball along one of the paths, when a thought struck him, and he called to her. "Hey you! You with the ball!"

She stopped what she was doing and looked around, then seeing Archie, she came up to the railings and asked, "What do you want?"

"I—er, I want to know if you saw a woman with a man holding a child go inside the house you just came out of."

She shook her head. "No," she said, "but I know who you mean."

"Well, who are they? Do they live there?"

The girl looked wary. "Why do you want to know?" she asked with suspicion.

"I think I know them!"

"I've never seen you before, and I know everyone who visits Lola," she said, still with suspicion.

"Lola!" he asked. "Is that the little girl?"

"That's Belinda. Lola is her mother. I thought you said you knew them?"

"I meant the man with them."

"Belinda's father?"

It was a blow, and it made his head reel. "What?" he asked in disbelief. "What did you say?"

Oblivious to the shock she had just given him, she said, "Belinda's father, but he doesn't live with them; he only visits. Daddy says he is a married man and that Lola is his mistress, and Belinda is their daughter. He also says—"

With anger and humiliation building up inside him, Archie cut her short. "Liar, liar!" he yelled. "How dare you say such things!"

Alarmed by his outburst, she mumbled. "I was only telling you what my father said."

He felt sick, and would have run away there and then if it hadn't been for that compelling curiosity of his. "Well," he asked more calmly, "what did he say?"

She eyed him defiantly. "I'm not going to tell you; you'll only shout at me again, and Mummy says that no one must shout at me."

"If you tell me, I won't shout at you, but if you don't...." He made a threatening face at her.

Uncertain, she hesitated, but unable to contain herself for long, she went on. "Well, he says that he is a famous lawyer. Daddy doesn't like him at all, but he likes Lola a lot. I heard him tell a friend, when Mummy was out, that she was a bit of all right, and that he wouldn't mind having it off with her himself. What does 'having it off' mean?"

Archie was horrified. It was his father she was speaking of, and he cried out, "You're disgusting, and I hate you. Tell your mother to wash your mouth out with soap!" And turning on his heels, he rushed down the street and as far away from the dumbfounded girl as possible.

Tears gushed down his cheeks as on and on he ran. He had never been so humiliated in his life. He hated that horrid little girl, he hated his father; he hated the whole world. How could they do this to him? On and on he ran until, exhausted and out of breath, he collapsed against the side of a wall and sobbed his heart out.

An hour later, or maybe more, the tears dried up, and he glanced around. He had no idea where he was. A passing stranger told him that he was in Paddington. St. Mary's Hospital, where he was born, was in

Paddington, and he knew that from there, he could find his way back to the Edgeware Road.

His feet dragged along the pavement. He was reluctant to return home, but he knew that he must. Sooner or later, he would have to face his father, and when he did, he wondered what he would say to him, and the thought of confronting his father filled him with apprehension. He wasn't the sort of man to whom you could speak your mind, and Archie had always been a little daunted by his presence anyhow. Even if you did have his ear, he was unbending. He swallowed. What was he going to do?

Suddenly, a thought came to him and filled him with even more anxiety. What if he left home for that woman? What would become of him? He would be nothing without his celebrated father behind him. He would have no prestige, no standing among his friends. *He mustn't leave home,* he thought in panic. All at once, he was running as if his life depended upon it. He had to get home as quickly as possible; he had to make certain that he was still there.

When his father opened the door to him, Archie wasn't certain which was stronger, his fear or relief. His father was an intimidating figure as he stood in the doorway, glaring down at him, and he cringed.

"So you decided to come home!" he exploded. "Have you any idea how long we have been waiting for you? You ungrateful, disrespectful, thoughtless little wretch! Isn't it about time that you give a thought to other people? And look at you, you are a mess. I am ashamed to have a son of mine running around looking like that. Now, get upstairs and make yourself presentable before coming down for dinner, and make it quick; I will not be kept waiting much longer."

Perhaps he should have said sorry, but the word stuck in his throat, and swallowing, he slid past his father into the hall and ran up to his room.

He felt frustrated and angry with himself. He had stood on the doorstep taking abuse from his father. He should have stood up to him. He should have said what was on his mind, but he was scared of what he might have done had he confronted him with what he knew. Tears stung his eyes. How he hated him. How he wished that he wasn't his father.

There was a soft knock on the door. He knew it had to be his mother. Perhaps he should tell her, he thought. It would certainly teach his father a lesson. Then she might not believe him. She never stood up to him, anyhow, why would she now? Suddenly, he was angry with her. "Go away!" he cried out.

The knock came again, the door opened, and his mother stepped inside his room. "Are you all right?" she asked.

He glared at her with resentment. "Yes!" he snapped.

She was used to her son's erratic temperament and took no notice. "Archie, I don't know why you were late coming home, but for whatever reason, you have made your father angry. Now he is waiting for dinner, so I suggest you come down right away before you provoke him further."

He kicked an imaginary ball, and without lifting his eyes he mumbled, "I'll be down in a minute."

She paused in the doorway for a second; then, with a sigh, turned and went back downstairs.

Reluctantly, Archie rose, crossed the room to where the hand basin stood, washed his face, combed his hair (his father hated to see untidy hair), and went down for dinner.

He could feel his father's eyes on him as he took his seat at the table; they would be unrelenting. He wasn't a man who could forgive or forget easily, if at all, and Archie braced himself for more to come. He didn't have to wait long.

"I have yet to hear a word of apology to your mother! Look what she does for you, pampers you like a baby. Sometimes, you act just like a baby, so I am not surprised. Well, I won't have it! Do you hear? Or are you deaf as well? The very least you can do is to be on time for dinner for her sake, if not for mine. You show no respect for anyone. I fail to understand you. I fail to understand how you can be a son of mine and behave the way you do!"

There was no abating once he got started. Archie bit his lip. *That's right,* he thought, *put it all on mother as if it had everything to do with her and nothing to do with what you want or expect. Not that you care about her; it just suits you. Well, you can't fool me any longer. I know you for what you are now. Try telling me you keep a mistress for her sake!* He glanced at his mother. She was chewing her food slowly, her eyes cast down in her plate the way they always were when she didn't want to get caught up in an argument between father and son, and it irritated him. He believed she owed it to him to come to his defense, but as ever, she didn't or wouldn't. Perhaps she just couldn't, out of fear of her husband. His mother was a mystery to him. Why did she marry his father in the first place? She came from an important family; she could have had anyone she wanted. Why did she have to choose him?

His father had finished speaking and was concentrating on eating. Archie watched him out of the corner of his eye. He could see that he was still in a bad mood, and hardly able to eat, Archie pushed his food around on his plate for a while, then asked to be excused.

***

Life had always been an emotional struggle for Archie. Perhaps a lot of it had to do with his personality, but his father's infidelity was another matter. He felt betrayed, and the anger inside him festered like an untreated wound. If only he could have confided in his mother, but she had also been betrayed and he had no idea what her reaction would have been. He was also afraid that it might open something that could never be closed.

He felt desperate, and decided that the only way to go on living under his father's roof was to pretend that nothing had changed within the family. In actual fact, it hadn't; it was all in his mind, but a young boy's mind could become a torturous thing.

On the surface, it seemed that he had succeeded, and for the next couple of years, life returned to normal, if anything could be termed as normal in that household. Nevertheless, he was unable to completely rid himself of the hurt and anger against his father, and concealing it as he did, he was like a ticking time bomb.

It was shortly after his sixteenth birthday that his father called him to his study. He rarely entered his father's study unless summoned, and that was only when he was annoyed with him over something, and he wondered what he had done to displease him this time.

His father looked somewhat uncomfortable when he entered, and for a moment Archie feared the worst—that he was going to tell him that he would be leaving to live with his mistress—so it came as a relief when he suddenly said, "Sex, Archie! Your mother thought it was high time that I discussed the subject with you." He paused, "When I was your age, we would talk about it in whispers in the schoolyard, but I would assume that now, with television, you are more enlightened than we were back then."

"Yes, sir, quite a bit more."

"Well," said his father with a sigh of relief, "that certainly makes this conversation somewhat easier for me. I don't suppose you have...?"

"No, sir. Not yet."

"Ah...! So what can I say about love and sex except, of course, that the two go together. It is possible, however, for a man to enjoy sex without love, but it is not possible to love without the expectation of sex.

"You will find it a very gratifying experience, Archie, to be intimate with the woman you love, and that will be yours to discover one of these days, and just as it has brought me, it will bring you great contentment."

They were just words, but as his father continued to speak about love and sex, they were enough to trigger his suppressed emotions, and all at once, his pent-up feelings came pouring out, taking his father by surprise.

"How can you speak to me, your son, of gratification when you are fucking a whore? Maybe you find it more gratifying than sleeping with your wife, but your wife is my mother, and I don't have to listen to you go on about how it fills you with contentment. Damn you, Father! Damn you."

The color drained from his father's face, and shaken, he gasped, "What is the meaning of this? What has got into you? How dare you use such language in my house! Now, you apologize at once, or I will have nothing more to do with you."

"You know exactly what I am talking about. You betrayed me and you betrayed your wife when you began to consort with that bitch of yours."

"I have no idea what you are talking about, and I doubt you do either. Now, if you have something to say to me, then say it clearly or don't say it at all. Do we understand each other?"

"Perfectly. I am talking about you and your mistress and that bastard of hers. Is that clear enough, Father?"

His face went a bright red, and he snapped, "I strongly suggest you take back that coarse and offensive remark and let us have done with this ridiculous accusation. I warn you, Archie, I am in no mood for this nonsense."

"If you find my remark offensive, how do you think I feel about your behavior? Wasn't it enough that you had a mistress? Did you have to have a child by her as well? Don't my feelings matter to you? Perhaps, they never have!"

His father stared at him for a moment, then he somewhat calmly asked, "How long have you known?"

"Long enough. Three years."

"Then why didn't you say something before this? Why didn't you come to me then?"

"Would you have told me the truth? You would have twisted everything until I thought I was imagining it. How many times have I heard you say that when caught: Deny! Deny! Deny! But I saw you with them; I saw you with them, sitting in Montague Square. You can't deny that!"

"What can I say? I am sorry you had to find out in such a way. Nevertheless, my association with them has never stopped me from doing what is right by you and your mother."

"Your association with a whore is hardly doing right by me and my mother. I think I have the right to expect better than that from you."

His father's anger rose once again. "I resent you calling her a whore. She is no such thing and never has been, and for the record, let me tell you what my rights are. I have a right to my own life, as long as what I do and feel doesn't affect the well-being of you or your mother, and I have never allowed it to. As for your rights, you have the right to expect me to do whatever it is that a father does for a child, and no more. You have never wanted for anything, and that only is what should concern you. The rest is my business alone!"

"Well, I beg to differ. You may have provided a roof over my head, put food in my belly and clothes on my back, but a child expects love as part of the deal, and where was your love? Those affections, that were denied me, were given freely elsewhere. All my life I have looked up to you, wanted to be just like you. You were my hero. It would have been nice if, just for once in that area, you could have lived up to my expectations. Perhaps Mother is satisfied with the way things are between you, but I could never be satisfied with the way they are between us!"

"I have said I was sorry once, I will not say it again. The last time I took a look at my life, I thought it belonged to me. As for your mother, I have no idea if she is satisfied with the way things are or not. If she is dis-satisfied, or suspects anything, then she is intelligent enough to keep it to herself. You would have been wiser to do the same."

"How very convenient that would have been!"

"Not convenient, Archie, simpler. Life is largely what we make of it and, rightly or wrongly, we owe it to ourselves to live by our own stan-dards, not other people's. If you have a quarrel with that, then perhaps it is time for you to take a look at your own life, and see if your banner can fly as high as you would have mine fly. Now, that is as much as I have to say on the subject, so if you will excuse me, I have an appointment that I must keep." And with those abrupt few words, Archie was dismissed.

It wasn't the first time that he had been dismissed or put in his place by his father, and it had never been a pleasant feeling, but this time, it sounded so final, so conclusive. Take it or leave it! What can you do when you are sixteen years old and living under your father's roof? You have no choice, and for good or bad, you take it.

Strangely, the effect of that conversation paved the way for a new understanding, a new relationship between father and son. Archie had got it off his chest, and now managed to come to terms with the idea of his father's affair. As for his father, he had gained a new respect for his son, and gave more time to him.

It was during the following year that Archie made an important decision about his career. He would not be following in his father's footsteps as he expected him to do; instead, he would take solicitor's articles. Much of the decision was due to the fear he had of not being able to live up to his father's reputation as a barrister. He had a strong jealous streak in him, and the concept of having people make comparisons between him and his father was anathema to him. The thought had also occurred to him that he would be free of his father's influence. He would be his own man once and for all.

Although his father was disappointed, he was pleased that he would be going to Cambridge to take an LL.B..and at the very same college from which he received his law degree. It also made him take a more active interest in his son's thirst for knowledge, and he would often discuss certain cases with him, especially those that he was prosecuting.

Archie had a bright mind, and it impressed him to see how well he could interpret the law; it also added value to their discussions as well as great pleasure. Their relationship was entering a harmonious period, and it was at this point that a rape case, of which his father would be the prosecuting counsel, came along, and he called Archie to his study so that they could discuss his approach to the case together. "Even though the victim is a pornographic actress who simulates the sexual act in front of the camera, I have never been more certain of a victory," he said. "The defendant is the director of one such film of hers, a young man who denies the charge. Only in this case, we have a witness who saw and heard everything—another actress who, at the time of the rape, was in one of the changing rooms attached to the set. Also, an examination, immediately after the attack, showed extensive bruising in and around the vaginal area consistent with forced entry.

"I expect the defense will raise the point that a sexual liaison between such an actress and her director is not unusual, and that it may well turn rough but only with the consent of both parties. However, given the nature of the crime, together with all the other evidence, I am confident of the outcome."

"But why should the testimony of a pornographic actress, such as the victim herself, be believed over the word of a director? Might not a jury think her testimony unreliable?"

"It is up to me to convince them that it isn't, and that shouldn't prove difficult with Dante's reputation in the film industry. He has, in fact, been charged with rape before, only that time there was no witness and he got off."

"Then, surely, it cannot be brought up."

"You are right, it cannot; but there is more. Not a year ago, he was charged with having intercourse with a minor. Although it was proved to be with her consent, it was still statutory rape, and he was put on probation."

"Then, are you saying that can be brought up?"

"I don't see why not. It is a similar offense, and he is still on probation."

"So you have him!"

His father smiled. "I think we can safely say so!"

Their relationship continued to improve and it was consoling to Archie to know that he had his father's ear at last. As well, it helped to disperse any remaining doubts and fears. They had become father and son in a way that they had never been before, and Archie felt that he could hold up his head with pride once again, and that was important to him.

He enjoyed going to court to listen to his father, to feel the aura that surrounded him, to see his riveting effect upon a jury. He had no equal in his field; no one had such a command of language or such a superb knowledge of the law. He had even known him to put one or two judges to shame, but he always did it in a nice way, even humbly, which was admittedly out of character. Then his father always knew the right pose to adopt, and the judges respected him for it.

When the rape case came on at the Old Bailey, Archie was determined not to let it go by without being there to share in his father's glory. He knew that he would never agree to him taking the day off from school, so on the morning of the trial, he dressed, as usual, in his uniform, and went down to breakfast with his father, leaving the impression that he would be going off to class soon after his father left for chambers.

It was while they were having breakfast that the phone rang, and Archie went out into the hall to answer it. It was for his father. "Who is it?" he asked when he returned to the dining room.

"I don't know, he refused to give his name," replied Archie. "Only that it was urgent he speak with you. I did notice that he had an accent. Italian I think."

His father looked disturbed as he rose and went to the study to take the call. Archie was supposed to replace the receiver in the hall the moment he heard his father on the line, but his curiosity had been aroused and, pretending to replace it with a quick click, he quietly listened in.

"I have told you never to phone my home!" sharply spoke his father.

"I wouldn't have if you had given me an answer," replied the man with the foreign accent.

"It's out of the question!"

"Then you know what I must do to protect my son."

"I don't take kindly to threats, Alfonso. Your son is guilty, and you know it as well as I do."

"Do you think I enjoy making threats? But I do not want him found guilty, and you can do something about it. Your reputation is beyond reproach; no one would suspect anything if you were to lose this case, but it will destroy my son if you don't!"

"Then he should have considered that before he did what he did. I will not risk my good name for a repeated rapist, so forget it."

"But you would risk it for your daughter's sake, wouldn't you? I know how much you love her, as much as I love my son. Have you forgotten the old days and how you met Lola? Why should either of our children be hurt because of some unfortunate incident?"

Archie felt sick as he listened. Who was this man, he wondered, and what did his father's mistress have to do with him?

His father was speaking now, and he listened breathlessly. "Why must you drag Belinda into this?" he said. "She's done you no harm; she is an innocent child. What happened a long time ago, happened, and has nothing to do with anything. Your son is guilty. You cannot—you must not ignore it; otherwise, he will go from bad to worse. Is that what you want? For heaven's sake, Alfonso, you used to be a fair-minded man."

"I will not see my son go to prison because of a whore who thinks she can accuse him of whatever she likes and get away with it. You know as well as I do what happens in the industry."

"A whore she may be, but even whores have rights, and he cannot be allowed to get away with rape again and again and again. I'm sorry, but that is my last word."

"Then I will see to it that you have a scandal on your hands; one that will not only rock your career, but also put pressure on your family, as well as your relationship with Lola. As for your daughter, the press will have a field day with her. You know how they will refer to her, don't you? Or do I have to spell it out?"

Archie went hot and cold, and he wondered what his father would say now. He didn't have long to wait. In the same deliberate, controlled tone that he used when angered or trying to make a point, he responded, "You piece of dirt! You are no better than your son. We are not talking about me here, not even Lola. We are talking about my daughter, and I have enough on you to put you behind bars with your son!"

"Fine, if that's what you want, but remember one thing—when you took Lola away from me, she was a minor. Have you forgotten? Have you forgotten that I didn't say a word? You owe me for that—you owe me big!"

There was a tense silence on the line. Archie barely breathed as again he waited for his father's response. It seemed forever before he heard him say in a suppressed tone, "I have no more time for this. I have to be in court."

"That's all right, as long as you bear in mind what I've said," replied the man.

Archie heard the click as his father replaced the receiver, and not wanting to get caught, he swiftly replaced it his end and stepped back from the phone. It wasn't a moment too soon; seconds later, his father emerged from the study. His face was gray, his mouth set in a grim line, and he looked right through Archie as he passed him, as if he wasn't there.

Anxiously, Archie's eyes followed him to the door, watched him pick up his briefcase from the console table, place his bowler hat on his head without his usual glance in the mirror, take his rolled umbrella from the stand, open the front door, and leave without a word to anyone.

He was still staring at the door when his mother came down the stairs. "Was that your father leaving?" she asked.

His gaze shifted to her face, and he nodded. Puzzled by the dazed look in his eyes, she asked, "Is something wrong?"

All of a sudden, his eyes flashed with resentment. "No!" he snapped and started for the stairs.

When Archie reached his room, he threw himself down in an armchair. He felt so uncertain; he was afraid of going to court, and afraid not to. God knows what his father would do, he thought. How did he get himself into such a position? he wondered, and he felt sick with apprehension. Surely, he wouldn't give in to blackmail. Not his father; there was too much at stake—his reputation, his name. Yet, at the same time, there was an uncomfortable little niggle at the back of his mind, and he knew that he had to be there, he had to know, he had to see for himself.

Somewhat sickened, he picked up his school satchel from the floor, placed it over his shoulder, went downstairs, and left the house without bothering to say goodbye to his mother.

The courtroom was filled to capacity when he got there, and if it were not for a clerk who recognized him, he might have been turned away. His father had a large following, especially among junior counsel, who would often turn out in numbers to see the "master" at work, and to learn from him.

He took his seat in the public gallery and waited tensely for the proceedings to begin. Almost from the onset of the trial, Archie knew that his worst fears were about to be realized. There was a total lack of authority in his father's bearing, and the usual command in his voice was missing as he addressed the jury with his early remarks. He sounded more like a junior stumbling through his first case than an eminent counsel.

It did not go unnoticed by the barristers in court that morning, and bewildered glances were exchanged on more than one occasion as the loose prosecution progressed. Finally, when a witness wasn't called to corroborate the victim's allegations, and the report of the doctor who examined her soon after the rape was made little of, whispers of disbelief were heard throughout the court. If the inadequate prosecution had managed to escape anyone, the defending counsel made certain that it was brought to the jury's notice in his closing remarks.

He looked so smug as he rose to his feet and walked over to the jury. He knew that he had it in the bag, and there was a note of satisfaction in his voice as he began his address. "Members of the jury," he said, and raised an eyebrow as if to say the whole prosecution was a farce, then continued, "why did not the prosecution produce the vital witness to the alleged rape, who gave evidence in the lower court? One can only assume that this witness is unreliable and would not stand up to cross-examination. Neither was the examining doctor called; his report was merely referred to. Again, one has to wonder why. Now, His Lordship will tell you that the offense must be proved beyond any reasonable doubt. I repeat, beyond any reasonable doubt!" He paused, glanced at Bingham for a second, and then faced the jury again. "And in the circumstances," he continued, "this case is not proven; therefore, you must bring in a verdict of not guilty."

No one in that courtroom could have missed the glint of triumph in his eyes as he returned to his place at the defense table. There was a shuffle of feet as they sat poised on the edge of their seats, waiting breathlessly, to see if Archibald Bingham would exonerate himself with a performance more in keeping with the usual flash and flair that they were accustomed to.

You could have heard a pin drop, and feeling uneasy, Archie glanced at his father's face. It was empty, and he knew then what he suspected from the very beginning, that it was over. He had given in, and not wanting to witness the final humiliation, he rose and left the court just as his father was rising to his feet.

He was devastated. His father had dishonored his name and his profession, and for whom? That's what hurt most; and he would never forget or forgive him as long as he lived.

He didn't make an appearance at dinner that evening, or for the rest of that week. He couldn't bear the thought of seeing his father and looking into his face as he made small talk as if nothing was wrong. His mother must have guessed that something had happened, because she didn't come knocking at his bedroom door and make a fuss about him not coming down for dinner. His father made no mention of it either as they passed each other in the hall the next day.

In the coming weeks, there were whispers of impropriety along the corridors of justice and an enquiry was held into the mishandling of the prosecution's case. How his father defended himself, Archie had no idea, but he must have satisfied the board of enquiry, because as soon as it was over, the gossip died down and life seemingly returned to normal in the Bingham household. Neither did his father suffer professionally; indeed, it was quite the reverse. Not two months after the fiasco, he was made a Q.C., and shortly before Archie left for Cambridge University, he and his mother accompanied his father to the palace, where he was knighted for his services in the profession.

CHAPTER THIRTEEN

Archie stood at the top of the stairs staring down into the hall below. He could see his luggage standing by the front door, two large cases and one small, waiting to be placed in the taxi that was due to arrive to take him to the railway station.

His father bade him goodbye earlier that morning, wished him good luck and all that, before leaving for chambers. It was an awkward moment; neither had spoken to each other, at length, since the trial. Archie wondered if his father was even aware that he had been in court that day. If he was, he gave no sign of it.

He could hear his mother's high-pitched voice on the phone in the library. She would be out any moment to wave him off. He glanced at the well-polished banister and let his fingers caress its silky smooth surface. Only once did he attempt to slide down the banister, but was caught by his father just as he was putting a leg over. "Just what do you think you're doing!" he yelled. "Get down at once. Dignity, Archie, dignity. Now, don't let me catch you doing it again."

He was ten years old at the time, and very much under his father's influence. He let his eyes follow the banister's curve to where the stairs widened at the bottom, and giving in to a sudden urge, he placed a leg over the top and slid all the way down. A grin of satisfaction spread across his face when he reached the bottom, and he whispered under his breath, "To hell with dignity!"

A bubble of excitement welled up inside him as the train neared Cambridge. This is what he had waited for, what he had worked hard at school for—to get away from home and start to live his own life without his father's interference. A porter boarded the train as soon as it came to a stop and carried his luggage out to the taxi rank. The last one had just left with a passenger, and he had to wait ten minutes before another arrived.

The air smelled fresh and clean after the city, and he took a deep breath, drawing it into his lungs and savoring it as if it were a glass of fine wine. Freedom at last, he thought, and the feeling was exhilarating.

Another young man, with extensive luggage, stood behind him at the taxi rank. His look of excitement, together with a certain expectation, left Archie in no doubt as to where he was heading. He thought he might ask him if he wanted to share a taxi, but changed his mind when one finally came.

He soon discovered that university was not only a new world, but also a vastly different one from the world he was used to. Unlike public school where you mixed with others of the same class, at Cambridge there was every class and creed under the sun, and he tended to seek out those with a background similar to his own, avoiding those whom he felt were not to his advantage.

However, there was one exception: Jack Williams. Had you asked him at the time why Jack, he could not have explained why he was drawn to him; they were so different.

Jack was orphaned by the time he was four years old, and raised by a maiden aunt who worked as a librarian for a living. It being their sole source of income, he went to the local grammar school, from which he won a scholarship to Cambridge. He had always been a likeable fellow, with a pleasant manner and a purpose about him that was in contradiction to his gentle nature.

He and Archie were complete opposites in every way except one. Where Archie was handsome and self-indulgent, Jack was "homely" and unspoiled. Where Archie was elegant, he was careless in dress. He was also shorter than Archie by more than six inches and wore thick-lensed glasses behind which were a pair of intelligent, if somewhat too serious, brown eyes. He was, however, every bit as bright as Archie, and the unlikely pair became the best of friends.

Archie took it upon himself to look out for Jack, and saw to it that he was invited everywhere he was. In fact, he made it quite clear to his friends that he would not accept an invitation unless it included Jack. When some would ask, with amusement, "What is it with you two?" He would jokingly reply, "Why, he's my conscience!"

Whether he realized it or not, there was some truth to it. He needed a mentor, and Jack was the one person who could talk to him and make him see sense. It was as though there was a pact between them. Each time Archie behaved in a scandalous fashion, Jack would step in with his practical wisdom, and once again, reason would prevail.

In many respects, Archie's good looks were his downfall. They seemed to attract the wrong kind of women, the kind who had nothing but sex, sex, and more sex on their minds. In fact, he was as much their victim as they were his; he had strong sexual desires, and they were all too willing to satisfy them, only as soon as he had what he wanted, he would treat them with disdain.

When Jack expressed disapproval, he laughed and replied, "Grow up. The truth is all women are whores and enjoy being treated as such. What's more, they are after two things—your money and your balls. Well, I'm damned if I will let them get their hands on any of my money, but I will fuck them as much as they can take!"

Jack, who had led a sheltered life before university, found such talk crude and offensive, and rebelled, "If you must speak like that, then save it for someone who can appreciate it because I don't!"

Archie chuckled. "Oh dear," he said, "it would seem that I have disgusted my poor straight-laced friend!"

"Yes, you have! And it's nothing to laugh at. Sometimes, I really don't understand where you are coming from. You were fortunate to be born into a good family and yet you delight in wallowing in the dirt. Why? Why? And why I put up with you, I can't imagine!"

"Then let me tell you why. You put up with me because you are my friend, and I am yours, and friends stick together through thick and thin, no matter what. Now promise me, Jack, that you will never let me down."

"You are doing a first-class job of that yourself, but, as you say, we are friends. If I can possibly help it, I won't ever let you down, but neither will I stand behind everything that you do."

"Fair enough!" agreed Archie. "Now, as my very best friend, have you some money to lend me until my allowance comes through at the end of the month?"

Archie had taken to gambling. From his first game of cards with the boys, he was hooked. Dice, horses, the dogs, you name it—he played it, and he lost big. Jack wasn't the only one to whom he owed money; he owed all his friends, but no one could accuse him of welshing. He paid up just as soon as his allowance was sitting in the bank, and he had a large circle of friends.

Archie's charismatic figure drew people to him like bees to honey, and soon, the circle widened to include an earl, a lord, an honorable, and

Harry, second son of one of England's premier families, who could trace their ancestry back to William the Conqueror.

Because of their monthly dinner parties, when formal attire was worn, they became known throughout the university as the Black Tie Gang. It was at one of these evenings, when discussion accompanied the cigars and brandy after dinner, that Jack saw another side to his friend's character—one that surprised him greatly, for he had never heard a prejudiced word leave his lips before that night.

The subject of discussion was heroes. Naturally, Archie named Napoleon as his, a name that aroused indignation from the more patriotic members of the set, but it was all taken in good humor, for the most part. Harry had been silent as he listened to the others expound the virtues of their particular hero, and when they had finished, Archie asked, "We have yet to hear who your hero is, Harry?"

"I don't know about hero," he said, "but I do have a great admiration for Ben Gurion."

His answer took everyone by surprise, but only Archie made a remark. "That little Jew, you must be joking! I mean, don't tell me that you, of all people, are a Jew lover?"

If Harry was hurt, he didn't show it. "You could say that," he replied pleasantly. "I have a Jewish grandfather whom I love dearly. As for Ben Gurion, is there another man in history who brought a nation together and gave them statehood against all odds? Even Stalin, one of the most evil dictators of the century, had to bow to his will and vote in favor of a Jewish state, and that was despite an inherent hatred for the Jew.

"My grandfather knew Ben Gurion, and he told me that he had never met a more impressive man in his life. He had a powerful presence, and a pair of piercing eyes that seemed to see right through you and leave you in awe. Yes indeed," said Harry. "I cannot think of anyone in history I admire more."

There was absolute silence when he finished speaking, and shortly afterwards, the gathering broke up.

When walking back to their rooms, Archie said to Jack. "I have never really liked Harry, and now I know why, the little Jew upstart!"

Jack was abhorrent. "That is not only insensitive and insulting, but unfair. Apart from his family, who happen to be one of England's oldest and most respected landowners, Harry is one of the best."

Archie glared at him. "What?" he sneered. "Another Jew lover?"

"What is it with you?" asked Jack. "I have never heard you talk like this before, and frankly, I don't like it. What have you got against Jews anyhow? What have they ever done to you?"

"That's beside the point."

"It is very much the point!"

"The truth is Harry gets my goat. He can be so damned condescending at times—he and his great family! Did you know that his allowance is twice that of anyone else? Yet does he put a hand in his pocket to help out a friend? Not he!"

"Ah!" exclaimed Jack. "Now I'm beginning to understand. He won't lend you money so that you can go gambling. Well, I say good for him. He is being a far better friend to you than the rest of us. Like Harry, we should not be encouraging you."

"He's a bloody Shylock, that's what he is; and now I know why."

Jack made no reply. He knew better than to argue with Archie when he was in a vicious mood. He was full of resentment of one kind or another, and there was no doubt in his mind that Archie was jealous of Harry's distinguished family history—one that even his prestigious background could not match.

As time went on, Archie's gambling grew worse. He was now betting more than his monthly allowance could cover and running up a debt that was impossible to keep up with, and soon he was barred from every betting shop in the area.

This gave Jack cause for relief. He thought it would be the end of his friend's gambling, but he reckoned without Archie's scheming nature, and before long, he had found a sleazy little backstreet bookie who didn't know him by sight, and gave the name of a fellow student as his own.

Hamish had never gambled, so Archie believed that the bookmaker would not be likely to discover the deception. Not that he intended Hamish any harm, he simply never gave the possibility a thought, and as his debt mounted and the bookie wasn't able to collect, it was to Hamish that he sent the "strong arm" boys. Despite all his denials, these thugs not only gave him a verbal warning, but also broke one of his legs to make certain he understood that they meant business should he not pay up smartly.

It would be a horrifying experience for anyone, but more so for Hamish, who had no idea whatsoever what they were talking about, and he would have gone to the police if it were not for his friends, who put two and two together and convinced him to take the matter to Archie's father instead.

It was Jack who informed Archie of the situation. "I swear," said Archie, "if I had known what they would do, I would not have given them his name. You must believe me, Jack."

"You're not a fool; you had to realize that they would want to collect their money when you didn't pay up. What did you think they would do? Ask politely?"

"I thought they would be aware of their mistake when they saw him."

"Well, you're lucky we stopped Hamish from going to the police. At least by taking the matter to your father, he should get some compensation for all his pain and suffering."

"I would rather face the police than my father, so don't expect any thanks from me."

"We are not doing it for you, Archie; we are doing it for Hamish. Don't you care about what you have done? Do people mean nothing to you? It was a criminal act; you can't go around doing things like that and get away with it."

"Neither can I take responsibility for what the bookmaker did, and it's unfair of you to expect it. Anyhow, his was the criminal act; mine was nothing more than a simple misdemeanor."

"There was nothing simple about it. For heaven's sake, Archie, they broke his leg! Have you no remorse?"

"So what do you want? That I should wear sackcloth and ashes for the rest of my life? I'm sorry but what is done is done, and it's not in my power to alter anything. All I can tell you is that I didn't intend for him to get hurt. Now, can we please forget all about it? It's going to be tough enough dealing with my father; he will make my life hell, especially if he has to dish out money."

"No more hell than you have made life for Hamish."

"Oh, to hell with Hamish! His leg will heal and all will be forgotten, but my father will never let me forget!"

"Have you ever thought that perhaps you shouldn't forget?"

"For heaven's sake, Jack, stop going on. I've just about had enough of your moralizing."

Jack shook his head in disbelief. "You're impossible. Everyone has to have accountability, and you are no exception. You don't give, Archie, you just take!"

"Who gives me? We are all in it for ourselves, and if you don't know that then you have a problem. You have to grab as much as you can in this life, or you end up with nothing, and I don't want to end up with nothing."

"Oh my poor friend, don't you get it…? We all end up with nothing. It's 'dust unto dust and under dust to lie, sans wine, sans song, sans singer, and sans end.'" And with a sad shake of his head, Jack walked out on him.

***

Archie had always been intimidated by his father's overpowering presence, and his natural reaction to it was belligerence. He felt that if he failed to assert himself, he would be lost forever. So when the expected call came, he was ready for it.

"What on earth do you think you have been up to?" cried his father. "Have you the least idea how much this escapade of yours has cost me? Not to mention the suffering you have caused this fellow—er, what's his name? Thank God, your friends came to me instead of going to the police—not that I would have blamed them if they had. You deserve to be punished, and strongly."

"Well, I am certain that you will see to it that I am!" said Archie.

"Don't you dare be insolent! Just imagine what the newspapers would have made of this if they had got hold of the story. Day after day, I have to stand up in court. I would have had to hide my face in shame. Have you no pride? Don't you care about the reputation of this family? Of our good name?"

"I leave that job to you, Father, and what a good job you do, even at the expense of your only son. Don't you care about my feelings in all this? I do have them, you know, or have you overlooked that? Think what it would have been like for me if it had reached the ears of the principal—I'd be finished at Cambridge. I could kiss my career goodbye!"

"How you make your bed, so you lie! Now, these are my terms, and I want no argument from you. There is to be no more gambling, no more womanizing, no drinking. You will see to it that you do nothing further to sully the reputation of this family. Furthermore, I will expect you to gain a first-class law degree. Nothing less will be acceptable from a son of mine. To finish with, I do not want any more phone calls informing me of this shocking behavior on your part. I shall not tolerate one moment more! Do I make myself clear?"

"Perfectly! I'm to crawl under a stone and only rear my head when it pleases you."

"You can drop the impudence for a start."

"Well, what do you expect? You are blaming me for something that was beyond my control. To listen to you, you would think that I ordered his leg to be broken. It's unfair, but then that's no big news, is it?"

"Fair has nothing to do with it. The facts have spoken, Archie, and they paint a decidedly nasty picture of you and the way you carry on. I'm disgusted, truly disgusted. Is it asking too much to want to hear something good about you for a change?"

Archie bit his lip. He could never win in an argument with his father, so what was the use? God, how he hated him for it. Anyhow, he thought, he still needed him and wasn't about to cut his nose off to spite his face, so he let him carry on without interrupting. When he finished, he said, "All I can promise is that you won't hear anything like that again," and he hung up before his father could reply.

He sat for a while, staring at the receiver he had just replaced, and thought about life at home. Nothing had ever been easy for him; but then, his father wasn't an easy man to deal with. He expected too much from him, even when he was a young boy. "Discipline, Archie, you must learn to control your natural instincts," he would say whenever he became too noisy, or too demanding. He was a child, for heaven's sake—how could a child grow up in such an atmosphere? You have to have room, and his father never gave him very much. It was always "Be quiet, Archie, you know that your father doesn't like noise" or "Be quiet, Archie, your father is working—he's on the phone—he has a headache." There was no freedom, only restraint; everyone needs a certain amount of freedom in their lives—even a child.

The funny thing, he realized, was that freedom was as much a state of mind as it was a state of being, and he knew now that he would never be free of his father's presence. It would always be there, looming over him like a giant shadow, inhibiting every move, every action.

His mother was different. She came from a background of prestige and wealth, and her life had been softer than his father's, whose parents were hard-nosed business people who saw everything in black and white. Being of a charitable nature, she came rushing up to Cambridge when she heard, more concerned with her son's feelings than with what he had done. "Oh, you poor darling," she cried, "what you must have gone through, but you know, it won't do. You really have to learn to curb your gambling."

"No need to worry, Mother," he replied. "I no longer have a taste for it."

"Then some good has come of it. What I would like to know is how you managed to get into such debt in the first place."

"You can thank Father for that! Really Mother, my allowance is pitiful; he has no idea what it costs to keep up an appearance these days."

"Why didn't you confide in me? I would have gladly seen that you were adequately looked after even if it meant dipping into my trust fund. I'll get in touch with the trustees as soon as I return home. I know that they will agree to advance you whatever money you may need."

"Will Father find out?" he asked anxiously.

"Not if I don't tell him."

"Then I accept," he said with a sigh of relief. "Er, how much do you think you might manage?"

"What if I double your father's allowance, would that be enough for your needs?"

"Triple would be better, if that's all right with you."

"Certainly. A son of mine should not have to go begging for a few extra pounds!"

With additional cash in his pocket, Archie began to throw wild parties to compensate for the friends who had begun to drift away. There was always an element of Cambridge society who were only too happy to take their place, and he now surrounded himself with these people. "They are nothing but a bunch of opportunists," complained Jack. "Just look at them! They play up to you for what they can get, not out of friendship. Does that really satisfy you?"

"What do you want me to do? I need people; you know that. Is it my fault if the others won't have anything to do with me?"

"What you are saying is that, as long as they are willing to pay you homage, you are content!"

"Is that so terrible?"

"Not if that's what it takes to satisfy you, but don't expect me to stand by and watch. I find it sickening."

"I thought you were my one true friend."

"I am, and that is why I feel I can tell you what is on my mind. You don't need the likes of them. There are enough decent people at Cambridge with whom you can mix; maybe they are not quite of your social standing, but it doesn't make them any less than you are. Times are changing, Archie. I thought you understood that when you chose me as a friend."

"Okay, you are right. I agree: no more wild parties; in fact, no more parties at all. They were beginning to bore me anyhow."

"Well, if nothing else, it is a start in the right direction!"

Despite everything, their friendship remained steadfast, that is, until Jack found himself a girlfriend, Penelope. Archie didn't like to share anything or anyone, and it really hit him hard. He had thought of Jack as belonging to him, and him alone; now he felt betrayed, just as he felt betrayed when he found out about his father's affair—and he was bitter.

There wasn't any logic to his feelings; there never was with Archie. He was as complicated a human being as ever you could find, and with a reasoning that defied any sort of rationality, and he made up his mind, even before he met Penelope, that he didn't like her.

When they were introduced, he was as cold as yesterday's dinner toward her. Not only did he not like her, but he also found her plain to look at and awkward in manner. He found fault with everything; she was too tall and lanky, and her voice sounded more like a squeak from a mouse than coming from a human being. "I really don't know what you see in her," he said when he and Jack were alone.

"Something very special," he replied.

"Hmmm! Well, are you going to tell me how you met this, er, special person?"

"In the library. We both reached for the same book of poetry, Keats. Immediately, we found that we had something in common."

"Poetry! The basis of a mushy relationship," he scoffed with exaggerated cynicism.

"Don't deride, Archie. In that split second, my whole life changed. Be happy for me. I am not confident with women the way you are, but when I am with her, I feel ten feet tall."

"And how long have you been ten feet tall?"

"Six weeks on Saturday."

"What? And you said nothing to me in all that time? Why not? Did you feel guilty or something? Anyhow, I don't know how you can allow a woman like her to come between us."

"What are you talking about? For heaven's sake, I've found a girl to whom I can relate, that's all! She hasn't come between us, and I didn't introduce you sooner because the opportunity never arose."

"But you said nothing; that isn't the action of a true friend."

"I said nothing because I wasn't sure of her until now, and I didn't want to appear a fool. We are in love, Archie, and just as soon as I qualify, we are going to get married."

"For heaven's sake! You don't marry the first girl that comes into your life; you fuck them, you fool!"

"That's your way, not mine."

"Then your way is the bourgeois way. People like us don't marry for love; we marry for convenience and then we take a mistress for the gratification of the body, and to hell with the soul!"

"Where do you get these ideas from, Archie? People like us! People like you! You're a snob at heart, aren't you? Well, people like me don't behave like people like you, and I'm glad of it."

"See what I mean? She has already turned you against me, and that's after everything I have done for you. I have gone out of my way for you. Do you think you would have been accepted into our circle if it were not for me? I have lifted you onto a different plane, and this is how you repay me?"

"Let us talk about what you have really done for me. You have bored me, disgusted me with tales of sordid behavior. You degrade the women you go with, and you degrade yourself. Well, I am not having you degrade my relationship with Penelope. The world doesn't owe you anything, and neither do I."

"We owe it to each other to be true."

"I don't think you know what truth is. The truth is that we are born and we die, and we are judged by what we do and how we behave between birth and death, and you, my friend, are not doing too well, so I wouldn't boast about your kind of people, if I were you. We are all equal, Archie; only our circumstances differ, and that has nothing to do with anything except pure chance and luck. Whether I had been accepted into your circle or not, I would still be me, and you would still be you, and I'm glad that I am nothing like you."

Archie could never take criticism, and coming from a friend whom he had always trusted, it was even harder. "Noted!" he said with a blast of sarcasm. "But it still doesn't alter the fact that you don't understand women. None of them are what they seem, and when you find that out for yourself, as most certainly you will, don't come crying to me, because I may not be there for you. Despite your moralizing, it is you who betrayed a friend, not me, and for whom? Some ordinary little nobody who is of little consequence, and that's what gets me—that someone like her can take you in so easily. What value is she to you?"

"I've heard enough!" cried Jack. "It's difficult trying to understand you when you are rational, but when you are irrational, it's damned impossible. Nevertheless, I've got the picture. Penelope is 'persona non grata,' and, in that case, so am I."

When Archie watched Jack walk out on him, it was as if he was losing a part of himself. He had never felt that close to anyone before. He also stung from the attack. The only other person who had ever criticized him was his father, and he hated his father; but this was different, and it hurt more. *It's all her fault,* he thought bitterly. *Penelope, she's to blame,* and he cursed her.

***

Without Jack, he felt like a lost sheep, and to replace him, he chose the unlikely figure of Philip Peel, a young man who had the dubious reputation of being homosexual. In a perverse way, Archie got a kick out of the speculation that arose from their association. The truth was Peel had no such tendencies. He was a victim of circumstance, no more, and for a while, their friendship flourished.

One of the reasons he had chosen Peel as a friend was because he reminded him of Jack in so many ways. He was quiet of manner, was studious like Jack, and had a similar build and the same round, baby face. They both wore glasses and neither paid any attention to fashion, but there the similarity ended. Where Jack was gentle yet strong of character, Peel was timid and seemingly devoid of any character; and where Jack had his own mind, Peel was apt to fall in with whatever anyone suggested, and Archie soon tired of him.

More and more, Archie found himself wanting Jack back in his life, and resented Penelope for having taken him from him, and his hatred for her grew. He also knew that if there was to be a chance of reconciliation, it would have to be on Jack's terms.

Apology had never come easily to Archie, but once Jack accepted the proverbial "olive branch," he won Penelope's acceptance as well, and soon the three of them became inseparable. Archie knew how to turn on the charm, and Penelope was captivated, much as Jack had been in the early days, and before long she was sharing little confidences with him, one being Jack's twenty-first birthday party that she was planning as a surprise for him. Unfortunately, she was also too trusting, and made the mistake of going to Archie's rooms to tell him of her change of plan and to ask for his opinion of her new ideas.

When Archie answered her knock, he was not only astonished to see her standing on his doorstep, but intrigued by the boldness of this timid creature. "Well hello!" he said in surprise. "Come in."

The obvious effect her sudden appearance had upon him made her feel awkward, and she stammered "Um—perhaps—perhaps I shouldn't have come. I mean…."

He grinned broadly. "I'm not going to eat you, if that's what's bothering you."

She laughed nervously, then took a hurried little step over the threshold, and stood there awkwardly, waiting for him to say something.

"Well, you better sit down," he said. "I barely have half an hour before a lecture."

The fact that he didn't have long seemed to make her feel less uncomfortable, and she looked for a place to sit. There was a couch against a wall, and a chair, piled with books, in a corner. She sat down on the couch, very stiff-backed and demure, at one end, while he sat on the edge of a desk, his legs crossed at the ankles, facing her.

She glanced up at him and blushed, then quickly looked away again.

"You better make it fast if I am to listen to what you have come to say," he said.

"Yes," she whispered. "Er, I was wondering what you would think of an intimate little dinner party for Jack. Something very special with champagne and caviar?"

"Does Jack like caviar? I don't even know."

"He told me once that he had never tried it. Too expensive, he said."

"Sounds good to me," said Archie, "but I think you should know that if you want all his friends to attend, then you better leave me off the guest list."

"Oh?" she murmured, looking somewhat perplexed. "But why?"

"Hasn't Jack told you anything about me and our so-called friends?"

"Like what?"

That was just like Jack, he thought; he was never one to talk about others. "Never mind," he said, "it's of no great importance. Now, what about this dinner?"

Her face suddenly sprang to life, and as she spoke of Jack and what she had in mind for him, there was a glow in her eyes, and quite unexpectedly, Archie felt jealous.

He found himself examining her closely; he had never seen her like that before. With her guard down, she was another person, and he noticed, for the first time, how deep blue her eyes were, and how large, with an incandescent quality about them that made them look quite lovely. He let his eyes wander down to her legs, so prim and properly placed together, and was surprised to see how well shaped they were. Then, lifting his eyes to her breasts, he thought how full and inviting they appeared as they strained against the silk of her blouse, and a ripple of excitement ran through him as he wondered what it would be like to uncover those soft peaks and fondle them.

She noticed the way he was looking at her, and in a state of confusion, she mumbled, "I ... I think I better leave," and rising to her feet, she took

a step toward the door. In a flash, Archie was between her and the doorway, blocking her from leaving. Her eyes widened in terror. "Please!" she
begged, but her plea fell on deaf ears.

What came over him, how or why, he could not have imagined. But he
suddenly wanted her in a way that he had never wanted a woman before. It
wasn't passion; it was a lust that seemed to have taken possession of him
and drove him to do terrible things, and suddenly he was tearing her clothes
and pinning her beneath him while she struggled with him to stop. The next
thing he heard was her pitiful wail when he thrust himself inside her.

When the consequences of what he had done hit him, it was too late.
Bruised and trembling, she was whimpering as she tried to put herself
together. Shaken, he stared down at her. He had never raped a woman
before, and this one, he didn't even find remotely attractive. What possessed him, he had no idea. Suddenly, the feeble sounds coming from her
lips got to him.... "Shut up, you silly bitch!" he bellowed.

Immediately, the whimpering stopped, and a pair of stark eyes stared
up at him in fear. He glared back, resenting her more than ever. Suddenly,
thoughts of Jack entered his head, and filled with anxiety, he grabbed her
by the shoulders and hissed, "If you dare say a word to Jack, or to anyone
else about this, I swear I will destroy your reputation. You came to my
room, remember? Explain that away if you can!"

She gasped, and the moment he let go, she picked up the rest of her
things and ran from the room as fast as her legs would carry her. He stood
by the door for a moment, listening to the clatter of her shoes on the stone
steps. When there was no longer a sound, he closed the door and sat down
to think.

He was filled with dread. He had done a terrible thing and was afraid
of what Jack might do, should he find out. The more he thought about it,
the more his anxiety grew, and he realized that if he wanted to save himself, he would have to get in first with his version of what took place. But
what could he say? What would be believable? Everyone knew him for
what he was. There was only one thing to do—be casual about it—and
later that day, people were chuckling. "What could I do?" he told everyone. "The lady came to my room looking for it, and being a gentleman,
I obliged!"

It was a cruel thing to say, to do to someone, and when it reached Jack's
ears, a pale and distraught figure came looking for him. "How could you?"
he cried. "How could you do something like that to me knowing how I
felt about her? You're rotten, rotten to the core. I've always known it, but

I never believed you would turn on me like that. We were supposed to be friends. Was it a joke to you? Or is that how your kind treat friends?"

He deserved Jack's anger, but it wasn't in his nature to admit to or apologize for anything. "What did she say happened?" he asked hesitantly.

"She didn't say anything. She's gone—gone before I had a chance to ask her about it. Just packed her bags and left Cambridge without so much as a note to me. I'll never forgive you for this, not as long as I live!"

Somewhat relieved, Archie said, "Well, there you have it! I did try to warn you about women, didn't I? None of them can be trusted, and now you know it as well as I."

Jack stared at him in disbelief. "You bastard!" he cried, and they were the last words he ever said to him.

Archie had lost the one true friend he had ever had, and if he could have, he would have gone back and changed everything, but "once the moving finger writes, it moves on." However misquoted, Jack would have appreciated that, he thought, and a great sadness descended upon him. He missed him very much. He missed his strength; he missed the scruples he had so often teased him about; but most of all, he missed the companionship of someone who really understood him when no one else cared or bothered to find out who he really was. Indeed, Jack understood him better than he understood himself.

One by one, his friends had deserted him; Jack was the last. In his wretchedness, he went from one degrading diversion to another in an attempt to relieve the loneliness, reaching depths of despair that he could never have imagined. He spent his days in despondency and his nights in wild abandonment. It was as if he was possessed by the devil; indeed, sometimes he believed that he was the devil, and hated himself for it, while at other times, the thought intrigued him. Jack had been his conscience, and without Jack, he had no conscience, and it gave him a form of freedom that had hitherto escaped him. Moral values no longer held him bound; yet this new freedom brought no happiness with it, only a price that he was all too willing to pay for a moment's diversion. The price was his soul and he destroyed it, along with everything else that crossed his path, and he almost destroyed Philip Peel for one moment of pleasure.

Peel's mother had come up to Cambridge to visit her son. Peel had never spoken of her; in fact, he kept her existence so quiet that Archie didn't even know if he still had a mother. So when he suddenly came face to face with her, he was not only surprised, but also completely struck by her extraordinary good looks. Add to this an earthy sex appeal and it was hard for Archie to imagine her as anyone's mother, let alone Peel's.

She was tiny like a doll and exquisitely proportioned. Platinum blonde curls framed a girlish face and exaggerated an already large and innocent-looking pair of blue eyes. Her full lips curled sensuously when she smiled, and made you want to kiss them passionately. The effect she had on the male population of Cambridge was riveting, and it embarrassed poor Peel no end, but it didn't bother her in the least; in fact, she reveled in it.

Archie had never experienced an older woman before, and here was a woman worth experiencing. Without a thought to Peel's feelings, he set out to seduce her, which, given her promiscuous nature, wasn't difficult, and before long, they were seen going off to his room together.

Everyone heard about it, and soon everyone was talking about it. The effect it had on poor Peel was devastating; he couldn't hold his head up, and had to suffer the indignity of smirks and eye rolling, and it drove him into a deep depression. When it was brought to Archie's attention, all he had to say was, "Am I to blame if his mother is such a tramp?"

Today, as he recalled making that insensitive remark, he shuddered at his lack of consideration. He had hurt Peel in the worst way that a young man can be hurt, and he was deeply sorry for the pain that he must have caused him. He was sorry for so many things that he did back then. He had been obsessed with living life to the fullest, with experiencing all the senses, the pure, the sordid, the noble, the base. Unfortunately, his experiences were more base than noble.

How many times had Jack tried to tell him how badly he was behaving? He would only brush him aside saying, "I only do what others think about. At least it's honest." Honest—is that what he really believed he was being? Wasn't he really deluding himself? he thought as he sat in the dark thinking back over his life.

Archie's last months at university were suddenly upon him. A lot of changes had taken place during the last year. A whole new breed of women was entering Cambridge. They were more aggressive, more in control of their lives, and unlike their former counterparts, whose only sexual drive was to lie on their backs, open their legs, and wait to receive, this modern woman called the tune. She knew exactly what pleased her and what didn't, and wasn't shy in making it known. She would also take the initiative when initiative was lacking in her partner.

The liberated woman was not to Archie's liking. He missed the fun of the chase; everything seemed to have changed in her favor, and when he was with one, he felt more like a puppet than a man.

He found it difficult to adjust. The majority of women were no longer fair game, and he had to be more selective in his choices. Of course, that his reputation was catching up with him didn't make things any easier; in fact, he was experiencing difficulty in many areas, including new friendships.

There was, however, an unsavory element who still enjoyed his company. They were a disreputable band who would frequent the more seedy cafés where marijuana was smoked and sometimes something a bit stronger. Drugs had never been Archie's scene, not that he hadn't tried marijuana, but he had never experienced that sense of potency that some claimed it gave them, and he saw it as a substance of the weak rather than the strong, and he believed in being strong. However, as an observer, the goings on did manage to amuse him, and he became a frequent visitor, along with his newfound friends.

There was a part-time waitress at one of the cafés, a young fifteen-year-old named Violet, who caught his eye. She worked evenings after school to make herself a little extra money. To look at, you would never have thought her the type to work in such a sleazy place. Whether it was because she was too shy, or too timid, she never spoke to anyone unless spoken to first, and even then, she would never look them in the eye.

She was too pretty to be left alone, and the boys would tease her mercilessly. For all the impact it had on her, she might have been deaf. Archie couldn't keep his eyes off her, with her fair skin and blue eyes that were fringed by the longest lashes he had even seen, she reminded him of his first girlfriend, when he was barely fourteen years old. She had come to visit an aunt and uncle who lived next door to him, and during her stay, they became friends, going to the cinema together, where they would hold hands. Sometimes, he would venture to put an arm around her and rub his thigh up against hers in the darkness. Whether she liked it or not, she never resisted.

It was his first taste of sensuality and he enjoyed it, and given the chance, he would have gone further. But as soon as his hand came near her breast, she would grab it and place it back on her shoulder once again.

When Archie's friends noticed how taken he appeared to be with Violet, they made a bet on how long it would take him to get her into bed. At first, he wanted nothing to do with it. He was no fool; the last thing he needed was to get caught making it with a minor. Nevertheless, knowing him, his friends increased the odds until it became too tempting for him to resist.

Even as he took on the bet, he knew that he was playing with fire, but it had been ages since he last gambled on anything, and he had almost forgotten what it was like to taste the excitement, to anticipate the big win, the kill. Not that this would be a big win, but it was enough to give that rush of adrenaline that he had so missed.

He knew women, and this one was like a timorous little mouse, running to hide at the least move. So he took it slowly, perhaps too slowly, and when she didn't respond as he expected, he was ready to give up when suddenly there was a turnaround on her part, and she agreed to go out with him.

Call it premonition, call it instinct, but it just didn't feel right. The turnaround was too swift and it troubled him somewhat, and if he could have, he would have backed out, but he was too much of a gambler; he had taken the bet, and now he had to stay with it.

They arranged to meet on Sunday. It was her suggestion that they make it for tea, as she had to be home by seven in the evening. He was not disappointed; in fact, he was glad. It was also her suggestion that he take her to a little village some ten miles north of Cambridge where there were some very pretty little tea shops. Again he was glad; he had no wish to be seen in town escorting such a young girl.

Not having a car at his disposal, they arranged to meet at the bus station at two in the afternoon. It was a lovely winter's day; the sun was shining and no wind to bite the flesh. She was already there, waiting, when he arrived. Despite the lipstick that was much too bright, she looked fresh and pretty, and any qualms that he might have had disappeared when he looked upon her sweet face.

The bus journey took forever, stopping every few minutes to pick up more passengers. Archie wished that he had a car. That was yet another grievance he held against his father. Suddenly, there was a long run between stops, and he tried to get her to talk about herself, but she was uncommonly reticent and he ended up telling her more about himself than he intended. Anyhow, from local gossip, he already knew quite a bit about her and her family. She came from a poor background. She had two older brothers. Her father was a drunk who hadn't worked in years. He was also thought to be abusive when drunk, especially to his wife and daughter. It was more speculation than fact; no one really knew the family that well—they kept very much to themselves.

Archie was relieved when they reached their destination. He was beginning to find her silence a bit of an ordeal and wanted to get the afternoon behind him as quickly as possible. He chose the first tea shop they came to. It was typical of the English countryside, with its bow windows, beamed ceiling, and a log fire burning in a brick fireplace.

They sat at a highly polished mahogany table. The chairs were wooden, straight-backed, and with little pallets to soften the hard seats. She didn't want anything but a cup of tea, and even that she didn't finish. He managed a scone with clotted cream and jam. The scone was heavy, and he only ate it for the want of something to do.

All through tea, Violet looked ill at ease, and not feeling all that comfortable himself, as soon as tea was over, he suggested that they return to Cambridge.

For the first time that afternoon, life crept into her eyes even if it was nothing more than a flicker of apprehension. "No!" she cried. Then somewhat confused, she said, "Er—I mean—well, a friend of mine has given me the key to her flat. It's just around the corner. I thought perhaps...." Her voice trailed off into a whisper, and her eyes filled with anxiety. "I'm sorry," she said, "I just thought that ... well, you know."

He stared at her, and seeing the look of disbelief on his face, she dropped her eyes in shame. "I'm sorry," she whispered again.

Unusually gentle, he said softly, "It's all right—it's all right. Anyhow, I think it best if I take you home right now."

Without lifting her eyes, she nodded.

On the bus back home, Archie asked, "Why did you agree to go out with me? It's pretty obvious that you are not comfortable about it."

She was staring out of the window, and the answer he received was a bare shrug of the shoulders. She was a strange girl, he thought, and decided not to press her further.

When they reached Cambridge, they waited for the bus to enter the bus yard before getting off. Somewhere along the route, the sun had gone behind the clouds that had gathered, and now it was dark and raining—that soft slow rain that went on for hours and hours. The streets, so bright and warm in the winter's sun, were now gray and cold. Archie lifted the hood of his duffle coat and shuddered. "I'm sorry," he said, "but I didn't bring an umbrella."

"I don't live far."

He hovered for a few seconds. The damp weather had made her skin glow, and he thought she really was pretty. "Well," he sighed, "I suppose I will see you at the café one evening."

"I suppose," she replied. Then, looking up at him for the first time since they left the tea shop, she asked anxiously, "Will you see me home?"

He hadn't expected her to ask, and after a moment's hesitation, he said, "Sure."

She lived in one of a terraced row of artisan cottages, and as they neared her house, the door suddenly opened and a man, with a huge belly that hung over the top of a pair of dirty gray trousers, came out onto the doorstep.

"Your father?" asked Archie.

Embarrassed, she nodded, and he thought that was all he needed.

When they reached the door, her father roughly grabbed hold of her arm and shoved her inside the house. "Everything in order?" abruptly he asked .

Archie glanced at her. Her reply was slow to come and strangely reluctant. "Yes," she whispered, and hung her head, but before he could give it any thought, her father turned on him.

"It better be," he barked, "or you'll be hearing from me."

Archie was confounded; he hadn't a clue as to what he meant, and it was a relief when the man slammed the door in his face and he was able to walk away without further ado.

When his friends saw him the next day, they were eager to hear all the details. It was a temptation that Archie couldn't resist, and grinning, he said, "There is nothing quite like deflowering a pretty young virgin!"

With a little over three months to the final examination, Archie used it as an excuse to avoid going back to the café where Violet worked. "If I don't get a first," he told his friends, "my 'old man' will surely disinherit me." If they were disappointed that he would no longer be joining them, he was much relieved. The last thing he wanted was to get himself entangled with Violet.

He did, in fact, throw himself into his work. He had grown up eating, sleeping, talking law. It was as much a part of him as the blood in his veins, and he wanted to do well. When June arrived, he was more than ready for it and went into the exam with every hope.

***

After a relatively mild winter and an early spring, summer burst forth in a blaze of flowers, warm breezes, and sunny days, and with the finals behind him, Archie was ready to enjoy what the season had to offer.

It was an exciting time, almost as exciting leaving Cambridge as it was entering the university on that first day. Archie glanced around the room. His clothes were packed. The bookshelves lay empty. The cupboards were bare, except for the hangers that dangled loosely, waiting for the next person to inhabit the room that was to become home to them for the next three years or so.

He opened all the drawers in the chest, to make certain that he hadn't forgotten anything; they were empty, and he closed them again. One last glance around, then suddenly the door burst open and one of his friends stood panting on the threshold. "Have you heard?" he asked breathlessly. "Violet is pregnant and her father is accusing you."

"What?" cried Archie in astonishment. "It's impossible. I had nothing to do with the girl, apart from that one afternoon!"

"It just takes once," said his friend.

"You don't understand; nothing happened that day."

"That's not what you told us."

Despite all his denials, no one believed him. He had a reputation, and it spoke for itself.

He arrived home that evening, only to be greeted by stony silence from his father. Immediately he guessed that he had somehow heard the news about Violet's pregnancy, and he braced himself for what was to come. At least, he thought, his father was bound to believe him when he heard all the facts.

No sooner was dinner over when his father rose and ordered him sharply, "In my study," then marched off.

Archie drew a deep breath. *This is it,* he thought, and glanced at his mother. She sighed heavily and gave him a pitying smile. He folded his serviette neatly, placed it in his serviette ring, rose slowly from the table, and followed his father out of the dining room and into his study.

His father's face was grim, and no sooner was Archie seated than he pounced. "You cannot keep out of trouble, can you? I warned you, I told you that I would not put up with your behavior forever! What have you to say for yourself under the circumstances?"

217

"I assume you are talking about Violet," he said. "I know that it looks bad, but there is no way that I could have made that girl pregnant. Her father is trying it on."

"Are you telling me that you did not seduce this minor?"

"I took her out for tea, then I took her home, and that was all. I swear!"

"That is not his version of what took place."

"I can't help what he says; he is lying!"

"Why would he lie? Someone made her pregnant, and he says that it's you. There must be more to it than you are telling me."

"There isn't. But you are right; there must be more to it. I think he knows who the father is, and that is why he is lying about it being me."

"You are not making any sense."

"I am if you knew the father and what he is capable of."

"What are you saying?"

"The man is a brute, he is a drunk, and he is abusive. You're a lawyer; put two and two together!"

Shocked, his father asked, "Do you know what you are saying?"

"I do, and I stand by it. There was something very strange about that girl; in fact, the whole afternoon was strange. I couldn't put my finger on it at the time, but now I am beginning to understand why she seemed so afraid of her father. There was a look of terror in her eyes when she saw him standing by the door, waiting for us. Perhaps, I better explain everything, then you might understand what I mean."

"I think perhaps you had better."

When Archie finished telling him about the café, the bet, and that Sunday afternoon when he took the girl out for tea, his father appeared thoughtful. "Hmm!" he murmured. "Did you confide your feelings, about that afternoon, to anyone else?"

The question took Archie by surprise. He had confided to his friends, but not the truth, and now he felt stupid. "I bragged about having her to some friends," he said embarrassed.

"What? What were you thinking of? Not only did you admit to something you claim you didn't do, but with a minor!"

"Well, you know how it is with boys," he said defensively, "we boast about such things, true or false."

"Well, true or false, you just might have landed yourself with a paternity suit."

"They wouldn't dare!"

"Why not? It's your word against theirs, and your boasting has provided them with ammunition."

"There are blood tests for such things that should prove I'm not the father."

"Only if your blood type differs from the child's, and who is to say that it will? Many people have the same blood type."

"I would be willing to take that chance."

"Well, I wouldn't! Whether he can prove you responsible or not, he is after money. I know the type, and only money will shut him up. He thinks he is onto a good thing. As for myself, I consider it a small price to pay to protect our good name."

Archie was appalled. "The truth is you don't believe me."

"Let's face it; you are not exactly a fountain of truth."

"That's unfair. I have never lied to you about something as important as this."

"There has never been something as important as this!"

"Thank you for that vote of confidence!"

"Believe me, Archie, nothing would please me more than to be proved wrong about you. Now, if you have given me all the necessary details, I think expediency is called for. So, if you will excuse me!" he said, and began to rummage through the papers on his desk.

It was his father's abrupt way of dismissing him, and filled with resentment, he slammed out of the room.

Although the matter with Violet's father appeared to be resolved, things were not going well between Archie and his father, and the thought of having to spend the rest of the summer at home with him breathing down his neck was not a pleasant one. When it seemed that he wouldn't be able to bear it much longer, he received an invitation from his mother's brother, Uncle Bertie, to spend time with him and his family at their summer home in Freshwater Bay on the Isle of Wight.

He had a sneaking suspicion that his mother had arranged for the invitation, but he was too relieved to be getting away to care one way or the other. Anyhow, he liked Uncle Bertie and his wife, Felicity. They were a great couple, if somewhat mismatched. His uncle was tall and as slim as a reed, and very serious about everything, while his wife was short, plump, and with a happy-go-lucky nature, yet somehow they managed to hit it off. Then there was Cousin Denise. She was great fun to be with, if a bit of a tomboy. The only fly in the ointment was their son, Cousin Bertram, who was a priggish bore, among other things, and Archie detested him.

He was twelve when he last spent two weeks at Uncle Bertie's home, and he remembered the time fondly. He and Denise got on like a house on fire, even though she was almost four years older than he. She was an unusual girl, with a razor-sharp wit and a tendency to play pranks, especially on her brother who always looked down on her with distaste. Archie thoroughly enjoyed her witty comments at Bertram's expense, and he and she became constant companions.

Two years later, he met her in London, quite by accident, and she told him that she had left home. Her parents had found out that she was a lesbian, and had made life unbearable for her, so she just left.

Archie had never suspected, and intrigued by the revelation, he asked, "What is it about men that makes you hate them?"

"I don't hate men; I simply prefer to be with a woman."

"Then do you actually … you know what?"

She laughed. "Of course."

"What's it like for you? I mean, is it the same as when you are with a man?" he asked with interest.

"I've never been with a man, but tell me, do you touch yourself?"

He went bright red. "I don't know what you mean!" he replied sheepishly.

"Oh, come on, Archie, all boys do it; it's nothing to be ashamed of."

No, it wasn't, he thought, and answered with a certain bravado. "All right! I do."

"Well, that's what it's like," she said. "Like touching yourself, only more exciting."

Once the invitation was accepted, his mother took him on a shopping spree. There were new outfits for tennis and for riding, not that he cared much for riding; he wasn't very good with horses, but his mother insisted. She had sat a horse very well in her day, and couldn't believe that a son of hers disliked riding. There were also some very natty clothes to go sailing in. Now, the thought of sailing excited him.

His uncle was a marine lawyer who loved the sea and kept a twenty-five-foot sloop at Cowes. The last time he was on the Isle of Wight, his uncle had taken him out a few times, but he wasn't interested back then. Now, he looked forward to learning more about sailing, especially as Denise was no longer at home to help amuse him.

Of course, Cousin Bertram never went out with his father; in fact, he never, ever went near the water if he could help it, much to his father's disappointment. He would get seasick simply thinking about sailing. He would have his uncle all to himself, and, as they got on so well, he was delighted not to have Bertram around to spoil what, he anticipated, would be a most pleasant time.

With so much to do, and so many new things to learn, the days passed quickly, and before he knew it, the end of September was near, and it was a bronzed and healthy-looking Archie who returned home to London.

While he was away, his parents received the news of his first-class law degree, and it was an unusually affable Sir Archibald who greeted him when he returned. He had even taken it upon himself to arrange articles for him with Haley & Son solicitors—a well-established and highly respected law firm in the West End of London. All that was left was for Archie to have an interview with Haley Sr., the outcome of which was a foregone conclusion.

As bad as they were before he left for Freshwater Bay, things between him and his father couldn't have been better upon his return. It seemed that those three little letters LL.B. made all the difference to him, and he actually treated Archie with some respect.

A few days after his interview with Haley Sr., Archie was reading the morning newspaper over breakfast, when an article, tucked away on the back page, caught his attention. The article was about a young girl, just turned sixteen, who had been found battered to death in an alley in the university town of Cambridge. Immediately, Archie's back stiffened and he anxiously read on. According to the pathologist's report, it said the murder had taken place elsewhere and the body was then dumped in the alley to make it look like a mugging had taken place. It also said that an autopsy revealed that the girl had recently given birth. No names were mentioned in the article, nor were there any clues as to the identity of the assailant or assailants.

Stunned, Archie put the paper down and stared across the table at his father. Noticing how the color had drained from his cheeks, his father asked with concern, "What is it?"

He passed the newspaper over to him and pointed out the article. After reading it, his father looked up and said, "It could be anyone."

He shook his head. "It's her," he said. "It's Violet. Don't ask me how, but I know it is."

Later that same day, they received a visit from the police. It appeared that Violet's father, when questioned, had told them that he saw Archie in the vicinity on the day the murdered body of his daughter was discovered. He also told them that he was the father of the child born to her, but that he had denied any responsibility.

On the day in question, Archie had been with his father all morning, and later, at an interview with Haley Sr. After checking his alibi, the police were satisfied that he could not have been in Cambridge, or anywhere near at the time the murder was reported to have taken place, and nothing further was heard from them.

They barely had time to draw a breath of relief, when Sir Archibald received a call from the dead girl's father. He wasn't satisfied with the outcome, and believed that, one way or another, Archie was involved in the death of his daughter, and swore that he would not rest until he was brought to justice.

Although he was aware that it was yet another shakedown, Sir Archibald made the decision to pay up anyhow, and went to Cambridge to resolve the matter once and for all, without letting his son know what he had decided.

When he returned, Archie was mad. "Why? There was no way that he could have made that accusation stick, you know that!"

"Maybe not," said his father, "but mud can and does, and I cannot afford a scandal; and as an aspiring lawyer, neither can you. Because of the nature of our profession, we have to be more careful than others."

"At least now you know that I have been telling the truth all along. The father is the villain here!"

"I know that you didn't kill that girl, and that is all that matters right now. As for her father, I never conjecture."

"No, you wouldn't, would you? You're too much the lawyer and not enough the father!" he said with a sneer. "All that concerns you is that your good name should remain intact. My innocence is inconsequential."

"That's not fair. Of course your innocence is important to me. I am your father, and what father wouldn't be relieved?"

"That is what I often ask myself! But the question here is, are you relieved for the right reasons?"

"Why must you always be so nitpicking? What is the matter with you, Archie? Why can't you be satisfied with what there is between us?"

"I wish I knew what that was. I'll bet you don't leave that illegitimate daughter of yours in any doubt."

His father's face hardened. "You don't know when to stop, do you? Well, for the record, you will never hold a candle to that child. Anyhow, I don't know what you have to complain about; you bear my name, she does not. If that doesn't satisfy you, then nothing I do ever will. Now be advised, I do not want to hear another word against her. Whatever my relationship is with her and her mother, I have seen to it that you have never lost by it."

"That goes to show how much you know or care."

"Enough, I say! There are limits to my patience, Archie, so don't push it. Now, I am fully prepared to overlook this entire conversation. I will simply put it down to stress on your part. We have both been through a very trying time. It is unfortunate for the young girl who was murdered, but it has nothing more to do with us, so let us put the incident behind us and get on with our lives."

Archie glared at his father. He had never hated him more than at that moment. Yes, he was going to put the incident, as his father called it, behind him and get on with his life, not because he said so, but because he realized that is exactly what had to be done, and it frightened him. He was more like his father than he cared to admit. Perhaps that was at the root of all their problems. They may have been cut from the same cloth, but he wasn't as strong as he was; his father never weakened, whereas he did, and he couldn't afford to weaken or he would be lost forever. So he took a deep breath and hardened his heart once and for all.

CHAPTER FOURTEEN

Archie thought of each phase of his life as a new beginning, and each time he made up his mind to do better, to be better. Whether trouble followed him around or he looked for trouble was a matter of opinion.

Haley & Son solicitors was a new beginning, and when Archie first walked into their offices, it was with the best of intentions. Perhaps if Alfred Sr. had been there to meet him, those intentions might not have evaporated as swiftly as they did. It was Alfred the son, a shrewd-eyed, haughty individual, who was on hand for his introduction into the firm, and the chemistry for a promising beginning simply wasn't there. Indeed, there was an instant dislike between them, and it showed in the manner in which Alfred greeted him. "I don't know what you expected from my father," he said sharply, "but he has left it to me to see that you get the proper grounding you need. He does nothing but trusts. Now if you will follow me, I will introduce you to the clerk with whom you will be working; then he can introduce you to the rest of the staff."

Immediately, Archie's back was up. He had expected VIP treatment and felt slighted by the absence of the senior partner. He was also indignant of the offhand manner with which his son spoke to him, and he decided not to let it pass without some show of displeasure. "Under the circumstances, it will do," he said somewhat haughtily.

Alfred's shrewd eyes glared at him with hostility. "One more thing," he said coldly. "I do not tolerate unpleasantness between my articled clerks, no matter who their father happens to be. Do I make myself clear?"

"Perfectly!" he replied with a smirk.

He could tell from Alfred's obvious annoyance that he had him ruffled, and it gave Archie a great amount of satisfaction. No one, he thought smugly as he followed him down the corridor to the general office, was going to get the better of him.

The first job he was given by the senior clerk was to acquaint himself with all the legal forms—a task he considered menial for someone of his education and background. But then, as the clerk pointed out, "We all have to start at the bottom, and that goes for you, too, Bingham!"

It wasn't so much what he said, but how he said it that irritated Archie. It was as if there was a conspiracy to humble the son of Sir Archibald Bingham, Q.C. Well, he had never been humble in his life and he wasn't about to begin, especially now, he thought. Maybe, as an articled clerk, a certain amount of humility was expected of him, but facts were facts; he could no more help having the weight of his father's eminence behind him than he could help being who he was, and if people did tend to find him a mite presumptuous, it was hardly his fault if the circumstances were such that they afforded him that particular luxury.

Indeed, it wasn't the best of beginnings. Nevertheless, if he had trouble getting along with members of his own gender, he got on superbly well with the females on staff. They would fall over themselves in an effort to please the handsome young gentleman in their midst. He never experienced the problems others had when they needed something to be done; his needs were attended to first and foremost. He didn't exactly gloat, but then neither was his attitude apologetic, and matters only grew worse between him and the rest of the male staff.

It wasn't until the end of his first week that Haley Sr. came by to see how he was fitting in with the office routine. No one could have denied Archie's capabilities; his quick brain had picked up on the day-to-day routine in record time, and he was now bored and wanted to be given something more important to dig his teeth into.

Haley smiled sympathetically when he complained to him. "You must learn patience," he said. "All in good time, Archie, all in good time!"

"If only I could work with you, sir. Everyone else seems to underestimate my intelligence, including your son."

"I do understand how you feel, but a good all-around grounding is necessary. Every young clerk has to go through it."

"But sir, it's holding me back."

"I can see that you are really bothered," he said with concern. "I'll tell you what. I'll speak to Alfred and see if he will take you under his wing. You would learn a lot from him."

"Why not from you, sir?"

"My work is trusts. It would only bore one so young."

"Never, sir, not with you as my teacher."

Haley laughed. "I don't know about that! But we can have another chat on Monday if you like," and without waiting for a reply, he shuffled back to his office.

***

When Archie made up his mind about something, neither hell nor high water could stop him from going after it. He had no intention of working under Alfred's direction; he couldn't abide the man, and it would only be a recipe for disaster. There was no love lost either way; he hadn't even come by once to see how he was doing. So much for his interest in him!

He knew exactly what he needed to do, and that weekend, he went to the reference library and took out as many books on trusts as he could find and studied all through Saturday and Sunday, burning the midnight oil in an effort to learn as much as he could on the subject.

Monday morning, well before the rest of the staff was due to arrive, he knocked on Haley's door. He knew that he would be there; it was known that he started at eight in the morning. "Come," called out Haley in that slow drawl of his.

Archie opened the door and stepped inside. He hadn't been in his office before and found it to be much larger than any of the others. Its walls were lined with books. A huge desk, piled high with papers, stood in the center; a few leather chairs were scattered around; and a large Persian carpet covered most of the woodblock floor. The only daylight came from a stained-glass window.

Haley's gray head was bent over some documents, and he murmured, without looking to see who it was, "Yes? What is it?"

"It's Monday, sir, you said we would have another chat."

Haley lifted his head in surprise. "My word! You are an eager beaver."

"Yes, sir, very eager to persuade you to take me under your wing. I really do have an interest in trusts, and I can promise that you won't regret it."

"I am certain that I wouldn't," he said, "but it's your interest that I have at heart, not mine. I really don't know what to do with you. I didn't think to concentrate on trusts until late in my career, and that is when I found I had a good head for the work. Of course, today, I am considered an authority on the subject."

"I am aware of it, sir. My father has often spoken of you and the fine work that you do. In fact, he holds you in high esteem, and that is why I hope to make you change your mind."

"Is that so?" he said, looking very pleased with himself. "I suppose it can be said that I know my stuff!"

"Indeed, sir!"

"Hmmm!" he murmured thoughtfully. "Upon further reflection, I could do with some help in my department. On the other hand, it would be unfair of me to keep you all to myself. I would be failing in my duty toward you if you were to leave here without the good general experience that you need."

Archie felt he had to convince him. He had a peculiar notion that his success or failure, somehow, depended upon it. "Sir," he cried in desperation, "you would not be failing in your duty toward me. Ever since I can remember, law has been an integral part of my life, and with my father's guidance, I have gained a deep understanding of it and its workings. Sir, it comes to me as naturally as breathing comes to a newborn child. It could not have been otherwise for the son of Sir Archibald Bingham! I know that I am more than capable of working with you and, at the same time, getting that all-around experience that is so essential to the making of a fine lawyer. All that remains is for you to give my request some serious consideration. Please, sir?" he finished with the edge of a begging tone in his voice.

There was a twinkle of amusement in Haley's tired old eyes. "You are making it very difficult for me to deny such an articulate appeal, but I'll tell you what—if you can answer my questions correctly, I will see what I can do. Is that fair enough?"

"Fair enough!" he sighed with relief.

Haley smiled kindly. "Now, let me see—I suppose the place to start would be with the basic elements of a trust. Tell me, what do you know of the rule against perpetuities?"

Archie could not have asked for a simpler question, and he smiled broadly. "A trust must not go beyond a lifetime plus twenty-one years," he replied smartly.

Haley nodded approval, then went on to his next question. "Explain the difference between a discretionary trust and an absolute trust?"

Again, it was an easy question, but he thought it wise to appear to be giving it some thought. "In a discretionary trust," he began with some deliberation, "the trustees can use their discretion as to what they invest the trust in. Now in the absolute one, they have to follow the wording of the trust document as to what they can invest in."

Haley stroked his chin. "You have done well," he said, "so this is what I propose: you will spend two afternoons a week looking into the documents with me, and the rest of the time, you will work in the general department. I cannot stress enough the importance of receiving proper instruction into the fundamentals of law. Now, what do you say to that?"

"You will not regret the decision. I will work very hard; and, sir, I cannot tell you how excited I am at the prospect of working under your guidance."

Haley laughed. "I wouldn't be too excited if I were you, I have every intention of making you work as hard as possible."

"And I would not have it any other way. I am here to learn, and from whom better than the master himself."

He smiled. "I don't know about that, but flattery will get you what you want. Now!" he exclaimed on a more serious note. "I must discuss the matter with my son and see which afternoons would be suitable. Either he or I will let you know in due course."

"What if he doesn't agree?" Archie asked anxiously.

"No need to fear; he will agree."

"Thank you, sir," he said, and took his leave.

Archie suspected that Alfred would try and put obstacles in the way of his working with his father, but "old man" Haley had a reputation for being as good as his word, and so he felt confident of victory. It was important to him; any victory over Alfred was important. He viewed him as being the enemy in his struggle against the powers that be. He was never able to bend to authority, and Alfred liked to flaunt his authority in his face.

When he arrived at the office next morning, just as he expected, an argument between father and son was in progress. The whole office could hear Alfred's raised voice as he shouted angrily at his father. "You had no right to make such a decision until you spoke to me first. If help is what you need, then we will engage someone who knows what they are doing, but Bingham! It's ridiculous! Apart from anything else, I don't trust him. Just because he happens to be the son of someone you admire doesn't mean that you should let him look into something as sensitive and important as a trust document. You can't go judging people solely by their family connections, and if you do, then you are a fool!"

For the first time since working at the firm, Archie heard Haley Sr. raise his voice above a murmur. "Are you calling me a fool? Because if you are, I take strong exception!"

Realizing his mistake, Alfred tried to smooth it over. "It's nothing more than a figure of speech; you know that, Father."

"Figure of speech or not, I am still the senior partner in this firm, and what I decide stands!"

"I haven't forgotten who is the senior partner, but as a partner and your son, I feel it is my duty to let you know when I think you are making a mistake, and I happen to think you are making a big one. I wouldn't want him snooping around in my office!"

"Then you have nothing to fear. After this little outburst, I would not think of letting Archie work in your office. Now on your way out, kindly have the decency to advise him that I want to see him right away. I will inform him myself of what has been decided."

"Good. The less I have to do with him, the better," he snapped as he stormed out.

Not wanting Alfred to catch him standing in the corridor listening, Archie ducked into an empty room and emerged just as he was passing. After a contemptuous glance in his direction, Alfred said brusquely, "My father wishes to see you immediately. For your information, you have what you want, but put a foot wrong and you will answer to me. Is that clear?"

Archie grinned and nodded in reply, then proceeded to Haley's office.

He was to work Tuesday and Thursday afternoons with Haley in his department, and the rest of the week he would be taking his orders from the senior clerk. It may not have been to his satisfaction, but it was an improvement over the previous arrangement, and for the moment, he was satisfied.

Archie's father was surprised when he told him about the decision and commented, "I had no idea that kind of work would be to your taste. You always seemed to me to be more suited to litigation. But then, you never know, do you?"

Archie just couldn't resist. "Is that a question, Father?" he asked contemptuously. "Because if it is, then my answer would have to be you, most certainly, wouldn't know!"

His father huffed. "You think you are being very clever, don't you? Well, sometimes a person can be too clever for his own good. Now, you just remember that."

"Oh, I certainly will, Father. I remember everything that comes from your hallowed lips."

"I was going to talk to you about getting a place of your own, but with this sarcastic mood you are in, I can see it would be useless talking to you about anything."

"On the contrary, I was ready to talk to you about it. As a matter of fact, I have found a nice little flat further down the Bayswater Road. The rent is reasonable and it's partly furnished, so it won't need much. A few extras, that's all, and I will be out from under your feet. That should please you."

"I will not qualify that remark with a reply, and as for the few extras, I am certain your mother will look after your needs—she always does. Now, if you don't mind, I have some work to do."

"Dismissed, Private Bingham!" exclaimed Archie. "Back to the trenches where you belong."

His father ignored his outburst the way he often did when he was being facetious. It wasn't that Archie intended any impertinence, but that is how his father affected him. Just being in the same room as he seemed to arouse defiance on his part. The tragedy was that, deep down, he yearned for his father's approval, but all that his rebellious nature was able to invite was exasperation.

The arrangement at the office appeared to work well. Archie was getting the general experience he needed and, at the same time, he was learning a great deal about trust deeds, and by the end of the first six months, the two afternoons a week in the trust department had stretched to two full days.

It had become a bone of contention between Alfred and his father, but the elderly Haley could be stubborn when he chose, and his son's complaints continued to fall on deaf ears.

It irritated him that Archie had the acceptance of his father, but never more so than when he confronted him and Archie had that gloating look of triumph on his face.

"You think you are winning, don't you?" Alfred said one day. "Well, you have two more years to go, and it may be another story by then."

"I wouldn't count on it!"

"We'll see!" he replied, and was about to walk away, when he suddenly asked with suspicion, "What's your real interest in trusts, Bingham? It can't be the work, not for someone with your temperament."

"I've had no complaints from your father. What's your complaint?" he asked with contempt.

Alfred glared at him for a few seconds, then turned and walked away.

Much to his surprise, Archie didn't find the work as boring as he thought he might. That is not to say that he found it particularly riveting, but he did find it intriguing. Some of the trusts were worth hundreds of millions of pounds, making his mother's trust of a few million appear positively paltry in comparison. He couldn't help wondering about the beneficiaries of such huge amounts. Who were they? What were they like? What kind of lives did they lead with so much wealth at their disposal? Sometimes, he would feel quite envious of these ghosts with a name but no faces to put to them, and then he would become dissatisfied with his own status, believing himself worthy of more.

One place where his worth was appreciated was in Haley's department. He found that he had a flair for the work, and Haley was delighted. Indeed, he had a flair for every aspect of the law and with the exception of Alfred, no one could find fault with anything that he did; and so time passed, a little too slowly for Archie, perhaps, but then he never did have much patience. When he wanted something, he wanted it now, and he could hardly wait to qualify and get out of there and be his own master.

A year went by, then eighteen months, and all appeared well. Alfred and he had managed to avoid one another, for most of the time. Haley and he had become very close, almost like father and son, and as for the rest of the office staff, they had got used to Archie and his flamboyant style and no one really took notice any longer.

Summer began during that second year with a heat wave, and without air-conditioning to cool the temperatures inside, the office became stifling. The coolest place was a back room, which was shielded from the heat of the sun by an inner courtyard. Archie would go there every now and then to cool down and enjoy a quiet cigarette.

That is where he was one afternoon, when a hurricane by the name of Abigail Stuart blew into the offices of Haley & Son. Abigail was a longtime friend of Alfred's and the rumor was that they were unofficially engaged. He'd heard stories of how attractive she was, but nothing that had been said prepared him for the vision of loveliness that was Abigail. By anyone's definition, she was a stunner. Flaming red hair hung loosely about a pair of exquisite shoulders, bared because of the heat. Extraordinary green eyes looked at you with more than a hint of flirtation. Her pale skin was flawless, her figure voluptuous, and her well-shaped legs seemed to go on forever. She was all woman, and she was breathtaking.

The very instant they made eye contact, he knew that he would have her—the only question was when. He knew women, and Alfred or no Alfred, she was as ready for an affair as ever he had seen. It took a week before a relationship began; it would have been sooner if she had come by the office sooner. But then, the unpredictable Abigail didn't like to appear anxious.

Abigail was a prize worthy of exhibit. A man's ego soared with a woman like that on his arm, and Archie was no exception. Soon everyone at the office was talking about their involvement, at first in whispers, then quite openly. It hit Alfred hard. She'd had affairs before; he never liked it, but he lived with it. Her affair with Archie was too much for him; there was no discretion on their part, and if that wasn't humiliating enough, he hated Archie with a vengeance.

"You don't care if you hurt Alfred, do you?" said Archie after he and Abigail had been out dancing one evening, and had bumped into him.

"Do you care?" asked Abigail.

"I am not the one who is practically engaged to him!"

"Neither am I!"

"But I thought––!"

"I can't help what you or anyone else thinks. Until there is a marriage agreement, I am free to do what I like and with whom I like."

"Marriage agreement? That sounds very cold to me."

Their relationship was wild and tempestuous. Abigail took great pleasure in teasing, and the torment drove Archie mad with desire. They were like two savages when they were together; she would claw and scratch, and draw blood when she was aroused. He would bite and bruise and take her with a viciousness that was drawn from a need to satisfy his animal instincts, and the more brutal he became, the more he aroused her.

For a while, it seemed that they would never be able to get enough of each other, but even their strong sexual appetite began to show signs of exhaustion. That was when Archie saw her in her true light; she could be devious, calculating, and spiteful. In other words, he had found his match.

What he disliked the most about her was her habit of overspending, especially when it was his money. She wanted the best and expected to have it. Whether it was the theatre, a restaurant, or a weekend away at an hotel in the country, only the best pleased her, and Archie found himself spending far more than he could afford. He had an inability to say no when it came to pleasure, and it was as if she had discovered his weakness and relied upon it to get what she wanted. It eventually reached a stage where it caused friction between them, and in his frustration, Archie turned to gambling.

Archie's addiction to gambling was like a smoker's addiction to nicotine: he may have been able to give it up for a while, but never for long. He missed the excitement—the adrenaline rush that accompanied the laying of a bet, the risk that was so compelling. It was a disease that, when awakened, needed to be fed, fed, and fed.

He managed an introduction into a private gaming club in Curzon Street, and that is where you could find him every evening, sitting at one of the tables waiting intensely for a wheel to stop or a card to be turned. The one time that Abigail accompanied him, he blamed her for his bad luck that evening, and a row broke out between them. They were asked to leave, and angered, he hit her when they got home.

She threatened to leave him, and might have done if it were not for the strong tie that kept them bound. If Archie was a slave to gambling, she was a slave to sex, and he had proved to be the best lover she had ever experienced, and so she stayed the course.

His gambling ended as abruptly as it began. His losses were heavier than usual one evening, when, without warning, credit was denied him. Offended, he demanded to see the manager of the establishment.

"Sorry, sir," said the croupier, "the order came from the manager."

"Then I want to see the owner," he cried indignantly.

"That's impossible; he sees no one," replied the croupier.

He was ready to lose his temper when a voice behind him said, "Let him have another thousand, Jimmy."

"Very good, Mr. Fellini," said the croupier, "if you say so."

Archie turned to take a look at his benefactor. He was a middle-aged man, shorter than average, with a swarthy complexion, dark eyes, and long dark hair that was greased back and worn in a ponytail. He didn't recognize him, but the name Fellini had a familiar ring to it; he just couldn't place it. "Thank you," he said, "but there must be some mistake. I don't know why I have been denied credit; they know I am good for it."

"But of course you are," said Fellini. "Why wouldn't the son of Sir Archibald Bingham be good for a measly few thousand!"

Archie didn't like the man's insolent tone, but then he was curious as to how he knew who his father was. "Have we met before?" he asked.

"Let me introduce myself. I am Armand Fellini, the brother of Dante. Now that is a name you should remember well!"

"I'm afraid not."

"Then let me remind you. Your father was the prosecuting council in a rape case against my brother. Your father made the front page, as always, but never quite in the way he did that time."

Archie resented the manner in which Fellini referred to his father and sneered with contempt. "My father is a crown prosecutor. There have been many such cases; I can't be expected to recall every one."

"I was in court that day, as you were, and I saw the look on your face when your father lost the case. Or should I have said, mishandled it? You wouldn't forget something like that."

Archie was trembling with anger. He wanted to punch the man in the jaw, and it took every ounce of strength to refrain. "Yes," he said. "I remember, and I remember your father's phone call that same morning, and his threat of blackmail, so if you will excuse me, I'm leaving right now. I have no need of dirty money!"

Fellini's hand caught hold of his arm and prevented him from turning away. It was a strong grip for such a slight man, and it bit into his flesh. "Don't try to play high and mighty with me," he said. "We have a lot in common, you and I!"

"I think not!"

"More than you think," replied Fellini. "There is your father's mistress; neither of us is happy about that, are we?"

"Remove your hand or I will call the manager," said Archie.

"Lola! You can't forget that name, and you can't forget her once you have seen her, and she is the woman your father loves."

"I'm not interested—not in her, not in you, not in anyone mixed up with your kind of people."

"And what kind of people is that? What kind of person do you think Lola is? Or Belinda, her daughter—the lovely, sweet, gentle Belinda. What kind of person is she?"

"I told you. I'm not interested in my father's whore or her daughter, and there is nothing that you can say that will make me change my mind."

"If you don't care, then why are you so bitter?"

"I'm not bitter. Why should I be? I am my father's son and legitimate heir; the whole world knows that. I am not some dark, dirty little backroom secret."

"Call them names if it makes you feel better, but it doesn't alter the fact that they have as much right to him as you have, perhaps more so. But I doubt you will ever hear the truth from your father, and that is what I am offering you—the truth—if it's what you really want to hear."

"You are holding me captive, so talk; not that I promise to listen to a word of what you have to say."

Fellini let go of his arm and spread his hands. "See?" he said. "I'm no longer stopping you. You are free to leave whenever you choose, but you won't leave because you do want to know. I can see it in your eyes, all the unanswered questions that have been building in your mind over the years like: When did they meet? How did they meet? Does he feel more for them than he does for me? Questions that can drive a young man crazy with not knowing."

"You're crazy if you think I am prepared to believe you."

"I don't care if you believe me or not, but you are going to hear what I have to say because it has to be said."

Archie swallowed. There was something mesmerizing about the man and the manner in which he spoke that held him to the spot. "Go on, if you must!"

"Yes," he whispered. "I am going to tell you everything you have ever wanted to know…. They met at my father's studio, long before he married your mother. That's right—long before! Lola was fifteen when her mother brought her to us for a screen test. Your father was there on some legal business that day, and he fell instantly in love with her, as we all did. She was so beautiful, more beautiful than anyone I had ever known, but no one had a chance against the handsome Archibald Bingham. Despite the fact that she was under age, he swept her off her feet, set her up in a flat, and she became his mistress. I was angry, so angry that I had in mind to go to the police. Statutory rape, that's what they call it. How many times since has he prosecuted someone for the very same offence! Sometimes I wish that I had gone to the police."

"Then why didn't you, if you felt so strongly about it? No guts?"

Fellini stared at him. "That would have solved all your problems, wouldn't it?" he said. "Well, I didn't go to the police because I realized that she loved him, and I couldn't hurt someone that I loved. If only your father had felt the same way, he would have married Lola instead of your mother; but then, Lola didn't have the right name or the right background, not to mention the wealth your mother brought to the marriage. All Lola could give him was love, and that wasn't enough for him. He wanted it all, and between them both, he had it all."

"That's a lie," cried Archie. "My grandparents would never have allowed my mother to marry someone who kept a mistress!"

"I didn't say they knew. Do you think your father would let it be known that he was sleeping with a minor?"

"A whore you mean! No decent woman would act in one of those filthy movies."

"You are right, they wouldn't, and neither did she. It was her mother's idea. She saw the potential for making money, and she would have done it if Lola had been that kind of person. If your father hadn't taken her when he did, she would have left the studio of her own free will. She was as pure and virginal on the inside as she was lovely on the outside. Not that it did her much good; it almost killed her when your father married your mother, and that was despite the love he professed to have for her."

"Rubbish! No moral woman would go on sleeping with a man after he marries another, so don't give me that stuff about how pure and virginal she was."

"Don't judge until you have heard the whole story. When your father got engaged to your mother, Lola was with child at the time, and she decided not to tell him in the hope that he would change his mind and marry her instead without any undue influence. It was a child's dream; but then, she was a child—a lovely, innocent, naïve child. The day your father married your mother, Lola was so distressed that she miscarried. She nearly died herself. You see, she didn't want to go on living without him.

"It was I who saw her through those dark days. I couldn't let her give up on life—it's so precious, she was so precious, and, despite everything, she pulled through. She never told your father about the miscarriage, or that she nearly died in losing their baby, and to this day, he knows nothing about it. She didn't want him to feel responsible in any way. Now, is that love or not? She was even ready to give him up for your mother's sake, but that didn't suit your father's plans. He still wanted her, and in the end, she weakened. Love didn't leave her much choice."

"She had a choice; she just didn't make it. But then, she is a whore after all."

Fellini's eyes blazed with anger, and, for a moment, Archie thought he was going to hit him. "Call her a whore once more and I'll knock your teeth out," he cried. "She wasn't the one who sold herself for gain; that was your father. So what do you call a man who does that?"

"How dare you! You are speaking of one of the most highly regarded lawyers in the country. Don't you compare him to a pimp like your-self!"

"Calling me names may give you satisfaction, but the truth will come out. It can only be kept hidden for so long. If you truly care about it, then go and take a good look at their daughter's face. That's where you will find the truth—in that child's beauty, in her gentleness, her sweetness. No whore brought that girl into this world; love did. They live in—"

"I know where they live. I don't need you to tell me anything, not about them or my father, so why the hell should I bother to take a look at her? She is nothing to me, less than nothing."

"Oh yes, you do. You're just burning with curiosity, and you will go and take a look at Belinda because I've got to you. Well, when you do, if you can still find it in your heart to hate or resent her, then you are no man, but a cold lump of flesh without a drop of red blood running through your veins. At least your father did one thing right in his life."

There was a gentleness in Fellini's hard eyes as he spoke of Belinda, and it stirred Archie's heart far more than anything he'd said. It was as if he had already looked upon her face and saw the truth that Fellini spoke of, and it made him feel uncertain. It is not easy to shed a hate that had grown with you over the years. It would be like losing an integral part of yourself, and he wasn't ready for it, if, indeed, he ever would be.

Fellini was staring at him with that distant look in his eyes that one has when gazing into the past. Archie swallowed. "I've heard enough," he said and turned away.

Fellini didn't try to stop him, and Archie walked out of the club, up Curzon Street, and on to Marble Arch which was close to where he had his flat. He felt empty, strange, not like himself. Fellini had managed to unsettle him, putting bizarre ideas into his head. Of course, he was lying; he wanted to get at him for some reason, and he had almost allowed him to.

Abigail was waiting for him when he got home. In the mood he was in, he had forgotten all about her. She came out of the bedroom when she heard him come in, and stood in front of him trying to entice him the way she usually did, wearing nothing but a black, see-through pair of cami-knickers. Normally she would have succeeded, but that evening, it only sickened him.

Perhaps if she hadn't come on to him in that slinky fashion of hers, he might not have struck her, but he did and with such force that it sent her reeling across the room. With a hand to a swelling jaw, she glared at him in disbelief. He took no notice, went over to her, pulled her to her feet, and drew her with him into the bedroom.

Without a word, this fiery creature followed him like a lamb to the slaughter, and allowed him to make love to her with an angry passion that had more to do with frustration than desire.

Theirs had been an intense relationship, love-hate, you might say, with moments of obsession and others of fury that were expressed in sexual exploits that were suited to both of their explosive personalities. In fact, Abigail was as complex a person as he was, and, if anything, more manipulating.

After meeting Fellini, a subtle change had come over Archie, and nothing was ever the same again between him and Abigail. "What is it?" she asked one evening. "You seem to be remote, different."

"In what way?"

"I don't know, but it makes me feel cheap whenever you make love to me."

"If you don't like it, you know what you can do," he said coldly.

It was the last straw. "That's it, as far as I'm concerned," and she leapt off the bed, scooped up her clothes from the floor, and took them with her to the bathroom.

"You'll be back," he called after her. "You always are."

"Never!" she cried.

He believed her this time. *Bitch!* he thought, and threw off the bed covers, followed her to the bathroom, tore the clothes out of her hands, pushed her against the wall, and took her.

Sex was at the very heart of their relationship. Without it, there would have been little to keep them together. It won Abigail over every time, and that evening was no different. Afterwards, she said to him, "You can be such a bastard. Alfred has never treated me the way you do. If I had any sense, I would have stuck to my guns and left."

"You couldn't do that because I give you too much pleasure, far more than that suffocating prig could ever give you, I'll bet."

"That's my business!"

"As long as you are with me, your business is my business, and don't forget it."

"I'm surprised you haven't asked me how I rate you as a lover."

"I already know how I rate."

"You really think you're it! Well, you are not the only fish in the sea."

He grinned wickedly. "The only fish that can satisfy you."

"Huh!" she exclaimed with indignation. Nevertheless, she couldn't help admitting to herself that he was right. No one had ever thrilled her the way he did.

Another evening he asked her, "Alfred isn't your type. What is it that you are after—his money?"

"We are friends. We grew up together."

"What about the rumor that you two will marry one day?"

"Since when do you take notice of rumors?"

"What, exactly, are you saying?"

"I am saying that I wouldn't pay too much attention to them if I were you."

"So does that mean you are waiting to see if you can do better before settling for him?"

Her green eyes flashed with anger. "You can be such a rotter when you choose."

His lips twisted into a facetious grin. "Because I see through you?"

He caught her wrist as she was about to slap him. "Because you don't really give a fig," she hissed angrily, and pulled her arm free.

Bound by one common denominator—desire—their stormy relation-ship continued despite its many trials. It was after making love with their usual fevered intensity, one late afternoon, that she suddenly rose from the bed and started to dress. "I have to leave," she said. "I have a dinner engagement. I could return later if you want."

He was angry. "Leave now and you don't ever come back!"

"Don't be such a pig, Archie. I'm not going because I want to. I prom-ised a girlfriend that I would have dinner with her and I am already late. She isn't someone I can afford to let down."

"Why? What has she got on you?"

"Why must you always think the worst?"

"Because, my dear, I know you better than anyone else does."

"Not as well as you think! As a matter of fact, she happens to be one of the richest women in London, probably in the whole of England if you don't count the Queen, and I am her best and only friend. So why would I let someone like that down, even for you?"

"If she is as rich as you say, I doubt you are her only friend!"

"Well, I am, and if you met her, you would understand why. She is not your average pretty little heiress, dressed to the hilt and eager to be seen dancing at the latest hot spot. She is retiring, has no dress sense whatso-ever; in fact, she is plain and dull by anyone's standard. Apart from hav-ing dinner with me occasionally, she never goes anywhere, except to one of her charities, that is."

"Then how come you?"

"We used to live next door to one another as children. That was before Daddy lost most of his money on a deal that went sour and we had to move to a more modest house. Anyhow, we never lost touch. The truth is she has been very generous to me over the years; so you see, I cannot afford to lose her."

"I knew there had to be a catch somewhere!"

"Well, why not?" she cried with indignation. "She has more money than she knows what to do with. She never goes on holiday. She never buys herself anything decent to wear. She just sits in that mansion of hers—day in, day out—with a bevy of servants to look after her every wish. Not that she ever wishes for anything—doesn't even decide on the food she eats—they just put whatever they want in front of her. It makes my blood boil when I think what I could do with all that money!"

"Well, as you said, she is generous to you!"

"I try my best for her, believe me, I do. She is not the easiest person in the world to be with; she is a first-class bore, so if I reap a few benefits, why not? She can afford it."

"I'm not arguing! What is the name of this benefactor of yours?"

"Patricia Nesbitt."

"What?" exclaimed Archie in surprise. "Not the Patricia Nesbitt of the Nesbitt Trust?"

"The very same."

"Oh, brother!"

"Now you know what I mean."

"Indeed, I do! What happened to her parents? Old man Haley is very tight-lipped when it comes to giving out personal information on a client."

"They died in a plane crash when she was fourteen. She was their only child. I really don't think she is aware of just how much she is worth. She is so mean to herself. I tell you, it's galling!"

"What does she look like?"

"I told you, plain and dull."

"No one can be plain and dull with that much money!"

"She can, trust me!"

"As far as I can see you!"

"That's not very funny. What's happened to us, Archie? We used to be closer than this."

"Things change. You've changed."

"I haven't changed, but you have."

He gave an unconcerned shrug. "Maybe," he said.

"Well, I have to go."

"I'll go with you."

"You're joking!"

"I'm serious. Take me with you."

"She will only bore you."

"Let me worry about that."

She gazed at him for a moment or two, then asked suspiciously. "Why would you want to meet her? What have you got up your sleeve?"

He stretched out his arms. "I don't see any sleeves. Do you?" he said with a grin.

"Stop playing the fool; it doesn't suit you."

"So am I going with you or not?

"All right, but afterwards, don't say that I didn't warn you."

The arrangement was to meet in the lounge of the Savoy Hotel. Patricia was already there when they arrived. The moment she saw Abigail, her pale lips broke into a smile. Then, when she noticed Archie with her, apprehension replaced the wan smile.

Archie, who had been eager to meet her, was filled with disappointment. Abigail hadn't exaggerated. She was plain, plain and dull, dressed in a gray tweed skirt and dark green twin set without a single piece of jewelry that did anything to liven it up. Her hair, a mousy brown, hung lifelessly around a long face that was somewhat flat in appearance.

She blushed when introduced to him, and dropped her eyes in embarrassment when he spoke to her. "I hope you don't mind my tagging along," he said. "Actually, it was Abigail's idea. You see, I was all alone this evening, feeling totally miserable, and you know Abigail, always concerned about others!" and he gave her one of his disarming smiles.

She mumbled something in confusion, and smiled awkwardly. At least her teeth were white and even, he thought as he continued to hold her limp hand.

They dined in the Savoy Grill. Patricia was too casually dressed for the main restaurant, and felt more comfortable in the less formal atmosphere. Abigail struggled to keep the conversation going during dinner, which wasn't easy with one so inhibited, and every now and then, Archie had to step in to keep it from dying altogether.

He could tell from the way she kept giving him shy little glances that she found him attractive. It didn't displease him. He loved attention, from whatever quarter it came, and with his spirit lifted somewhat, he encouraged her to add a word here and there, even to laugh.

There was no doubt that he had made a good impression, and for the sake of appearances, he took the bill out of her hands when it arrived. She was obviously impressed; he wasn't when he saw the amount of the bill. They had eaten well, and Abigail, with her love of the best, had chosen an expensive bottle of French champagne. Nevertheless, he managed to put a brave face on it, and even left a generous tip.

After leaving the restaurant, they walked Patricia to her car—an old "banger" that looked ready for the junk heap. Abigail had her Jaguar sports car parked a little further down the road, a present from Patricia when she turned twenty-one. Archie didn't have a car of his own. His father had promised him one when be began his articles but, like most of his promises, he failed to keep it. He did, however, have the use of his mother's Mercedes whenever he needed a car, but not that evening.

Patricia was somewhat more at ease with Archie than when they met earlier, and allowed her hand to linger in his while saying goodnight. Archie kissed the back of it, which made her blush profusely. "It was an enchanting evening," he murmured. "I enjoyed every minute of it."

Uncertain of herself, she pulled her hand away and whispered shyly, "Yes."

Archie smiled to himself. "I hope it won't be long before we meet again," he said.

It was all too fast, too unexpected, and trembling she rummaged through her handbag for the car keys, and tried to fit them into the car door. Gently, Archie took the keys out of her hand and opened it for her. With barely a glance at him, she got in behind the steering wheel, murmuring, "Thank you," and then drove away.

Abigail, who had been watching the little scene from a few paces away, burned with resentment. "Overdoing it a bit, weren't you?" then she mimicked with exaggeration his parting words to Patricia. "*I hope it won't be long before we meet again!*"

She was a surprisingly good mimic, and it made him laugh. "You're jealous," he said with amusement.

She was walking on ahead of him to her car, and when she reached it, she got in behind the wheel and slammed the door after her. Archie got in beside her. He could see that she was still fuming, her lips tight, her eyes fixed in that way people have when they are angry with someone. "Come on," he said, "they were only words; they didn't mean anything."

Still with that fixed look, she put the car in gear and drove off, going through a red light as she turned into the main road. "Jealous?" she muttered to herself. "That will be the day!"

"Being a bit childish, aren't you? I thought you would want me to be nice to her, seeing how important she is to you."

"Nice, yes, but you were practically licking her boots. You're up to no good. I can smell it. I knew it was a mistake taking you along."

He was in no mood for her tiresome behavior and shouted, "Now look here, what I do or how I behave is none of your bloody business. We are having an affair, that's all. I promised you nothing."

She was driving fast. He could see the needle going from thirty to fifty miles an hour in seconds. "You bastard," she yelled. "I should have driven off and left you standing at the curb!"

"If that's how you feel, why didn't you?"

They were now traveling at sixty miles an hour, and without warning, she slammed her foot down hard on the brake pedal, nearly sending him through the windscreen as the car came to an abrupt stop. Her eyes ablaze, she turned to him. "You're going after her, and don't bother to deny it because I can see right through your little game."

"Go to hell! I don't have to answer to you."

She slapped his face. He slapped hers. "Do that again," he said, "and you'll regret it."

Her breathing was heavy, her chest heaving with emotion. "Get out of this bloody car," she screamed.

He glared at her with contempt. "You disgust me!" and opening the door, he got out, not bothering to shut it after him.

She bent across the passenger's seat, and in a cold, hard voice said, "You'll be the one to regret it!" Then she closed the door and drove off at breakneck speed.

Seething with anger, he watched the car disappear down the road, then began to look around for a taxi. There were none to be had, and he started the long walk back to his flat.

The affair had to end sooner or later, he thought. She was becoming too possessive, so it was time to move on. What disturbed him most was that they were too alike for comfort. It was like seeing himself through the eyes of somebody else, and her reaction worried him.

Anyhow, he had bigger fish to fry. Strange how things worked out, he thought. If it were not for Abigail, he would never have been introduced to Patricia; so for that, he was grateful to her. He smiled at the thought of all that money. Shy, awkward, unworldly. Probably had never been out with a man. He could not have wished for an easier mark.

An excitement took hold of him. *The richest woman in London!* he thought. *Well, here comes the richest man!*

CHAPTER FIFTEEN

We can't all be born attractive but when we are, it is an advantage. It is also an advantage when we are endowed with that very special ingredient known as charisma, appeal if you prefer; and therein lies a charm that goes on and on when beauty is long passed and forgotten.

Patricia Nesbitt was born with neither beauty nor charm—only a large pot of gold, and when Archie set out to win her, it was the gold he had his eye on.

For all her seeming simplicity, Patricia was not an easy target. Having been brought up to be wary of potential gold diggers, she was filled with inhibitions and chose a life of partial seclusion as a means of protecting herself against unwanted advances, and Archie had a more difficult time breaking through the barrier than he anticipated.

From an early age, she was painfully aware of her homely appearance. When other girls began to experiment with cosmetics, she wouldn't dare, afraid that makeup would draw too much attention to her plain features. In fact, if it were not for Abigail, she would have been happy to shrink into a corner and never be noticed.

Suddenly, a young man comes along and turns her safe little world upside down, and it was a frightening experience, even more so because of the unexpected feelings he aroused in her. Like any woman in love, it made her vulnerable; but she wasn't just any woman, she was Patricia Nesbitt, heiress to a fortune, whose upbringing made it difficult for her to yield to the magic of being swept off her feet by a handsome suitor. Nevertheless, in the end, she was nothing more than a woman with all her longings, hopes, and dreams, and eventually she succumbed to the attentions of Archie Bingham.

Desire overwhelmed her, and for the first time in her life, she came to understand what it was to want a man. It was a discovery that was both devastating and wonderful, and when he seemed to return her feelings, her feet never touched the ground again.

If she had to acclimate herself to these new emotions, Archie also had to do some adjusting. He had never been faithful to one woman in his life. Neither had he ever tried to curb his appetite for sex. Now he had to, but it was a price he was willing to pay for what he expected to receive.

Patricia delighted in a few kisses. She had never had that much, and to want more would never have entered her mind. It suited Archie to have few demands made upon him; he still hadn't got used to the idea of being with a woman he found unattractive, to say the least. At times, he wasn't sure he would even be able to do what was expected of him; and then, all he had to think of was the fortune that would be in his hands once he married Patricia, and he knew he would have no trouble in fulfilling his obligation.

As their relationship developed, the threat of Abigail and what she might do began to worry him. He knew he would have no peace until he was able to get Patricia to break their friendship. He also knew that it would be difficult to achieve. They had grown up together, and in many ways, Patricia relied upon her for advice in certain areas. There would have to be a good reason for a breakup, and so he waited for such an opportunity to arise.

The opportunity presented itself when meeting Abigail, unexpectedly, one evening. It was obvious she wasn't pleased to see them together, and he said to Patricia afterwards, "You know, she isn't the friend you think she is. She uses you just as she uses everyone. Did you notice how cold she was? She doesn't like to see you happy."

Her response wasn't quite what he expected. "There is nothing you can tell me about Abigail that I don't already know," she said, "and I really don't mind if she uses me, as you say. We have been good friends ever since I can remember. I think that gives her some entitlement."

"You don't understand. She isn't the sort who is content to come second in a relationship. She is also jealous of you, and she can be very unpredictable when jealous. It makes me worry about what she might do to upset you. You must be aware of how much you mean to me."

She blushed. "I, er—don't know," she stammered, "but I do know how much you have come to mean to me."

"In that case, please see less of her." She appeared hesitant. "What is it?" he asked.

"Abigail said that the breakup between you was mutual. Is it true?"

"Does it matter?"

"I wouldn't want to think that I was the cause of it."

"You weren't. She and I were through when I met you; it was only a question of time. Abigail doesn't leave a man room to breathe. Anyhow, I was never in love with her, no matter what she may have said; but I did fall in love with you, and she can't forgive me for that."

She couldn't have looked more astonished if he had admitted to murder. "You did?" she asked incredulously.

"Why do you find it so hard to believe?"

She was obviously flustered. "I, er … I mean Abigail is so beautiful and glamorous. I'm not even pretty!"

"You mustn't put yourself down. The truth is I don't put Abigail in the same class as you. Her looks will fade, and then what will she have? You have the qualities that a man looks for in a wife, qualities that endure, like goodness and generosity. Physical beauty can't compete with those attributes."

She was staring at him with a stunned expression, and he suddenly realized that he had all but proposed to her. He hadn't intended to say anything at that point, but having gone so far he decided to go all the way. "I think we have both been taken by surprise by my admission," he said.

"Yes!" she whispered shyly and cast her eyes down.

"Patricia, you have touched my heart and I can't bear to think of a life without you. I suppose now is a good time to declare my intentions. Patricia, will you do me the honor of becoming my wife?"

Perhaps deep down, she knew it for the lie it was, but when a woman desperately wants to believe, she can fool herself into believing anything, and there was nothing in this world that she wanted more. "Yes!" she whispered, and those pale uninspiring eyes of hers suddenly shone with love.

For the next few days, she walked as if in a dream. Her step was light; her heart was brimming with happiness. She loved and was loved in return. It was a miracle that she thought would never happen to her, and it had.

When Haley received the news, he was overjoyed. He had been like a father to her ever since the death of her parents, and his dearest wish had been to find her a suitable match and get her married. Now, it seemed, she had found such a match in Archie.

He had always liked the boy, despite rumors of unseemly behavior. He came from good stock, and he believed it would show in the end. Anyhow, he had nothing against a full-blooded young man sowing a few wild oats before settling down, and he was certain that he would settle down as soon as he married Patricia.

His son Alfred was of a different opinion. He was angry when he heard the news, and marched into his father's office to protest the match. "How could you even consider letting her marry that unscrupulous bastard? He doesn't love her; he's after her money. I knew he should never have had access to those documents of yours. He only picked out the wealthiest woman in London for himself, and that little idiot fell for the line he must have given her. You have to do something to stop it from going any further. She has to know what the score is with Archie."

"And what will that achieve? The poor girl has found happiness at last, and I, for one, am pleased for her. As for her money—the sort of wealth she has was bound to have some influence on a man, and many a good marriage has been founded on just that."

"I should have realized this would be your reaction! You have always been partial to that rotter, but you cannot ignore the fact that he is a womanizer of the worst kind. How long do you think it will be before he's fooling around again?"

"Really, Alfred! If every young woman took a man's past into consideration, there would be few marriages. But this isn't about your concern for Patricia, is it? It's about you and Abigail and her affair with Archie. You can't forgive him for that, can you? Neither have you ever liked him, not from the day he first stepped foot in this office."

"If you think I'm jealous, you're wrong. I have always understood Abigail's needs. She is a very sensual and desirable woman, and men tend to come on to her. So she plays around occasionally, but it's never serious. Once we are married, things will be different. She will have me to keep her occupied."

Haley arched his eyebrows. "I hope so," he said dubiously, "for your sake."

Archie's father greeted the news with enthusiasm. "Patricia Nesbitt!" he said in wonder. "You certainly have done well for yourself. I am proud of you, dear boy."

Archie had long craved his father's approval; now that he seemed to have it, instead of it pleasing him, it gnawed away at him. "I thought it would please you," he said with a sarcastic twist of his lips. "After all, I am keeping up the family tradition of marrying for money. Right, Father?"

His father gave him a reproving glance. "If this is going to turn into one of those unpleasant arguments of yours, I want nothing to do with it."

No, of course, he wouldn't, thought Archie with disdain. He knew, only too well, where it would lead. He had made it quite clear that anything he had to say about his association with that whore of his and her bastard daughter was off-limits. So what was the use? he thought bitterly. "No," he said resignedly, "it's not going to turn into another of those arguments."

Relief spread across his father's face. "I'm glad to hear it. Now, I will leave it to you and your mother to arrange a suitable dinner date so that we can meet your young lady, and I must say that I am looking forward to it."

"I bet you are!" mumbled Archie under his breath.

"What was that you said?" asked his father.

"I said great, fine, whatever you say. That's what it always comes down to in the end, anyhow," and turning on his heels, he marched out of his father's study.

His mother was standing by the stairs when he came out into the hall.

"Another argument?" she asked with concern.

"Actually, I did very well today. I managed to keep my temper in check."

"You know, you could get on really well with him if you wanted to."

"How? By looking aside, the way you do when he does something despicable like—well, never mind."

He had hurt her cruelly and knew it by the way she began to fuss with an imaginary speck of dust on the banister. Why had he been so wretched to her? She didn't deserve it. "I'm sorry," he said. "I had no place saying that."

She looked up at him, and as though nothing had been said, she asked, "So, when would you like to bring your young lady over for dinner?"

"When would you suggest?"

"Thursday. Your father never goes out on a Thursday."

"Then Thursday it is," he said more kindly.

Patricia was nervous. "Do you really think I look all right?" she asked for the tenth time since leaving her house. "Do you think your parents will like me?"

He was driving her old car. The gears kept sticking and the exhaust pipe kept spluttering, and to cap it all, she was getting on his nerves with her incessant worries. "For Pete's sake, does it matter? And why must we always use this old thing when there is a perfectly good Rolls sitting in the garage doing nothing?"

"I'm sorry," she said. "It belonged to my parents, and I never think of using it myself."

"That's another thing," he complained. "You are always being sorry for something. For once, can't you give a reply without being sorry?"

"I'm sorry," she whispered apologetically.

"Oh, what's the use!" he cried in exasperation, and kept his eyes fixed on the road ahead.

She sat there, looking meek and pathetic, and he was angry, angry with himself for being so short with her. It wasn't her fault that she irritated him. He ought to be more sympathetic; after all, she was trying. He glanced at her out of the corner of his eye. She was wearing a pearl necklace and ear-rings to match, not that they did much for her—with her lack of poise, they looked more like a string of cheap beads than the expensive jewels that they were. What would his father make of her? he wondered. He heaved a sigh and set his jaw in a determined line.

When they reached his parents' house, he parked outside, switched off the engine, and turned to her. "I'm sorry," he said. "I didn't mean to get angry with you. I suppose I am as anxious as you."

Her dull eyes looked at him with apology, and she whispered, "It's all right. I understand."

"Do you, I wonder?" he said, as if to himself.

In many respects, the evening was a success. His father was attentive, enchanting her with his courtly manner, and keeping her amused with little anecdotes relating to his profession, and before long, she was under his spell.

Archie watched him work his magic with mixed feelings. He had never understood what it was that women saw in his father; now he did. It was that same mesmerizing quality that swayed many a jury in his favor—and he felt jealous.

His mother, as usual, was content with her husband holding center stage. If she had any thoughts about Patricia, one way or the other, you would never have guessed. She was gracious, as always, and helped put her at ease.

By the time they left the house, Patricia was beaming. Archie had never seen her look so excited. "Your father is such an extraordinary man! You know, I think he really liked me," she said with surprise.

"Why wouldn't he? You have all the right qualities."

The sarcasm was lost on her, and still excited she went on. "Uncle Alfred says that he never loses a case."

"Then dear Uncle Alfred doesn't know him that well," he said with irony.

His tone made her glance at him. "Have I said something to annoy you?"

His eyes left the road to look at her for a second. "Don't tell me you are going to apologize again?" he said with contempt.

Uncertain of herself and even more uncertain of him, she shrank back in her seat and remained silent for the rest of the journey home.

Bright and early the next morning before he left for work, he received a call from his mother. "She is very nice, dear," she said, "but not for you."

"Why do you say that? Father seemed delighted!"

"I know better than your father. She will bore you to death before the honeymoon is over."

"She is rich beyond belief mother. It will more than compensate for any lack on her part. Think of it: I will be able to have everything I want. I will be able to do anything I want. That's freedom, real freedom."

"If you believe that, you're a fool. Being financially dependent upon a wife isn't freedom; it's a string around your neck."

"It never deterred father!"

"That's unfair, Archie. Your father married me under different circumstances, and for your information, he is, and always has been, the breadwinner in this family. It is his income and not mine that has kept us, and you would do well to remember it."

"Well, whatever! Anyhow, once I am married to Patricia and in charge of the purse strings, I won't need anything more from him."

"Her money is in trust, Archie. Do you really think Haley will allow her to give you control over the income? You better think again, my boy, if you do."

"Haley likes me; he trusts me. You have seen what she's like. I'll have her eating out of my hand before long."

"It's one thing before marriage, and quite another after. Don't make the same mistake most men make about women. We have more going on in our head than we are given credit for."

"I'll take that chance!"

"It's your life. I just hate to think of you wasting it. Anyhow, that isn't the only reason for the early call. Haley phoned after you left last night. He wants to give the engagement party as soon as it becomes official. Also, your father and I discussed the engagement ring, and the suggestion is that you take Patricia to Aspreys, in Bond Street, to pick out something suitable. We have an account there and, of course, you will not have to worry about the cost. It is our gift to you."

"Thank you, Mother. You don't know what a relief that is. What figure did you have in mind?"

"Twenty thousand. That should buy her something very nice."

"Was that his suggestion or yours?"

"Does it matter?"

"Just interested!"

"It was mine, but under the circumstances, he had no objection."

A round of social events followed the engagement party. It seemed an endless stream of people were anxious to meet the man the heiress to a fortune was about to marry. Archie enjoyed being the center of attention, and took it in his stride. For Patricia, who had always been a very private person, it was emotionally draining. She left the planning, as well as the cost of reciprocating, to Archie who found it well beyond his means, and he soon got deeper and deeper into debt.

Had he gone to her and explained his predicament, he knew there would have been no problem, but Archie had his pride. What he would do after the marriage was one thing, but before? That was unthinkable.

He had to find another source of income, and quickly. Going to his father was definitely out. He would only lecture him on the value of money and then, in all probability, refuse to help. His mother was already subsidizing his salary to a large extent, and so there was only one source available to him—Sally!

Sally, a buxom wench with a pretty face and a saucy pair of eyes, was a secretary in the office. She was also in charge of the petty cash box. For some time, Archie had been aware of her strong feelings for him, but because of his situation, he had never thought to take advantage of them. Now he looked upon those feelings as propitious.

Sally was not only quick tongued and quick witted; she was also an opportunist, and was all too willing to oblige Archie, as long as she got what she wanted out of it, and a bargain was struck.

Sex in exchange for what he wanted couldn't have suited Archie more. He had denied himself for so long he was as ripe as he could ever be for an affair, and the thought of getting his hands on those extravagant thighs of Sally's and fondling that mountainous bosom filled him with excitement.

Her only concern was that he repay the loan from the petty cash at least one day before the end of each month, when a check on the funds was taken, and he readily agreed.

To add to his delight, Archie discovered that she had the most amazing body for one so plump. Those voluptuous curves were as firm as a rock, and those magnificent breasts that caught the attention of many a roving eye were like twin torpedoes poised ready for launching, the sight of which aroused him more than he could have imagined, and so the arrangement proved satisfactory to both parties.

Had the unforeseen been taken into account, their little pact might have gone on forever, but it hadn't been. There came a day when the chief clerk, whose job it was to check the funds in the box against the petty cash vouchers, suddenly took it into his head to do a check earlier than usual, only to find a discrepancy of three hundred pounds.

With no satisfactory explanation for the missing funds, poor Sally was at her wit's end and asked for a few days in order to look into the matter. She was given twenty-four hours. Shaken, she went to Archie's flat that evening to see what could be done.

He was more concerned with the inconvenience it might cause him than with her predicament. "You didn't mention me, did you?" he asked.

"Of course not. What do you think I am?" she replied.

"Well, you must have let something slip or why would he have made a check this early?"

"I didn't, I promise you. Anyhow, it will be all right as long as I can replace the money first thing tomorrow morning. I'll come up with some excuse for it not being there in the first place."

"Well, don't look at me. I'm broke until the end of the month."

"What about your family? They're rich!"

"Forget it. We would never have needed the arrangement if I could have gone to them in the first place."

Her face fell. "Well, you have to do something. Where will I find that kind of money?"

"You have always been resourceful. You'll think of something."

"Like robbing a bank? For God's sake, Archie, I'm desperate. What if he already suspects?"

"You know, for a bright girl, you have really been stupid. You should have realized that something like this could happen and had the situation covered. It's not my fault that you didn't."

She was beginning to see the light. "You bastard!" she cried out. "If it weren't for you, I wouldn't be in this mess."

"You got what you wanted out of it. Now, if you just use your head the way you use your body, you'll do all right."

She gasped. "You pig, you rotten pig! Everyone's been saying you're no good, but I didn't expect this, not after everything."

"I don't care what you did or didn't expect, as long as you keep my name out of it."

"Why should I take the fall for you?"

"You stupid bitch! Whatever you do or say, you are still implicated; drag me into it as well and you will be sorry."

"I'm already sorry. How much worse can it be?"

"A lot worse!" he hissed.

There was no doubt in her mind that he meant it, and fearful of him, she whispered, "I won't say anything," and left immediately.

Archie sat down to think when she had gone. It was a right mess. If only he could be sure she wouldn't implicate him; but then, how could he trust a woman? They were such an unpredictable lot. Damn her, damn the whole bloody business! What would he do if she did let him down? What could he do?

He needn't have worried. When he turned up a little later than usual at the office next morning, Sally had already been dismissed. No one quite knew what happened, except that she had been called into Alfred's office the moment she arrived. Ten minutes later, a tearful Sally collected her things and left without a word to anyone. It became apparent, as the day wore on, that she had kept her word and hadn't mentioned Archie.

That evening, however, she came knocking at his door once again. He thought it was her and opened it immediately. She was a sight—her eyes were red, her face puffy from crying. Not wanting any of his neighbors to see her, he pulled her inside at once and closed the door.

"I've been fired!" she said in that flat way people have when they have run out of emotion.

"I heard. What happened?"

"They didn't even give me the twenty-four hours they promised. It was Alfred. He wouldn't listen to anything I had to say, and if it were not for his father, who stepped in, I truly believe he would have called the police and had me prosecuted for stealing. As it was, I was told to collect my things and leave immediately."

"Are you certain they don't suspect my involvement?" he asked anxiously.

"Don't worry," she said with contempt. "I'm the only one in a bloody mess."

He sighed with relief. "What are you going to do?"

"What can I do without a reference? Who do you think will employ me?" She suddenly burst into tears. "You have to help me, Archie. I have nothing—no money, nothing! You owe me."

"There is nothing I can do.... Here," he said dipping his hand into his pocket and pulling out a few notes, "there must be close to a hundred. It's yours."

She stared at it in disbelief. "And how far do you think that will go?"

"At least it's something until you get settled in a job."

"What job? Don't you understand? I have no references, unless you can fix it for me," she said doubtfully.

He knew she was right. It would be tough going, and after giving it some thought, he said, "I'll tell you what. Come by tomorrow at this time. I think I may be able to solve your problem."

Her eyes narrowed with suspicion. "You're not saying that to get rid of me, are you?"

"Just be here," he replied.

There was still some uncertainty in her mind, but then, what did she have to lose? "All right," she said, "but please, Archie, don't let me down again."

Archie knew that his father kept some headed notepaper in his study at home, and the next morning, when his father would have left for chambers, he went to the house, took a few of those sheets of paper, together with an appropriate envelope, and left for the office. That evening, he wrote Sally a glowing reference and signed his father's name to it.

"Here," he said, handing it to her when she arrived, "this should more than satisfy a prospective employer."

She glanced at the envelope. "This is from your father's office!" she said in surprise.

"And you couldn't wish for a better reference."

She looked dubious. "He doesn't know, does he?" When he didn't reply, she asked, "What if someone gets in touch with him?"

"Why would they? His signature carries a lot of weight; it's recommendation enough for anyone."

"I don't know! It just doesn't feel right."

"Oh, for heaven's sake!" he cried. "You better take it because there is nothing else I can do, and what's more, I don't ever want you coming here again!"

She hesitated for a moment, and then placed the envelope in her handbag. "Thanks," she said, "maybe it will work out after all."

Someone did get in touch with the office of Sir Archibald Bingham. Fortunately, it was Phipps, his chief clerk, who answered the phone. He immediately put two and two together and acknowledged the reference, and so all went well for Sally.

Not so for Archie, however. Phipps was fuming when he got hold of him. "What were you thinking? If your father had answered the phone instead of me, I wouldn't want to be in your shoes! Don't ever pull a stunt like that again."

"Are you going to tell him?"

"If I don't, it's for his sake and not yours. He has enough grief to put up with without me adding to it. But don't think that because I let you get away with it this time that I will again."

"It won't happen again. I didn't know what to do, Phipps. The poor girl was beside herself. She has a sick mother to look after and she needed a good job—one that pays well. I had to do something for her; one has to help the downtrodden sometimes, Phipps."

Phipps had known Archie since he was a baby, and there wasn't much that he could put over on him. "Sick mother or not," he said scornfully, "just remember that this is the last time I help you out."

"I'll remember, and I do appreciate it, Phipps, I really do!"

A short time later, preparations were made for the wedding. The Brompton Oratory was booked for the ceremony and Claridges for the reception afterwards. Patricia's engagement gift to Archie had been the dark green Aston Martin that he admired at the showroom in Sloane Street a few weeks earlier. Now, with the wedding so close, she offered him the beautiful guest suite on the top floor of her house. With so much to do before the big day, she thought it would be more convenient if he were close at hand.

He accepted, if with mixed feelings. It was hard to resist the sumptuous accommodation, with its own sitting room, as well as a bevy of servants to attend to his every need. The question did arise in his mind, however, whether she would expect more from him than just a brief kiss. Such closeness couldn't help but put their relationship on a more intimate level, and he worried about how he would deal with it. But, sooner or later, he would have to deal with it, so he put all disagreeable thoughts behind him and moved in.

It was a mistake. Not that she expected more from him, at least not in the way he feared, but he was expected to dine with her every evening and listen as she gave a minute-by-minute account of how she spent her day. If she bored him before, he was now bored out of his mind. Unable to take such petty conversation for any length of time, he began to make excuses and disappear into the night, soon after dinner, and not return until he was ready to retire.

She didn't complain. She didn't ask where he was going or where he had been. She accepted it in that passive way she had of accepting everything.

Saturdays, he would find more excuses to leave the house and not return until late afternoon. He would spend the time tramping the streets of that part of London he loved best: Wigmore Street, with its old established antique shops, coffee shops, and other pricey establishments; Wimpole Street, with its stately houses; Bentinck Street, with its quaint aristocratic character; narrow Marylebone Lane, with its village atmosphere; and then there was George Street, where elegant Bryanstone and Montague Square were situated.

He would dream, as he walked through the streets, promising himself that as soon as he got his hands on Patricia's money, he would buy a flat in the area—a place that he could call his own, where he could go when he felt the need to escape and be alone.

Sometimes, when he walked past Montague Square, he would experience a twinge of pain, even apprehension; and then there were times when he was drawn to it, as if by an invisible hand, and he would stand outside the house where his father's mistress lived, staring up at the windows, wondering which one was hers and whether his father was inside at that very moment.

At other times, he would just stand there feeling bitter and resentful, hating all of them especially his father. That is where he was, one Saturday afternoon, when the door suddenly opened and a young girl of about fifteen came tripping down the front steps.

For a moment, he was in a panic and wanted to run, but then the dazzling radiance of the girl's lovely face held him captive. Who was she? he wondered in awe.

As if in answer, the door opened again and a woman, with that same radiance about her, came out onto the doorstep and called, "Belinda!"

The sound of that name being called was enough to make his heart sink, and he began to tremble, and for a brief moment, he was filled with a strange foreboding. Then she turned and smiled at the woman, and once again, he was captivated by that wonderful face of hers.

"Yes, Mother?" she asked.

Archie's gaze turned to the woman on the stairs. "Don't forget," she said, "your father will be here early this afternoon."

The mention of his father made Archie feel betrayed all over again. Yet something strange had taken place inside him. All the hatred, all the anger he had for that woman and her daughter, suddenly seemed misplaced, and it left him confused.

He glanced back at the girl. She was saying, "I won't forget." And her smile broadened and her eyes sparkled with joy. Then she turned again, and it seemed to him that she floated along the pavement as she walked away.

He couldn't stop himself from staring after her, his heart a mix of pain, frustration, and so many other unexpected emotions. Fellini was right, he thought. How could any man look upon that face and not be moved? And all at once, he was frightened by his feelings.

When he returned home and looked at Patricia, it was like coming in out of the sunshine into the darkness. He had glimpsed paradise in a young girl's eyes, and he knew that nothing would ever be the same for him again, and he became more depressed than ever.

The closer it got to the wedding, the more unsettled he was. Day and night, he was tormented by the image of Belinda and that wonderful smile of hers. To escape, he began to drink to excess, telling himself that he needed to in order to get through an evening with Patricia.

If she noticed, she said nothing. Sometimes he wished that she would. At least, then they could have an argument; anything to relieve the boredom of her company. At one time, he became rude to her, trying to goad her into saying something. When she still wouldn't, he could no longer bear it and cried, "What's wrong with you? Can't you see what I am doing? For heaven's sake, Patricia, have you no pride? Look how I treat you, and instead of telling me to bugger off, you say nothing. Are you alive or dead?"

She simply lowered her eyes and said with embarrassment, "Abigail says that it's wedding nerves and that I shouldn't take notice."

"Abigail?" he cried, incensed. "Abigail? Since when did you start to confide in that bitch?"

"I have to talk to someone, and she is my best friend."

"Some friend! I thought you weren't going to see so much of her?"

"I haven't been, but since she agreed to be my bridesmaid, we can't help spending more time together. I don't know why you object, Archie; she has been very supportive of both you and me."

"That bitch doesn't know how to be supportive of anyone but herself; you are too naïve to see it. Why didn't you tell me that you asked her to be your bridesmaid?"

"But I did."

"I would have remembered if you had."

She blushed. "You were, er—preoccupied," she said awkwardly.

He gave a harsh laugh. "Preoccupied? That's a good one. I was drunk, you mean."

"I would never have said that!"

"Well, you should have, or have you no stomach for the truth?"

She looked as if she were on the verge of tears. "Please, Archie," she whimpered, "I don't want to argue with you."

"You never do. Perhaps that's what's wrong. You never say what you think, and I have to guess. Right now, I guess you are thinking that I'm a sodding bastard and a bloody drunk! And you would be right."

He knew how she hated him to use bad language, and that was probably why he used it all the more. It gave him a perverse sense of satisfaction to see her reaction to it. He smiled to himself when he saw her turning a bright red, and heard her cry out, "Stop! Stop! I can't take it."

Suddenly, the anguish in her voice got to him. He knew what an unrelenting bastard he could be, and realized that she didn't deserve the punishment he was handing out. His frustration had nothing to do with her. It was his problem, and he was the only one who could solve it. "Look, I'm sorry," he said. "Sometimes, I don't know what comes over me." She had started to cry, with every sob sounding like a reprimand to his ears, and it made him feel bad. "Don't," he said, "please!"

"I can't help it," she wept. "I try so hard to please you, but I don't seem able to."

"Then don't try, just be yourself. I am the one who must try harder. Do you think that you could bring yourself to forgive me?"

She dabbed her eyes with a white tissue, and nodded.

Archie couldn't help thinking, as he watched her, that Abigail would have used a lace-edged handkerchief. "Do you feel better now?" he asked.

Again, she nodded.

"Good! Now, let us put this unpleasant business behind us and get on with the wedding plans. You do still want to go on?"

There was a trace of a smile around her thin lips, and once again, she nodded.

He forced himself to return her smile, and with a sigh of resignation, he thought, *Well, that's it, back to square one!* Not that the prospect was as comforting as it should have been.

With one week to go before the wedding, Haley Sr. gave Archie the time off to prepare. There wasn't much left to prepare. His wardrobe was already full of new clothes, and he'd had his last fitting for the morning suit, and was expecting it to be delivered Friday, together with a top hat and all the other necessary accessories. Nevertheless, it was appreciated. His mind hadn't been on his work of late; in fact, his mind hadn't been on anything much. It was as though he had closed it down in order to blot out all thought, and exist only from moment to moment. Is that what the condemned do? he wondered with irony.

He did consider staying with his parents for the week, but then he would have his father to contend with, and that would not have been pleasant, so he soon dismissed that idea.

Staying put, he concluded, wouldn't be so bad after all. Patricia was busy with her own preparations and was hardly at home during the day, so he would have the house to himself for the most part, and that idea appealed to him.

He had never really taken advantage of all that the house had to offer. There was the indoor swimming pool, with an adjoining exercise room complete with a full range of body-building equipment. Patricia never went near it. Apparently, her father had been very keen on keeping himself fit, and the servants continued to look after it as though it was still being used. There was also an extensive library with shelf after shelf of the great works of the famous, both dead and living. Here again, Patricia kept her distance. It was filled with too many memories of her father, to whom she had been very attached.

Of course, there was the celebrated wine cellar, with its range of fine wines from all over the world, once the pride of her father. He had already sampled a good many of them and intended to sample a good many more during the week. Last but not least, there was the superb chef. The story was that Patricia's father was having dinner in a country restaurant in France, and so enjoyed the meal that he asked to see the chef. To his surprise, out came a young girl of seventeen from the kitchen, and then and there, he offered her the position of cook, and brought her back home with him. Patricia never made use of her culinary skills; she went in for plain food, the plainer the better. Well, he would change all that starting that very week, and so he did. After a morning of leisurely pleasures, he would dine sumptuously on lobster, fillet mignon, veal in a brandy sauce, followed by a soufflé or some other delicious concoction.

In the afternoons, well satisfied and feeling somewhat lazy from over-indulging, he would spend the time in the library with a bottle of brandy, a fine cigar from her late father's collection, and some masterpiece taken down from one of the bookshelves. As a boy, he had loved to read. He could lose himself in the pages that sprang to life with every word, every line written by the author. Somehow, he never managed to get around to a good book since leaving Cambridge. Now here he was, with a great wealth of literature at his fingertips. It was a life he felt well suited to, and he could have gone on like that forever. If only, he thought with a sigh, Patricia would lose herself!

The very afternoon before the wedding, he was in the library, as usual, halfway through a bottle of Napoleon brandy, his head in that woozy stage between sobriety and intoxication, when the butler entered and announced the arrival of Abigail.

"What?" he cried in surprise. "What's she doing here?"

The question had barely left his lips when she came prancing in and, with an air of authority, dismissed the butler. Immediately, she noticed the half-empty bottle of brandy. "You've been drinking," she said with amusement. "What are you trying to drown, Archie? Or should I have said who?"

He glared angrily at her. "What do you want?"

"Why nothing! I'm here to deliver a present—a present especially for you and you alone."

"You know what you can do with your present! I already have all that I want."

"Not all!" she said teasingly, and began to unbutton the tight bodice of her dress, ripping carelessly at the buttons.

If he had any sense, that is when he should have gotten rid of her. He should have taken her by the scruff of her neck and thrown her out, but as he watched her undress, he couldn't bring himself to. She looked so seduc-

tive in that slinky dress she wore and he knew from experience that she wouldn't be wearing underwear, and the thought excited him to the point where he could feel himself rising. His eyes swept greedily over her body. "We shouldn't!" he said lamely.

She knew that she had him, and arching an eyebrow mockingly, she finished unbuttoning her dress, and then slid her hands down over her hips and around her thighs, tempting him with the thought of what those long, tapering fingers were capable of.

His desire was overwhelming. "What if she should return?" he gasped.

She was moving toward him now, her breasts exposed, her hips swaying provocatively. "She won't be back for hours," she whispered. "Come on, Archie, do me. I know you want to."

"The butler!" he murmured breathlessly.

"The door's locked." She was up close, her thighs rubbing against his, her hot breath caressing his ear as she spoke. "Do it now. Fuck me as you have never fucked me before."

He was lost, and pressing himself hard against her, he drew her down onto the carpet, and in a heated frenzy almost tore the dress as he ripped it away to reveal her complete nakedness.

She lay there, her eyes closed, waiting for him. He forced her legs apart with his knee. He could hardly wait, when suddenly it was as if all hell had broken loose. She began to claw at his chest with her nails, and at the same time screamed for him to stop. At first, he thought it was one of her games, and he pinned her arms down and tried to enter her, but she continued to fight and scream until something snapped inside him and he struck her across the face, splitting her lip. "What's the matter with you?" he cried.

She began to weep now, begging him, like some frightened animal, to stop. For a moment, he was mystified, and then he heard a horrified gasp coming from the doorway. With a shock of realization, he lifted his head in time to see the back of Patricia as she fled the scene.

It took seconds for his brain to piece it together. He had been tricked, and staring down at Abigail, he hissed, "You lousy bitch. I'll see that you pay for this!"

Her eyes filled with triumph as they looked up into his, and it was as much as he could do to stop himself from hitting her again. He rose to his feet and put himself together. He stared down at her once more. She was still laying there, her bare skin gleaming white as milk, her smile victorious. He had never hated anyone as much as he hated her at that moment,

and, angry with himself for having been fooled, he turned and went after Patricia.

She was already upstairs in her room, with the door locked against him. He knocked, banged, called out, and begged her to listen to him, but all in vain. When he finally realized that she wasn't going to open the door, he left and trudged up the stairs to his suite on the top floor of the house.

He had lost, but what made it even more bitter was that Abigail had won. Now there was nothing left but to pack his things and move out as soon as possible.

He glanced around at the luxury he had been living in. He was going to miss it, he thought with disappointment. Perhaps he should have left a lot earlier. At least then he would have saved himself, and everyone one else, a lot of humiliation. *Now what?* he wondered with a sigh. Pulling himself together, he took out his suitcases from a closet in the dressing room and started to pack his clothes.

He had almost finished when there was a knock on the door, and thinking that it might be Patricia, he hurried to open it. It was the butler with a letter from her. He took it, closed the door, sat down on the settee, and tore open the envelope. Her engagement ring fell out onto the floor. He picked it up and carelessly dropped it into his pocket, then read the enclosed note.

"Kindly remove your things and be gone by the time I come down to breakfast in the morning."

It went straight to the point, with no words of regret, or any heartfelt response to what she had encountered. She hadn't even bothered to add her signature. He was dismissed, just like that!

He sat staring at it for a while, then he let it fall from his hand, lifted the internal phone, and called the butler to help him down to the car with his luggage.

He must have driven around for a long time as he tried to sort things out in his mind. One thing was clear: as the shock wore off, he began to feel relieved. He was out of a situation he should never have been in in the first place. His main concern now was how to tell his father.

Without thinking, he suddenly found himself pulling up outside his parents' home. He gazed up at the windows. There was a light on in the library. It could only have been his father, and the thought of facing him filled him with apprehension; he wasn't going to like what he had to say. He turned off the engine, got out of the car, mounted the steps to the front door, and rang the bell. His mother answered.

"Oh!" she cried in surprise when she saw who it was. "I didn't expect to see you this evening."

He entered, closed the door, and then looked her straight in the eyes.

"Is something the matter?" she asked, seeing the tense expression on his face.

"I think it's best that I speak to both you and Father at the same time. Is that him in the library?"

She gave him a worried glance. "Yes. He is on the phone speaking to Haley. He phoned a little while ago."

"Oh dear! I had hoped to be the first to tell him."

"That bad?" she asked.

"I suppose from Father's point of view, it is."

"Come," she said, and accompanied him to the library.

His father was still on the phone when they entered, his voice solemn, his face grim as he glanced up at Archie while continuing his conversation with Haley. "Needless to say, this has come as a terrible shock," he said, his eyes hostile as they glared at his son, "and under the circumstances, it was very good of you to let me know as quickly as you did. I feel that an apology for Archie's behavior simply isn't sufficient. Nevertheless, please convey my sincere regrets to Patricia, and tell her how deeply sorry my wife and I are for the pain this family has caused her."

To whatever Haley said, his father answered, "Yes, I will, and thank you once again," and he replaced the receiver.

He continued to glare at his son, and puzzled, his wife asked, "What is it? What has happened?"

His eyes turned to her. "Well, you may ask," he snapped. "Your son, here, is beyond contempt. I have never been so ashamed in my entire life." Then with eyes flaring, he turned back to Archie. "Is there no end to the amount of deceit you are capable of? You lie, you cheat, you philander and worse, if I am to believe what I have just heard, and I have no reason to doubt it! Were you born without an ounce of decency? Or did you happen to lose it upon growing up? Either way, I am embarrassed to call you my son."

"What did he do?" asked his mother in bewilderment.

"Why don't you ask him? I also would be interested to hear an explanation of his conduct, not that I put much faith in anything he says!"

"Then what's the point?" responded Archie in indignation. "You have never had any faith in me, period; so why should today be different?"

"You are right; for once, it isn't." Then turning to his wife, he said, "Your son, madam, had the impertinence to bring a woman into his fiancé's home, the very day before the wedding, then proceeded to rape her on the library floor. What have you to say to that?"

She glanced from one to the other in horror. "I don't believe it!" she gasped.

"No. Of course, you wouldn't! Your precious son can't do wrong, in your eyes." Turning to Archie, he said, "Tell her—tell your mother what you did."

Her eyes searched her son's. "Is it true?"

"No!" he replied. "Haley wasn't there; he doesn't know what went on."

"But Patricia was," cried his father. "Are you now calling her a liar?"

"She saw what she was supposed to see. The whole thing was a set up to make me look bad in her eyes."

"Why would anyone want to do that?" asked his mother.

"It's a long story. The truth is it has nothing to do with anything except revenge by a very spiteful person."

"Revenge?" exclaimed his father. "I have heard rape called many things, but never revenge. Who was this woman you consorted with? Some cheap rubbish, no doubt!"

Archie suddenly realized that his father didn't know that it was Abigail, and that meant Haley didn't either. For some reason, Patricia was protecting her identity. Well, perhaps it was for the best. "You are right," he said. "She was a bit of rubbish, but as it turns out, she did me a big favor. I was about to make the biggest mistake of my life. Now, I am free again," and taking the engagement ring from his pocket, he threw it on to the library-table.

Bristling with anger, his father continued, "You should have thought about that before you allowed things to get this far. It was not only selfish, it was inexcusable and unacceptable. Have you no remorse for what you put that poor girl through? I give up on you, Archie. I can't understand how a son of mine could do such a thing. I blame you, madam, I blame you," he said angrily to his wife. "You have given in to him time and time again. He can't do wrong in your eyes. Well, see what your son has done now?"

His mother, usually so submissive, took them both by surprise and stood up for herself. "He is also your son," she said calmly, "and if I have had a hand in his upbringing, then you have had a greater one, and any blame is as much yours as mine, if not more so."

His father went red in the face and exploded. "How dare you contradict me in front of that boy of yours! Do you know what you are doing? You are undermining my authority, and I will not have it."

"Authority has always been important to you. Whatever happened to love and understanding? Isn't that how it is supposed to be between father and son? He is your son, and perhaps that is the problem between you. You see too much of yourself in him."

Her husband, speechless with rage, looked as if he wanted to say something, but could only manage a choking sound.

She watched him spluttering a second, and then said with satisfaction, "Now that we agree on something, what else did Haley have to say?"

"Wasn't that enough?" he growled.

"I am referring to finishing his articles. I don't suppose he will want him to stay on at the firm?"

Somewhat less agitated, he replied, "On the contrary, he has agreed to allow him to stay on. With only a month to go, he realizes that it would look bad if he were to change firms at this late stage. The man is a gentleman. I doubt I could be as generous under the circumstances!"

"I have no intention of returning to the firm," responded Archie, "under any circumstances!"

"You will do as you are told. You have done enough damage to this family's good name. The less people speculate about what happened, the better."

"Ah!" cried Archie. "Now I see it all. All your anger—it's not about what I did or didn't do, it's about your precious name. That's all that ever matters to you!"

"It's your name as well!"

"And there are times when I would rather forget it!"

His father's temper flared. "You—you!" he gasped, and lifted a hand as though to strike him.

Fearing he might have a stroke, his wife stepped in. "Enough!" she cried. "Let us behave like adults for once. What is done is done. Now we must think ahead."

Sir Archibald calmed down. "You think ahead," he said to her. "I've had enough. Just get him out of my sight."

Archie, being Archie, liked to push his father to the limit. "Which is it to be? Out of sight or out of the house?" he asked with a sneer.

"I couldn't care less!" replied his father.

"In that case, I have no intention of staying under your roof a minute longer."

"Oh?" questioned his father. "And where do you propose going? What will you use for money? I have no intention of giving you any, and I gather that you are already in debt up to your eyes."

"If that is supposed to be concern, Father, I think I prefer it when you couldn't care less. At least then you are being honest!"

Before it went any further, his mother came to the rescue once again. "Please leave, Archie, before any more damage is done."

Once in the hall, she asked her son, "What do you propose doing?"

"Well, I can't stay here, that's for sure."

She went to the hall table, took a check from her handbag, and wrote on it. "You will need this," she said, handing it to him. "It will see you through the next few months."

"Thank you, Mother, and thank you for being so understanding."

"You have always had my sympathy, Archie. I know how difficult it is to be the son of a successful man, but as for understanding, I have never understood you or your father. You do and say things that, sometimes, are beyond my comprehension. It's as though both of you are hell-bent on destruction, especially you. Nonetheless, I love you both, not that either of you has ever made it easy for me."

Once again Archie was taken by surprise. He had never heard his mother express her feelings before, and it was as though he was seeing her for the first time as a person in her own right, instead of just his mother, or his father's wife, and it was revealing. "I'm sorry if I have caused you pain," he said.

She smiled and touched his cheek. "Not pain, my darling, only bewilderment."

Before setting off in his car, Archie glanced at the check in his hand. It was generous. As his mother said, enough to see him through the next few months and longer, if he was careful; only he had never been careful in his life. What he wanted, he had to have without giving a thought to whether he could afford it or not. So, putting the car into drive, he headed toward Mayfair, and then on to the Ritz Hotel.

Perhaps deep down, there had always been a twinge of guilt attached to his extravagance, not that it had ever prevented him from enjoying it to the fullest; but the next morning, when he awoke in his expensive suite at the Ritz, it was more than a twinge that made him go in search of a flat directly after breakfast.

Furnished flats didn't come cheaply in elegant Knightsbridge, the area that he decided upon. However, as chance would have it, he found what seemed like the ideal accommodation, advertised in the window of Estate

Agents Bartlett & Bow, and full of eagerness, he went in to inquire about it.

The agent on duty put him on to his assistant, a rather tricky-looking young man named Wilkes. "Is it just for yourself?" he asked, his crafty eyes giving Archie the once-over.

"Yes," he replied.

"Then I would say you're in luck," he said with a crooked grin. "It's on the small side, but reasonable, and where can you find anything reasonable in this part of London?"

"What's wrong with it?" asked Archie with suspicion.

Wilkes laughed. "Not a bloody thing," he said, "if you'll pardon my French."

Archie smiled. He rather liked his cheeky attitude. "So what's the story?"

"The entire building is for sale and the owner wants it filled quickly for a better deal. It's a good block. You came along in the nick of time. I only put it in the window this morning, and if I know anything about the market, it will be snapped up by this afternoon. Let me show it to you. We can walk—it's only a couple of minutes away."

It was, indeed, a very good block, with porterage and garage facilities, difficult to come by in that area. The flat itself was small but pleasantly laid out, with an interconnecting living room and bedroom. The kitchen was tiny, with a back door to the fire escape. But the bathroom was the big surprise—it had a separate shower stall as well as an oversized bath, which was unusual for such a small place. "I'll take it," said Archie.

"Knew you would," said Wilkes with that crooked grin of his. "The owner will only give a six-month lease. Is that all right with you? I'm certain we could get it extended if you wish?"

"No, that's perfect. By the end of six months, I will want something a lot better than this. How soon may I move in?"

"As soon as the lease is signed and a deposit taken, it's all yours."

"This afternoon?"

"Sure!"

"Then let's return to your office."

After looking through the lease, Archie signed it and gave Wilkes a check for the deposit and the first month's rent. "Now, if you'll give me the keys, I'll be off," he said.

"Not so fast!" said Wilkes. "I can't give you the keys until the check has cleared."

"But you said I could move in this afternoon?"

"For cash. You walk in here off the street, what do I know about you? I don't know if your check is any good, and I have my client to look after."

"That is an insult! Here," he cried, taking his mother's check out of his pocket and pointing to the signature. "Lady Bingham, she is my mother, and as you can see, it's made out to me. My father is Sir Archibald Bingham, one of England's foremost barristers. And if you take a look out of the window, you will see my Aston Martin parked on the other side of the road. I would say that is reference enough!"

He took a look and whistled. "Very nice," he said, "but cash if you don't mind!"

Archie was exasperated. "I don't carry that kind of cash on me, and it could take until mid-week before the check is cleared. Surely, under the circumstances, an exception can be made."

"Sorry," he replied, shaking his head, "but I have my orders."

"Then I will have the money for you on Monday."

"Suit yourself, but I think it only fair to warn you that it could be gone by then. It's too attractive a proposition to stay on the market for long, and I can't hold it for you."

"Then what do you suggest I do?"

Wilkes's eyes narrowed into two crafty slits. "I like you," he said. "Maybe there is something I can do for you, and that you can do for me. If you get what I mean!"

Archie got the message. "Fair enough," he said. "How much?"

"Mmm!" he murmured, stroking his long chin. "I'm not a greedy man, Mr. Bingham. Say—twenty-five quid?"

"I can't leave myself short over the weekend, but I might be able to manage twenty, and the rest on Monday."

"I accept. A fine gentleman like yourself won't do me for a fiver!"

It took Archie no time at all to move into the flat. His clothes were already packed and waiting at the hotel. All he had to do was collect them and be off. Later that afternoon, he stocked the refrigerator with supplies from the food hall at Harrods: a cooked chicken, a pizza, a few tins of baked beans, some cheese, a French stick of bread, and some fruit.

There was no fruit bowl in the flat, so he filled a plastic dish with the fruit and placed it in the center of the glass dining table, then glanced around. It would take more than a bowl of fruit to make it look like home, he thought, but for now, it would do.

Sunday, he explored the area. The girls were sexy with their short skirts, long hair, and even longer legs. There were a few pubs where a good cheap meal could be had and, of course, the traditional tea shops with their assortment of delectable pastries and gateaux. Not that he had a sweet tooth, but sometimes it was nice just to sit, sipping tea, eating cake, and watching the world pass by the window.

Monday morning, he awoke to the daunting realization that it was a workday. He lingered in bed, wishing that it were still Sunday. The last place on earth he wanted to be was in the office of Haley & Son. But he had no choice, so he dragged himself off the bed, washed, shaved, dressed, and grabbing an apple from the fruit dish, he made his way to the tube station.

He didn't know what kind of reception he would receive, and braced himself for the worst as he rode up in the lift to their offices on the top floor of the building. He need not have worried; there was no reception whatsoever, almost as though he wasn't expected, and he was left to twiddle his thumbs for the whole of that day. It wasn't until the afternoon of the following day that Ambrose, the chief clerk, called him into his office.

"It has been left to me to deal with the situation," he said uncomfortably. "I wish it hadn't been, but then it's not for me to argue with anyone about it."

"If you mean Alfred, I know exactly how you feel."

"That may be so!" said Ambrose. "Anyhow, it has been suggested that your knowledge of the office routine might be in need of refreshing. But you don't need me for that; anyone of the junior clerks can help you there."

Archie's brow shot up. "I don't believe it," he cried. "Ambrose, you know me. You know what I am capable of. No way am I going to deal with some junior clerk!"

"I'm only passing on orders, not giving them. If you have a quarrel with anything, take it up with Alfred."

"You know why he is doing this, don't you? He wants to humiliate me in front of the entire office."

"That's between the two of you. I want no part of it; so take it or leave it, it's up to you."

"If only it were! Well, I suppose I can put up with his nonsense for a month, but no one is going to demean me, and you can tell him so, for all I care."

"I just told you what the score is. Now you do what you like."

***

The moment Archie entered the general office, the busy typewriters stilled and a hush fell over the room. Fingers were poised above the mute keys, and every eye followed him as he made his way to one of the empty desks.

The strained silence might have unnerved the tentative; not so Archie. He was a lot of things, but timid was not one of them. And with an amused grin, he glanced around, then broke the silence. "Show's over," he said, "back to work everyone."

Immediately the tension eased, the clatter of the keys resumed, and once again, the room filled with the sound of uninhibited conversation.

Left to himself, Archie had to search for work to fill the time. Ambrose had given him no clear direction, or any particular duties to perform. In some respects, it was a relief; in others, it wasn't the happiest state of affairs. Nevertheless, he managed to get through the main part of the week without incident.

Friday afternoon, moments before the office was due to close for the weekend, Alfred walked in and went directly to Archie.

Surprised by his unexpected appearance, everyone in the office stopped what they were doing and watched with interest as the two men came face to face. Somewhat bemused, Archie asked, "Is there something you want?"

"Not I!" his eyes glaring with hate as they locked with Archie's. "I bring you a message from Patricia," he said loudly enough for everyone to hear. "She says she is willing to let you keep the Aston Martin, should you wish—but, of course, under the circumstances," he added in a condescending manner, "I doubt you will."

Archie seethed. No one was going to demean him in front of a room full of people and get away with it. "So you are now her errand boy!" he said with an impudent air. "Well, you can go back and tell Patricia that I would be only too happy to return her gift, as long as the request comes directly from her, and not from any lackey."

Alfred went red in the face. The deep silence in the room was fraught with expectation. He opened his mouth to say something, then thought better of it, turned on his heels, and marched out in a huff.

The moment he was gone, activity returned to the office. Covers were placed over machines, desks were cleared, and chairs were mounted on top in readiness for the cleaners.

***

The last weeks flew by in relative peace. Apart from a brief glimpse in passing, he didn't see Alfred again. As for Haley Sr., he didn't see him at all. Archie's one regret was having hurt him. Haley had been good to him, and they had grown very close. There were even times when he wished that he had been his father. How different things might have turned out if, indeed, he had been.

No office is without rumors, and there were plenty running around as to the cause of the breakup between Archie and Patricia, none of which came anywhere close to the truth. There was one piece of gossip, however, that proved to be true. It seemed that Abigail had moved in with Patricia, supposedly to help her through the bad time she was having dealing with the situation. It was no surprise. Archie knew that, one way or another, the cunning bitch would get a foot in the door again. He did wonder, though, how much Alfred actually knew, or perhaps guessed. Not that it concerned him any longer.

When his final day arrived, it was with great relief, not only to him, but to all. The atmosphere at work had been rather stiff and unpleasant. However, there was one cute little secretary, who had worked for the firm for a few weeks, who expressed some regret at his leaving. "If you should ever pass by Albert Mansions in Paddington, look me up," she said with a flirtatious grin. "I live alone."

Any other time he might have been interested, but not then. "Sure," he said, "if I ever pass that way."

Walking out of the office into the late September sunshine that afternoon was like walking out of a prison. The sun had never felt so good, or the air so fresh. He gazed up at the sky. It was a vast ocean of blue, without a cloud to be seen. Like his future, he thought—a future that would be of his own making, with no one to stand in the way or to press their will upon him. He was free at last!

CHAPTER SIXTEEN

Archie spent the first few weeks of freedom luxuriating in his new-found independence. There was a lot to decide, whether he should opt for more experience in a large firm, or start out on his own immediately. The latter was more appealing, but there was plenty of time for decision making. What he needed, at the moment, was to recuperate from the ordeal of the past month. He also wanted time to feel his feet.

He still had his prized Aston Martin, he thought smugly. He knew, when he suggested it to Alfred, that Patricia would never have the nerve to face him and ask for its return. He could have gambled on it.

From time to time, his mother phoned inviting him over for dinner. He refused every invitation, saying he was too busy making plans for the future. Exasperated, she turned up at his flat one day. "I know why you're avoiding us," she said, "but you will have to make peace with your father sooner or later. So why not now?"

"If he wanted to make peace with me, he had the opportunity to do so the day I qualified."

"He doesn't need you, Archie. You need him, and he is in a position to do you a lot of good."

"Sounds as if you doubt I could make it on my own."

"Of course you could, but it would take a lot longer. Why go through the ordeal when all you have to do is apologize to him? He is still your father; he will come around."

"If I beg, and I don't beg anymore. I finished with that the day I completed my articles."

"You can't let your pride get in the way, Archie. We all need a helping hand now and again, and you were fortunate enough to be born into an influential family. Don't allow that arrogance of yours to throw good fortune away. Now, promise you will give it some serious consideration."

"I promise, but I can't say I will act upon it. It's more than a matter of pride, Mother. I don't want to remain under his thumb forever. I have to stand on my own two feet, if I am to make it."

***

Two weeks later, he changed his mind and accepted an invitation to Sunday lunch. His parents always went to morning service, and he thought it a good idea to accompany them. He hadn't been to church since a boy. He never enjoyed it then, and wasn't looking forward to it now, but he guessed it would please them. He needed as much going for him as possible, if he was to get through lunch with his father.

Indeed, it was appreciated and somewhat improved the climate between father and son.

After lunch, at his mother's suggestion, his father and he retired to the library for coffee and brandy. It was obvious that she had spoken to her husband and cleared the way for a discussion about Archie's future.

"So," enquired his father, after a few sips of brandy, "have you given thought to what you want to do?"

Archie welcomed his interest with enthusiasm. "Yes, sir, I have. I've decided to start out on my own."

"Do you think it wise? It's important to get as much practical experience as you can before even considering such a step."

"I received vast experience working for Haley & Son. Their clientele was varied, and I had access to most of them. I learned a great deal, Father, I really did, and I'm not afraid to go out on my own."

"It's not a matter of being afraid. It's a matter of being realistic. You will be thrown in the deep end before you can swim."

"Then I will have to learn fast, won't I?"

"And what of your clients while you are learning?"

"That is something I want to talk to you about," he said with excitement. "A few days ago, I met with the surviving partner of an old established firm that's for sale. It has a small but quality list of clients, and the price is reasonable. Mr. Jessop, who is close to eighty, is anxious to sell to the right person. I know I could make a go of it."

"And the name of this firm?"

"Jessop, Jessop & Jessop."

"Can't say that I've heard of them."

"I've looked into the practice and find that it has a good reputation. As well Mr. Jessop is willing to stay on for a six-month period to familiarize me with his clients and their particular needs. Of course, I won't let it rest there. I intend to build it up, and with our family connections, I should have no problem."

"How much is Mr. Jessop expecting for the practice—considering it's a small concern?"

"We haven't worked out the exact figure, but I reckon thirty thousand pounds would not only buy it but would also leave me with a good working capital to begin with."

"And from whom will you get that kind of finance?"

Archie bit his lip. "I haven't approached the banks as yet," he said tentatively. "I thought I would talk to you first."

"In other words, you want me to lend it to you?"

"If it goes as well as I expect, I should be in a position to repay the loan in a year—two at the most."

"And if it doesn't?"

"Do you doubt my competence?"

"It is your lack of patience and ability to get along with people that worries me. Clients need a good rapport with their lawyer if they are to be retained."

"Then, is that a no?"

His father considered for a moment, and then said, "I'll have Phipps make some inquiries, and if I am satisfied with what he finds, then we will discuss the matter further."

"It will go fast, Father. I can't afford to wait long."

"We are not talking about buying a pair of shoes, Archie. It will take as long as necessary."

His father was right about one thing, Archie didn't have much patience, and the waiting made him extremely irritable. However, when he did hear from his father, it was with good news.

"I'm happy to say Phipps was rather impressed with the setup," he said. "It seems Mr. Jessop is one of the good old-time lawyers who really knows his stuff. Some of his clients go back sixty years, or more, to when his father started the firm. That is not to say you won't lose a certain amount during the first months of taking over, but with the right approach and patience, Archie, you should retain a good majority. Yes indeed, I think we may go ahead and start the negotiations."

"Not we, Father. I am quite capable of negotiating on my own."

"If you are going to be unreasonable about it, I will have nothing more to do with it. You have no experience in dealing with such matters. I am sending Phipps with you. I know he will secure the best terms possible."

"Is it being unreasonable to expect my father not to undermine my authority? I'm a fully qualified lawyer, for heaven's sake. I don't need anyone to hold my hand!"

"And I don't throw my money away! No one learns at my expense. So take it or leave it, which is it?"

His father never failed to ruffle his feathers, but this was one time that he thought better of walking out in a huff. "You give me no choice," he said.

"Not if you want the practice."

"Before we go any further, are there other conditions that I should be aware of?" he asked facetiously.

"Yes, but I would call it a wise decision. The firm's managing clerk is also retiring. Now, Phipps has suggested that his son Thomas might be available. He has had a great deal of experience working for a big law firm in the city, and he assures me that his knowledge is excellent. Phipps has already spoken to him and he is considering the position very seriously. He is just the man you need, Archie. He can be of enormous help to you."

"As what? A spy in the camp?"

"That is totally uncalled for!" remarked his father. "We are doing this for your good, not ours!"

"I couldn't afford to pay him what he's worth, even if I wanted to."

"I have taken that into account, and I am prepared to take on the responsibility until you find your feet."

"It's very noble of you, Father, but if you pay his salary, he'll be working for you, not me, and that I don't like."

"Why can't you take what is handed to you graciously? The sole purpose here is to give you every opportunity to succeed. Have you a quarrel with that?"

"My quarrel is that I will remain under your thumb for a lot longer than I intended to. That's what this is really about, isn't it? You can't pull the wool over my eyes, Father. I have lived with you for far too long for that."

"I will ignore that bit of insolence for your mother's sake. Now once and for all, do you want me to lend you the money or not? There are plenty of other uses I can put it to if you don't."

"No doubt, and I know a few of them!"

His father's face turned dark and ugly. "That's enough from you," he snarled. "A person can only take so much and no more, and you would do well to remember it."

"So what do you want me to say? You know I can't refuse the money at this late stage."

"I'm not looking for gratitude, but I would appreciate some good taste on your part."

"I suppose you will also want everything in writing, or do you trust me?"

"It's a matter of business, not trust."

"Between father and son? I would say that's definitely a lack of trust."

His father glared at him. "I shan't miss a penny of the money if you never repay me," was his angry response, "but that is not the point of the exercise. You have to learn to be accountable. An agreement will be drawn up!"

Phipps proved to be a superb negotiator, and they bought the practice at a steal. Jessop stayed on for the transitional period and, as promised, introduced him to his clients in glowing terms. Archie soon discovered the clientele, mostly in their seventies and eighties, were as outdated as the doddering old man himself. Well, he thought smugly, he would soon shake them up.

Once he was well settled in, his father began to send the odd client his way. No one substantial, but solid enough for the type of firm. That, too, would change, determined Archie. He was out to make a name for himself, and come rain or shine, nothing was going to stop him.

Although he was reluctant to admit it, Phipps Jr. was a godsend. His knowledge of the law, together with his level-headed approach, helped Archie out on more than one occasion. Tom, as he called him, had his head screwed well on, and against all odds, including losing a lot more than a few old clients, when the accounts came out at the end of the first year, they were in the black, if only just.

"So what are you going to report to my father?" asked Archie.

"Now why would I report anything to him, Mr. Bingham? I'm working for you," he replied.

"Come off it, Tom. We both know why you're here."

"Look, when I took this job, I was asked to look after your interest. Well, that's exactly what I've been doing, yours and yours alone."

"In that case, we have to do better next year. Any suggestions?"

"As it happens, I know a clerk of the court. Now, if I were to slip him a few quid, I'm certain he would send some clients our way."

"Why didn't you say so before?

"You're a wildcard, Mr. Bingham. Do you think you could handle court work?"

"Well, there is nothing like finding out for yourself, is there?"

"Then a word of advice. You keep that temper of yours in check when it comes to the police. Treat them with kid gloves and you'll get what you want. Rub them up the wrong way and you've made an enemy."

"Are you telling me how to handle myself in a police court? I'm my father's son. I think I've seen him at work enough times to know what the score is."

"Good, that's what I want to hear."

Archie discovered that he had a talent for advocacy, especially criminal work, but that wasn't what he really wanted. He wanted the big stuff, and so he targeted the property boys, and he got them to come to him by defending the small man against them, and winning too often to be ignored. Soon, he was acting for some of the top businessmen in the city. With this newfound success, he dropped the criminal element in favor of the latter, and he went from strength to strength. After two years in practice, he found he was able to repay the loan his father made him. He also decided it was time to buy himself a decent place to live and got in touch with Wilkes, who had been very helpful to him in the past.

"What did you have in mind?" asked Wilkes.

"A flat, but I don't like large buildings—no character. I want something classy and discreet."

"How do you feel about conversions?"

"Depends where, and if it's a good conversion."

"Then you're in luck. I have the very thing for you in Wimpole Street. The entire house has been exquisitely renovated and there is only one flat left. It's ground floor, and has a gourmet kitchen with dinette large enough to entertain in. There are two bedrooms, and the master suite has a marble bathroom. The lounge has an original Adam fireplace. It doesn't come cheap, but when does anything good come cheap!"

"I've always had a fancy for Wimpole Street. Let's take a look."

The price was very high indeed, but then the flat was most desirable. "I'll take it," said Archie.

"That's what I like about you!" said Wilkes. "You don't mess about. Need a mortgage?"

"Why? Are you going to get me one?"

"I could put you onto my bank. The manager is very accommodating to any client of mine."

"Oh, yeah?" laughed Archie. "And what's in it for you?"

"A quick sale, that's all. I swear on my mother's grave."

"You would."

Wilkes grinned. "Now is that a nice thing to say? And when I'm in a position to do you some good ... tut! tut!"

"Such as?"

Wilkes gave Archie a probing glance. "Did I tell you I got married recently? A baby on the way as well," he said. "Damn expensive babies, they need good schools, the right home to bring their friends to. God, you wouldn't believe how much they need these days. It's not easy to make ends meet. True, I'm in line for a partnership, but that won't happen for a long time yet. The old buggers won't retire and make way for the young, and I can't wait. I want it all now, Mr. Bingham. We're a lot alike, you and I. I knew it the first time I laid eyes on you. I said to myself, 'Wilkes, here is a gent you can do business with.'"

"That depends on the business," said Archie.

"I'm with you there. Trust me, I wouldn't do anything illegal. We have a property on our books. It's going for a song. The owner is desperate and needs cash quickly. It could turn out to be a very lucrative deal for someone like you."

"I can't afford to buy this flat and purchase a property, no mater how reasonably priced."

"I didn't think you could, and I can't buy it because I don't know how my firm would look upon it, them being a stodgy lot, conflict of interest and all that rubbish! But what if I worked it so that you could buy and sell the property at the same time, and without having to put a single penny down? There could be a hundred thousand profit in it, maybe more."

"For you or me?"

The agent grinned. "Both."

"And your end of the deal would be...?"

"We split fifty-fifty."

"Sixty-forty. I'm out on a limb if you don't come up with a purchaser in time."

"Not the way I'd work it. By the time contracts are ready to be exchanged, I'll have a purchaser at our price. I will then arrange it so that contracts are signed simultaneously, and on completion you and I are a hundred grand to the good."

"Sounds simple enough. But what if you don't find a purchaser? And even if you do, what's to stop things from going wrong at the last minute?"

"If I can't find a purchaser, you can back out before anything is signed, and that lets you off the hook. As for something going wrong during the exchange, it will be my job to see that nothing does. I will be with our purchaser in one room while you are with the owner's solicitor in another. If ours won't sign, for some reason, I will let you know before you sign your end."

"How will you get over the down payment?"

"I'm the agent. Leave that side of it to me."

"I'd like to think it over."

"Do, but don't take long. This property will go fast. We can't afford to piddle around here."

"I don't intend to. You will have your answer in the morning."

The idea excited Archie. How far could he trust Wilkes, he didn't know. But he was smart, and obviously had it all figured out. Anyhow, if he couldn't trust his sense of decency, he knew he could trust his greed, and he was a very greedy bugger.

Of course, he would have to be discreet. He didn't want Phipps to know anything about his dealings with the man. Not that it was any of his business, but he might let slip to his father, and Archie wasn't sure how he might take it. He was a lawyer, first and foremost, and anything to do with business, he frowned upon as though it was beneath him.... Yes! He decided he would go ahead. An opportunity like that didn't come along every day of the week.

It turned out to be a money-spinner. The property market was hot. Wilkes was in the know, and Archie's bank balance swelled beyond all expectation. The practice also did well out of Wilkes, who referred some very influential people in the property world, and Archie soon gained a reputation for being a smart real estate lawyer. In the process, he became a very substantial young man.

He was in the fast lane, and it seemed to him that his luck would never run out. The money was pouring in, and with all that ready cash at his disposal, he turned to his first love—gambling. It wasn't his only vice; also there were fast women, booze, fancy clothes, and exorbitant restaurants. Yet, with all that, there was a constant nagging inside him, a hunger that couldn't be satisfied, no matter what. Something was missing from his life, and it gave rise to self-doubt.

Naturally, he blamed his father for this. All his uncertainties, his anxieties—he was at the root of them. Wasn't he to blame for the lack of love in his life. Had he ever given him more than a measly few minutes of his time? And that begrudgingly. It seemed everything that should have been his was bestowed on another. Belinda—the girl with the chestnut-colored hair that framed a face more lovely than anyone he had ever seen. She was the apple of his father's eye, and he hated her for it.

It was a strange kind of hate that obsessed him. He couldn't get her out of his mind, even now, after two years had passed since he saw her. Was she still as lovely? he wondered. Would she still be able to excite his imagination? Would he melt at the sight of her as before?

With Wimpole Street so close to Montague Square, the urge to go and see for himself became too strong to ignore. All he needed was a glimpse, he told himself, and he would be able to get on with his life and never think of her again. After all, she was nothing to him, nothing!

Week after week, on Saturday afternoon, he would take a walk past the square, and stop for a while to gaze at the house where she lived before walking on. It was on one such Saturday in October, a month that often began the day with a mist and ended with the sun filtering through a soft haze, that Archie stopped, as usual, to gaze at the house. All of a sudden, the door opened and she came tripping down the steps just as she had done the first time he saw her, and his heart stood still, just as it had then. She was even more lovely than he remembered, and he couldn't stop staring at her as she passed him on the street. He felt like a fool, a schoolboy with a crush; only he was no schoolboy, but she was a schoolgirl. Damn her, he thought. After all, what was she but the daughter of a whore, and was probably as wanton as her mother.

Despite his feelings about her, he couldn't get her out of his mind. At night, in bed, thoughts of her drove him mad, and he knew that he had to see her once more if he was to get her out of his system.

The following Saturday, he was there at the corner of George Street and Montague Square, tense, as he waited for her to appear. When it seemed unlikely that she would, the door opened and there she was, coming down the front steps and walking toward him as she had the previous week.

The closer she came, the wilder beat his heart, and this time she smiled at him as she passed. It left him breathless, and he had to steady himself before he could move on. It made him angry; once more he had behaved like a fool, and he made up his mind never to let it happen again.

But it did, the following week, when she spoke to him. "Hello," she said. "Are you waiting for someone or just looking?"

That she should speak to him took him by surprise, and he asked, "Is it usual for you to talk to strangers like this?"

She smiled that wonderful smile that made his heart soar. "My father would have a fit if he thought that I did, but I have seen you here so often that I feel I know you."

The mention of his father reminded him of who she was and he snapped angrily, "Then you should do as your father tells you and not talk to strangers in this way."

Her eyes opened wide, and in all innocence she asked, "Then how would we become acquainted?"

She had a way with her that took him off guard. "Why would you want to?" he asked.

"There are some things that cannot be explained, like what I felt when I first saw you from my window."

"You could get yourself into a lot of trouble saying things like that to a man you don't know."

"What is wrong with saying what you think or feel? My father says it is better to tell the truth than to lie. Lies have a way of catching up with you."

There was a bitter edge to his voice as he said, "Spoken from experience no doubt."

She regarded him with surprise. "You sound so angry. Are you always like this? Or is it something or someone, perhaps, who makes you unhappy?"

"What is happiness? Are you happy?"

She smiled. "That's my father's trick, to answer a question with a question."

"And you are far too inquisitive for a young lady."

"Does it offend you?"

"No! But it is disconcerting."

"Perhaps if I introduce myself, you won't find it so disconcerting. I'm Belinda."

"Belinda! Pretty name."

"What's your name?" she asked.

"Does it matter?"

"I told you mine."

This was the last thing he expected. What could he tell her…? "Arthur," he said with some discomfort.

"Arthur!" she repeated. " 'A'—the same initial as my father. I like it." She waited for him to respond, and when he didn't, she said hesitantly, "Well … I better be going … goodbye." Again she waited for a response, and when none was forthcoming, she turned, slowly, and started to walk away.

He watched her for a moment, and then, on a sudden impulse, called out, "Wait a minute!"

She stopped and turned. "Yes?" she asked eagerly.

He was at a loss. Why did he call after her? "Would you have tea with me?" he asked, and his heart missed a beat.

A smile hovered about her lips. "Now?"

"Yes!"

"I would love to," she replied.

He was six feet tall, but she made him feel taller as he walked beside her up George Street to a little café in Marylebone Lane where they served the most delectable cakes made on the premises.

She couldn't have been more than five foot two, and when he noticed the struggle she had to keep pace with him, he asked, "Am I going too fast for you?"

She laughed happily. "I'm used to it," she assured him. "My father is as tall as you. In fact, there is so much about you that reminds me of him. I noticed it the first time I saw you from my window. Maybe that's why I feel so at ease with you. Do you feel the same way? Or is it just me?"

"No," he said sharply, "I don't."

She was taken aback by the harsh tone of his voice. "Have I said something wrong?" she asked anxiously.

He stared down at her. What was he getting himself into? "… I, um, I get uptight sometimes, that's all," he replied.

"We all do," she said.

It was that time of day, between lunch and tea, when the café was deserted. A waitress sauntered over, as if she resented the intrusion, and sat them by the window. "This all right?" she asked with a bored sigh.

"Perfect," said Belinda.

"Thought it might be," she said indifferently. "Everyone likes to sit by a window." She took their order, and then slouched away.

Belinda's gaze followed her to the kitchen. "It must be terrible to be so bored with life!"

Archie shrugged. "I think people are more bored with themselves than with life. It takes a certain capacity to enjoy living, and not all have it."

"Do you have it?"

"I'm never bored."

"Neither am I."

"Does that mean there is nothing missing in your life?"

"One has nothing to do with the other."

He knew what she was referring to, and it gave him a measure of satisfaction. Why should he be the only one to suffer because of his father? "I suppose we all have something missing in our lives," he said.

"Yes!" she whispered sadly.

"Want to talk about it?"

"No."

"Then we won't."

She was suddenly hesitant, and he wondered what was coming. "My mother says we should always look at what we have and not at what we haven't," she said

"If everyone looked at life that way, how would anyone achieve their goals?"

"I have never thought about it in that sense," she said thoughtfully.

"Have you no goals?"

There was a faraway look in her eyes. "Simple ones ... like love and happiness, but they are always the hardest to achieve ... you would think God would have made them the easiest."

"You believe in God?"

"Of course. Don't you?"

"He's a myth, like everything else in the Bible."

"We all need something or someone to believe in, or life has no meaning."

"I believe in myself. Some of the most powerful men in history have believed in none other than themselves."

"In themselves? Or in the destiny that God chose for them?"

He laughed. "Now, that would make a good argument for another time," he said, and gave her an admiring glance. "You know, you're quite intelligent for a beautiful young woman."

She blushed. Fortunately, the waitress arrived with their tea and cake and saved her from further embarrassment. "My favorite," she declared when she saw the light sponge cake filled with whipped cream and a layer of strawberry jam.

Archie watched as she tucked into the cream cake, thinking to himself he shouldn't be there with her, and that if he had any sense, he would leave right away. But he knew he couldn't. There was so much more that he needed to know; how she felt about her father—his father. Most of all, he wanted to hear that she was hurting. "Tell me more about yourself," he asked.

She stopped eating and looked directly at him. "There isn't much to tell."

"You make it sound as though you lead an empty life."

A sadness crept into her eyes. "A good part of my life is empty," she said. "Then there are moments when it is brimming with happiness. But I don't want to talk about me; I want to know about you. You seem interesting. You must lead an interesting life."

"I don't know about interesting; a different kind of life to most, I suppose."

"Definitely interesting," she said, "but there is something else … I can't quite make out what, and it confuses me; but then, I should know all about being confused. There are times in my life when I am not sure who I am supposed to be."

"That's a strange thing to say. You have a mother and father, haven't you? What is so confusing about that?"

She lowered her eyes and whispered, "Things!"

He was familiar with those … things, as she called them, and still he couldn't find it in his heart to spare her. "Such as?" he asked, searching her face for a hint of suffering.

She looked away from him for a moment, and when her eyes returned, there it was—what he wanted to see: anguish. "My parents aren't married," she said slowly. "You see … my father is already married to someone else. It isn't easy for me or my mother to share him with others. I want to be with him all the time, like any daughter would be." She swallowed. "It doesn't make for a very happy situation."

Archie went cold. Was he supposed to feel sorry for her? Is that what she expected: sympathy? Well, he had no sympathy, none whatsoever. "How do you think his family feels? Don't you think it makes them unhappy to have to share him with you?" he asked bitterly.

She glanced at him in surprise. "I have never thought about it," she said. "Perhaps they don't know that we exist."

"And what if they do? Do you think your father is being fair to them? Perhaps they are hurting just as you are; after all, they are the ones being betrayed."

She gasped in horror. "No!" she cried. "My father isn't like that."

"Isn't he? He sounds very much like that. He sounds like a bastard."

She was hurt and angry. "Why would you say something so horrible; you know nothing about him or his love for me and my mother. It's not as if they were having an affair … they truly love each other. That must count for something."

"If he really loves your mother, then why is he still married to his wife? It would seem to me that his first love is himself."

Tears of frustration welled up in her eyes. "I should never have told you about them. I thought you would understand. I think … I think I would like to go home now."

Her tears, her gentleness, everything about her was getting to him. Where was all the hatred, the bitterness? What happened to it? He needed it. Without it he was vulnerable—stripped naked. Abruptly, he called for the bill, and as soon as it was taken care of, they left.

There was a certain hesitation in their step as they wandered back to Montague Square. When they reached the corner, Archie stopped. "This is where we part," he said.

Her eyes doleful, she glanced up at him. "It sounds so final," she whispered.

He looked down at the ground. "It is!" he said.

"Because I told you that my parents weren't married?"

His eyes returned to her face, such a lovely face, he thought with a pang. "We are wrong for each other; there are too many differences, too many problems."

"I don't believe it. Somehow I have offended you, and I don't know why."

"Then let us leave it there. It's for the best."

"Not for me."

"Especially for you."

"Then tell me why." When he didn't reply, the tears welled up again and she was barely able to whisper, "Goodbye," before she turned and ran home.

He stared after her, his heart a mix of pain and relief. The unthinkable had happened—he had fallen in love with the one person in the world he should never have.

***

The following week was the worst of his life. He couldn't eat; he couldn't sleep. All he could think of was Belinda. He yearned to see her again, to be with her and to look into those wonderful eyes of hers. The promise of the world was in those eyes, and he wanted the world, and he was racked with guilt over it.

But guilt or not, he couldn't keep away, and the following Saturday, he was there at the corner of George Street and Montague Square, hoping for a glimpse of her.

She must have been watching for him from her window, for no sooner had he arrived at the corner, then out she came and flew down the street to meet him, her face radiant as she cried, "I knew you would come, I knew it!"

His heart soared at the sight of her, and, lost for words, all he could do was stare. Eventually, he managed to ask, "Tea?" and he laughed when she nodded with childlike eagerness.

Side by side, they walked up George Street. The air smelled different. The wind on his face felt different. It was filled with her—with her joy, her presence—and oh, how good it was.

They turned into Marylebone Lane, and there was the café, their café, as they came to call it, looking warm and cozy on that dull November day, not that they noticed the weather. They could have been in the middle of a blinding snowstorm, and they would only have noticed each other.

The same waitress sat them at the same table. Her weary expression softened when she saw them, for indeed, how could anyone not soften in the presence of young love? "Same as last week?" she asked.

Her face flushed, her eyes glowing, "Please!" said Belinda.

She smiled and went off to get the order.

For a while, they sat and stared at one another, taking pleasure from simply being together. Suddenly, Belinda asked, "What made you change your mind?"

"Does it matter? I'm here."

"It would be nice to know, that's all."

"Why must women question the obvious?"

"Perhaps because we are not certain of ourselves. Perhaps we simply like to hear men say it."

He laughed. "Perhaps you simply like to have us grovel."

She became serious. "No, that's not it. We like to hear that we are wanted."

286

He felt uncomfortable. It was not the kind of conversation he wished to pursue "Tell me how you spent the week."

Her face brightened. "I go to college during the day, and study hard at night. I don't know what I want to do yet. I am giving thought to becoming a barrister like my father. Did I tell you that he was a barrister?" she asked proudly.

His heart sank. "I don't think so," he said, frowning.

"What do you do?" she asked.

He hesitated. From one lie comes so many, he thought. "I, er—I buy and sell property, that sort of thing. But let's not talk about me. I want to know all about you. Do you have a boyfriend?"

"No, of course not," she cried. "I wouldn't be here with you if I did."

"This isn't exactly the same as having a boyfriend, is it?"

"Then what is it?"

What could he say? He wasn't sure what it was himself.... "Friends," he said at last. "We're friends."

"That, too," she replied.

"No!" he said firmly. "Just friends!"

Her face fell. "Something is the matter. I can sense it."

"Look, you mustn't attach more to this than there is. You mustn't romanticize a situation. It's not good for you and it certainly isn't good for me."

"I don't understand. I'm not romanticizing anything. I know what I feel. I thought you felt the same way."

"You have to understand something; it's just not possible!"

"Then why were my prayers answered when I prayed to see you again?"

"I would be careful what I pray for if I were you."

"Not all my prayers are answered like this one."

"And this is the one prayer that shouldn't have been."

"I don't understand. You talk in riddles."

Her sweet face was anxious as she waited for a reply. "Listen to me, Belinda," he said softly. "We can never be more than friends. I would be lying if I said that we could."

"But why? Aren't you well? Because if you aren't, I don't care. I just want to be with you."

"There is nothing physically wrong with me. It's just how it is."

"Are you married?"

"I am not married."

"Then everything is all right!"

She was beginning to frustrate him and he snapped. "You are making it difficult for me with all your questions. I should never have come here today."

"More riddles. Why are men so full of riddles? I just want to go on seeing you, that's all. Please?"

He should have stood firm, but he had always been weak when it came to what he wanted, and he wanted to go on seeing her as much as she wanted to go on seeing him. "I'll tell you what," he said. "We will make a pact to meet here, at the café, every Saturday. But should one of us decide not to come, then the pact ends and we get on with our lives. Can you make that promise to me Belinda?"

"But!"

"No buts, Belinda. Just a yes or no."

"Yes!" she said, and those marvelous eyes of hers lit with joy.

For the next few weeks, Saturdays came and went. They would talk about everything and anything, but never something serious. When he was with her, he was filled with guilt. When they weren't together, his heart ached with longing and he couldn't wait to see her.

How simple it was for her, he thought. As it was, the stress was becoming intolerable and, on more than one occasion, he thought of not turning up.

The first Saturday in December was a cold day with gray skies and snow flurries that dissolved to water as they touched the ground. He was already at the café, waiting, when he saw her from the window, walking slower than usual, the snowflakes covering her dark hair like a lace handkerchief.

He could see that she was upset about something, and with a stab of fear, he wondered if it had anything to do with him. "What's wrong?" he asked the moment she took her seat beside him.

She turned a pair of tearful eyes to him. "It's my father," she said. "We haven't seen or heard from him for a week. It's not like him and we are worried."

"Oh, is that all!" he sighed with relief. "I thought it might be something important."

"It is important. He had a bad cold when we last saw him. It might have turned into pneumonia. He had it once before, and that was after a cold."

"I'm certain he's all right. He's probably busy, that's all."

"He must be ill; otherwise, he would have phoned to let us know that he wouldn't be coming."

It annoyed him when she spoke of his father as if he belonged to her; but then, she didn't know the truth. What would she feel if she did? he wondered. Would she still love him as much? She was beginning to get on his nerves. "For God's sake, Belinda," he cried, "do you think he really cares about you the way you care about him?"

She looked somewhat puzzled. "Of course he cares about me; he loves me," she said.

"Don't you understand? All he cares about is himself. You don't put a man like that on a pedestal; he doesn't deserve it."

"Why do you hate him so?" she asked in bewilderment. "Is that how you feel about your father?"

"What I feel about my father ... well, it doesn't matter."

"It does. You frighten me when you talk like that. It makes me realize that I know so little about you. We talk, but you don't say anything important. What are you afraid of?"

"You are the one who should be afraid; but then, how can you know?"

"Know what?"

"I think we should call it a day," he said. "It was silly to have started this strange relationship of ours in the first place. Now it's time to move on."

"No!" she cried. "We can't stop seeing each other, not now. I'll do anything you want. I'll never mention my father again if it makes you angry. Only please, don't stop seeing me. I couldn't bear that."

"It's not that I want to; it's just that we must stop. Believe me, it's for the best."

"That's what you said once before; but whose best?"

"It's too complicated to explain. Now, I'm going to pay the bill; and then, I am going to get up and walk out of here on my own. As soon as I have gone, go home to your mother and forget all about me. Please, Belinda, for my sake, if not for yours?"

She was in tears. "You ask too much," she wept. "I'll never forget you, and I'll be here waiting for you, next week, the week after, and for the rest of my life, if that's how long it takes for you to return. I love you, and although you have never said it, I know you love me. So don't deny it because I won't believe you."

The ache in his heart was too much. He closed his eyes for fear of look-ing into her face and changing his mind…. He rose slowly, turned, and without a last glance her way, walked out of the café, and out of her life.

She may have been out of his life, but not his heart. He had to throw himself into work during the day, and play hard at night, to forget her. Sometimes it worked. Mostly, it didn't, especially when he dreamt of her only to awaken with his limbs throbbing with desire, and he began to dread sleep. It took its toll on him, and he became irritable and short-tempered with everyone, including some of his best clients.

Phipps expressed his concern in no uncertain terms. "Look here," he said. "I don't know what's going on with you, but whatever it is, you had better get a hold of yourself. We can't afford to lose clients, and we will if you carry on like this."

"It's none of your bloody business!" responded Archie.

"That's where you're wrong. I've put a lot of effort into helping you build up this firm, and I don't like wasting my time. So don't tell me it's none of my business when you behave like some bloody fool who puts the practice at risk."

"If you're not happy with the way things are, you know what you can do!"

"And I just might. Who needs to work for an ungrateful bugger?"

"You watch it! Have some respect."

"I give respect where respect is due. You watch it! I could get myself a good job just like that!" he said, snapping his fingers.

As a rule, Archie never backed down, but he knew Phipps was right, and he didn't dare let him go; he was too valuable. If the truth be told, he didn't know what he would do without him. "Look," he said somewhat apologetically, "I've been through a rough time lately. I know I shouldn't be taking it out on the clients, or you, for that matter. It won't happen again. Okay?"

"Okay. As long as you keep your personal problems at home where they belong, I'll continue to do my best for you."

While things improved at the office, it was the reverse in his private life. Thoughts of Belinda drove him crazy. He found himself going from one woman to another, trying to find someone, anyone who could help ease the pain he was going through. None of them could, and they would leave him feeling as empty afterwards as he was before, if not more so.

He longed to see her again, to catch a glimpse of her face, to hear the sound of her voice. If only he could wave a magic wand and banish all thought of her. If only he could get her out of his system and get on with his life.

The Saturday before Christmas, the longing became too unbearable to ignore. He had to see her or go out of his mind. That afternoon, he put on his overcoat, took an umbrella from the stand, and ventured out in the driving rain. He didn't even know if she would be at the café, but he had to find out; he had to know if she was suffering as much as he was.

The moment he turned the corner into the lane, he saw her sitting by the window, looking sad and forlorn, staring out at the rain that splashed heavily against the pavement. Immediately, his heart went out to her, and he knew then that he couldn't put her through the hope and despair all over again, but neither could he leave until his eyes had their fill of her. So cold and wet, he pressed himself back into a doorway, and continued to gaze out at her sweet face.

Suddenly, she rose, lifted her coat from the back of her chair, and put it on. His heart fell. It was time for him to leave the shelter of the doorway and return home. The last thing he wanted was for her to see him when she left the café. It was painful enough for him; it would only make it painful for both of them if they were to meet. He opened his umbrella. The rain was heavier than before, and with the wind driving it, it swept against his legs, making his trousers cling against his shins as he strode home.

He spent Christmas day with his parents. He would have gotten out of it if he could, but then he would have upset his mother, and he didn't want to do that. She deserved better from him. Unlike his father, she had always been there when he needed her. It was the thought of having to suffer his father all through dinner and listen to him moralizing about something or other that filled him with distaste.

Why was it, he wondered, that those least qualified were always the first to spout morality at others? He watched him carving the turkey, in that exact way of his, his face a mask of respectability, and he wanted to spit.

He knew that he must have seen Belinda and her mother the night before. She had told him, "Father always spends Christmas Eve with us," and her eyes had glowed with happiness for a second before turning sad the next. "He spends Christmas Day with his other family." She always referred to them as his other family, as though it made it more acceptable to her. "Wouldn't it be wonderful if we could all spend Christmas together as one family?" she said wistfully. "I know it's an impossible dream, but wouldn't it be wonderful?"

His heart filled with pain at the thought of her. God, how he missed her!

He watched his father place a turkey leg on a plate, saying, "I know you like the drumstick," and passing it to him.

"Actually, I prefer the breast," he replied, just to be contrary, and passed it back.

His father gave him an exasperated glance, removed the leg from the plate, and replaced it with breast.

February was Belinda's birthday month—the fifteenth, to be exact. How could he forget? When she mentioned it to him, he planned to get her something special to remember him by. He found the ideal gift a week before they last saw each other, in a little antique shop in Jermyn Street, which runs behind Simpson's in Piccadilly. It was a Victorian broach made up of five garnets with a tiny seed pearl in the center of each one, and set in gold filigree in the shape of a square, or cross, if worn at an angle. It caught his eye at once, and he went in and bought it. Now, it was lying in a drawer at his flat, and would probably remain there forever, he thought sadly.

Friday, the day of her birthday, he opened the drawer, took it out, and fingered it gently. It was hers, he thought. It always would be, but she would never know. He then placed it back in the drawer and closed it quickly, as if it was an act of shutting her out of his life once and for all.

Saturday morning, he awoke from a restless sleep and knew that he would never have peace until he had given her the broach. He wanted to see her wearing it. He wanted to see her face light with joy, as he knew it would when she saw it.

It was a spur-of-the-moment decision, without any thought to the consequences, or even that she might not be there. After all, almost two months had passed since they last met.

It was a cold afternoon, with a bitter north wind blowing, but he was warm with excitement as he placed the little velvet box, with the broach inside, in his coat pocket and went out to the car. Normally, he would have walked but he was in a hurry to get to the café; he was scared she might leave before he got there. He parked in Wigmore Street, and went the rest of the way on foot.

He prayed that she hadn't left, as he turned the corner into the lane. Whether it was God or the devil who heard him, his prayer was answered. As the café came into sight, so did she, sitting at their table by the window, her eyes sad, her mouth turned down at the corners as if ready to cry. The lump in his throat almost choked him, and he stood still, wavering as to whether he should stay or leave. The decision was made for him. She noticed him standing there, his hair swept across his forehead, the scarf he had wrapped around his neck flying in the wind, and joy mixed with wonder spread across her face, lifting the corners of her mouth and making her eyes glow.

She rose immediately and almost knocked him over with excitement as he entered the café. "I knew you couldn't stay away today of all days. I knew you would remember my birthday," she cried happily.

They sat opposite each other; she in her usual seat, he in his, as though it were a week ago when they last saw one another. He stared at her for a while. She gazed back, unable to take her eyes off him. He dipped his hand into his coat pocket, and brought out the little box and placed it in front of her. "I came to give you this," he said. "It has been lying in my drawer for the past two months."

She stared at the box. "Two months!" she murmured. "It felt like two years since I last saw you."

"Open it," he said softly.

She lifted the lid slowly, then gasped with delight. "Oh!" and taking the broach from the box, she handed it to him. "Pin it on," she said.

Their hands touched as he took it from her, and a wave of pleasure rippled through him. He swallowed, leaned across the table, and pinned the broach at the neck of her blouse. Immediately, her hand lifted, and she traced it with her fingertips. "Thank you," she whispered. "I will cherish it always."

It was a bittersweet moment, making it all the more difficult for him. "I should leave," he said.

"Please!" she begged. "Don't go. Don't leave me again."

"I have to."

"You can't give me hope and then take it away without an explanation. It's more than I can bear."

He shook his head in despair. "If I stayed, I would want to hold you, touch you."

"Then hold me, touch me. It's what I dream about."

"You don't understand!"

"Then make me understand."

She was right, he thought, she should know. He hesitated for a moment, and then said, "Look at me, Belinda ... really look at me ... can't you see the resemblance?"

"What resemblance?"

"To your father!"

She stared at him in disbelief.

"I'm his son," he said simply.

She turned pale. "That's a cruel joke."

"If only it were."

"No. You're lying."

"When we first met, didn't you remark how like your father I was? If you think it was by coincidence, then you are lying to yourself. I am his son. It's not a lie."

"You're frightening me. I don't want to hear anymore."

"The way I feel about you frightens me. That's why we can't see each other."

"It's an excuse not to go on seeing me. That's all it is," she cried.

She was being difficult, stubbornly refusing to believe who he was, and it was driving him mad. "Can't you see what you are doing? Just looking at you torments me. What can I say that will convince you of the truth?"

She was close to tears. "Why do you keep lying to me? Why did you come here if you never want to see me again?"

Suddenly, he was angry. "Damn you!" he burst out. "If you won't believe me, then you will have to believe your own eyes. Put on your coat; we're leaving."

"I don't want to go with you. I want to go home."

His temper rising, he stood up and pulled her to her feet. "Now get your coat!"

He was glaring at her, his eyes sparked with anger, and it scared her. "Why have you changed like this? I don't know you anymore ... leave me alone," she cried.

He didn't reply, and taking her coat from the back of her chair, he made her put it on, and then pulled her from the café and along the street to his car.

Partly running, partly stumbling along the pavement, she followed him, too afraid to resist, and when he commanded her to get in his car, she did so immediately.

She watched him out of the corner of her eye as he drove. "Where ... where are you taking me?" she asked feebly.

His eyes had become glazed and she didn't know if he heard her or not. She didn't ask again, but just sat there, her heart thumping with fear.

Soon, they were pulling up in front of a large townhouse in the Bayswater area. He got out of the car, came around her side, opened the door, and dragged her out. Then, grabbing her by the arm, he walked with her up the stairs to the door of the house, opened it, and pushed her inside.

Her eyes wide like a frightened kitten, she glanced around. She was having trouble breathing and barely whispered, "Where are we?"

"This is his house, my father's house. That's his library," he said, pointing to one of the rooms. "Go on … see for yourself."

Alarmed by the crazed look in his eyes, she backed away. "No!" she cried, and glanced at the door, looking to run.

"Go on, go inside," he shouted.

She jumped in fright. "I don't want to."

His frustration with her growing, he again grabbed her by the arm and pulled her into the library. "There!" he said, pointing triumphantly to the portrait of his father hanging over the mantelpiece. "Our *father.*"

Slowly, her eyes lifted until they were staring at the portrait. Horror spread across her face, and then, shaking her head in disbelief, she pulled away from him. "It's a trick," she cried, and ran for the front door.

In a flash, he was after her and brought her back. "Oh no! You don't leave this house until you accept the truth about that man. I have suffered long enough on my own. Now you can suffer with me."

She was staring at him in fear, repeating over and over, "It's a lie, a lie."

He was at breaking point, and, no longer in control of himself, he struck her across the face. "You stupid bitch!" he screamed. "You're no better than that slut of a mother of yours. You think you have a claim on my father? Well, whores don't have claims; they are just whores."

Terrified of him, she began to whimper. "I want to go home. I want to go home."

The whining enraged him even more, and he threw her on to the couch, and pinning her down, he tore at her clothes, and started to assault her.

The more she struggled, the more violent he became, and in desperation she uttered a piercing cry, *"Noooo!"*

Perhaps it was the sound of that heart-rendering appeal that brought him to his senses, but whatever it was, he was suddenly filled with horror, and, staggering back from the couch, he gasped, "Oh my God!"

Her eyes were wild with fear as they stared up at him.

"I'm sorry! I'm sorry!" he kept repeating. "Forgive me, I beg you, forgive me," and going over to her, he tried to help her up from the couch.

Still in terror, she shrank from his touch.

"Please," he begged.

She shrank back even further while her eyes watched his every move, and when she saw her chance, she swiftly rose and fled the house as quickly as her feet would carry her.

He stared after her, too dazed to stop her. Moments later, he heard the sound of screeching brakes, followed by a sickening thud. Heart in mouth, he ran to the front door only to see her lying in the road, her body mangled like a rag doll that had been twisted out of shape.

He froze, his mind too numb to think or feel, and he stood there, staring down at her, unable to move, unable to run to her side to see if she was still alive or dead.

People were pouring out of their homes, running over to see what could be done. The man who was driving the car that hit her was in a daze. "I didn't see her," he cried. "One minute the road was clear, the next she was in front of me. I couldn't stop. Oh God, I couldn't stop!"

He was beside himself with grief. A few people were trying to calm him, while others were standing over Belinda, watching, as one of them tried to find a pulse. "Phone for an ambulance," he called out. "I'll do it," cried another, and ran to his house.

Still numb, Archie watched the activity through glazed eyes. Nothing seemed real, as in a dream.

Suddenly, a siren was heard in the distance, growing louder and louder as an ambulance came into view, its wail winding down when it came to a halt in the road. "Quick, over here!" cried the man bending over her.

Two paramedics came out of the ambulance, bringing a stretcher with them, and ran over. One took her pulse; the other put a stethoscope to her chest. After a few seconds, the one with the stethoscope shook his head.

Archie's heart sank. It was his first feeling since seeing her lying in the road, and the pain was excruciating.

The police arrived on the scene just as they were covering her body with a blanket. They walked over, pulled it back, took a quick look, and then threw the blanket back again, giving the ambulance men a nod. They then lifted her onto the stretcher, carefully placed her in the ambulance, and drove away.

Archie swallowed. He should have gone with her, not just left her in the hands of strangers, but it was too late now—it was done. When it came down to it, he was a coward, and felt ashamed.

The police were taking notes from those around. One of the officers came up the steps to talk to Archie. "Shocking business," he said. "Is this where you were standing when it happened?"

"I was inside. By the time I came out to see what was going on, she was lying in the road."

"Apparently, she was seen running from this house?"

"Yes. I suppose she was."

"Why was she running? Were you chasing her?"

Archie's heart sank. "No, of course not. Look, Officer, I feel a bit groggy. Can we go inside?"

"Certainly, sir. I can see you're upset."

He followed Archie into the living room and gave a quick look around before giving Archie a probing glance. "So why was she running?" he asked.

He swallowed. "We had a bit of an argument."

"A bit of an argument? A bit extreme to run away from a bit of an argument," he said.

"I know it may sound ridiculous, but that's how it was. I—I couldn't stop her."

"Did you want to stop her?"

"What is that supposed to mean?"

"It was just a question."

"It happened so fast, Officer. I didn't have time to think."

He gave another glance around. "Is this your house, sir?"

"My parents."

"They are not home, I gather?"

"No."

"Is this the room where the argument took place?"

"The library," he replied without thinking.

"And where would that be?"

Archie was beginning to feel uncomfortable. "Across the hall," he said hesitantly.

The officer gave him a searching look before crossing the hall to the library. His sharp eyes took the room in at a glance, and when he caught sight of the painting over the mantelpiece, he asked in surprise. "Isn't that Sir Archibald Bingham?"

"He's my father," said Archie.

"It is a small world! I can't count the times I've given evidence for your father. He's a good man. Knows how to treat the police, unlike some snotty-nose lawyers who think they're it! Are you a lawyer then?"

"Solicitor."

"Didn't want to follow in your father's footsteps? Then I can see how he would be a hard act to follow. No offense intended, of course."

"None taken, Officer."

"So, do you live here with your parents?"

"No!"

"Then what, may I ask, were you and the young lady doing here?"

The questions were unsettling, and he wished they would stop. "We were close by … we just popped in," he said cautiously.

"Then your parents knew the deceased?"

Deceased, thought Archie; it was such a cold, impersonal word. He swallowed. "No."

"Hmm!" murmured the officer. "Let me get it straight. You just popped in to your parents' house, when they weren't here, and when they didn't even know the girl. If you don't live here, why would you do that?"

Damn the man, he thought, and took a deep breath. "Put like that, it does sound ridiculous. But that isn't how it was. I don't know why we stopped by. There was no ulterior motive behind it; we just did. This is my parents' home after all, Officer, and I'm entitled to come and go as I please."

"I can't recall having mentioned an ulterior motive. Then again, I am curious and tend to ask a lot of questions. There is also this report I have to make out for my superior. Now, he asks some very tough questions, and I want to have all the answers ready."

"Well, I can't tell you any more than I already have. This has been very traumatic for me. I still can't believe it!"

"I'm sure you can't! However, as soon as you give me the girl's name and address, I'll be gone."

"… Belinda!" he said softly.

He took out a notepad and began to write…. "Last name?" he asked.

Last name? wondered Archie. He had never thought to ask. He assumed she bore his father's name, but, of course, how could she have? "I—I don't know," he said. "We only knew each other a short time."

"What about an address?"

"Montague Square. I don't know the number of the house. We'd meet at a café."

"Do you know if she lived with her parents?"

"Her mother. She never mentioned a father," he paused. "Perhaps he's dead."

"Or her parents don't live together. It's not uncommon these days," he said, and his eyes scanned the room once again. "There was no identification on the body. Neither was there a handbag. Could she have left it behind when she ran from the house?"

"I don't know."

"Would you mind if I took a look around?"

"Why would I?"

"Exactly!" he exclaimed with a grin, while his eyes remained examining.

Archie stood by, nervously, while the officer searched for a handbag. A few minutes later, he came up from behind the couch, waving his find triumphantly. "Knew there had to be one," he said. "Never known a woman to go anywhere without her handbag." Then he emptied the contents on to the library-table and rummaged through them.

Archie watched the procedure intently, worried about what he might find among the odd assortment of articles a woman keeps in her bag. Suddenly, the officer gave a cry of victory. "Got it! A credit card. Should have no trouble in getting a name and address from this."

He shoved the articles back into the bag, snapped it shut, and looked up at Archie. "Are you certain she never mentioned a father, or any other relative? It would make it a lot easier on the poor woman if she had someone with her when I break the news of her daughter's death."

Archie hesitated, but for a second. "I'm certain."

"Pity—this is part of my job I hate. Oh yes, I would like your address and phone number, just in case I need to ask further questions. Doubt I will, though."

"Archie took a piece of notepaper from the library-table and wrote his address down, then handed it to the officer.

He glanced at it and whistled. "Wimpole Street! You must be doing well!"

"Well enough," he replied.

"You know, it makes me even more curious. With an address like that to impress a young lady, why would you want to bring her here?"

"I explained all that, Officer. We were passing."

"Oh yes, so you did," he said with a dubious gleam in his eyes.

"Why do you find it so hard to accept?" asked Archie.

"Did I say I did? Anyhow, it doesn't matter what I believe at this point, but I can see how a reporter would have a field day with it. I mean, a young, beautiful girl seen running from an eminent barrister's home and, obviously, too distraught to notice a car coming toward her. If there isn't a story behind it, they will make one out of it. You can bet on that."

Sick at the thought, Archie asked, "About that, Officer, is it necessary to report that she was seen running from this house? I'm thinking of my father, you understand. He's a very public figure, and the attention he would receive—well, it could make it most uncomfortable for him. It's not as though it would bring her back, is it?"

"I see your point," he replied. "The last thing I would want is for Sir Archibald to come under any undue pressure from the press or anyone for that matter. He's a real toff, your father. Contributes generously to the policeman's ball every year. No promises, mind, but I will see what can be done."

"That's good enough for me," replied Archie.

"Well, that's that then," he said with a sigh, put away his notebook, and started toward the door. He stopped suddenly and turned. "What I still don't understand is why she would run into the road like that without looking. She must have been really, really upset by this argument of yours."

Archie's back stiffened. "I can't tell you what was in her mind, if that's what you are asking me."

"No! No, I don't suppose you can," he said. "Well, it's time I was on my way. Give my regards to your father when you see him. Officer Brady—I'm sure he'll remember me. Never forgets anyone, your father."

Archie forced a smile, waited until he had reached the pavement, then closed the door and leaned back against it with a sigh of relief. He thought the questions would never end. Hadn't he suffered enough without him probing and probing? If only he could go back and start the day all over again. Oh God! How did it come to this? What madness possessed him? What would his father do about it? Whatever … nothing could be worse than the hell he was already going through.

He went back into the library. It looked the same; it only felt different—empty, cold, removed from all that had happened in that room, from all the secrets it held.

He gazed up at the portrait of his father. His eyes seemed to be staring down at him accusingly, and all at once, he was angry and cried out, "I hate you. Do you hear me? I hate you and everything you stand for. None of this would have happened if it were not for you. She would still be alive if it were not for you. I hope you burn in hell for what you have done!"

He was beside himself with grief, and falling to his knees, he sobbed his heart out, crying her name over and over again. *"Belinda! Belinda!"*

CHAPTER SEVENTEEN

Archie didn't leave his flat all day, Sunday. He ignored the telephone when it rang. He wasn't ready to talk to anyone, especially his father. He would know about the accident by then, and it must have been a terrible shock. What would his reaction be? he wondered. His father wasn't a fool; he must have figured out how she happened to be in his particular street on Saturday. He felt sick. What would he say to him? How would he defend himself when they faced each other?

It was late afternoon and the Sunday paper was still in the letterbox. He was afraid to read what it had to say about the accident. It was evening before he plucked up enough courage to take a look. There was nothing at all about it.

Monday morning, there were two little lines on the back page of the daily newspaper, and, heart in mouth, he read: "YOUNG GIRL IN FATAL ACCIDENT IN POSH ALBION STREET—IDENTITY YET TO BE RELEASED." It was so cold, detached, and it broke his heart. She was flesh and blood, not just a statistic!

He pushed the paper aside, drank his coffee, and got ready for the office. Somehow, he had to get through the day. He knew it wouldn't be easy. He also had to prepare himself for a visit from his father. If he didn't come by that day, it would be the next. It would be after hours. He was a private person, and wouldn't want anyone to hear what he had to say to his son.

Phipps was already in the office when he arrived, sorting out the post. His eyes became alert with curiosity when he saw Archie. "Did you read about that girl getting killed in your father's street?" he asked. "I wonder if he saw the accident."

His morbid interest riled Archie and he barked, "Have you nothing better to think about?"

He stared at him in surprise. "Why are you so touchy this morning?"

"I have a lot on my mind, and I can't be bothered by what you've read in the newspaper. Does that answer your question?"

"You are in a bad mood. Has it something to do with that slimy fellow Wilkes?"

"What do you know about Wilkes?" he asked testily.

"This is me, Phipps, you're talking to. Don't you think I've figured out what you two have going? I just can't believe you would trust him, that's all. I know I wouldn't, but then that's your business, isn't it?

"Damn right, it is!" he snapped.

Phipps raised his brow. It was a long time since he had seen Archie in such a foul mood. "I think it best that I leave you to your work and I'll get on with mine," and he marched out of his office.

Impudent bastard, thought Archie, *thinks he runs the place. Well, I'll do something about that one day!*

His heart wasn't in anything, and with nothing to distract him, the hours ticked by slowly. Phipps didn't show his face all day. He was relieved. He had an uncanny knack of putting his finger on the crux of the matter, and it was the last thing he needed.

The sudden bustle in the outer office announced five o'clock, as the staff was getting ready to leave for the day. He waited until it was quiet again, then rose, opened the door, and peered out. It was dark everywhere except for the corridor and Phipps's room, which was next to his. He was always the last to leave. Impatiently, Archie poked his head around the door. "Still here?" he asked.

Phipps raised his eyes and gave him a curious glance. "I have some paperwork to clear up. Why?"

"No reason. How much longer do you think you'll be?"

"I don't know. I don't watch the clock. What's the hurry?"

"I have to stay on a bit myself. I'm expecting a visitor and it's private."

"I'll be as quick as I can."

"Leave the light on in the corridor when you go. I'll lock up myself tonight."

"Sure," he said, still with that curious look in his eyes, and returned to his work.

Archie was on edge as he waited for his father. He prayed that he would come that evening. It was going to be nasty and he wanted to get it over with as soon as possible.

How long he sat there, nervously, twiddling his thumbs, he wasn't sure. But, all at once, he heard the door to the outer office open, and then creak on its dry hinges as it closed again. Had to be Phipps leaving, he thought, and then he heard the all-too-familiar steps along the wood floor of the hallway.

He stiffened, his eyes glued on the door to his office, when it suddenly eased open to reveal the figure of his father, his shoulders bent, his face ashen, his eyes dark and sunken with that haunted look of the bereaved. Shocked by his appearance, Archie stared at him in alarm.

Their eyes met and remained fixed on one another, as his father moved slowly into the center of the room. This was it, thought Archie, and held his breath in anticipation of an angry outburst. Instead, he received the quiet outpouring of a grief-stricken father, and it was harder to bear than any amount of words spoken in anger.

"I have just come from the examining pathologist's office," he said, his voice barely audible. "She looked so cold as she lay on that marble slab. I wanted to hold her, to warm life back into her." He stopped, and collected himself before going on. "He said that her underwear was in shreds, as when someone tries to tear them off. If he had found that she had been entered, by force or otherwise, I would have killed you."

His words quietly spoken, wounded like no instrument could, burying themselves deep in his heart. What could he say? Nothing. He could only stare at his father in dismay.

"Why? Why?" he asked. "What did you have against her? What did she ever do to you? If there was a fault, it was mine—not hers. She was innocent of any wrongdoing. Why did you have to involve her in your quest for revenge against me?"

Archie cringed. "No one could have foreseen the accident."

"So am I to forgive you because you couldn't foresee an accident? Is that your excuse for your cowardly behavior? She wasn't aware of who you were until you brought her to my house, was she?"

Archie hung his head in answer.

"You destroyed the joy of my life," his father went on. "How on earth did I bring you into the same world as I brought her?"

Couldn't he see that he was also bleeding? thought Archie. Wasn't he suffering enough already? He would gladly give both arms if he could bring her back, but how could he tell that to his father? He had made up his mind about him long before Belinda was born, and knew there was nothing he could say or do to change it.

His father was wiping a tear from his eye, and when he finished, he said, in a voice that was as dull and flat as the look in his eyes, "I have said what I came to say, and they are the last words that I shall ever speak to you. I never want to see you again, not for as long as I live."

It was the final blow—the knife through the heart. He watched his father turn from him and walk back along the corridor, his shoulders more bent than when he arrived, his step a little wearier, as though life itself was too much for him to bear. Filled with anguish, Archie suddenly called out to him. "I loved her, too. I didn't want any harm to come to her."

His father stopped dead, turned slowly, and the look in his eyes as they glared at him made Archie shrivel. Then his father turned again and walked out.

He continued to stare, his heart aching, when a hesitant voice filled the emptiness his father had left behind. "Will you be leaving shortly?" asked Phipps.

He blinked in surprise. "What? Oh, it's you! I thought you had gone."

"I was longer than I expected," he replied sheepishly. "Do you want me to wait and lock up?"

Giving him a searching glance, Archie said slowly, "I'll do it myself."

"Well, goodnight then."

Archie's eyes followed him down the hallway, just as they had followed his father a short while ago. Damn the man, he thought, and wondered how much he had heard.

With a heavy sigh, he rose, looked around, turned out the lights, and left for the night. It had been one hell of a day, one hell of a weekend, and he wondered if it would ever be over. His father had had his say. He knew exactly where he stood with him. Funny, he thought, for years he had wished him out of his life, and now that he had his wish, all he felt was regret. The price had been too high.

How do you get over something like that—the guilt that was with you day and night? How do you convince yourself that it wasn't your fault? Work wasn't the answer; neither was play, although he tried. God, how he tried! All the deviancy that had worked before now left him cold. All he could think about, morning, noon, and night, was Belinda, and suddenly he was impotent of all desire except one—gambling. Only when he was gambling was there any relief at all.

Night after night he was at the gaming table, watching the wheel turn, waiting for it to stop. It was the escape he needed, the drug that helped him through the night, and he gambled big—bigger than he had ever gambled before.

Wilkes and he were still doing deals together; only now, as quickly as the money flowed in, so it flowed out. He was losing more than he could afford, not that it worried him; he was past caring about anything. He had always sought pleasure; now gambling was his only pleasure.

Suddenly, after years of prosperity, England found itself in the grip of a recession. Property prices began to slump, and there were fewer deals to be done. Conveyancing, a big part of Archie's practice, was also drying up, and before he realized what was happening, he was deep in debt to the gambling establishments. Not even his precious Aston Martin fetched enough to pay it off; and without giving a thought to the consequences, he turned to the funds in his clients' account, which held, at any given time, close to three million. It was easy money—all that he had to do was rob Peter to pay Paul as the money was called upon, and no one would be the wiser.

It might have gone on unnoticed forever if the recession hadn't turned into a full-blown depression and the property market collapsed completely, leaving the fund very deficient.

It was Phipps who discovered it on the same day that a completion was to have taken place. Shocked when he found the fund short two hundred thousand pounds, he came barging into Archie's office demanding to know where the money had gone.

Archie was as shocked as he; he just couldn't believe that there wasn't enough to cover the purchase. "It has to be a mistake," he cried. "Have you had a word with the bank manager?"

"I have, and it's no mistake. There can be only one reason for the deficiency—misappropriation! What the hell has been going on?"

"That is an insult!"

"You are the only one who had access to the money."

"All right. I borrowed, from time to time, but I have always replaced whatever I took, so I don't know what the fuss is about."

"I'll tell you what the fuss is about. It's called embezzling, not borrowing."

"Oh, for heaven's sake, Phipps, don't be so dramatic. I'll have a talk with the bank manager myself. We've put millions through his bank. The least he can do, in return, is help us out at a time like this."

"I wouldn't talk to him, if I were you. It seems he has your number. It was he who suggested you might have been using the money for other than what it was intended. He didn't say so in as many words, but I think he was referring to your gambling."

Archie fell silent. It seemed everyone was aware of his gambling. "Well, don't just stand there," he suddenly cried. "Do something! What do I pay you for?"

Phipps knew better than to argue with him, and he rushed from the office, and returned twenty minutes later. "I've spoken to your father, and informed him of the situation. He is on his way to his bank now to arrange for a banker's draft for the full amount of two hundred thousand. I have also arranged for the completion to take place tomorrow morning. The client was very unhappy, I can tell you. I had to promise him compensation for the delay."

Archie was enraged. "You did what?" he cried. "What right had you to approach my father without first asking me?"

"You wanted something done, I did the only thing that could save your neck."

"I'll go to the loan sharks before I go to my father!"

"They would screw you so hard, you would never get out of debt. Who would you turn to then … your friend Wilkes? I doubt that money-grabbing little weasel would come through for you."

Archie knew he was right. Wilkes was out for himself, and if there was nothing in it for him, he wouldn't want to know. It was exasperating. "Is there nothing else we can do?" he asked.

"Only your father."

"Never!" he cried.

"Never is a long time, Mr. Bingham, and in the meantime, you could end up spending a big part of that never behind bars. Do you know what happens to handsome men like you in prison? They are used, not once, not twice, but over and over, and by more than one inmate. Trust me, it's a world you don't want to know."

Archie swallowed. He had heard such stories and didn't think that he could survive it. "What did my father say when you told him? How did he react?" he asked tentatively.

"He wasn't happy, that's for sure."

"But what did he actually say to you?"

"For a while, there was nothing but silence on the line and I thought he had hung up on me, and then suddenly, he asked, 'How much?' I told him, and again, there was silence before he asked questions like the name of the client, what kind of property he was purchasing, who was acting for

307

the other side. Stuff like that. Then he said that he would be going to his bank right away, and as soon as he heard from me that the completion was on, he would attend to the matter in person."

"In person? You see what he's doing? He's out to make me look small in front of everyone."

"I'm just reporting what he told me. I don't know what goes on between you and your father, and I don't want to know. He has promised to make good on your behalf, and that's what counts. Now, if you want to mess with loan sharks and put this firm in a very precarious position, you do so without me, because I don't want to stand by and watch you and the firm go down the tube."

"Are you threatening me?"

"Call it what you like, but you would have to be a fool not to accept your father's offer. He is even willing to pay the man compensation to get you off the hook, so I don't understand your complaint."

"So you and my father have it all fixed up between you. How cozy."

"Just tell me. Do I give him the all clear, or not?"

"What choice do I have? Make that phone call."

Sir Archibald Bingham had a code of conduct—conduct by which he lived, and although he would, on occasion, bend the law to suit himself, it was always within the bounds of those principles. His son had stepped over the line, and he would have to pay for it. When he told Phipps the conditions attached to the help he was giving, it stunned him, and he was somewhat embarrassed when he reported back to Archie. "The completion will take place tomorrow morning as arranged," he said quietly.

From the sorry look on his face, Archie knew there had to be more. "What is it?" he asked. "What does my father want from me in return?"

Phipps had avoided his eyes until that moment; now he looked him straight in the face. "He—he doesn't want you practicing law in this country ever again," he replied somewhat awkwardly.

Archie's mouth dropped open in disbelief. "I should have guessed," he said. "Now you know why I didn't want to go to him in the first place. He is using the situation to get back at me. That's what he's doing!"

"He's helping you out."

"He is saving his precious name. That is all he has ever cared about."

"So what do you want me to do?" asked Phipps.

"What else? Take his offer."

Archie leaned back in his brown leather swivel chair when Phipps had gone. He was angry with himself. The whole damned thing could have been avoided if he had had his mind where it should have been. It was yet another point against him, and another homerun for his father. How smug he must feel.

God how he hated the man! His father always had so much going for him; what did he have except scorn and rejection? The only person his father ever cared about was Belinda, aside from himself, that is.

Belinda! he thought with a pang. What a price she paid for the love she received. The funny thing was, having known her, he could understand how his father loved her so much. Didn't he love her despite himself? Who couldn't have loved her...? If only the pain would end!

With a heavy sigh, he put all thoughts of her out of his mind and turned his attention to the present dilemma.

The practice wasn't as easy to sell as he expected. There was the recession, of course, and the figures were not good, but then he didn't want to give it away. After months of advertising the firm, he received a reasonable offer from a recently qualified lawyer eager to start out on his own. Listening to him, Archie was reminded of himself when he first started.

"I'm good," the young man exclaimed with a proud lift of his head. "Came top of my year at university, and as for articles, my superior put most of the work onto me while he played around with one of the girls in the office. Indeed, why should I work for anyone for a mere pittance when I can work for myself and keep what is mine? I intend to make a go of this firm. Put it on the map!"

Archie stared at him. "Indeed!" he smirked.

Phipps stayed with him to the end. He had already secured a good position at another firm, and was only waiting for Archie to hand over the practice before leaving. "Well, this is it!" he said on their last day together.

"Yes," said Archie, "this is it. I know that I wasn't always easy to get along with, and if I snapped at you a bit too often, then I'm sorry."

"I didn't mind you snapping," he replied. "It was being so pig-headed that I objected to. I don't know if you know it, but there were times when I went out on a limb for you."

"I realize it now. We certainly had our moments, didn't we?"

"Quite a few of them! To be honest, there was a lot I didn't like about you, but then there were a few qualities that I admired."

"Really? Such as?"

"Well, for one, you were loyal to your staff. It may have been in your own interest, but your interest or theirs, it was still loyalty."

"You said a few things?"

Phipps laughed. "So I did, but I am a bit hard-pressed to think of anything else."

Archie grinned. "That's what I've always liked best about you: you never tried to bullshit me!"

The smile left Phipps's face. "I really am sorry it ended the way it has. At least your father's good name is still intact. I know how much it means to him. I was afraid, for a while, that the Law Society would find out about the … well, you know! I didn't say anything, at the time, because I didn't want to worry you, but the client did threaten to go to them if we didn't make good."

"You told my father, of course."

"I thought it wise to mention it."

"I knew there had to be a good reason for him to compensate the man so quickly. Involving the Law Society would have been the last straw for him." With a sigh, Archie asked, "How do you get along with your father?"

"All right, I guess," he replied with a careless shrug. "But then, we are simple folk with simple needs and simple expectations. Greatness like your father's wouldn't fit in with our lifestyle anyhow. All we are concerned with is making a living. That's what life is about for the likes of us."

"Isn't that what life is about for all of us?"

"Maybe, but you tend to let your pride get in the way. Of course, we have our pride, too, but no airs or graces accompany it. We are part of the common herd, the faceless masses, and, in many respects, it works to our advantage."

"Then I envy you. Sometimes a person can have too much to live up to."

"And I have always envied you, having more to live up to."

"Don't be fooled by appearances. Nothing is as easy or simple as you seem to think it is."

"Perhaps not, but it would be nice to know what it's like to walk on the other side of the fence once in a while."

"The grass is greener, right?" said Archie. "Well, not always; neither does the air smell any fresher. In fact, at times, it can be damned suffocating."

"Only if you have a tendency to expect too much."

"Which I have, I suppose!"

"Well, you can't win at everything." Phipps suddenly looked awkward. "Bad choice of words," he said.

"No, you're right. Actually, you do pretty well with words. You have taught me quite a bit. I'm glad I had you aboard."

Not one for compliments, Phipps turned pink. "Yes, well…. Goodbye, sir," he said, "and good luck to you."

Archie rose and shook his hand. "Good luck to you, Tom, and thank you for everything."

With Phipps gone, he suddenly felt very alone. Even the room had an unfamiliar air about it, as if he were seeing it for the first time. He glanced around, his eyes coming to rest on the mahogany bookcase that his mother had given him the day he bought the practice, a big glass-fronted antique that stretched from wall to wall, filled with a vast variety of legal books all bound in fine leather. "Nothing but the best will do for my son," she had said. His world was filled with such promise back then. What happened? he wondered sadly. How could his star fade so quickly?

He hadn't heard from his mother for some time. It was obvious that his father hadn't told her about the affair, or she would have been on the phone to him like a shot. He wasn't surprised; nothing he did was of any real concern to his father. He might have been dead, for all he cared; perhaps he was dead to him, as dead as his precious daughter. How it hurt. His father should have loved him, if not more than, then at least as much as he had loved her.

Suddenly, he was angry. He was the injured party, not his father. So how come he always made him feel that he was in the wrong? In a moment of bitter resentment, Archie lifted the phone and dialed the number of the Law Society of England.

Had the call not been answered immediately, it might have given him time to think about what he was doing. But it was, and without a thought to the outcome, he anonymously tipped them off to the improper use of clients' funds that had taken place in the firm of Jessop, Jessop & Jessop.

He had to catch his breath when he replaced the receiver. He had set the wheels in motion. Disbarment was inevitable, and suddenly he realized that it wasn't only his father that he was punishing, but himself as well.

***

After a full inquiry into the matter, Archie was called before the disciplinary committee and subsequently struck off the rolls, prohibiting him from practicing law in England. Although he expected it, when it took place, it was as bitter a moment in his life as any he had experienced.

The following morning, it made the headlines of just about every daily newspaper. "SON OF EMINENT Q.C. SIR ARCHIBALD BINGHAM DISBARRED FOR EMBEZZLEMENT." He had done what he set out to do, to humiliate his father, but the only satisfaction was in the knowledge that he wouldn't be able to buy himself out of that one.

With a pang, he placed the paper face down on the table. He had no stomach to read on. He poured coffee that tasted bitter on his tongue, and he pushed it aside and rose from the table. At the very same moment, the phone rang. He hesitated. It could only be his mother. In carrying out his revenge, he hadn't given a thought to her and how she would feel, and he was sorry. He went over to the telephone and, somewhat apprehensive, lifted the receiver.

"Oh Archie!" she cried. "Please tell me it's all a horrid mistake."

"I wish I could," he answered.

"When your father saw the headlines, I thought he was going to have a stroke. Why didn't you warn us?"

"I didn't think it would go that far, especially as father made good the deficiency."

"He knew about it?"

"Not that I was disbarred."

"I worry what this will do to him. You know what a proud man he is. But I don't understand. If he made good the deficiency, how did the Law Society get to know about it?"

"I have no idea!"

"Obviously, someone spiteful, and after everything he has suffered this last year. He still hasn't recovered from the loss of his daughter. Now, this on top of it!"

"You knew about his daughter?"

"Of course. I know more about his affairs than you think. You can't keep something like that a secret forever."

"Then how did you go on living with him? He betrayed you. Weren't you resentful?"

"At first!"

"But not now, it seems. I would have thought you would hate him."

"I did, for a while. But then, I was still Lady Bingham, wife of Sir Archibald Bingham, and it meant a great deal to me. I know you find it hard to understand, but people look up to your father, and when I'm on his arm, they look up to me. All I would be without him is another lonely woman without a partner, and I wouldn't much care for that. Despite what you may think, it has been a good marriage. There is love, of a sort, between us, if not passion. And at my age, stability is far more desirable than passion."

"Doesn't it hurt to know that he loves another?"

"Less and less, as time goes on. Anyhow, there is no such thing as love without pain of some kind. If anyone tells you that there is, then they have never loved."

"I could never be that forbearing!"

"Well, you are who you are, and I am who I am."

"That doesn't excuse him."

"I didn't say that it did…. He blames you for the death of his daughter, doesn't he?"

"Why do you say that?" he asked, trying not to appear defensive.

"I know how he thinks, and he hasn't mentioned your name in a year, not since her death. Neither have you stopped by the house in all that time. There had to be a reason."

"I could have explained what happened, if he had only listened. But then, when has he ever taken the time to listen to anything I have to say?"

"Neither of you seem to have the time to listen to each other. You are more alike than you think."

"How can you say that? He was my hero, Mother. As a boy I loved him unconditionally. He has never loved me unconditionally, conditionally, or any other way. The love that should have been mine was given to another."

"There are different kinds of love, Archie. He may not have spoiled you, but don't confuse the lack of being spoiled with the lack of being loved. He loves us both, in his way, but like everything in your father's life, it has to be on his terms. And that is what you have never been able to reconcile yourself with, have you?"

"I don't consider that love."

"Because you refuse to understand him and his needs, but I didn't phone you to argue. I heard a rumor that you sold the practice?"

"It's more than a rumor. I could hardly continue under the circumstances."

"What will you do?"

"I'm still thinking about it."

"How are you off for money?"

"Fine, so far."

"You need only ask, you know that."

"I do, and I appreciate it."

There was a moment's hesitation, when suddenly she cried, "It's all so unfair. Where did I go wrong? Your father has always said that I spoil you too much. Do I? Do I spoil you? Is that why I'm being punished?"

Damn! thought Archie. It was the very reaction he dreaded. "Mother, you are not being punished, and if you feel that you are, I'm sorry. I wish I could alter things, but I can't. So please, for my sake, don't feel that way."

"Oh my darling, I've upset you. I didn't mean to. I'm sorry."

"I'm the one to apologize, not you. I would like to go on talking," he said, "but I still have a lot to do. Look, as soon as I have decided on something, I'll call you and we can have lunch together."

"I would like that."

It took Archie a month to make a final decision about his future. Law was all that he had ever known. It had played an important part in his life ever since he could remember. At breakfast, at dinner, the law and its effect upon society, was the only subject that held his interest. It had been the dominating factor behind everything in his life. Now, suddenly, he was at a loss, robbed of that essential ingredient that had been so clearly a part of him; therefore, as soon as his flat was sold, and there was nothing left to keep him trapped, he made the only decision that was available—to leave England.

"Where will you go?" asked his mother over lunch. "This is your home. I cannot imagine you being happy anywhere else."

"I haven't been happy here. This sceptered isle, this paradise that you seem to think it is, has left me no choice."

"Perhaps after a while, the Law Society will reinstate you."

"I seriously doubt it! Anyhow, Father made it abundantly clear that he didn't want me practicing in this country ever again. He worries more about his reputation than he does about my feelings."

"I can't believe he meant it."

"Whether he did or not, circumstances have taken it out of his hands, and I am beginning to think that it's for the best after all. I have decided to go to America."

"America!" his mother exclaimed in horror. "But darling, America is for those poor souls who can't make it over here."

"Mother, you are living in the past when fathers would send their errant sons across the ocean to try and make something of themselves." He suddenly gave an ironic laugh. "I suppose you could apply that sentiment to me after all."

"Nonsense, darling! Anyhow, America is a country full of crime. People go around with guns in their belts, shooting at each other."

"New York isn't exactly the wild and wooly West! As well, America is the powerhouse now, not England. I could do a lot worse."

"Don't you need a visa or something to live in America?"

"I've applied to Harvard Law School. With my LL.B. from Cambridge, I cannot imagine being refused. And once I have an American law degree, there should be no trouble in getting permission to stay."

"University costs money."

"The proceeds from the sale of the flat will take care of the fees; nevertheless, there is a little matter of living expenses."

"If you are really intent on going, I could have a word with my trustees. They'll not argue; they will agree to whatever I want."

"And Father?"

"He won't object. Anyhow, I doubt he will ask questions."

"I don't suppose he will!"

"How long, do you think, before you are ready to leave?"

"I expect a reply any day now, and I will leave soon thereafter."

"Oh no!" she cried in alarm. "But that doesn't give us much time. When will I see you again?"

"As soon as the arrangements have been made, we will fix something up."

"Will you fly? Or go by boat?"

"Boat is expensive, not that I wouldn't prefer it."

"Then as soon as you tell me everything is settled, leave the arrangements to me, my darling."

Archie arrived in America in style. The finest suite, aboard the Queen Elizabeth, was his for the crossing—a gift from his mother. It had been a tearful parting, but not for him; he couldn't get away quickly enough. There was nothing left for him in England except bad memories. He had had enough of those to last a lifetime, he thought as he stood at the rail of the ship, a lump in his throat despite himself, as they slipped quietly from the quay into the So'lent, before making for the open sea.

315

***

He found New York to be alive, bustling like no city he had ever seen, and his pulse raced to its compelling rhythm. He had made the right choice, he decided. America was the ideal place to start afresh, and he was keen on fresh starts. He never did like carrying yesterday's baggage around with him.

If he expected Harvard to be anything like Cambridge, he was mistaken. It had a totally different feel about it. Firstly, he was a mature student. Secondly, the character of the American was in complete contrast to the British. In many respects, the Americans were more open-minded and accepting of others, while the British were more reserved, not only in their thinking, but also in their attitude toward others.

Either way, he had no desire to make friends at Harvard. The last thing he needed was to repeat the mistakes of Cambridge. Looking back, he realized that it was one of the unhappiest times of his life. He had made enemies of friends, and friends of undesirables when there was no one left to turn to. How could he go wrong if he kept to himself? he reasoned.

His mother corresponded with him regularly during the following year, giving him news about this and that, but never mentioning a word about his father—what he was doing, or how he was—so it came as a shock when he received a letter from her after two months of silence.

> My darling son,
>
> We buried your father yesterday in a quiet little church-yard near Branksome, where, as you know, we went to live soon after he retired.
>
> It was a private funeral, none of the judiciary or members of the bar in attendance. No reporters to spread the news of his demise—only a handful of close relatives. I thought he would prefer it that way after everything.
>
> From the first day when the Law Society published its findings in the *Gazette* regarding the embezzlement, his health deteriorated. You wouldn't have recognized him in the end. He, who stood so tall and proud, became withered and wasted. The only time he found strength enough to leave the house was to go down to the local post office and collect the letters his mistress wrote him. Naturally, he didn't have them delivered to the house in order to spare my feelings, but he couldn't hide it from me for long. I knew him too well.

It didn't hurt as much as it would have done earlier in our marriage. I passed that stage a long time ago, after I learned to accept the situation. As well, he seemed so much brighter after one of her letters that I welcomed them.

I had my solicitors inform her of his death. I thought it was the right thing to do. They were together a long time. To my relief, she had the grace not to attend the funeral. I felt sorry for her; she never had the chance to say goodbye to the man she loved. That privilege was mine alone. In a way, it made up for everything. It is sad, though; I am sure she is suffering over her loss, as I am over mine.

Try to forgive his shortcomings, my darling; it will help you find peace in your heart. He was, after all, only human.

I miss you, Archie, especially now.

Your adoring mother

There were tears in his eyes when he finished reading the letter. It pained him to think of the man he once revered without the pride that had been so much a part of his character. What had he done to him? All he really intended was for him to know what it felt like to be betrayed.

Tears were damp on his cheeks as he folded the letter carefully and placed it in a drawer. The bitter truth, he now knew, was that he had never stopped loving him, and the knowledge made his heart ache the more.

Suddenly, the lights in the apartment came on. The refrigerator started to hum, and the air-conditioning began to clear the room of the suffocating heat.

Archie's eyes wandered to the drawer, which, after ten years, still held the letter from his mother. He rose, went over, took it out, and read it for the hundredth time. Tears fell, as on the first day he read it. After all the years between, it had lost none of its power to move him; only now, it seemed more poignant than ever.

What had it all been for? he wondered. What had he achieved in the end, except pain, pain, and more pain? Where was the glory? The joy in life? Was happiness meant to be momentary, like a rainbow that vanishes soon after the rain? Why wasn't there more? Why did everything have to end so finally? What was it all about?

He wiped his eyes dry, put the letter back in the drawer, and stood by the window. It was early, not quite six in the morning, and yet the city streets were alive with the sound of traffic. Taxi drivers were arguing loudly over this or that. A fire engine, its wail drowning out all other sounds, raced to a fire somewhere in the metropolis. An ambulance followed, its wail just as loud. It was to this vibrant tune, this beat, that the seasoned New Yorker danced, and it was exciting.

Is that how life can be summed up, a moment's excitement, and then nothing but the earth beneath which you lie? He turned from the window and glanced at the telephone. It was time to get it over with. What else could he do but give in to Frankie Leeman's demands? What did it matter, in the end, if he nailed the Mafia or not? There was always another Mob boss to take the place of the last one. It was all a political game, and he had never really been a political animal. You had to kiss up too often, and it wasn't in his nature. What was in his nature...? Not much it seemed.

Leeman's card, with his private phone number, was beside the telephone. He lifted the receiver slowly, dialed, and then waited. The phone seemed to ring forever before it was answered. "Yes?" asked the voice at the other end.

Archie's heart skipped a beat. His mind was swaying with uncertainty. He swallowed. Again, the voice at the other end, impatiently this time, said, "Yes?"

The words refused to leave his tongue. His breath came in short, sharp bursts. "No deal!" he gasped, and then replaced the receiver quickly before giving himself a chance to change his mind.

It took but seconds for him to realize that he was finished. His whole life, his career, was at an end. Thoughts of Belinda crept into his head. It was a long time since he last thought of her, and suddenly, all the feelings that he'd had for her came rushing back and filled him with pain all over again. Would he ever find peace, he wondered, or was his penance to go on loving a ghost?

All at once, it became too much for him—thoughts of his father, of Belinda, the whole damn sham that had been his life, and in a moment of absolute hopelessness, he went to the bathroom, took out a razor, and slashed his wrists.

Blood gushed forth rich, red, and thick, and horrified by what he had done, he sank to the floor in shock. As he sat there, his head leaning back against a wall, his mind a jumble of mixed thoughts, a vision of his father appeared before him. His eyes were full of criticism as they stared down at him. "You can't blame this on me, Archie," he said. "You know what your trouble was? You couldn't come to terms with life. Well, you will have long enough to come to terms with death!"

He held out his hand to him. "Father!" he cried. "Father!" But the vision was already fading, and his hand dropped to his side, his life's blood oozing into crimson puddles of despair.

What depth the misery? What measure of desperation drives a person to suicide? What stopped Archie from telephoning for help, when confronted by the horror of what he had done? To understand, you would have to understand the complexities of Archie Bingham, and that had never been easy. What could be said, with certainty, was that he was too possessive by far, too egocentric, and it proved his undoing.

After an investigation into the suicide of Archie Bingham, certain irregularities, carried out on his behalf, came to light, one of them being the planting of evidence by an undercover officer involved in the case of Guido Bocacci. The charge was subsequently dropped.

QUOTES/REFERENCES

1. Chapter 7, page 157, quotation from *The Story of Mankind* by Hendrik Willem Van Loon.

2. Chapter 12, page 254, reference to the history lesson on Napoleon. Subject matter taken from *The Story of Mankind* by Hendrik Willem Van Loon.

3. Chapter 13 quotes from *The Rubaiyat of Omar Khayyam*.

4. Reference to the facts on art and the artists' aim taken from the *Picture Encyclopaedia of Art*, published by Thames & Hudson, London.

Printed in the United States
44865LVS00004B/1-87